me take a closer look. If ~~~
back with wire cutters."

Meyer hesitated, then ~~~ careful. There might
be guards on the oth~~~

Rall's white tee~~~ ows. "I've a date
tomorrow night. You thin~ I'm going to miss it?"

633 SQUADRON
LOSES A FRIEND

Pouring smoke from both its starboard engines,
the B.17 lurched drunkenly from the tight formation. As its pilot tried to bring it under control,
two Focke Wulfs attacked from opposite sides.
With five gunners already slumped over their
weapons, the end was near. Cannon shells blasted
huge holes in the massive wings and tore off the
weakened wing assembly. With air screaming eerily inside its fuselage, the B.17 began its long fall
to earth. Incredibly, a gunner in the upper turret,
his parachute pack blown to ribbons by gunfire,
went on firing defiantly as the two Focke Wulfs
followed the bomber down.

It was the first B.17 to be lost since 633 Squadron had come to the Americans' aid, but all the
Mosquito crews knew it would not be the last . . .

DEPT. 24

633
SQUADRON

OPERATION RHINE MAIDEN

BY
FREDERICK E. SMITH

BANTAM BOOKS · TORONTO · NEW YORK · LONDON

*This low-priced Bantam Book
has been completely reset in a type face
designed for easy reading, and was printed
from new plates. It contains the complete
text of the original hard-cover edition.*
NOT ONE WORD HAS BEEN OMITTED.

**633 SQUADRON
OPERATION RHINE MAIDEN**
A Bantam Book / published by arrangement with the author.

PRINTING HISTORY
*First published in Great Britain by Cassell and Company, Ltd.
in 1975*
Bantam edition / April 1979

ISBN 0–553–12778–0

Published simultaneously in the United States and Canada

PRINTED IN THE UNITED STATES OF AMERICA

To
my old and dear friend
JOHNNIE GEMMELL,
who will be greately missed

The author wishes to acknowledge his debt to the authors of the following works of reference:

Bekker, *The Luftwaffe War Diaries* (Macdonald); Adolf Galland, *The First and the Last* (Methuen); Alfred Price, *Instruments of Darkness* (Wm Kimber); Richards and Saunders, *Royal Air Force 1939–1945* (H.M.S.O.); C. Martin Sharp and Martin F. Bowyer, *Mosquito* (Faber); Sir C. Webster and N. Frankland, *The Strategic Air Offensive against Germany 1939–1945* (H.M.S.O.).

And, last but not least, to his good friend Group Captain T. G. Mahaddie, D.S.O., D.F.C., A.F.C.

1

The small group of mechanics, all smoking cigarettes, were standing in the summer sunshine outside a dispersal hut. An FBVI Mosquito with modifications was at rest twenty yards away. Beneath its nose a young Aircraftman IInd Class, whose chubby face was shining in the heat, was trying to replace a gun bay panel. As he struggled to locate the spring-loaded screws, a Leading Aircraftman detached himself from the group. An old sweat with a long, dismal face and a sharp nose, he was wearing a filthy pair of overalls held together at the waist by a single button. Ducking his head he gazed at the sweating youngster.

"Takin' your time, aren't you?"

"I'm going as quick as I can," the ACII muttered.

"You'd better get a jildi on, mate. If Chiefy has to ground this kite, he'll have the lot of us workin' on it all night. And then you'll be real popular."

The youngster was having difficulty in lining up the screws with their sockets. "Couldn't you hold the panel for me?" he asked tentatively.

The old sweat, by name McTyre, looked shocked. "You want to get me into trouble, Ellis? I'm a fitter, not a bloody armourer."

"But I only want it holding while I fasten the screws," the young ACII wailed.

McTyre was clearly shaken by the youngster's readiness to bend the sacred lines of demarcation. "Out of the question, mate. By the centre . . . ." Shaking his head, the old sweat retreated to the group of mechanics. "You hear that? He'll be askin' Chiefy to give 'im a hand next."

A telephone was heard ringing. A corporal ran into the dispersal hut, to return fifteen seconds later. "Hey, Ellis. Is that gun serviceable yet?"

The cherubim-faced youngster had got the panel on at last. "Yes, I think so, corp."

The corporal went back to the telephone. McTyre

1

met him in the hut doorway as he was coming out. "Is it right Lacy's not flyin' with Harvey today?"

"Yeh. Lacy's got appendicitis."

"Who's flyin' in his place?"

"One of the sprogs. Blackburn."

McTyre gave a whistle. "Christ! That'll make Harvey happy."

By this time Ellis was carrying his equipment away from the nose of the Mosquito. When the way was clear McTyre stepped loftily forward and climbed into the cockpit. A few seconds later the starboard engine fired, followed by the port. A flight of starlings, grubbing in the short grass near by, took off with a clatter of wings.

The Merlins began to thunder as McTyre warmed them up. A shower of dust and stones made the group of mechanics take shelter on the lee side of the hut. Three minutes later McTyre waved an underling into the cockpit and swung his legs to the ground. As he scribbled his initials on the Form 700 that the corporal pushed at him, the roar of the engines died into a rhythmical murmur. It allowed the mechanics to hear the roar of other Merlins around the airfield where the same routine was being carried out.

A 25-cwt. transport began circling the perimeter track, dropping off crews at their dispersal points. A second vehicle, a station wagon befitting a Flight Commander, drew up a few yards from McTyre whose muted wolf whistle at the pretty Waaf driver brought only a toss of curls.

The tall, powerfully-built pilot who jumped out was Frank Harvey, A Flight Commander and Acting Squadron Commander for the operation. With the warm evening obviating the need for flying clothes, he was wearing service uniform. A Yorkshireman with withdrawn eyes and a face that was all planes and angles, Harvey was not famous for his sociability at the best of times. This evening his mood was forbidding as he dragged his parachute from the station wagon.

Two other men followed him out. One, a stocky youngster carrying a canvas bag as well as his parachute, was Blackburn, Harvey's new navigator and the innocent cause of the Yorkshireman's mood. The other man was "Sandy" Powell, an affable Australian who, like Harvey, was a survivor from the original squadron. Wounded over Bergen, he had been hospitalized during the climactic raid, an accident that had probably saved his life. Harvey's dourness was an obstacle to friendship, but Powell was the closest to a friend on the squadron that the Yorkshireman had, and, although Harvey would have died rather than admit it, he valued the Australian accordingly.

As Harvey started for the dispersal hut, Powell caught his arm. "Wait a minute. You still haven't given me the name of those gee-gees."

Harvey did his best to be affable. "You can have 'em when we get back."

"You kidding? What if you get the chop?"

Harvey gave an impatient scowl. "It's Sun King for the two-thirty and Jason II for the three o'clock. The other one's Blue something—maybe Blue Stocking. I'll have to check on it."

"Great. If they come up we're in Scarborough tomorrow night for dinner. O.K.?"

Harvey nodded, humped his parachute over one shoulder, and started again for the dispersal hut. As the stocky Blackburn followed somewhat ruefully after him, Powell clapped him on his shoulder. "You'll be all right, cobber. His bark's worse than his bite."

Blackburn gave him a grateful look, and Powell ran back to the station wagon, which shot away. At the dispersal hut Harvey barely glanced at the Form 700 before signing it and shoving it back at the corporal. Ignoring Blackburn he strode over to the Mosquito, ordered the mechanic out, and took his place in the pilot's seat. Feeling the eyes of the ground crew on him, Blackburn took a deep breath, threw his bag and parachute through the open cockpit door, and pulled himself in after them. Almost instantly the two Merlins began to roar as Harvey tested them. A green Very light soared up from the Control Tower and D-Danny began to roll forward.

McTyre was grinning unsympathetically. "I'd hate to be in his shoes. Harvey looks mad enough to pitch him into the drink."

Ellis, still new and young enough to feel wonder at it all, ventured a question. "Where are they going, Mac?"

McTyre gave him a look of pity. "You've helped to bomb up the bloody thing and don't know where they're going."

"Nobody's told me," the young armourer complained.

Across the airfield Mosquito after Mosquito was moving from its hard-standing and taxi-ing in procession for take-off. As another Very light soared from the Control Tower, Harvey's D-Danny came swooping along the runway and climbed into the sunlit evening sky with a crackling roar. McTyre jerked an oily thumb eastward. "They're goin' to prang a Jerry convoy. Somewhere off the Danish coast." As another of the graceful planes took off and banked round the airfield, the old sweat followed its flight with a rare pride.

"Look at 'em, mate. Miracle kites, that's what they are. Made of wood and yet able to outfly anything Jerry can put up. And carry a 4,000-lb. cookie if they want to."

The youngster's ingenuous blue eyes, bright with envy, watched the orbiting planes break and follow Harvey eastward. Flying in a loose gaggle, they swept so low over the fields that their shadows pursued them like sharks. Reaching the coast just south of Flamborough Head, they leapt over a sunlit beach still sprinkled with holiday-makers. Men leapt to their feet and excited girls waved towels. The gaggle swept over a line of inshore fishing boats, then the sea that led to the enemy coast reached out blue and dangerous before them. Within seconds they were only a cluster of specks to the watching holiday-makers. The time was 1915 hours. The month was July 1943.

It was later the same evening that Frank Adams, the Station Intelligence Officer, took a walk round the airfield perimeter. Since the teleprinters had started clacking that afternoon he had been working at full stretch, and in an hour or less, when the squadron returned, de-briefing might keep him busy until midnight. This was the lull period when the ground staff could take a breather, and Adams had discovered that a walk helped to ease his tension.

The murmur of voices drifting towards him told him that inside the dispersal huts mechanics were smoking cigarettes and brewing cups of tea. The distant row of poplars were black against the fading sky and an arrow-head of homing birds was winging its way towards Bishop's Wood. Adams glanced at his watch. The evenings would begin closing in soon. In less than three months those icy, north-east winds would be back, probing through the Nissen huts and sweeping unmolested across the cement-stained ground. Adams had never been able to decide which season he preferred since putting on uniform. In spite of its discomforts, winter did at least match the black mood of war.

The turf-lined mound on Adams' left was the bomb dump. As he passed a gun-post he could feel the crew watching him and had to restrain his impulse to call out a greeting. That most other ranks found familiarity from officers an embarrassment was another unwelcome fact Adams had learned.

He walked until a hillock hid him from the gun-post, then pushed through a tangle of sweet-smelling grass to the perimeter fence. The fence here was only three feet high and down the road, set back behind its garden, he could see the Black Swan. With all the personnel of the airfield on duty tonight, its bars would be almost empty.

In the hedgerow across the quiet road a blackbird had begun its evening song. With the sentimentalist in him unable to equate such moments with war, Adams found his thoughts turning paradoxically to the time ten weeks previously when the aircrews of 633 Squadron, weighing their lives against the threat to their country, had chosen to fly straight into the murderous steel trap of the Swartfjord.

It had been an evening of equal beauty when the armourers had loaded the earthquake bombs into the waiting Mosquitoes. And Adams could distinctly remember hearing a blackbird singing during the cold dawn vigil when he, Davies and the Brigadier had waited for survivors. Blackbirds seemed an integral part of Sutton Craddock, but when only one crippled Mosquito had landed and the full extent of the disaster was known, Adams had wondered bitterly what the hell they had to sing about.

It was a memory that was still painful to Adams, yet certain scenes of it were etched for ever on his mind. The numbed expression of Marsden, the Signals Officer, as he tried to understand he would never see ninety per cent of his friends again. The mercurial Davies, struggling to balance the loss against his euphoria at the success of the mission. The elderly Brigadier's shame at the relief he could not hide. But of all the fragmented memories, the most painful was Hilde Bergman's reaction on hearing Grenville had not returned. There had been the small fluttering motion of her hand that Adams had come to know so well and now epitomized her grief. The few unsteady steps she had taken across the room, her single sob, and then, incredibly, her melodic voice addressing him.

"Thank you for coming over to tell me, Frank. I know how painful all this must be for you."

That she could think of him at such a moment and express sympathy had been the breaking point for Adams. Wanting above all else to comfort her, he had instead stumbled back to his billet where, cursing his cowardice, he had drunk almost a full bottle of whisky. It had not helped. The next twenty-four hours had contained all the elements of a black nightmare for Adams.

His eyes focused again over the perimeter fence. Two months had not been long enough to hide the fire-blackened scars in the cornfield where Gillibrand had made his supreme sacrifice, although when the field was ploughed in the autumn the scars would disappear. While the sentimentalist in Adams protested at the thought, the realist in him knew the world seldom sorrowed long over its martyrs.

He stirred impatiently at his habit of extracting melancholy from memory. The news he had been able to give Hilde three days ago ought to have erased some of the sadness of the past. He had heard from the Red Cross that Grenville, although seriously wounded, was making good progress in a German prison hospital. Adams had run all the way to the Black Swan to tell Hilde. Her reaction had made Adams think of his childhood and the tale of the Sleeping Beauty who had come back to shining life at the kiss from her Prince. "I have felt it, Frank. But it is something I have never dared to believe."

Adams told her that apart from Harvey and his observer who had escaped capture and been brought back to England by the Norwegian Linge, the Red Cross reported only two other men alive in German hands. Her decision when the full import of Grenville's survival had sunk in had dismayed Adams but not surprised him. "I've wasted enough time feeling sorry for myself, Frank. Now I must go and make myself useful like the rest of you." She had phoned a military nursing unit in Whitby and had left Sutton Craddock only that morning.

Perhaps, then, there was an excuse for his mood to-night, Adams thought. When his wife, Valerie, had decided to leave the Black Swan and live with her parents until the war ended, Adams had been free to spend his off-duty time as he wished and much of it had been spent seeing Hilde. They had become close friends and after a day or night assessing how many enemy aircraft had been shot down, how many German factories had been destroyed, or how some young friend had been killed, Adams' need to see the girl had often been as urgent as a wounded man needing a sedative. He sometimes felt the madness of war would go on for ever and the realization tonight that he would have to face it without her was crushing.

About to sit on the top rail of the fence, Adams decided it was too rickety. As he leaned his elbows on it instead, he remembered almost with surprise that it was Sunday. In the village churches that dotted the Yorkshire countryside the faithful would be in their pews reaffirming their allegiance to the Prince of Peace. Listening to the blackbird's song again Adams discovered that a coarse background of sound was adulterating it. Back where the shadows were thickening between the billets and hangars, orders were being shouted and engines were starting up. With a sigh Adams pushed himself away from the fence. Signals must have been alerted that the squadron was nearing its base and Sue Spencer, his assistant, would be wondering what had happened to him.

An unmilitary figure with his spectacles and stocky build, Adams started back along the perimeter track. In the dusk ahead the activity was quickening. As the dim lights of the Control Tower came on, darkness seemed to close in and envelop the airfield.

As Adams passed one of the sandbagged gun-posts he heard the hum of an approaching aircraft. A moment later he saw its navigation lights in the darkening sky and he quickened his stride. Half a minute later the Mosquito passed over him with a roar of engines and began orbiting the field.

Hurrying now, Adams passed a row of Nissen huts and the transport park. To the east he could hear more aircraft approaching. As he crossed the tarmac apron in front of No. 1 hangar, he passed close to a frail mono-plane. It was a Miles Messenger, flown in two hours ago by Air Commodore Davies. Davies, a small, alert man with a choleric temperament, had been the link man with the Special Operations Executive in the Swartfjord affair. An officer with a high pride in his service, Davies had a particular affection for 633 Squadron and consequently, in the way of love, was prone to criticize it when it fell below his expectations. A good-looking young Wing Commander had flown in with him but as Davies had offered no introductions, Adams could only speculate on the reason for the visit. For the last ninety minutes they had been closeted in the Control Tower with Henderson. Henderson, nick-named "Pop" by the crews, was a huge, middle-aged Scot who had taken over the squadron after Barrett's death. A taciturn man, he exercised his authority with the minimum of fuss and so was a popular C.O.

As Adams was passing the door of the Control Tower the landing lights flashed on, a dazzling corridor of brilliance that made Adams' eyes blink behind his spectacles. Navigation lights flashing, the first Mosquito began its landing approach. Engines purring and airfoils whining, it positioned itself between the two rows of lights and sank down. There was the squeal of tyres and brakes and the graceful shape disappeared into the luminous haze at the far end of the field.

The second Mosquito appeared to have suffered damage and Adams paused to watch it. One engine was coughing like a man with asthma and there was an unsteadiness in its approach as it entered the lane of lights. But its wheels were locked down and it was sinking into a safe landing when, to Adams' horror, a dark shape hurled itself out of the darkness like a hawk on a pigeon. The hammer of cannon fire was followed by a muffled explosion and a great gush of flame. The stricken Mosquito lurched helplessly and crashed fifty yards to the left of the landing lights. As the fireball slithered along the ground it left behind it huge patches of burning petrol and wreckage.

The German night intruder, who had carried out his mission so successfully, escaped into the darkness before the stunned crews above or the ground staff below knew what was happening. One gunner did let go a burst of Hispano cannon fire but the wildly-aimed shells were a greater threat to the orbiting Mosquitoes than the Ju.88. In the few seconds of chaos that followed, men ran in panic for the air-raid shelters and other men yelled orders that no one obeyed. From the platform of the Control Tower someone was firing pointless Very lights into the red-stained sky.

Then training asserted itself. As if a giant's black sleeve had swept across the field, the landing lights went out, giving Adams a moment of vertigo. Around him men were assuming their duties and fire engines and an ambulance were already gathering speed in their dash to the distant funeral pyre.

The Control Tower door burst open and Davies, Henderson and the young Wing Commander appeared. Seeing Adams, Davies ran over to him. "How many of the bastards are there? Any idea?"

"Only one, I think," Adams said, hating the unsteadiness of his voice.

Henderson joined them. The swinging headlights of a fast-moving ambulance momentarily lit up his face. Normally ruddy, it was pale and shocked. "Let's hope you're right." As he turned to flag down a crash wagon, Davies caught his arm.

"There's no point to it, Jock. You'd be wasting your time."

For a moment it seemed Henderson might resist. Then his huge body relaxed. "I suppose you're right." His Scots voice held a dash of resentment.

Overhead the orbiting Mosquitoes had switched off their navigation lights. Adams' imagination lifted him up there. Weary from hours of action, in imminent danger of collision with their comrades, the crews had no way of knowing if other intruders were waiting to pounce on them when they came in to land. Turning to Henderson, whose shocked eyes were still fixed on the burning aircraft, Adams found his question difficult to ask.

"Do you know who it was, sir?"

Henderson nodded. "Yes. It was Sandy Powell and Irving."

"Sandy Powell! Oh, Christ," Adams breathed.

Davies, birdlike in his quick glance at both men, gave neither time for reflection. He pushed Henderson and the young Wing Commander, who had not spoken, towards the Control Tower. "If we don't get the rest of 'em down, there might be another disaster. Come on."

The three men disappeared through the door. Over on the airfield crash wagons were now pouring foam on the wreckage. With a last look Adams followed them inside.

2

The blackout in Wilberforce Street, Highgate, was

The atmosphere in the Intelligence Room that evening had a hardness that a sharp knife might have had difficulty in cutting. Adams was seated at a large table. A detailed map of the Danish province of Jutland was spread out before him. His assistant, Sue Spencer, was seated at a table against the opposite wall. She was a tall, willowy girl whose sensitive face and gentle voice belied her efficiency. At the opposite end of the long hut, standing on either side of the door, were two groups of aircrew, and it was from them that the tension was radiating. Afraid of an eruption at any moment, Adams was finding concentration on his task a problem.

His method of interrogation was to give the crews some small privacy when they spoke to him, his belief being that privacy made them more likely to discuss their own mistakes and the mistakes of their comrades. Stan Baldwin, lapsed Catholic from Barbados, called his hut the "Confessional" and the name had taken on.

Hopkinson was the navigator Adams was interrogating. Hoppy, as he was affectionately known among the older aircrew members, had once been Grenville's navigator but an injury received in an earlier mission had kept him out of the Swartfjord raid. A small astute Cockney with a pinched face and the eyes of a sparrowhawk, he was wearing flying overalls which carried an evocative smell of combat—oil, cordite, and a dozen other indefinable odours—to Adams' nostrils. Condemned to ground duties by his eyesight and his age, Adams had discovered that the odours always stirred envy in him, and this envy puzzled him because in general Adams found war abhorrent.

He stole another quick glance at the two groups of aircrew. Their sullen muttering and antagonistic glances at one another made him think of the two electrodes of a giant condenser into which an overcharge of current had been poured. Apprehensive, he glanced up at Hopkinson

11

again. Usually one of the most cheerful men on the station, the Cockney was looking disgusted and resentful.

"So you don't think any ships were hit?" Adams asked.

Hopkinson's laugh was caustic. "It would have needed a miracle, wouldn't it?"

"Why?"

"I've just told you. Because there was a bloody great smoke-screen right over the convoy."

"But that means they must have had wind of your coming."

"Of course they'd wind of it. Is anyone surprised?"

With Hopkinson usually a helpful as well as a polite collaborator, and with everyone shocked by the intruder attack, Adams had thought it prudent to allow a loose rein. Now he decided things were getting out of hand.

"All right. You're not happy and you've shown it. Now pull yourself together and tell me specifically what went wrong. And while we're being civil to one another, put that cigarette out."

The jolt to Hopkinson was the more severe because it came from Adams, usually the mildest of men. His nicotine-stained fingers holding the smoking cigarette ground it into an ashtray on the desk. "I thought you'd already heard about the flak ship," the Cockney muttered sullenly.

"If you'd been keeping your eyes open instead of grumbling to those old sweats of yours, you'd have realized you're the first navigator I've interrogated. What flak ship?"

"The one you warned us about at our briefing."

Adams gave a start. "The one south of the convoy?"

"Yes. You pointed out that if it sighted us it would tip off the convoy. That's what happened."

Adams winced. The German convoy, protected from the Royal Navy by off-shore minefields, was believed to be carrying precious iron ore from Narvik to the Baltic ports. Adams was not looking forward to the rocket Group would dispatch when it learned the convoy was now safe in the Skagerrak.

"But you were routed well north of it. So how did it see you?"

"You're forgetting Harvey was given a sprog navigator. The fool took us in sight of it. I spotted the bloody thing on the horizon and broke R/T silence to warn Harvey, but he decided to keep going and hope for the best. We didn't run into any fighters, thank Christ—maybe they thought we were making for the coast—but the convoy hadn't taken any chances. The smoke was like a London pea-souper when we reached it."

"How can you be sure it wasn't your R/T that alerted them?" Adams asked.

Hopkinson tried unsuccessfully to hide his contempt at the question. "A Jerry flak ship doesn't miss two gaggles of Mossies only six or seven miles away. With the Banff Wing scaring the shit out of them, that's what they're looking for all the time."

Although Adams knew he was right, he felt a need to put in a word for the unfortunate Blackburn. "By the time you got there the convoy and the flak ship can't have been more than thirty miles apart. It's not difficult to drift a few miles off course over the sea—as a navigator you know that well enough."

Hopkinson's lack of charity was as uncharacteristic as was Adams' severity. "I know this—if it isn't one bloody thing, it's another. Christ knows when we last hit the button. The lads have had a bellyful. Once we were a squadron. Now we're just a shower."

Hiding his thoughts beneath a frown, Adams tapped his questionnaire with a pencil. "Let's make that the last of the moans, shall we? What type were the destroyers?"

"Elbings, I think," the Cockney muttered.

"Any flak ships in the escort?"

"I saw one. There might have been others."

"Was there much flak?"

"Enough for me."

"Radar controlled?"

"It had to be in all that smoke."

"Any damage?"

"I didn't see any. I saw them hit Powell though. Just under his starboard engine."

"Did he start straight back?"

"No, he dropped his bombs first. Then Harvey told him to piss off. Not that it did him much good," Hopkinson added as an afterthought.

Adams wrote it down. At the nearby table Sue Spencer had finished interrogating a freckle-faced navigator and a tall young pilot was now walking down the Nissen hut towards her. As he neared the girl, Adams, who could not resist a sideward glance, saw that her eyes held a faint trace of moisture.

It was a scene Adams had witnessed at least a dozen times as the girl gave silent thanksgiving for the pilot's return. Worship seemed the only appropriate word to express Sue Spencer's feelings for Tony St. Claire, and yet Adams felt even a hardened cynic would excuse its extravagance, for the slim young officer with the Byronic head and long, sensitive hands was the handsomest man Adams had ever seen. Nor was his artistic appearance deceptive. After studying the piano at the Royal College of Music, St. Claire had just been making a name for himself on the concert platform when the war had claimed him for service. In the six weeks since the young pilot's posting to Sutton Craddock, Adams had more than once pondered on the unfairness of a world that could pour such lavish gifts on one man and leave others so impoverished.

Only a trained observer would have noticed how Sue Spencer brushed her hand against St. Claire's as she handed him a leaflet. Occasionally Adams had felt a certain professional unease at allowing the girl to interrogate him: at the same time he knew she was not one to put personal relationships before her duty. Watching their faces in that brief moment and knowing they were already together in that magic world where he always walked alone, Adams felt a tug of pain as he turned back to Hopkinson.

"Did you see Millburn and Gabby get hit?"

"No. But that wasn't anything serious, was it?"

"Gabby got a scratch and a bang in the ribs and the M.O. sent him to the County Hospital for an X-ray. We're expecting him back tonight. Have your photographs gone in?"

A sudden shout interrupted Hopkinson's reply. The voice had a north-country accent that was exaggerated by anger. "You! St. Claire. Over here! At the double!"

The sullen hum of conversation stopped dead as all eyes turned on the doorway. Looking enraged enough to commit murder, Harvey was moving stiff-legged into the hut. Hiding his apprehension well, St. Claire turned away from the startled Sue Spencer and approached him. "Yes, sir?"

Adams could hear the Yorkshireman's heavy breathing. "You bastard," Harvey gritted.

St. Claire's good-looking face turned pale. "I beg your pardon, sir."

Harvey was trembling with fury as he moved to within three feet of the young pilot officer. "Don't beg pardon me, you bastard. I ought to bloody kill you."

There was a low gasp as Sue Spencer rose to her feet. Afraid she would intervene Adams caught her arm. Down the hut, although he was as shaken as the girl, St. Claire was giving no ground. "You keep on abusing me, sir, but I still don't know what I have done."

A large vein was visible on the Yorkshireman's forehead as he fought for control. "You wouldn't know, would you, you stupid sod. What orders did I give you after Powell was hit?"

"You said I had to fly back with him."

"That's right. And what do you think that was for—to play a duet with him?" The loss of his friend was almost choking Harvey. "Your job was to provide him with cover. And what happened? You let a bloody intruder give him the chop."

A few cries of assent rose from the smaller group and loud shouts of protest from the larger. As the dismayed Adams watched he saw a big pilot officer with a shock of black hair detach himself from the latter group. Tommy Millburn, an American of Irish descent, had joined the RAF before the United States had entered the war and in spite of repeated overtures from the 8th Air force and the promise of pay that was astronomical by British standards, Millburn had resolutely refused to exchange uniforms. Rich with humour and the darling of the Waafs, the American was showing the quixotic side of his nature as he faced Harvey.

"You've got it all wrong, sir. That Ju.88 wasn't behind Powell—he came in at ninety degrees. I was right behind St. Claire and saw the Hun cross the flarepath. There was nothing anybody could have done."

Frustrated by a witness who could clear St. Claire, Harvey was only too glad to turn his resentment on to the American. "So you were right behind the dreamy bastard! What were you doing? Listening to him playing Beethoven?"

A fighter to his fingertips, Millburn was only too willing to trade punches with the Flight Commander. "No one could have stopped that 88. Why don't you ask the guys on the ground? They must have seen it too."

There was a shout of agreement from the larger group. Knowing his case was lost but with his pain still demanding a victim, Harvey moved closer to the American. "Neither of you thought of helping him down? Or giving him cover on either flank?"

Millburn's contempt was pure provocation. "How could we know an intruder was waiting for him? Control thought he was fit to land on his own and so did Powell. Anyway, what difference would it have made? If we'd been in line with Powell that Hun would have got one of us as well. Maybe both."

It was the wrong thing to say. Harvey rammed his incensed face into Millburn's. "I'll tell you what difference it would have made. I'd trade half a dozen of your lot for Powell, Millburn. Any day of the week."

Millburn's cheeks paled. As men shouted their protest it seemed for a moment that the American might put himself straight in front of a court martial. Instead, regaining control with an effort, he muttered something and turned away. Instantly Harvey grabbed his arm and swung him round.

"Don't you turn away from me, Millburn! Not until you've been given permission."

His tug was the spark to the powderkeg. With a curse Millburn shoved him away. Eyes blazing with relief, Harvey was moving in to a fight that would have destroyed his career when an urgent bellow halted him.

"Harvey! Millburn! Attention!"

Training made both men stiffen. The horrified Adams, who by this time was running down the hut, saw Henderson inside the doorway. The bluff Scot was looking incredulous as he came forward. "What the hell's going on in here? What do you two think you're doing?"

When neither man spoke, Henderson turned his anger on Adams. "You—Adams! This is your office. Can't you keep order in it?"

Seeing that Davies and the young Wing Commander had followed Henderson into the hut, Adams was able to appreciate even more the big Scotsman's indignation. "I'm sorry, sir. That intruder raid seems to have upset everyone's nerves. I think you'll find it's only a mis-understanding."

Henderson was taking in the two groups of airmen and the expressions of Harvey and Millburn. Acutely conscious that the splenetic Davies was dying to get in on the act, he knew he had to act fast and firmly. The Intelligence Officer's explanation, weak though it sounded to Adams, gave the Scot the excuse he needed.

"It'd bloody better be," he said grimly, turning to Harvey and Millburn. "You two get to my office. I'll be along in a minute. If you exchange another word on the way, you're straight in front of a court martial. Under-stand?"

The two men nodded. Glancing at one another, they went out. Feeling Davies's critical eyes on him, Henderson turned to the hushed crews. "As none of you appear to have hit anything, I'm canceling this de-briefing session. Go to the Ops. Room and wait for me. It's time you and me had a long talk. That means no one leaves the air-field tonight. All right—move!"

As the men filed silently out Henderson turned his at-tention on Adams. "I want you to stay but not your assis-tant."

The shaken girl collected her papers and left. The door had barely closed before Davies, whose efforts to remain silent had almost choked him, came forward like a tru-culent cockerel.

"That was a bloody disgraceful scene, Adams. A Flight Commander brawling with a pilot officer. . . . Christ, this is a military establishment, not a taproom. What the hell was it about?"

Adams could see no harm in telling the truth. "It's the old problem, sir. When Harvey's navigator was taken ill, we had to give him a fresher, a man called Blackburn. It seems the youngster's mistake gave the convoy the tip-off."

"That doesn't call for a punch-up, does it? Where do St. Claire and that American fit in?"

Adams could only hope he wasn't making matters worse. "St. Claire and Millburn were following Powell down. It wasn't their fault—I saw myself that the 88 attacked across the flarepath—but Harvey thought they hadn't given Powell cover. I suppose it was one thing piling on another—Harvey and Powell were friends."

Davies swore and swung round on Henderson. "This isn't a squadron—it's a pack of squabbling mongrels. You've got to sort it out, Henderson. And bloody quick at that."

Somehow the Scot hid his displeasure. "Yes, sir. I'll do my best."

"You do that," Davies snapped. "Once this was the best squadron in the Group. I want it the best again. So I'd like some fingers pulled out. All right?"

Henderson's burly face turned red. "I said yes, sir!"

Giving him a sharp look, Davies motioned the young pilot forward and turned back to Adams. "You two had better be introduced. Adams, meet Wing Commander Moore. You'll be seeing a good deal of him in the future because he's your new Squadron Commander."

3

Adams' start and the glance he gave Henderson brought a terse nod from Davies. "I know. Harvey's not going to like it, but that's something he'll have to live with. In any case, after this ding-dong tonight he must know he's blown any chance he had."

Adams held out his hand. The man facing him was fresh-complexioned, with wavy fair hair and a good forehead. A very English face was Adams' first thought—the kind one associates with cricket matches and regattas at Henley. He had a small scar on his right cheek, and the crinkles round his eyes when he smiled suggested he was somewhat older than the squadron average—perhaps twenty-six or -seven. He was slim in build and his uniform was beautifully tailored, but any suggestions that the wrappings were more impressive than the contents were dispelled by the DSO and DFC ribbons beneath his pilot's brevet. His reaction to the fracas and Davies's sarcasm had been little more than a quirk of the mouth. With storms eddying all around him, Adams found this composure a most attractive feature.

He said the first thing that came to him and wanted to kick himself for it half a second later. "You've picked quite a night to arrive."

Moore's voice was much what he expected. English, cultured, and laconic. "These things happen."

Davies jumped in quickly at that. "They bloody shouldn't." He turned to Henderson. "Mind if I come to the bollocking?"

The big Scot made no attempt to hide his lack of enthusiasm. "If you want to."

"I do. I've a few things I want to say myself. And we can introduce Moore to them. All right?"

Henderson sighed audibly. "All right, sir."

"What about Harvey and that American? You going to talk to them first?"

"Yes, I suppose I'd better."

"You wouldn't like me to handle that while you go along to the Ops. Room?"

This time Adams was certain he saw Moore's lips quirk as the big Scot reacted. "No, sir. It's a Station disciplinary matter and I'd rather take care of it myself. But of course you're welcome as an observer."

Davies glowered. "No. I'll make a couple of phone calls instead. I suppose I am allowed to use the Adjutant's office?" he asked sarcastically.

"Of course, sir." Henderson's face was pink but expressionless as he turned to Moore. "If you don't mind waiting here, I'll collect you on my way back. If there's anything you want to know in the meantime, Adams will take care of you."

Looking like two dogs—one very large and one very small—who had squabbled over a bone, the two men left the hut. Unsure what Moore's half-smile signified, Adams proceeded with caution. "Feel like a seat while you're waiting?"

The two men sank into a couple of chairs that flanked the long hut. As the younger man pulled out a cigarette case, Adams shook his head.

"No, thanks. I'm a pipe smoker myself."

Moore extracted a cigarette and snapped the case closed. "Don't they say pipes are more soothing for the nerves?"

Adams could not help following the cigarette case back into the Wing Commander's inner pocket. Unless it was a fake—and spurious possessions did not seem to go hand in hand with this self-confident young man—the metal was gold. Before Adams could think of a reply, the need was taken from him as Moore flicked on an equally expensive lighter.

"Talking about nerves, this seems a pretty edgy squadron. What's your version of it?"

Knowing that both Davies and Henderson must have briefed him, Adams proceeded carefully. "I feel that any squadron that's suffered the losses we've suffered would have the same problems."

Somewhat to his surprise, the young officer nodded. "You're probably right. I'm told you have ten left of your original crews. Tell me again how that number's made up, will you?"

"Ten until tonight," Adams said with some bitterness.

"Young and his navigator were the only ones who flew back from the Swartfjord. He's now B Flight Commander. Harvey and his navigator, Lacy, escaped capture after being shot down and were smuggled back to the U.K. by the Norwegians. The other six come from crews wounded over Bergen before the Swartfjord raid who have now come back to us from hospital."

"So you needed massive replacements?"

"Right. And with the newspapers having plastered 633 Squadron's sacrifice in the Swartfjord on every front page, it's hardly surprising they didn't arrive here full of confidence."

The young officer looked sceptical. "You're not suggesting they saw this as a suicide unit?"

"No. But they saw it as an élite one. And with the Press constantly reminding them of it, it's not surprising they arrived here feeling inadequate."

"Did the old sweats behave like a *corps d'élite?*"

"They're a bit clannish," Adams admitted. "With their common bond of survival, I suppose it's natural in one way. And with three times their number of recruits pouring in, self-protection must have had some part in it."

"So the recruits felt they were being patronized, got chips on their shoulders, and things have got steadily worse?"

Either he knew something about men, Adams thought, or else Davies's briefing had been very perceptive. Rightly or wrongly, the recruits had felt themselves patronized. And the old sweats, mistaking their resentment for envy, had started making comparisons. As comparisons, in the nature of things, could hardly be anything else but unfavourable, they had closed their ranks even further. Polarization of the two groups had led to bad feeling and inefficiency, inefficiency to a series of abortive missions, recriminations to even more drastic polarization. Before Adams could comment further on the vicious circle, Moore put another question to him.

"What action did your last Squadron Commander take to put things right?"

Sweet nothing would have been Adams' reply if he hadn't disliked speaking ill of the dead. Alan Prentice, sent to the squadron a week after Grenville had been reported missing, had been a stiff, unimaginative officer, and although he had led the squadron courageously enough, he had been at sea in handling the psychological tensions that were tearing it apart. So his death in action three weeks previously had been no setback to the squadron's difficult convalescence, unless one argued that it had led to Harvey's temporary accession to the leadership. What that had done to squadron morale, in particular his behavior tonight, Adams was still trying to sort out in his mind.

"I believe he thought that time would put things right," was the best Adams could say for the unfortunate Prentice.

Moore did not pursue the subject. "How do the ground crews line up?"

"They tend to make matters worse. In Grenville's days they were members of an élite force and could look down their nose at other squadrons. Now the other erks are taking their revenge and ours don't like it. We try to keep them in line but they show their contempt of the new men in a hundred ways."

Moore was examining Adams' round, bespectacled face. "What would you like to see done?"

The directness of the question surprised Adams. "Me? I suppose I'd like to see them pull off a few successful operations. Their tails would come up and they might get a new respect for one another." Conscious of the obviousness of his solution, Adams suddenly felt embarrassed. "I know it's over-simple but I can't think of anything else."

The younger man gave no sign of noticing his discomfort. "Fair enough, but what comes first—the chicken or the egg? I suppose all the old sweats fly together?" When Adams nodded, Moore went on quietly: "Have you ever thought there might be a solution there?"

Adams gave a jump. "You don't mean split up the crews?"

"Not so much the crews as the flights. That way they might gain a new respect for one another."

Harvey loomed large in Adams' mind. An ambitious man, the Yorkshireman must have had high hopes that his role of Squadron Commander would be substantiated, yet in a few minutes he would learn he had been used only until Group had found a man more to their taste. After such a day of disaster, it was hard to visualize what his reaction would be to his replacement's suggestion.

"I'm afraid you'd have a revolution on your hands. You know how crews stick together. And most of the old sweats are in Harvey's flight. He'd go berserk if he lost them."

Moore's shrug suggested nothing could worry him less. "Tell me about your kites. They're a modification of the FBVI fighter-bomber, aren't they?"

"Yes, but by leaving in only the two outer cannon and giving us the short-barreled version, the manufacturers have given us a longer bomb bay and room for a bombsight in the cockpit. It's a bit of a squeeze but it does make us a very flexible unit."

Moore nodded. "How long have you been with the squadron?"

Adams had to think. "Over sixteen months."

"Then you must know the men as well or better than anyone. Will you advise me on reshuffling the flights?"

Adams procrastinated. "Have you discussed this with the Old Man?"

"Not yet. But I'm sure he won't object. I've been told I've got a relatively free hand to sort things out."

"I'm a coward," Adams told him. "I'll give you my advice but only on condition you don't tell even the station cat."

Moore gave his likeable smile. "It's a deal. When? After the C.O. has introduced me to the men?"

"If you like." Adams slanted a glance at his crowded desk. "In any case I'll be here for at least an hour—I haven't filled in my reports yet."

"Fine. Then I'll be back."

Adams hesitated then decided to say it. "Don't be too hard on Harvey and the old sweats. They've taken a hell of a beating and I think half their trouble is they're miserable that the squadron has slipped so much."

He saw a twinkle in the younger man's eyes. "Do you know something, Adams?"

"What?"

"You're just as sold on the old crowd as those erks you were talking about."

Behind his spectacles Adams looked resentful. "They were a fine crowd. So what's wrong with admiring them?"

"Nothing. Except I'm wondering what the difference is between you and the others."

"I don't blame the new men. That's the difference."

"Don't blame them for what? For not matching up?"

Discovering his muscles were tight, Adams made himself relax. "All right, you've made your point. I'll watch it and be as objective as I can."

"Good man."

Heavy footsteps sounded outside, and a moment later the burly figure of Henderson appeared in the doorway. His expression suggested he had got something off his mind and was feeling the better for it.

"You ready, Moore?"

"Coming, sir." With a friendly nod at Adams, the immaculate young officer walked unhurriedly towards the door. Watching him with a certain grudging respect, Adams, prone to irrelevant thoughts at such moments, found himself wishing he knew the name of his tailor.

The bright moonlight made the woods an eerie place of old light and jet-black shadows. The hoot of the distant train, reverberating among the mountains, added to the atmosphere. Hidden in a bush among the trees that flanked the cutting, Hausmann pulled aside a branch. The moonlight enabled him to see the single-line railway track that ran past him. Fifty yards down the track a heavy steel gate, linked to a high mesh fence, straddled it. Both were glinting dully in the moonlight. Defences could not be seen because of the darkness, but from the lights that had appeared when the guard was changed an hour ago, Hausmann knew there was a large blockhouse only thirty yards from the gate.

His eyes followed the high mesh fence that disappeared into the woods on either side of the track. Probably electrified and surrounding the entire valley, was his guess. He gave the railway track his attention again. Once it passed the steel gates, the tall firs closed tightly on either side, giving the appearance that the track was running into a dark tunnel. Probably it was, Hausmann thought. If the valley held the secret he and his comrades believed, German thoroughness would almost certainly ensure the track was camouflaged from the air.

The mournful hoot of the train sounded again. This time, as he listened, Hausmann could pick out the rhythmical pounding of its steam engine. With sounds carrying far in the mountain air, he knew it was still some distance away, but now it seemed certain this heavily-guarded valley was its destination.

He let the branch swing back into place, but not before the moonlight showed a weatherbeaten face and a burly, middle-aged figure wearing a pair of workman's overalls. As he sank back, a sharp root that had been jabbing into his body for the last ninety minutes no matter what position he assumed, took on new venom and dug into his right groin. With a silent curse he drew himself forward and took the pressure on his thigh. The sudden movement brought a loud clatter as a jay in the trees above took fright and flew away. Holding his breath, Hausmann drew the branch aside again, but to his relief no signs of alarm showed at the gate.

He wondered what Meyer and Rall were doing. They had been gone forty minutes: surely they had determined the extent of the fence by this time. On the other hand, the woods here were dense and vast: it was easy enough to get lost in them in the daylight, never mind at night.

A pain in his left leg was growing by the minute. Günter Hausmann suffered from arthritis which, although seldom severe enough to incapacitate him, could cause considerable pain when he was subjected to damp, and heavy dew was an integral part of summer night in these parts. He could feel its wetness as leaves brushed his face and knew that in the morning he would have difficulty in getting to work. The bloody war, he thought, that made a man of his age crawl about damp woods when he ought to be in bed with some plump woman. It was typical of his character that Hausmann could concern himself with rheumatism when one security slip could end in torture and death.

There was a singing in the telephone wires that ran alongside the track. As the night wind dropped, the wail of the train was heard again. By this time Hausmann knew it had passed through the small town at the head of the approach valley: the rumble of its freight cars and pounding of its engine had taken on a sterner note as it began its climb through the mountains. Under the waiting man the ground began to tremble.

Half a minute later a dazzling light shone through the bush as an arc light above the gates was switched on. Drawing the branch cautiously aside, Hausmann saw that the massive barrier, the high fence, the grim blockhouse, and a platoon of soldiers were standing out like a stage set against the black woods. To a yell of orders, the soldiers ran forward and manned the gates.

A shaded blue headlight appeared among the trees to Hausmann's right. Edging forward, he watched the freight train approach the gates. Although it was travelling slowly, the red glow of its firebox and the dull glint of its metal surfaces gave an impression of crushing weight and power. As it came opposite him there was a hiss of vacuum brakes. With a clanking of couplings and screech of metal wheels, the chain of wagons halted in front of the gates. As a searchlight flashed on and began playing down the track, Hausmann ducked back out of sight.

At the gates the driver and fireman were called down from the engine to show their papers. Soldiers from the blockhouse began moving down the train, shining their torches into and under the freight cars. The search for possible intruders was exhaustive: even soldiers who were manning the flak wagon at the rear of the train were called down for interrogation.

Fifteen minutes passed before the train was cleared and the steel gates opened. When the tail light of the flak wagon disappeared into the woods, Hausmann began counting in an effort to see how far the train ran into the woods before reaching its destination. As he counted, the steel gates swung back across the track and the arc light went out. He had reached only nine seconds when far into the valley there was a bright flash and a dull explosion. Dogs began barking immediately and there was a fusillade of automatic fire. Showing alarm, Hausmann backed a few yards into the woods. Then, forgetting his aching leg, he began to run.

"There it is!" Rall's whisper had a youthful sound as he raised an arm. His taller companion, little more than a shadow behind him, pushed forward to his side. Thirty yards ahead was a corridor of felled trees and down its centre the heavy-gauge wire of a mesh fence glinted in the moonlight. Meyer's whisper suggested an older man. Both men spoke in German, their native tongue

"So it does go right down the valley. Probably all the way round. Let's go back and tell Hausmann."

Below them they could hear the freight train pene-
ating deeper into the valley. Rall caught Meyer's arm.
We've got to find out what's going on down there. Let
e take a closer look. If it's not electrified, we can come
ack with wire cutters."

Meyer hesitated, then nodded. "Be careful. There might
e guards on the other side."

Rall's white teeth flashed in the shadows. "I've a date
morrow night. You think I'm going to miss it?"

The youth crept forward while Meyer kept watch. A
ight breeze, bringing the sound of the train nearer,
emed to emphasize the size and loneliness of the
oods. The youth managed to keep in shadow until he
ached the bright corridor of moonlight that lay be-
een him and the fence. As he paused, Meyer straight-
ed anxiously. "That's enough. You can see all you want
om there."

Rall either did not hear him or ignored his advice.
ending low, he began running towards the fence. He
as half-way towards it when there was an eruption of
ame and a shattering explosion that threw his body like
rag doll against a felled tree.

For a moment Meyer was too horrified to move. Then
e ran to the edge of the moonlit corridor. One glance
the dead youth was enough: he drew back gagging. As
s ears recovered from the explosion he heard the barking
dogs, followed by automatic fire. Fighting to control
s stomach, he ran back into the trees and made for the
alley entrance.

He took a path that led him away from the fence, but
e sound of dogs and shouting men was growing louder.
e thanked God they came from the other side of the
nce but he knew there must be access points along it,
d if his presence were suspected and the dogs re-
ased ahead of him, he was as good as dead. Stumbling
d falling, running until he felt his heart would burst,
e kept going until the sounds grew faint behind him. By
e time he reached his prearranged rendezvous with Haus-
ann he was retching again, this time from exhaustion.

"Mines," he gasped. "All along the fence. The youngster
n right on top of one."

As he dropped to the ground Hausmann's fingers dug
to his shoulder. "Could he talk?"

"Talk? Christ—what with?"

Hausmann relaxed. "Then they can't be sure. It coul have been anybody—a forester or a poacher."

Chest heaving painfully, Meyer managed to sit up. Lea in build, he had gaunt, sardonic features. "Did you get look at the wagons?"

"Yes. They were covered with tarpaulins but their seri al numbers tallied."

In the moonlight Meyer looked pale. "Then it look as if you're right."

Hausmann motioned him to be quiet. The dogs ha ceased barking and the train could no longer be heard Yet the deep silence was broken by the distant sound o machinery and the throb of powerful engines. Comin; from the vast stretch of forest, the sound was both mys terious and intimidating. Hausmann listened a moment then put an urgent arm beneath Meyer's shoulder. "Come on. We must get a message through to London."

The weary Meyer stumbled alongside him. As they dis appeared a night breeze swept down the valley, agitatin; the tall firs and drowning the alien sound. When the breeze dropped, the woods were silent again.

4

"Parade! Attention!"

There was a loud rumble of chairs and benches as the crews rose. Henderson, his ruddy face still showing resentment, waited at the foot of the platform for Davies to precede him before starting towards the end door of the Operations Room. Towering a good eight inches over the diminutive Davies and weighing at least a hundred pounds more, the Scot had the thought they must look a bloody ridiculous pair, particularly as they had unconsciously fallen into step. In his sensitive mood he wondered if Moore, who had stayed behind to chat with Young, wasn't being smart in avoiding the walk up the aisle with them. A suspicious glance at the crews showed their faces were expressionless but nevertheless Henderson broke step before they reached the door.

It was held open by Marsden, the Station Signals Officer. Giving him a nod, Henderson followed Davies outside, not failing to hear the muted cat-calls and murmurs of discontent the second he was out of sight. Nor did Davies either. The red spots on his cheekbones made him look more like a truculent cockerel than ever as he turned to the C.O.

"You've got your fair share of comedians among that lot. If you take my advice you'll keep swinging the big stick from now on. Otherwise they could get on top of you."

Although he needed to clench his jaw to do it, the big Scot kept silent. Outside on the airfield the rescue crews were still sifting through the wreckage to find the remains of Powell and his navigator. "The bastards!" Davies snapped to no one in particular. "A bloody dirty way to fight."

As things stood Henderson could see no percentage in reminding him that both sides practised it. Still bristling from the indiscipline he had witnessed, Davies marched stiff-legged across the tarmac to the Headquarters Block and down the corridor to the C.O.'s office. There, as if setting an example to all who abused protocol, he waited for Henderson to open the door and invite him inside. Muttering to himself, he tossed his cap on the Scot's crowded desk.

"I'll say this—you laid it on. Let's hope it makes 'em pull finger in the future."

Henderson decided it was time to speak up for his team. "There's nothing basically wrong with these lads, sir. They've had a run of bad luck and it's had an effect on them but they'll pull through."

Davies scowled. "They'd better, Jock, because I had to fight every sod from the C.-in-C. down to get this squadron. Nobody seemed able to grasp that one day a vital target might come along that only an élite squadron could clobber. Then that Swartfjord job arrived—and Christ, wasn't that important—and the boys did me proud." With memory ousting all else, Davies' birdlike eyes turned as bright as new pennies. "Nobody else could have done that job, Jock—not the Army, the Navy, or Main Force itself. This squadron did it—*my* squadron. So doesn't that give me the right to jump on 'em when they start falling from grace?"

Recognizing love and pride when he saw them, Henderson was mollified. "These boys won't let you down, sir. Just give them a bit more time and you'll find out."

Davies' remark was addressed to himself more than Henderson. 'That's the trouble. Time's running out.'

The Scot's ears pricked up. "Does that mean another big job's coming along?"

Regretting his lapse, Davies gave another scowl to cover it. "If we don't pull finger we won't have 'em for any job, big or small. There are dozens of gloating bastards up top who can't wait to shove 'em back in Main Force again."

Henderson's eyes were on his face. "Is that why you've brought in Moore?"

"Yes. If anyone can make a team of them, he will. But he might be a bit drastic at first—in fact I've told him to be. Back him up, will you, Jock? He knows what he's doing and I must have a first-class unit again." Before Henderson could comment, Davies went on: "You know who he is, don't you?"

'No. Who?"

You must have heard of Moore's Footwear. Shops in ry town in the U.K., Army contracts, the lot. He's the y son."

The Scot grimaced. "At least he shouldn't have prob- s meeting his Mess bills."

Loaded," Davies told him. "Somehow his old man's t the business private. Rumour has it he's on his last s, so any day the lad could inherit the lot."

'Let's hope it doesn't take his mind off his job," Hen- son said, conscious of his malice.

'Not a chance of that. He was one of Pathfinder Force's men and you know what that means. I'd nearly to dynamite to get him here."

At that moment the phone rang and the Scot picked the receiver. "Oh, hello, Bill. What's your problem?"

Davies, whose sharp eyes missed nothing, saw Hender- 's brow furrow as he listened. "Marsh? Yes, of course member. But you know what my orders were."

The indecipherable metallic voice made hurried ex- nations. After hesitating, Henderson appeared to relent. ll right. Let him go. But no one else. Got it?"

Before the caller could reply he slammed the receiver wn. "Trouble?" Davies asked casually.

'No," the Scot said shortly. "An administration mat- . It's settled now."

Davies changed the subject. "I'd like a favour, Jock. n I borrow your office for the night?"

Looking surprised, Henderson glanced down at his tch. "You mean you want to work?"

"No. I want to sleep in here. Will you arrange to have ed brought in?" Catching Henderson's look, Davies de- ed some explanation was called for. "I'm expecting important phone call but it won't come until the early rning. So there's no point in your staying up."

"I don't mind," the curious Scot offered.

"No. In any case it's something I have to handle alone. x it up, will you?"

Henderson had two thoughts as he dropped into his air and picked up the receiver. One was that he was w certain the Old Man had something big up his sleeve. e other was that the request for a charpoy would rt the rumour that he was knocking off a Waaf in his

office. Not wanting to hear the Duty officer's surprise, ▮
let the receiver fall the moment he made his dema▮
known. "Anything else, sir?"

"No. I've got all my kit with me." Davies was picking ▮
his cap from the desk. "Now what about a drink?"

Henderson, who could be tactful in spite of his blu▮
exterior, hesitated. "You mean in the Mess?"

"Where else?"

"You don't feel after all that's happened tonight, ▮
might be a good idea to stay out and let the lads blo▮
off a bit of steam?"

Davies stared at him. "Because you've given 'em a b▮
locking? Good God, no. Face 'em and let 'em know y▮
meant every word of it."

About to argue and then realizing the futility, the bur▮
Scot gave a semi-humorous shrug and followed Davi▮
outside.

Unlike Young, Frank Harvey did not stay in the Oper▮
tions Room to talk to Moore. As soon as Davies and He▮
derson had disappeared outside, he pushed back his cha▮
and followed them. Conscious that men were nudgir▮
one another as they watched him, he looked neither le▮
nor right. Out in the corridor he saw that Davies a▮
Henderson had not yet reached the exit door and ▮
paused. The last thing in the world the Yorkshirema▮
wanted at that moment was an exchange of words wi▮
either.

As dangerous as a goaded animal, he gave a start ar▮
swung round as a hand tapped his arm. For one who po▮
sessed his full measure of Irish temper, Millburn wa▮
looking contrite. "I'm sorry, sir. I'd forgotten back in t▮
Intelligence Room that you and Powell were friends."

"What the hell had that to do with it?"

Seeing how things were, Millburn took it cautiously. ▮
guess it makes me understand better how you feel. Only ▮
had to put in a word for St. Claire. The kid real▮
wasn't to blame."

"So you said."

Although the American felt he was hammering at ▮
brick wall he decided he might as well say it all. "It▮
tough about the job too. I guess all the guys feel the sam▮
way."

The crews were now leaving the Operations Room an▮

:ir glances at the two men were curious as they
tled past. The embittered Harvey jerked a thumb.
hey look it, don't they? Don't give me a load of crap.
llburn."

The embarrassed American was wishing he'd never
rendered to his impulse. "You are coming over to
: Mess, aren't you? Taff Wilson got a case of whisky
lay."

Harvey swung away. "No. I'm turning in."

Glad the painful scene was over, Millburn watched the
•rkshireman's powerful figure clump down the corridor
d disappear. They came all shapes and sizes, the
nerican thought, but that awkward sonofabitch led
: field. Then thoughts of Harvey vanished as a hand
pped across his shoulders and pushed him forward. "You
»oding about the bollocking, Yank? Forget it. There's
isky in the Mess."

The dog began barking when Harvey was still fifty yards
•m his billet. As he pushed open the door it rushed
ward and leapt against his legs. Closing the door he
itched on the light. The dog, a large black mongrel
:h Labrador leanings, tried to leap up and lick his face.
shing it away, Harvey stripped off his tunic. The dog,
ising his distress, ceased its fussing and watched him
xiously as he dropped on the iron-framed bed.

Christ, he thought, what a day. A ballsed-up operation,
•well's death, and now this. After they'd raised his hopes
letting him lead the squadron for nearly three weeks.
rvey's big hands closed into fists but before he could
ease the dam gates of his bitterness he saw again the
eral pyre that had incinerated Powell and Irving. His
:lamation of protest as he jumped to his feet and went
his locker brought a bark from the anxious dog. Dis-
vering he had locked the doors earlier, Harvey put a foot
ainst one door and heaved on the other. With a ren-
:ing of wood the lock burst open. Pulling out a bottle
whisky and a tin mug, he returned to the bed where he
e off his tie. A mat of chest hair showed as he unbut-
led his shirt and ran a hand round his sweating neck.
iring down at his wet palm, he cursed and swilled whis-
into the mug.

The neat spirit warmed his stomach and for a moment
: blood-red image in his mind faded. Before it could
urn he grabbed and held on to his resentment. The

hatred it engendered was like an analgesic and Harv
surrendered himself to it.

The effing, sodding country—nothing ever change
When Prentice had got the chop they'd used him as a sto
gap. Now, with the heat off, things were back to norm:
You could sweat your guts dry with fear, you could i
until the oxygen burned your lungs out, but the mome
they looked at your documents and saw your backgroun
up went their bloody toffee noses. They called in the bo
with the old school ties like this bugger Moore and y
were out on your arse.

Harvey raised the mug again. You could always t
'em. Their looks, their accent, their manner—most of
their manner. Harvey, who was nobody's fool, knew th
education and polish gave a man the confidence he cou
never have, but it was knowledge that only put a sha
point on his bitterness. The bastards denied you that poli
and then punished you for the rest of your life becau
you lacked it.

The whisky was warming the Yorkshireman's hostili
as well as his stomach. You had to hand it to 'em, thoug
They hadn't survived down the centuries for nothin
Carrots were their secret. Dangle one before a donke
and he'd follow you to hell and back. They were doi
it now. Every newsreel and broadcast told you the wa
was destroying for ever the old class system, and if we a
fought hard enough and won it, we'd all march should
to shoulder into a bright egalitarian future. Harvey gave
belch of disgust. When the war was over, the toffee-nose
bastards would climb back into their Daimlers and man:
gerial chairs, and buggers like himself would be back i
the factories and coal mines.

Another vision of Powell's funeral pyre came to Harve
as he slumped back on the bed. As he stiffened, the an:
ious dog barked and tried to jump up alongside hin
Harvey wiped an arm across his sweating face. Better th
bitter prewar memories than that.

His eyes settled on a faded photograph on a chest
drawers. The middle-aged woman was plump and dowd
the balding man showing unease in his Sunday-best sui
Kicked from arsehole to breakfast time all their lives an
as poor as church mice, the poor sods. To give him an
his kid brother, Jack, a Christmas stocking they'd had
put a sixpence a week away in a Christmas Club fro

January to December. If he or Jack had torn a shirt or a pair of shorts in play, it had been a major disaster. Yet in his entire life Harvey could never remember hearing either of them complain. His mother had sometimes cried but that had been for other reasons than self-pity. That was as far as Harvey could think about his mother: as always his mind shied away from the painful memories.

His father, Arthur Harvey, was a veteran of Ypres and the Somme. Although he had known nothing but menial work and poverty since leaving school he had tried to rejoin the Army on the outbreak of war. Disappointed by his rejection, he had joined the Home Guard. In Harvey's harsh terms—and oblivious of the fact he himself was an RAF volunteer reservist—his father was being loyal to the very bastards who had shit on him. Today, in his middle fifties, Arthur Harvey was a vanman receiving less than fifty shillings a week. With his younger son, Jack, crippled in North Africa and now back home receiving only a private's disability allowance, he would have been unable to keep the home together without the allowance Frank Harvey sent him.

Harvey had long ago decided there wasn't a single institution of society he could believe in. Parliament, the Law, and the Police were in his judgment a Machiavellian syndicate to help predators rob the poor and then protect the loot they seized. The Church's primary function, in spite of the casting of pious eyes upwards, was the preservation of its power and the power of its sponsors. What was that prayer in the Anglican High Church Service? "Thank God for the gift of great leaders." Ramsay MacDonald, Stanley Baldwin, Neville Chamberlain—Thank you very much, dear God! Something Harvey had once read had made him grin with pleasure—that the greatest charlatans in any society were those who wore gowns, be they white, pulpit-black, or lined with ermine. The fact that the wide net could embrace doctors and university dons had not diminished the Yorkshireman's approval.

By the time Harvey had drained the second mug of whisky, his thoughts were as blurred as the outlines of the sparsely-furnished billet. Attempting to get cigarettes from his tunic pocket, he fell back on the bed and his hard laugh echoed round the room. "Hey, Sam. I'm drunk! I'm bloody pie-eyed drunk!"

The delighted dog reacted instantly with a fusillade of

barks. Abandoning his attempt, Harvey tried to swing his legs up instead. It took him two attempts before he was able to lie back full length on the blankets. More confidant of him now, the dog jumped up and when it was not pushed away, crept up to lay its head on the man's chest, a position it often assumed when the Yorkshireman was sleeping. The dog lay quiet for a minute, then reached up and licked the man's face. There was no response. Harvey was fast asleep.

5

The Black Swan was quiet that night. Maisie, the barmaid, a big, handsome girl with dark hair and bold features, was leaning moodily against the counter of the lounge. A massive structure, the bar was scarred and weathered by centuries of use. The lounge beyond it, like the rest of the old inn, was also of great age, and had panelled walls and a timbered ceiling. Wooden tables, the cross-sections of some huge and ancient tree, stood round the walls. Like all the timber in the room they had the rich black patina that came from centuries of wood and tobacco smoke. Copper and brass ornaments flanked the wide stone hearth while others winked back light from the massive beam that made the lintel over the bar.

The girl was wearing a thin but tight-fitting sweater that accentuated her large breasts. The only other occupants of the lounge were four locals who were playing dominoes at a table near the fireplace. At the opposite side of the room blackout curtains were drawn across a huge mullioned window.

The public bar was hidden from the girl by a stand of oak shelves but she could hear the voices of the half-dozen farm labourers who were playing darts there. Usually jocular, they sounded muted tonight. As the girl listened a door opened and closed and a voice called out a greeting. Reacting immediately she hurried to the end of the counter where she had a view into the bar. Her face clouding, she drifted back to her original position and moodily lit a cigarette.

The innkeeper came round from the bar a minute later. Stoutly-built, with a countryman's ruddy face and thinning white hair, Joe Kearns was a man in his middle fifties. Like the girl he had a North Yorkshire accent.

"Young Jack Wilkinson has just come in. Seems he's had a word with the Special Policeman on the gate. No one's been allowed out of camp tonight."

The girl nodded sarcastically at the near-empty lounge. "Jack's always first with the news. Didn't he find out what happened?"

"The S.P. wouldn't say. But Jerry attacked 'em, I'm sure of it. I heard gunfire just before the crash."

The girl shifted restlessly. "So we still don't know who it was?"

Kearns shook his head. "What makes it worse they'd all got back. I counted 'em going out and coming home."

The girl's generous mouth was sullen. "You'd think someone would phone us and let us know."

"You know better than that, Lass. They put a blackout on the station when there's an emergency on."

The sound of an opening door made both of them turn but it was only one of the domino players going to the toilet. Kearns pulled out a huge pocket watch, then nodded at the remaining three men.

"Make that their lot tonight. We mightn't get a delivery tomorrow and I don't want the lads to go short when they're allowed over."

Maisie nodded and Kearns returned to the public bar. As the man returned from the toilet, one of his companions showed him an empty glass. The man, wearing a sports coat and corduroy trousers, nodded and approached the counter.

"What about another round, luv?"

Maisie gave him a stare. "What's the matter, Jack Foster? Can't you count? You've already had your two pints."

"Come on, luv. You can't be short tonight. Give us another round and have a drink yourself."

"I'm surprised at you, Jack Foster. If everyone tried to get more than his ration, where would the country be?"

"You don't ration that RAF crowd when they come over," the man complained.

Maisie bristled instantly. "I should bloody think not. Those lads earn their beer." Stalking from behind the counter she approached the men's table. "Come on, you lot. I'm closing up now."

Grumbling, but without malice, the men packed up their dominoes and said their goodnights to her. Listening at the door to their cheerful voices growing fainter, the girl caught the scent of geraniums and on impulse walked down the garden to the wicker gate. Over the wooden fence opposite she could see the Control Tower and the roofs of the hangars. With the airfield unusually quiet, the distant sound of a crane and the clink of metal were audible. Guessing the nature of the sounds the girl stood listening while a light breeze rustled the leaves of the crab apple tree behind her. It carried on it a smell of burnt rubber that drowned the scent of the flowers.

The small man wearing a service shirt and slacks was standing in front of a mirror on the billet wall. His right shirt sleeve was rolled back and he was peering at the back of his forearm. As he held it up to the mirror he showed his dissatisfaction and rubbed it with something he was holding in his left hand. This time he appeared more pleased with the result. As he was about to rub it again the billet door suddenly crashed open and Millburn entered. Dishevelled and clearly drunk, the American stumbled over the step. His cap clinging precariously to his shock of black hair, he peered at the small man then gave a wide grin.

"So you're back, kid. Hiya. How'd it go?"

The other airman, startled by the unexpected visit, had whipped his left hand behind his back. His voice had an undertone of guilt as well as a Welsh accent. "Not too bad, boyo. It can't have been, because they let me out."

Millburn waved a hand vaguely at the billet door. "You've missed a great party, kid. A whole case of whisky. We've drunk the lot."

The Welshman showed his disgust. "Greedy sods. You could have kept a bottle for me."

A wiry man with sharp features that looked comically young or shrewdly old at will, Johnnie Gabriel was one of 633 Squadron's characters. Nicknamed Gabby or The Gremlin either because of his appearance or his madcap pranks, his youthful image was in fact an illusion because at 28 he was the oldest aircrew member on the Station. In the late thirties he had flown as a fighter pilot for the Government in the Spanish Civil War and had shot down three planes before being shot down himself and captured. When threatened with death by firing squad, he had offered to fly for Franco and incredibly his offer had been accepted. The first time Gabby had flown solo he had flown straight out of Spain into France.

At the outbreak of World War II, Gabby had volunteered to fly for the RAF, not unreasonably expecting to receive pilot training. Instead, in its infinite wisdom, the RAF had kept him waiting in civvie street for eighteen months and then, to his high indignation, trained him as a navigator instead. His present rank of pilot officer was the same rank that his pilot, Millburn, held.

Incongruous in appearance as the American and the small Welshman were, they were an inseparable couple and notorious on the station for their mad pranks and tireless pursuit of women. Unlike most of the other recruits, who had come straight from the pool, they had served for six months on a Mitchell Squadron which in April 1943 had been posted to the Middle East. At that time Millburn had been in hospital recovering from a foot wound and Gabby's protestations had been so vehement that he had been allowed to remain in the U.K. until his pilot was fit again. The outcome had been a posting to the famous 633 Squadron which at the time had flattered and delighted the two men. Now, faced with the dissension that threatened the very existence of the unit, they were less happy with their posting.

Sensing with a drunk's perception there was something wrong with the Welshman, Millburn showed concern and lurched towards him. "What'd they say about your back, kid? It isn't broken or anything, is it?"

"Of course it isn't bloody broken. But I've got a hell of a bruise."

Millburn gave him a lecherous grin. "You didn't waste your time in there, did you, kid? You've got a couple of nurses lined up for us?"

"Not nurses," Gabby told him. "But there was a bint in the Waiting Room I chatted up. Her mother was having a finger stitched and this girl was waiting for her."

"Nice looking?"

"Great. Long blond hair and all the trimmings. Looked like Veronica Lake."

"I go for Veronica Lake. She got a girl friend?"

Gabby nodded. "I said we'd see 'em on Saturday if we're not flying."

"What's the girl friend like?" Millburn asked suspiciously.

"How do I know? Gwen said she's all right. But you don't have to come if you don't want to."

Grunting something, the American sank down heavily

on his bed. "I'm in trouble, kid. I had a scrap with Harvey and Pop Henderson heard it. Called us both in and gave us hell."

Gabby was edging towards his locker. "What was it about?"

"Harvey was going for St. Claire. Said it was his fault Powell got the chop. He's as touchy as hell tonight. Maybe this new skipper's got something to do with it."

Gabby halted. "New skipper?"

"Don't you know anything, kid?" Then Millburn remembered. "The Old Man had us in the Ops. Room while you were away. Tore us off a strip for not pulling together and then introduced us to this new guy, Moore."

"Moore?"

"Yeah." Millburn grinned maliciously. "He looks like one of your upper crust. Got a row of gongs, though."

"Harvey must be shaken up."

"You're not kidding. He didn't come into the Mess tonight." It was then Millburn noticed Gabby's rolled-up sleeve and the hand he was still holding behind his back. "What the hell are you doing?"

Gabby's start and look of guilt was all the big American needed. Moving fast for a man in his condition he grabbed the indignant Gabby by the arm and stared down at it. A thin weal, raw and inflamed, ran across the outer forearm. Glancing round, the puzzled Millburn saw a discarded bandage lying over the back of a chair. "What's the idea?"

As the small Welshman tried to pull away, the American spun him round and forced his other hand open. He stared down at the toothbrush that Gabby had been trying to hide, then let out an enormous guffaw. "You little bastard! Now I've seen everything."

Caught in the act, Gabby reacted defiantly. "Listen who's talking! If I were in your outfit they'd give me the Purple Heart for this."

Millburn's hysterical laugh was echoing round the billet. "You were rubbing it, weren't you? Making it worse so you could show it off to the broads." Howling with laughter he released Gabby and collapsed on the bed.

"Jesus Christ, the Conquering Hero. . . . Pity it's not across your arse, kid. Then you could give 'em a real eyeful." Millburn wiped tears from his eyes. "I can't wait to tell this to the boys."

Gabby looked aghast. "You wouldn't do that?"

"Kid, I couldn't stop myself. It's a lulu."

"You do and our date's off," Gabby threatened.

Alcoholic cunning came to Millburn's aid when he saw Gabby was serious. "I'll make a deal with you, kid."

"What kind of a deal?"

"I have Veronica Lake on Saturday and you get the blind date. Right?"

Gabby, who in spite of his stature liked tall girls, did not give in without a fight. "You could lose out. The other one might be terrific."

"Yeah, that's likely. You've caught me that way before, you little bum. Make up your mind. It's Veronica Lake or I'll take your arm and that toothbrush and lay 'em both on the Mess table."

Gabby's voice was bitter. "Now I know why you don't join the Yank Air Force. They're too bloody smart to have you."

"Right. Is it a deal?"

"It's a deal," the small Welshman choked.

6

The blackout in Wilberforce Street, Highgate, was
complete that night. The only light Julie Marsh could see as
she sat at the window of the upstairs room was the moonlight glistening on the roofs of the prim, semi-detached
houses. Wilberforce Street lay in the suburbs of the small
Yorkshire market town, and its inhabitants were mostly
elderly and law-abiding citizens.

In the semi-darkness of the sitting room the girl's hands
were picking fretfully at the arms of her chair. As she
heard the sound of an engine her pale face appeared at
the window. Seeing it was only a car moving down the
street with hooded headlights she turned restlessly and entered a bedroom where she tip-toed to a cot and listened.
Satisfied the child was asleep she adjusted the coverings
and withdrew.

Holding her watch to the moonlit window she saw it
was almost midnight. Time for the news if she wanted to
hear it again. She did not and yet she switched on the
battered old radio that stood on a small table near the
fireplace. Music sounded for a couple of minutes and
then the announcer's voice she had come both to need and
fear. "This is the late night news read by Alvar Lidell.
The battle in the Orel sector is still raging and latest
reports indicate the Russians are inflicting heavy losses
on the enemy and are advancing on all fronts. In the
Pacific the Americans claim to have shot down 45 Japa-
nese bombers over the Central Solomons. In Italy the
Canadians have captured Caltagirone. . . ."

Years of war had taught Julie Marsh to sift through
the propaganda and only hear what was relevant to her.
The relevance came at the end of the bulletin. "This
evening, light aircraft of Bomber Command struck at
enemy shipping off the Danish coast. Enemy merchant
ships were damaged and one believed sunk. Only one of
our aircraft is missing."

That was what it had come to now, the girl thought.

43

Suffering was measured in numbers. One missing aircraft was nothing—if it were a Mosquito it meant only two bereaved families. Fifty missing aircraft were different. Fifty plus was bad—unless the results came up to expectations in which case the losses in military terms were still insignificant.

The girl could taste blood where she had bitten her lip. She had been listening to the news bulletins since nine o'clock and with Peter still not home had convinced herself the light aircraft referred to belonged to his squadron, for she knew they had used 633 on shipping strikes in Danish waters before.

Feeling panic clawing at her mind she tried to obey Peter's appeal to stay calm. Ninety-nine times out of hundred, he had told her, there was an innocent reason why he was late. It might be a hold-up at de-briefing or an unexpected order to see the Flight Commander. It might very easily be a breakdown of his old motorbike. There were dozens of innocuous things that could make him late.

If only he were able to contact her, the girl thought. Needing a target for her pent-up emotion, she found one. Why hadn't those two old bitches downstairs got a telephone? For the rent they charged they ought to have one in every room. Although Julie knew that half the time Peter would not be allowed to phone her, reason had no place in her resentment. You saw selfish bitches like them every day. Women whose husbands had no more dangerous jobs than running the local bank or cinema and yet who grumbled because the sound of our own planes kept them awake. The war had split society right down the middle. On the one hand profiteers were making killing from it and their wives were gloating over their newly-found wealth. On the other hand were mugs like Peter and herself, living in two threadbare rooms and wondering if each day would be the end of their world.

Julie Marsh discovered she was trembling and went to the sideboard for the pills the doctor had prescribed her. Needing water, she started downstairs to the kitchen she shared with the elderly sisters. They had long retired to bed and six months of conditioning made the girl tiptoe down the staircase. Then she realized what she was doing and a sudden rush of defiance made her leave the chen door open as she ran the tap. The jet of water, umming into an enamel basin, drowned noises from the eet and it was only when she heard the sound of a otorcycle being leaned against the passage wall outside at she knew her vigil was over for one more night. For-ting the blackout, she fumbled with the lock and tore e door open. As a uniformed figure appeared in the ctangle of darkness, she flung herself forward. "Oh, ank God, Peter. Thank God!"

He could feel the trembling of her thin body. "I'm rry, love. I knew you'd be worried."

"Worried! . . ." She was holding him with the urgency one trying to press through the barrier of flesh to make e only unity death could not sever. He made an effort enter the kitchen but her arms were binding him like es. His rush of impatience shocked him. "Careful, e, for Christ's sake! There's light streaming out all over e garden." As her arms slackened he disengaged them d closed the door. "That's better. Another minute and u'd have had the police round."

Marsh was a 24-year-old pilot officer. Orphaned in s late teens, he had been studying to become an ac-untant when he met Julie at a Christmas dance in 1938. scovering she was an orphan herself and that they ared the same serious-minded tastes, Marsh had fallen love with the girl almost at first sight and they had arried while he had been waiting his call-up into the AF. At the time Julie had been living with an ageing nt and it had been agreed she should remain there til Marsh's pay would allow them to rent their own me.

Their child, Mark, had been born one month after arsh's posting to 633 Squadron and had been a dis-trous turning-point in their marriage. Until then Julie d seemed to bear his aircrew activities if not with uanimity at least with the nervous fortitude other pilots' ives displayed. But with the birth of Mark had been rn a fear that no pleas of Marsh's, no visit to the doc-r, no frantic calls on the Church for help, could di-inish. With only her old aunt for a relative, what would appen to her child if Marsh were killed?

It proved a fear as progressive as a chronic disease. n his doctor's advice Marsh had asked for living-out per-

mission. Although in general aircrews were not allowe
to have their wives within forty miles of their airfield
Barrett, the old C.O., had let himself be influenced b
medical reports, and Marsh had found two rooms for th
girl in Highgate.

It was a move the young pilot officer had regrette
almost as soon as it was made. Now Julie had facts a
well as imagination to torture her, and her discover
that Marsh was a member of an élite squadron, with a
that status implied, did nothing to help her. As the un
had trained for its climactic mission in the Swartfjor
her neurotic apprehensions had grown, and it had com
as a relief when Marsh had been seriously wounded i
the arm during the ambush over Bergen. Longing for hir
to be grounded, she had secretly prayed for amputatio
and so had added guilt to her neurosis. Instead Marsh ha
made a complete recovery and now that he was back o
active service every day was a crucifixion for Julie.

Marsh had lost count of the times the girl had begge
him to ask for ground duties and his procrastination wa
not helped by the fact he had flown over forty mission
In Main Force he would have automatically qualified fc
a rest: in an élite squadron it was almost a prerequisit
that one stayed on for a second tour because a high de
gree of efficiency could only be obtained with exper
enced crews. Nor had the situation been helped by 633'
terrible mauling in the Swartfjord. With such a small nu
cleus of survivors to build on, Davies had practically ir
sisted that all men volunteer for a second tour, and now
as things stood between the older crews and the new, th
survivors would bitterly resent one of their member
shaming them by withdrawing from combat.

Yet the strain on the young pilot officer was grea
Unlike most of his comrades who, in spite of their ex
perience, seldom thought of personal death because the
were young enough to believe themselves immorta
Marsh was made to think of death every time he returne
home. And death contained no subconscious illusions o
glory. Knowing what it would do to the girl, Marsh feare
it not for its pain or its mystery but for its stark breac
of faith. He was needed, and so death would be a de
sertion that in moments of despair he felt would keep hir
chained to the earth in an attempt to expiate it. Tha
Marsh could hold such thoughts was perhaps the bes

idence of his deteriorating health and the love he had
r this sick and frightened girl.

In appearance he was thinly-built with a sallow face
d thin locks of black hair that tended to straggle over
s bony forehead. Strain and battle fatigue showed in his
ithdrawn eyes, nervous movements, and sudden bouts
irritation.

Hurt and confused by his tone, Julie had drawn back
to the kitchen. "Have you had anything to eat?"

He tried to make amends. "Yes, love. But I wouldn't
ind a cup of coffee."

Glad to have a task, the girl turned to a cupboard that
ing over an enamel-topped table. As she fumbled in-
de, a tin tumbled down with a loud clatter. "Watch it,
r Christ's sake," Marsh muttered, picking up the tin.
e was returning it to the cupboard when he heard a
oor creak. Looking dismayed, the young couple turned
see a woman of late middle age advancing down the
all towards them. With curlers in her frizzled hair and
er mottled legs thrust into a pair of fluffy slippers, the
parition was wrapped in a grey woollen dressing gown
at in her displeasure she was wearing like a suit of
ail. Her initial attack was directed at the white-faced
rl.

"Really, Mrs. Marsh, I do feel you ought to be more
nsiderate. Do you know what the time is?"

The girl's voice had a cracked sound. "Yes, Miss Tay-
r. I know what the time is."

"Then how do you justify this kind of behaviour? First
ou come clattering down the stairs and wake me and my
ster up and now you make all this noise in the kitchen.
ou're not thinking of cooking a meal at this time of
ght, are you?"

"No, Miss Taylor. I'm making my husband a cup of
offee."

"Then do you have to make so much noise?" The elder-
woman, who was in fact the younger of the two
sters, transferred her resentment to the dismayed young
an. "It's very late, Mr. Marsh. Nearly half-past twelve."

The trembling Julie pushed past Marsh before he could
aswer. "Unfortunately the enemy aren't very considerate
out the time, Miss Taylor. Sometimes they sail their ships
d fly their aircraft right through the night."

The unexpected counter-attack made the woman stiffen.

"There's no need for sarcasm, Mrs. Marsh. We're just a
aware as you are what the Germans do."

Marsh moved fast before the situation got out of hand
"My wife's a little overwrought tonight, Miss Taylor. Sh
knew I'd been out on a raid and was worried becaus
I'm late home."

He received a sniff of disapproval. "Mrs. Marsh get
overwrought a little too easily, Mr. Marsh. I think you
should explain to her that my sister and I can hardly b
blamed for the war or that you are in the Air Force."

Marsh felt the girl contract and squeezed her arn
warningly. "No one's blaming you, Miss Taylor."

"Most people of our age wouldn't dream of taking in a
young couple with a baby. Loss of one's privacy is quit
a sacrifice at our age, you know."

"We know that, Miss Taylor. And we do appreciat
it."

"I'm glad of that, Mr. Marsh. Because with Highgat
crowded with evacuees accommodation isn't easy to find
these days."

The girl's eyes were tightly closed. You're doing thi
for me, aren't you, Peter? You fly out day after day an
put your life on the line and then have to come back an
crawl on your belly to people like this. Just for the privi
lege of being with me for a few hours. Julie Marsh sud
denly felt sick as she listened to the woman's mollifie
voice. "If you really need a cup of coffee, please be a
quick as you can about it. My sister and I find it ver
difficult to sleep when someone is pottering about in th
kitchen."

The girl waited until the door closed before openin
her eyes. "Dear God Almighty," she breathed. "Is thi
what the war is all about? Protecting the possessions o
millions of people like that?"

He sighed. "Never mind the coffee. Let's get to bed."

For the first time she saw how weary he looked. "No
First you're going to have a drink and something to eat."

Upstairs the bedroom was chilly: the old house with it
stone walls exuded dankness even in the summer. Witl
the one-bag-a-week ration of coal firmly in the hands o
the Taylor sisters, and with the Allocation Board arguin
that Marsh was taken care of by the RAF and his wif
ought not to be billeted so near the airfield, heating wa

other problem the young pilot officer could only try to
[pu]sh to the back of his mind until the autumn.

He was drawing back the cot blankets but afraid he
[wo]uld waken the child, Julie pulled him away. "I didn't
[ge]t him to sleep until nine o'clock. I think a tooth is
[bo]thering him."

Marsh moved reluctantly away and stripped off his uni-
[fo]rm, the gaslight giving his thin arms and torso a pal-
[lid] appearance. By the time he had climbed into his
[pa]jamas Julie was already in bed. As he turned off the gas-
[lig]ht and opened the blackout curtains to let the moon-
[lig]ht in, she turned back the bedclothes for him. He sank
[do]wn beside her with a sigh. "Heavens, that's good."

She reached out and felt his hand. "You feel cold."

[ ]I am cold, he thought, his mind on Powell and Irving
[an]d the way they had died. Her question was the one he
[ha]d been expecting since his arrival home. "It was you
[w]ho lost that aircraft, wasn't it?"

"No," he lied.

"Yes it was. I can always tell. Who was it?"

He lay staring at the ceiling. With his eyes now ac-
[cu]stomed to the moonlight he could just make out the
[da]mp stain in the corner caused by the rain the previous
[da]y. "Have you told Miss Taylor about the ceiling? It's
[go]t to be fixed before the autumn."

"Yes. But they said it's difficult to get workmen with a
[w]ar on."

He gave a groan. "Not that again."

There was no way of side-tracking her. "Who was it,
[Pe]ter? You've got to tell me. Otherwise I'll be wondering
[al]l night."

Someone has to help her, Marsh thought in panic, but
[w]ho? The medicos she had seen had fobbed her off with
[pi]lls that only made her feel worse afterwards and the
[ch]urchmen had made her feel guilty for not having faith
[th]at her husband, who statistically should already be dead,
[w]ould live to be a hundred and fifty. The only name that
[of]fered hope was Squadron Leader Adams. Unlike any
[ot]her Administration officer that Marsh had known, Adams
[se]emed genuinely concerned with the problems of his
[m]en, and the one time Marsh had confided in him had
[b]rought Adams straight round to No. 30. Not being pres-
[en]t at the interview, Marsh had never known what Adams

had said, but for at least a week afterwards Julie ha
seemed brighter. Marsh made a mental note to see Adam
the next day.

"I have told you," he said. "We all got back. All fiftee
of us."

Her hand, gripping his own tightly, brought a lump t
his throat. It was all so bloody pitiful—she did not believ
him and yet desperately wanted to. Perhaps if he mad
love to her it would release the tension in them both. He
voice, small with shame, checked him as he was turnin
towards her. "I was an awful coward tonight, Peter.
was certain it was you."

Suddenly, as real as if it were in the bedroom, he caugh
the smell of burnt flesh that had hung around the ashes o
the Mosquito. He sank back. "We were dropping leaflet
from 30,000 feet over France. You can't have anythin
safer than that. They haven't a fighter that can touch us.'

At least it was as good a lie as any to sleep on, h
thought. As he kissed her he tasted the salt of her fear
"Are you going to sleep now?"

"Yes," she whispered. It was another lie: how did on
resolve one's desperate need for rest when every secon
with him was so precious?

He kissed her again. "Good girl. Dream about tha
leave I'm getting. It's only six weeks away."

For a moment she did not speak. Then she held ou
her arms to him. "I love you, Peter," she whispered.

At that he made love to her. Afterwards, with hand
entwined, they lay quietly side by side in the old-fashioned
bed with its brass fittings. Their bodies had just been one
but their minds were already a thousand miles apart in
their thoughts and fears. Both were too young to know
their loneliness was shared by all mankind.

7

A moonbeam was slanting across Henderson's office when the scrambler telephone rang. In precise time it was 0246 hours. A comical figure in striped pyjamas, Davies leapt from his camp bed and promptly stubbed his toe against a chair. Cursing loudly he limped towards the desk and snatched up the receiver. His irascibility died at the voice that greeted him and it was nearly three minutes before he spoke again. His tone had changed to sobriety and a barely-concealed excitement. "That's bad luck, sir. But at least we know our suspicions were right. Yes; I'll organize that right away. With luck I should have the photographs by noon or thereabouts. How shall I get them to you?"

As Davies listened to the reply, his sore toe was rubbing itself ruefully against his bare ankle. "I agree, sir—it'll be more convenient. Right, providing all goes well I'll drive round with the plates tomorrow afternoon. Yes; I'll organize that too—I'm pretty certain there's room. No, we'll keep that hush-hush but it's going to be difficult not to tell Henderson and Adams about the valley: can I play that as it comes? I can—good. What's that? The squadron? Oh, Christ, no. You've nothing to worry about there. When we want 'em they'll be ready. All right, sir—I'll see you tomorrow."

Lowering the receiver, Davies stood motionless for a moment. Out of uniform, his small pyjama-clad body looked oddly vulnerable. Nothing to worry about—Christ. You know your trouble, Davies? You're a sentimentalist as far as this squadron is concerned and unless you're lucky or Moore is a miracle worker, they're going to drop you right into it. And then those bastards up top will have your guts for garters. Suppressing a sigh, Davies picked up the second telephone.

"Hello, switchboard. This is Air Commodore Davies. I want you to get me the Photo-Reconnaissance Unit base at

Benson. What's that? Of course I know the time, you silly little man! Pull your finger out and put me through."

The Waaf sergeant at the sunlit window gave a start. A pretty girl with freckles, she was finding it difficult to hide her excitement. "I think some of them are coming now, sir."

Moore, who was inspecting a plan of the station with Adams at his elbow, did not look up. "Are they, sergeant? How many?"

"Eight, sir."

"Is the Flight Commander, Harvey, among them?"

"Yes, sir."

Moore slanted an amused glance at Adams. "It sounds like your old sweats. Good. There's nothing like killing all the birds with one stone."

Adams wondered at the young man's imperturbability. After helping him with the crew reorganization the previous evening, he had agreed to give Moore a conducted tour of the airfield. Believing the new lists would not go up in the Flight offices until Harvey had a chance to see them, Adams had suggested the tour be made directly after breakfast. Now, trapped with Moore in the Squadron Office, with over half of A Flight marching in for a showdown, Adams was feeling like a criminal caught in the act.

The flushed Waaf moved to her ante-room door. "What shall I do, sir? Let them in one at a time?"

Appearing not to hear her, Moore was pointing at the station blueprint. "What's that?"

"Our SCI stores," Adams told him. "We keep them away from the bomb dump. Just in case."

"I take it they're inspected regularly?" As Adams nodded, Moore's voice ran on with no change of inflection. "No, sergeant. Let 'em all in together if that's what they want."

Adams could now hear the tramp of outraged feet in the corridor. Giving him an agitated glance, the girl ran into her office. A moment later Adams heard a door flung open. The gruff voice that followed made him wince. "I want to see the Squadron Commander."

The girl sounded breathless. "I'll see if he's free, sir."

For a reply there was a cross between a growl and a snarl. The flustered Waaf appeared in the ante-room doorway. "Flight Commander Harvey would like to see you, sir."

Adams, aware of his cowardice, broke in quickly. "Would you like to handle this alone?"

"No. It shouldn't take more than a couple of minutes." Expecting Moore to keep Harvey waiting in a gambit to draw his steam, Adams was surprised when the young Squadron Commander gave the Waaf a nod. "Ask him to come in, will you, sergeant?"

The glowering figure of Harvey, wearing a uniform that had known much wear and tear in Mosquito cockpits, entered the office. Already on his feet, Moore held out an amiable hand. "Hello, Harvey. I'm sorry we didn't get the chance of a chat last night. But it's good of you to come along like this and introduce yourself."

The coolness of it took Adams' breath away. As Harvey stopped dead in his tracks, Adams had an incongruous vision of a fighting bull, breathing fire and brimstone, being confronted by a smiling matador holding a bouquet of flowers.

The handshake the Yorkshireman was compelled to make was little more than a hostile crunching of palms. Before any more courtesies could frustrate him, he launched his attack.

"I've come about these new flight lists pinned up in the office. Are you responsible?"

"Yes, of course."

"You gone out of your mind? You've not only split up the flights, you've even split up some of the crews. What the hell's the idea?"

Moore indicated a chair. "Like to sit down while you discuss it?"

The Yorkshireman's face was as black as a fell in a thunderstorm. "No, I wouldn't. You've only been here five minutes. How the hell can you learn anything about my crews in that time?"

Moore dropped into his chair and sat back. "It was a bit of a problem, I admit. But I managed to get expert advice."

Harvey's glare almost knocked Adams' spectacles off. "From him?"

"There are plenty of people on the station who know your crews, Harvey. So it wasn't difficult to put two and two together."

"And get what? Five, six, a bloody dozen? You come barging in, tear apart lads who've been flying together for months, even years, and stick sprogs in their places. Do you realize how the lads in my flight feel? If you don't pull those flight lists down, every man-jack of 'em will ask for a posting."

Moore nodded at the ante-room door behind which sullen voices could be heard. "Are those your men?"

"Yes."

"Which ones? The crews who flew under Grenville?"

"That's right. When this was a real squadron."

"Do they want to see me?"

"To a bloody man."

"Then call them in. It'll save time that way."

Glaring at Moore suspiciously, Harvey stalked to the door and gave a growl. Led by Hopkinson, men began filing into the office. Some looked openly rebellious, all looked upset. Among the latter was Peter Marsh. Moore, who had risen to his feet again, gave each man a smile. "This is an informal get-together, chaps, so take what chairs there are and smoke if you want to."

Although a few puzzled glances were exchanged, no one took advantage of his offer. Giving no sign he noticed, Moore seated himself again. Standing fascinated by a filing cabinet, Adams saw Hopkinson throw a glance at Harvey and then step forward. He guessed the Cockney, as Grenville's old navigator, had been chosen to speak for the rest of the flight.

"We're here about these new crew lists, sir. We can't make any sense out of 'em. As things stand we've got one good flight. Split us up and all we've got is a shower."

"Go on," Moore encouraged as a mutter of assent ran round the office.

"Splittin' up the flights is bad enough. But you've broken up some of the crews as well." Hopkinson nodded at a rangy, satirical-faced New Zealander. "I've been flyin' with Andy Larkin ever since I came out of hospital. Now you've given him one of the sprog navigators. Where does that leave me?"

Moore's laugh surprised even Adams. "You've all my sympathy, Hopkinson. A new boy arrives one evening and the next day wholesale changes are made. It does seem a bit of a bastard, I agree."

Although Harvey's scowl deepened at this show of forebearance, it clearly threw Hopkinson. "We're sore because we're the old crowd who flew with Grenville. It's bad enough to change flights: it's the bloody end to be crewed up with a fresher."

Moore nodded sympathetically. "I agree. Losing your crew mate is worse than losing your girl friend. That's why it's only done when necessary. I'm sorry you're one of the victims, Hopkinson."

A puzzled murmur ran round the office. Hopkinson voiced the men's bewilderment. "Can I get somethin' straight, sir? Was it you who made those changes or wasn't it?"

"Oh, I made them. With help, of course."

"Then I don't bloody get it," Hopkinson said bluntly.

With a laugh, Moore walked round to the front of the desk and leaned against it. Watching his performance with admiration, Adams found himself thinking of a young college tutor lecturing his students. "It's really quite simple. Wellington used to do it in all his battles. And it was very effective."

"Did what, sir?" The open-mouthed question came from Bernard Ross, a Scottish navigator.

"When Wellington had a lot of rookies—and he was always given half-trained troops—he used to slip in one seasoned soldier among every three or four of 'em. That way he never had a completely inexperienced battle line and of course the recruits soon learned all the tricks from the veterans. I suppose in botany they'd call it self-propagation."

Another of the "old" hands—in this case a 21-year-old called Frank Day whose pink cheeks suggested only a passing acquaintance with a razor, was frowning. "What has that to do with us, sir?"

"That's easy. You are one of the seasoned veterans. When a fresher has you around, either as a member of his crew or in the kite alongside him, he feels much more confidence."

Adams could have sworn he saw the youngster grow a couple of inches. "I see. Thank you, sir."

Moore's gaze travelled round the eight men, most of whom were now listening intently. "The truth is, this squadron can't afford the luxury of super crews all flying in the same flight any longer. Look at the situation as it stands. A Flight has four experienced crews. B Flight has only two, Young and Millburn, and although Millburn is experienced he tends to associate himself with the more recent arrivals. If I transfer two of your crews to B Flight and at the same time split the two remaining experienced crews into two units, I have in effect four experienced crews in each flight, a far better balance. Doesn't it make sense?"

Seeing from the mens' expressions and the couple of hesitant nods that Moore's argument was gaining ground, Harvey launched a counter-attack. "That's all theory. In practice look what happened to me yesterday with a sprog navigator. It'll be bloody chaos. No one will know his arse from his elbow."

His pugnacity earned no more than a grin from Moore. "Then we'll have to teach everyone the difference, won't we? I've asked Air Commodore Davies to take us off ops. for a few days." As the men gave an interested stir, Moore went on: "We'll spend them getting to know one another better. I want you all in the Ops. Room at 1100 hours to brief you on a practice exercise. In the meantime get your kites air-tested. Any more questions?"

"Yes." As expected, the growl came from Harvey. "Does the C.O. know about this?"

"Of course. I had to get authorization from him before I could ask Davies to take us off ops."

"I didn't mean that. Does he approve of your buggering about with the crews?"

"He had a few reservations, just as we all have, but he felt it was worth a trial."

It answered the question Adams had asked himself. "So he's not as sold on it as you are?"

"I'm not sure I know what you mean by sold. He's given his permission for it to go ahead. That means he will back its enforcement. Is that what you are asking?"

For the first time Adams felt the iron fist in the velvet glove. Harvey's grim expression suggested he felt it as well. "It's not going to work. It's better you know it now than later."

Ignoring him, Moore glanced round the half-circle of thoughtful faces. "As the survivors of the old squadron, you must be more aware than anybody there's a need for change. I don't believe what's happened recently is your fault or even the fault of the new men. I believe it's one of those things that happen to any squadron that suffers the casualties you've suffered. 617 were in an even worse mess after the dam raids—at one time it looked as if they might be disbanded. But they've pulled through and become a crack squadron again and so will you. But because you're the seasoned crews I need your cooperation and it's my guess you'll give it. All right, that's all. You can get your kites tested now."

Looking more rueful now than militant, the men began filing from the office. Seeing Harvey was still standing his ground, Hopkinson hesitated, then said something and followed the others out. Moore, who had walked back behind his desk, feigned surprise on seeing Harvey was still there.

"Is there something I haven't covered?"

Although deserted by his army, Harvey was still defiant. "This isn't the way to improve squadron morale. You're only going to make more problems."

"Have you any better suggestions of improving it?"

"Yes. Give those bloody freshers a dressing down. Tell them to stop thinkin' they know everything."

Moore grinned at him. "But I'm giving you the chance to do that. Right inside your flight office."

Harvey's temper broke. "I'm warning you. I'm not taking this and neither will my lads when they see through your flannel."

Moore's voice checked him in the doorway. "Harvey, let me give you some advice. If you have thoughts of influencing your men against me, I would think again. Otherwise you'll find yourself in very serious trouble. Do I make myself clear?"

For a moment the Yorkshireman's huge frame seemed to expand in the doorway. Then, with a curse, he lurched out. As Adams released his breath he received a comical glance from Moore.

"I don't think he approves of me, do you?"

"Whether he approves or not, you talked the others round."

"Not all. Don't forget there are still the new men."

"Do you think they'll also make a protest?"

"From what I saw in your office last night, I wouldn't be surprised."

Before Adams could reply Moore's phone rang. "Moore here. Oh, hello, sir. Yes; he's with me now."

He replaced the receiver thirty seconds later. "We'll

have to postpone the crew briefing. That was Davies; he wants us both in his office later in the morning."

"What time?" Adams asked.

"He can't say exactly. It seems there's a PR Mossie dropping in some time before lunch with photographs. Davies wants us when the photographs are developed."

Suspicions that had collected almost unnoticed in Adams' mind since the previous evening suddenly surfaced. Davies' prolonged stay at the airfield, his anxiety to get the squadron shipshape, Moore's almost indecent haste in reshuffling the crews, and now this PR Mossie . . . .
"Do you think Davies has something lined up for us?"

Moore's shrug gave nothing away. "If he has, perhaps he'll tell us about it when the photographs arrive. What about this inspection tour of ours? Have we still time to make it?"

Convinced now that he was right, Adams could only hope Davies knew how deep the squadron's troubles went. "We can try. It's up to you."

At that moment the Waaf sergeant put her freckled face round the door. "Pilot Officer Millburn's on the phone, sir. He's asking if he and some others can have an interview."

Moore's laugh was aimed at Adams. "There goes our tour. Let's try to make it this afternoon." He turned to the girl. "All right, sergeant. But tell them to hurry it up."

Adams moved towards the door. "I'll go and catch up with my work in the meantime. Shall I drop in when the Mossie lands?"

"If you would. Then we can go to the C.O.'s office together."

8

Adams heard the Mosquito just after 1130 hours and walked out on the tarmac in front of No. 1 hangar. The dazzling morning sky made his eyes blink behind his spectacles and he was a few seconds spotting the aircraft. Painted sky blue, it was banking gracefully over the gunposts along the southern perimeter. As Adams watched, it banked more steeply and began flattening out for a landing.

His eyes lowered to two jeeps that were waiting on the airfield. The moment the Mosquito's wheels touched the runway, the jeeps began moving forward. As the aircraft lost its forward momentum its propellers became golden bangles in the sunlight. The jeeps had now made contact and were running alongside the taxi-ing plane. A man was standing up in the leading jeep and waving an arm. Obeying his signals, the sky-blue aircraft turned off the runway and came to a halt alongside a dispersal hut. The pilot and observer climbed into the first jeep which drove off immediately for the Headquarters Block. The second jeep parked between the aircraft's stationary propellers and Adams saw a mechanic and a Waaf jump out and remove the camera pack. Half a minute later the jeep span round and headed at speed towards the photographic section.

In his turn Adams made for the Squadron Commander's office. The freckle-faced Waaf was checking her curls in a mirror on the wall as he entered. "Tell Wing Commander Moore that the PR Mossie has landed, will you?"

"He's gone to see the Armament Officer, sir. He shouldn't be more than a few minutes."

"How did his interview with Millburn and company go?"

The girl's giggle told Adams she had fallen for the debonair Moore. "He told them it was important they flew with the older members because, as they'd been at OTU more recently, they were better acquainted with the latest equipment."

Adams stared at her. "Did it work?"

"It seemed to cool them down. It's the way he does it, sir. I think he could charm the birds from the trees if he wanted to."

Walking with Moore five minutes later to the C.O.'s office, Adams asked the question that had been worrying him for the last two hours. "That business about Wellington. Did he really space his seasoned veterans out like that?"

Moore's amused laugh echoed down the corridor. "I haven't the faintest idea. But it sounds the kind of thing he might have done, don't you think?"

Unteroffizier Klaus's earphones crackled. "Wildcat Two! Steer 122 degrees for practice interception. Altitude 1,600 metres. Grid reference Anne-Marie 15."

"Got that, Fritz?" Klaus asked in his throat microphone.

Behind him little Fritz Neumann already had his map open and was tracing his finger along the intersecting A and M references. "Ludwigshafen," he announced.

The Bavarian countryside with its mountains, forests, and ripening rye fields tilted and revolved as Klaus set the Me. 110 on its new course. A pleasant-faced young man, Klaus was wearing shorts, for the July day was hot and the cupola of the 110 had a hothouse effect. His shirt was a South African bush jacket on which his girl friend, Heidi, had sewn his insignia of rank and his pilot's wings. Klaus, young in years but old in experience, had flown in North Africa the previous year and the bush jacket was a gift from a South African he had shot down near Benghazi. The plane had been a Mitchell and all its crew had survived. Klaus had entertained them at his airfield that same evening and before the drinking had ended he and the South African pilot had exchanged shirts like rugby players after a hard-fought match. As the Mitchell had been his first kill Klaus had looked on the bush jacket as a lucky charm and even during the winter had worn it under his flying suit.

With his kills now totalling six, the young German felt he had reason to believe in the efficacy of the souvenir. Four more kills and he would be an ace and receive the Iron Cross. The difference that decoration made! Even a small man like Kuhnel, who couldn't scale 130 lb., had seemed to grow six inches once it dangled around his neck.

And the effect on girls was magnetic. Klaus had promised himself he would notch up his tenth kill before his leave in August when he and Heidi were to be married. To go home and greet Heidi an ace and a hero seemed to young Klaus the ultimate in human happiness.

Fighter control came in somewhat snappishly: "Wildcat Two. You're drifting off course. Turn on to 122 degrees."

The order roused Klaus from his dreams of glory and he turned and gazed into every quarter of the blue sky. Satisfied it was clear of hostile aircraft, he threw a glance back at Neumann. "Anything showing yet?"

The radar operator was peering at his three opaque screens. "No. We must still be out of range."

Klaus felt the Messerschmitt yaw slightly and swore as he corrected her. The cause was the contraption of aerials and reflectors sticking out of the 110's nose. Part of her Lichtenstein air-borne radar, it reduced her speed by at least eight knots and made her more clumsy to handle. At the same time, Klaus reflected, the cat's eyes that the radar set provided more than made up for its defects. Since his transfer to a night fighter squadron he had made four kills in as many weeks and all had been four-engined bombers. Many of his comrades had been equally successful: the *Tommis* were taking a terrific beating. Klaus's one fear was that their losses under the Kummhuber defences would stop them coming and so frustrate his ambitions.

Like the target plane it was stalking for practice, the 110 was under the control of "Kassel," one of the many Kummhuber radar stations that by July 1943 formed a complete defence chain from Denmark to the Swiss frontier. Picking up an approaching bomber on its "Freya" beam, a station would hand over its image to one of its "giant Würzburg" beams when the plane came within their range. With a second "giant Würzburg" locked on to radar-equipped Me.110s or Ju.88s whose nightly task was to patrol the beacons, the fighter controllers could vector their hunting aircraft near enough to an unsuspecting bomber for their air-borne radar to take over. Kassel was one of the latest beacons, built in depth behind the main radar chain, to take care of any Allied bombers who broke through into the heart of the Reich.

Fritz Neumann could hear Klaus humming the latest

popular song through the intercom. Neumann was a Bavarian from the small town of Bad Heilbrunn at the foot of the Austrian Alps. At school he had wanted to be a journalist but the war had scotched that ambition. As a member of the Jungvolk he had been in Hamburg during the early 1941 RAF raids, and although they had been small-scale compared to what was to come later, the sights the impressionable Neumann had seen had determined him to join the Luftwaffe. He had hoped to become a pilot but there had been a glut of pilot cadets at that time and he had been trained as a navigator instead. During this time the bombing offensive on Germany had greatly increased in severity and a desire for revenge on the *Tommi* flyers had been strong in the young Bavarian. From navigational school he had been sent for a two months' course on radar equipment before his posting to the Pool. There he had been crewed up with Klaus whose North African tour had ended in a spectacular crash that had killed Klaus's navigator and brought the young pilot back to Germany in a flying ambulance. Somewhat prone to hero-worship, Fritz had at first been flattered at becoming Klaus's navigator. Now his hero-worship, if not altogether gone, was growing thin.

For now that Fritz Neumann had become an experienced airman and taken part in the destruction of four Allied aircraft, his desire for revenge had totally vanished. These days he saw the enemy as men like himself—ordered by their political leaders to do a filthy job and doing it at the risk of their lives. He had never dared tell Klaus that more than once he had retched when he saw the Messerschmitt's cannon shells rake open the belly of a helpless bomber and flames engulf its wounded occupants. At such times he envied Klaus who, like so many other fighter pilots, seemed to see enemy aircraft as clay pigeons to be shot down for sport rather than vehicles containing men of flesh and blood like himself. Sometimes Neumann wondered if the very imagination that had made him sob for revenge in the flaming streets of Hamburg was now responsible for his feeling of identity with the *Tommi* fliers whose charred bodies were strewn over France and Germany.

The huge, blue mirror of Lake Constance lay to the right of the 110. It fell behind as "Kassel," whose instruc-

tions were coming through more frequently, made Klaus
turn thirty degrees north. "Any luck yet?" he asked Neumann.

Neumann was scanning the screens of his "Emil-
Emil," the night-fighters' code name for their Lichtenstein
radar, with some exasperation. The fighter controller's instructions to Klaus told him they should be well within
A.I. range of their target. "Nothing yet," he called back.
"I think these mountains must be interfering with the
blips."

Klaus switched off his R/T so his words wouldn't reach
Kassel. "If the stupid fools had set the exercise at 3,500
metres instead of on the deck, there wouldn't be any
problems. Forget the Emil and look out of the bloody
window."

Neumann was about to obey when he saw a flicker of
light appear on one of his screens. He made quick adjust-
ments to his controls. "Got it," he shouted. "Range 5,000
metres."

Klaus has spotted the target plane visually at almost the
same moment. It was an old Dornier 11 flying over a
wooded hill. He switched on the R/T to inform Kassel
that contact had been made and pushed forward the yellow throttle knobs. The note of the engines rose a full
octave. Behind him, to satisfy Kassel and the demands of
the exercise, Neumann was giving instructions from his
radar set but Klaus was paying little attention. Swinging
in a wide arc on the slower Dornier, he approached it on
a parallel head-on course. At a closing speed of over five
hundred miles an hour the Dornier grew from a black
speck to twenty tons of power-packed metal in seconds.
Klaus waited his moment and just before the two aircraft
shot past one another he banked steeply into a half-
circle and pulled up under the Dornier's tail.

He could not resist putting his thumb on his cannon
firing button as he crept in closer. Two hundred metres,
one-fifty, one hundred. . . . He was now in the perfect
position for the kill, so close he could see the penumbra of
the sunlight round the turning propellers, the blue oxide
flame of the exhausts, the patched scars from old battles
on the bomber's wings and fuselage. The graticule of his
sights moved to the junction of body and wings. In his
mind's eye he pressed the firing button and the aircraft

reeled away like a stricken fish. It took a yell from Neumann to pull him together. "Look out! You're getting too close."

With a smile Klaus swung the stick over and the Messerschmitt dived away. Only four more bombers needed and over a month to go before his leave. He would double, perhaps treble, that number of kills before then.

9

The two rooms on either side of the C.O.'s office had
been vacated of staff when Moore and Adams came down
the corridor. An S.P. posted on guard stiffened to attention. Certain now that his suspicions were well-founded,
Adams followed Moore into the office. Davies, who with
Henderson alongside him was bending over a map on the
desk, glanced up irascibly.

"You've both taken your time, haven't you?"

Moore's voice was imperturbable. "You said when the
photographs were developed, sir. Are they here?"

Davies scowled. "No. But they bloody well ought to be
by this time."

Taking the hint Henderson picked up a telephone and
put a call through to the photographic section. While he
was talking Adams noticed two young airmen standing in
the corner by the door. Although they had removed their
helmets, both were wearing flying suits which suggested
they had been flying at altitude. Now back on the ground
they were looking uncomfortably warm. One was tall,
dark-haired, and sported a huge moustache. His colleague
had sandy hair and a nose that looked as if it had been
bent in a rugby scrum.

As Henderson replaced the receiver, Davies motioned
Adams and Moore towards the map. They saw it was a
large-scale map of Bavaria with a red ring drawn round
an area west of Salzburg. Davies jabbed a finger at the
ring. "I want you to take a look at that. It's where these
two PR wallahs have just been."

Neither man could see anything but the contours of
mountains and the dots of Alpine villages as Henderson
passed on the news of the photographs to Davies. "They
hope to have the plates over within ten minutes, sir."

As Davies gave an ambiguous grunt, Moore turned to
two PR airmen. "What was the trip like?"

The taller man answered him. Very self-possessed, he

sounded in accent and manner as if he had just returned from a successful conference in the City. "Frightfully good, sir. Top-class weather all the way. Lucky, really, because we only got wind of the job early this morning."

"That's all the notice I could give 'em," Davies snapped to no one in particular. Then, to the pilot and navigator: "Tell us again what you saw."

At the pilot's glance, the sandy-haired navigator stepped forward. Adams caught a lilt of Welsh in his voice as he stood over the map. "There wasn't very much, sir. Just a railway track running from this village up into the valley" —the navigator's finger traced a line between two mountain contours—"but then it vanished into the woods."

"No suspicious buildings of any kind?"

"There was something that might have been a blockhouse, sir. But apart from that, only a few farms and forest huts."

"What about firebreaks?"

"Yes, sir, there were some of them. But don't all woods have them?"

Davies shifted his gaze to the pilot. "Did you say there was no flak at all?"

"Not over the valley." The pilot's quip was clearly intended for his Celtic colleague. "It was as quiet as a Swansea Sunday."

Davies' scowl suggested he did not approve of this young man's self-possession. "Some people have it easy, don't they? All right, you'd better go and have something to eat until we've seen these photographs. Remember your briefing. Not a word about this to a soul—not even to your mothers. Off you go."

The two men nodded. As they disappeared outside, a Mosquito climbed over the building with a crackling roar.

"Air-testing?" Davies asked.

Moore nodded. Through the window Adams could see a second Mosquito taxi-ing towards the runway. Davies sounded curious.

"How did they take your shuffle-up?"

"Not too badly."

"Think they'll settle down in a couple of days?"

"I'm hoping so, sir."

"So am I," Davies growled. Motioning the men nearer again, he lowered his voice. "What I'm about to tell you is something you don't even tell yourselves once you've left this room. Understand?"

Both men nodded.

"All right. Here it is. As you must have heard, there have been rumours buzzing about for years that the Jerries are miles ahead of us in rocketry and recently a Waaf Intelligence Officer, Babington-Smith, has identified what looks like a flying bomb of some kind on a ramp at Peenemünde in the Baltic. They're keeping tight-lipped about it but I gather PR kites have located factories and laboratories there as well, so we can assume it's due for a Main Force raid at any time. That's one side of it. We're on to something a bit different. It seems Jerry's clearing house for reports on secret weapons, code-named ZWB, has been infiltrated by one of our agents and he's confirmed that Jerry is developing an entire range of rockets: rocket fighters, long-range bombardment rockets, radar-controlled flak rockets, and Christ knows what else. Until now, apart from Peenemünde which is believed to be specializing only in this flying bomb, no one has known where these developments are taking place. However, we've known for some time that a certain factory near Hoffenscheim in north Germany is turning out servo-mechanisms and our agents have been trying to trace their destination. With the rerouting Jerry does with his wagons, you can imagine the problem and until a week ago they'd had no dice. Then, by sheer chance, someone discovered a high-security zone in Southern Bavaria. Agents were put on surveillance there and the outcome is disturbing."

Letting the point sink home Davies lit a cigarette and as an afterthought offered the packet round. As the three men declined, another Mosquito could be heard taking off on its air-test. Glancing upwards, Davies waited until the roar of engines faded.

"I don't have to tell you that our aircraft losses are climbing again. Jerry's a resilient sod and he's pulling out all the stops to defend the Fatherland. At the moment it's not his flak but his fighters that are the main threat. The Yanks are taking a hell of a beating on their daylight raids and the radar-controlled night fighters are clobbering us hard. If losses continue to rise, Jerry could win back control of his air space and that wouldn't only put paid to our policy of strategic bombing but would also have a drastic effect on our invasion plans. And if invasion is delayed another year or so, who knows the effect it might have on Russia and the fate of Europe. So the stakes are bloody high."

Satisfied from his listeners' faces that he had their full attention, Davies laid a finger on the map again. "Which brings us back to this Bavarian valley. Although Jerry is working on a dozen rocket projects, we've reason to believe he is giving top priority to two. One is a bombardment rocket that can be radar controlled for about forty miles. Imagine what that would do to an invasion fleet. The other, code-named Rhine Maiden, is a radar-controlled anti-aircraft rocket with a proximity fuse. If we don't like their fighters, imagine what these bastards would do to us. Our armament and speed would be useless and among tightly-packed formations such as the Yanks use, their effect would be catastrophic."

In the tight hush that followed Davies' revelation, Adams felt that someone was expected to ask a question. "You're saying that these servomechanisms have been traced to this valley, sir?"

"Correct. I got the news last night. A train entered the valley and its wagon numbers corresponded with those seen leaving Hoffenscheim."

"Do the agents know the exact location of the plant?" Moore asked.

"No. You know what those Bavarian valleys are like— all high mountains and bloody huge forests. You've only to lop off the lower branches of the firs and you can hide a railway track and anything else in 'em. And the population's sparse. That's why we've only just discovered it's a security area. The peasants have probably been told it's a training centre or some guff like that." Irascible again, Davies swung round on Henderson. "Where the hell are those photographs?"

The Scot was turning back to the telephone when running footsteps were heard in the corridor, followed by a half-hearted challenge by the S.P. Pushing past Adams, Davies yanked the door open, to reveal a breathless Waaf carrying a tin box. Davies's bark made the girl jump as if the S.P. had pinched her bottom.

"You've taken your time, haven't you?"

"We've been as quick as possible, sir."

"How have they come out?"

"Quite well, sir. We've enlarged two of the best as you asked."

Davies snatched the box from her. "All right. Off you go."

As Adams closed the door, Davies put the box on the office floor and opened it. As he lifted out the first photograph, a wet print sandwiched between two plates of glass, he gave a satisfied grunt. "That PR pilot was right. We have been bloody lucky with the weather." He examined the rest of the prints, then, motioning Henderson to clear the desk, laid two prints on it. "The one on the left is of the main valley and the town at its entrance, Ruhpolding. The other is a blow-up of the town itself."

The other three men gathered round him curiously. The first photograph, taken from a great height, made the Bavarian landscape resemble a heavily-wrinkled tablecloth. A short, wide valley occupied the centre of the print and Adams knew that the dark shadows on the flanking mountainsides were dense forests. Half-way along its length the valley bifurcated, the eastern leg of the Y being longer and narrower than the western. Davies laid the point of a pencil on the parent valley entrance.

"Ruhpolding's here. Now take a look at the blow-up. This is the railway station. I've already been told that the line used to end here. Now see where it goes," and his pencil ran up the photograph and off the glass.

He replaced the print with two others. The first was a long-range shot of the eastern branch of the valley. The sides were densely wooded and although minute squares of fields dotted its length, most of the floor was dense in timber. The second print was a blow-up of the junction of the two valleys and heavy enlargement showed a cotton-thin black line swinging into the eastern leg. Tracing it Davies gave an exclamation of triumph. "You see. It ends in a forest. Doesn't that prove that it has to mean something?"

Henderson was looking doubtful. "It could be just for removing timber. Or it could go right through the valley to somewhere else."

"Then why the hell would they throw a high-security net round it?"

The unconvinced Scot gazed down at the photographs. "What security measures have they taken?"

Davies, who was clearly holding something back, turned to Adams. "You're the expert. What do you see?"

Adams was studying the thin lines of firebreaks that were criss-crossing the timber. Two ran along the mountains that flanked the valley and two others lay across it, forming a huge rectangle. He pointed them out. "These firebreaks look a bit too symmetrical. Could there be fences along them?"

Adams had never expected to get a beam of approval from Davies but he received one now. "That's good work, Adams. Our tip-off says the fence is mined and that the trains have to pass through a check-point before they enter the valley. So you see Jerry's security is tighter than a bull's arse in fly time."

"What's our first move?" Henderson asked.

"First we have to be certain we're right about the nature of the target and where it's sited. That's a job for our agents and with all this tight security they've got a problem. Our problem—assuming our guesses are correct—is that we don't know how long the plant has been there and what stage its research has reached. So time could be running out for us."

Adams, still euphoric from Davies' praise, interrupted him. "Excuse me, sir, but if the target is so important and time is at a premium, wouldn't the simplest thing be to send in a force of heavies?"

The glance he received was withering. "Send in thousands of trained men and millions of pounds' worth of machinery without knowing what we're bombing? Into a narrow valley as far away as Berlin? You losing your grip, Adams?"

"Sorry, sir. I didn't give it proper thought," Adams said hastily.

"You can say that again. Christ, they're queuing up in front of Harris with their priorities. We're not even certain it's not an elaborate spoof—Jerry's clever enough —and then think what clots we'd look! But in any case heavies could never bomb this place at night, even if they used Pathfinders and knew what they were bombing. Don't you know those forests stretch for miles?"

Moore's intervention brought Adams relief. "Have you considered B.17s? They would solve your daylight problem."

Davies' scowl was an admission he had dabbled with

the idea of calling on the Americans for help. "No one would choose an out-of-the-way valley like this out of pure cussedness. We feel it's a hundred to one the plant is sited so a high-level raid can't touch it. And if it has to be done at low level, Mossies are the only kites with the necessary range and capability."

Nodding, Moore spanned the map with his hand. "I make it around six hundred miles. More with dog-legs."

Davies expressed his uneasiness in irritability. "I know that."

"What time of day would the attack have to be made?"

"The experts think about noon. In the early morning and evening the mountains throw too many shadows."

"That's what I thought. So it would mean a round trip of 1,200 miles in daylight over enemy territory with a low-level attack thrown in. As things are at the moment, I'd say it was just about impossible."

Although Adams was shocked by the risks involved in the operation, it was clear Davies had not expected his young Squadron Commander to hold the same doubts.

"Nothing's impossible, for Christ's sake. We're working on it, and if the job has to be done, we'll find a way. But as far as the primary target goes we can't do anything until our agents confirm their suspicions and then pinpoint the target for us. Unfortunately that might take some time although they're making it a top priority job."

"How can they get near the plant if security is so tight?" Adams had the temerity to ask.

"Leave their problems to them," Davies snapped. "You're going to have enough of your own because I'm making the entire operation this squadron's pigeon. Your first job, now we know where the servomechanisms are going, is to flatten the Hoffenscheim factory. This might give our agents a bit of breathing space to do their stuff. Also, as Hoffenscheim is in a valley, it'll give your lads a taste of what the real job might be like. After that, if the agents are still in the dark, we'll clobber another factory that's making gyros. It's on the outskirts of Miesbach, near the Swiss frontier. Even if we're wrong about the whole thing, it won't do any harm to knock out two of Jerry's highly-specialized factories. You'll get more details later. All right?"

The three men nodded. Adams, the only man other than Davies who had been present at a similar briefing

four months ago, was feeling the same dry throat and
sense of presentiment. Moving from face to face, Davies'
eyes stopped on Moore.

"I hope it's clear now why I want this shakedown doing
fast. If Jerry's research is completed before we've the
chance to hit him and his blueprints go out to factories
all over Germany, we can forget about stopping production. In three months he'll have his long-range rockets
targeted on our Channel ports and his Rhine Maidens
will be knocking us and the Yanks out of the sky like
pheasants, so work your boys until they drop. Plenty of
low-level stuff. Use the Loch Ness range if you like—I'll
get clearance for you. Your deadline for Hoffenscheim is
0600 hours on Thursday. O.K.?"

"Yes, sir."

Satisfied the urgency of the situation had sunk in, Davies stood back from the desk. "Then that's it for the moment. I'm away for a day or two but will be back before
Thursday. In the meantime, not a word to the fleas on the
station cat. Off you go."

As Adams followed Moore into the corridor, Davies appeared in the doorway. "Hang on, Adams. You're pretty
friendly with the innkeeper of the Black Swan, aren't
you?"

Adams showed his surprise. "Yes, sir."

"What's the accommodation situation over there? Do
you know?"

"He hasn't anyone at the moment. He doesn't like letting rooms because it's impossible to get help to do the
cooking."

"But wasn't your wife over there for a time? And Miss
Bergman?"

Adams saw this was going to be difficult. "I could ask
him, sir. As a favour."

"I'd like you to. For two weeks. Starting on Thursday."

"You mean for yourself, sir?"

"What the hell would I want a room for? No; it's for a
girl."

"A girl? I see, sir."

"Don't look so bloody salacious, Adams! I'm not planting myself a bit of crumpet across the road. It's the
daughter of some friends of ours. Swiss people who came
over to this country in 1939. The girl teaches German and
until now hasn't been north of the Thames, so while the

schoolkids are on holiday I promised to see if I could fix her up. The moors might suit her because she likes walking and she'll also get a chance of meeting some young people from the station. Anyway, it's the best I can do, so speak to the innkeeper for me, will you?"

"Yes, sir. I'll do it right away."

"Good man. Tell him I'll take care of the bill. Her name's Reinhardt, by the way. Anna Reinhardt."

Both excited and apprehensive at Davies' disclosures, Adams would have given much to discuss them with Moore as the two men walked down the corridor, but with Orderly Room staff passing by he contented himself with the remark: "Am I right in thinking you'd a hint of this when you arrived?"

Moore glanced round them before answering. "A hint but that's all. I hadn't any details."

Satisfied, Adams changed the subject. "As you've cancelled the briefing of the crews until this afternoon, what about coming over to the Black Swan with me? We've just time for a quick one before lunch."

Half-expecting a refusal, he was gratified by Moore's reply. "Why not? It'll be my last chance to relax this week. Let's take a look at this famous pub of yours."

10

As Adams led Moore into the pub lounge, Maisie was chatting to two young farm labourers at the counter. The only other occupants were two middle-aged couples drinking beer at a table near the fireplace. The girl's eyes brightened at the sight of Adams and she gave a shout. "Joe! Frank's here."

Conscious that all six people in the lounge had suspended conversation to watch them, Adams led Moore forward. As Kearns came hurrying in from the public bar, his greeting expressed his relief.

"Hello, Frank. It seems a long time since Saturday."

Privately Adams agreed with him. "Hello, Joe. One way and another we've been kept busy. Let me introduce our new Squadron Commander—Wing Commander Moore."

As Kearns shook hands with the pilot, Maisie was taking in his appearance. Under thirty, good-looking, a row of medals a mile long, and a scar on his cheek that made Maisie think of a romantic film she had once seen in which students gave one another sabre cuts to attract women. Forgetting the two young labourers, she took a quick glance at herself in a mirror behind the bar. Although as concerned as ever about the crash the previous evening— and beneath her sweater Maisie had a heart as big as her mammaries—the sex in her could always be relied on to lighten her mood if a presentable man came into her orbit. As Adams turned to her, she smoothed down her sweater.

"This is Maisie. If you're extra nice to her, she sometimes reaches beneath the counter and finds a bottle of whisky."

Maisie leaned her hemispheroids provocatively over the counter and offered her hand in the way she had seen it done on films.

"I'm pleased to meet you, sir, I'm sure."

Moore gave her a smile. "I'm pleased to meet you, Maisie."

Too posh for her, Maisie was thinking without the slightest resentment. You'd only to look at his uniform and listen to his voice to know that. But who cared? The fun was in the trying, wasn't it? There was an archness in her movements as she stood back.

"What would you gentlemen like to drink?"

Kearns gave a chuckle. "After what Frank said, I don't think we've much choice, lass."

Winking at the two officers, Maisie leaned voluptuously down, to reappear fifteen seconds later with two half-filled glasses of whisky. Her tone changed as she saw hope light up the faces of the watching locals. "It's no use you lot lookin' at me like that! It's the last of the bottle and there's no more due for another week."

At any other time Kearns would have asked Adams about the accident the previous evening but with Moore an unknown factor and with civilians present, he decided to wait until he and Adams were alone. Maisie, however, had no such inhibitions.

"What was the trouble last night? We heard 'em come back and then there was some firing and a terrific crash. We could see flames from upstairs."

Unsure of Moore himself, Adams decided to make the locals his excuse and slanted a warning glance in their direction. "I'm afraid it's all a bit hush-hush at the moment."

His expression made Maisie forget her role of the femme fatale. "Someone was killed, wasn't he? Is it anyone we knew?"

Kearns took her by the arm. "We'll find that out soon enough, lass. Run in and take my place in the bar, will you?"

The girl hesitated, then, with a troubled look at Adams, obeyed. Kearns addressed his apologetic murmur to Moore. "Sorry about that, sir. But the lass is as fond of the lads as I am and it's a strain not knowing what happened."

Adams was glad he had another subject to broach. "Joe, have you ever met Air Commodore Davies?"

Kearns had to think. "I seem to remember he came over here once. Is he a small man?" As Adams nodded, Kearns glanced at Moore and judged his man to a nicety. "With all respect, as spry and sharp as a fox terrier?"

Both men laughed. "You've got him," Adams said. "He wants to know if you'll let him have a room for a couple of weeks. From Thursday." As the innkeeper's mouth opened in protest, Adams went on quickly: "I told him the difficulty you have in getting help but the snag is he knows my wife and Hilde were here recently. So I had to say I'd ask you."

Although recognizing Adams' problem, Kearns was looking doubtful. "It's very difficult, Frank. Mrs. Billan might help again but I'd have to ask her first. The trouble is, a man makes more work than a woman."

Adams saw a ray of hope. "It isn't for him. It's for the daughter of some family friends of his." He went on to explain. "The girl's Swiss. Aren't they supposed to be very domesticated?"

The piety of his hope made the innkeeper's eyes twinkle. "Let me have a word with Maisie. She's in touch with all the help around here."

He returned a minute later. "All right, Frank. Maisie thinks Mrs. Billan will help but if she won't the two of us will manage. You did say it was only for a fortnight?"

Adams was moved to relief. "That's all. Thanks, Joe. I appreciate it." He glanced at Moore. "Time for another?"

Moore emptied his glass and set it down on the counter. "No; I must get back now. I've still a few jobs to do before the fireworks start this afternoon." He turned to the white-headed innkeeper. "Nice to have met you. I'm hoping you'll see plenty more of me in the weeks ahead."

"I hope so too, sir. Good luck in your new job."

Maisie, who had been keeping an ear open for their departure, popped her head round the corner. "If you two come in this evenin', I might find half a bottle of brandy in a cupboard."

Moore was smiling. "Keep it until the weekend, will you? By then we'll appreciate it." He glanced back at Kearns. "Don't worry if you don't see many of the boys in here for a few days. As a new man I have to show them my way of doing things and it'll probably keep us busy until the weekend. Then I'm hoping things will get back to normal."

Kearns hid his curiosity well. "I see, sir. Thanks for letting us know."

As the innkeeper stood watching the two men go out,

Maisie left the bar and joined him. "What did Frank say he was?"

"He's the new Squadron Commander. Roy Grenville's old job." Kearns' expression was reflective as he packed flakes of tobacco into a blackened pipe. "I hope he'll handle the squadron as well. Things haven't been the same since Grenville went."

Maisie's big eyes were dreamy. "I don't know how he'll handle the boys but one thing's for certain, he could handle me. Did you ever see such a dreamboat?"

The Waaf with freckles put her head round the door. "Pilot officer Hopkinson's here, sir."

Moore lowered a file of papers and sat back in his chair. "Tell him to come in, sergeant."

The Cockney, still looking resentful, marched in and saluted. "You wanted to see me, sir."

Moore indicated a chair. "Yes. Sit down and make yourself comfortable. Smoke?"

The Cockney remained standing. "No, thanks, sir."

Grinning wryly, Moore leaned back. "You're sore with me, aren't you, Hopkinson? You're angry because I've split up your partnership with Larkin and puzzled why I haven't crewed you with anyone else. Right?"

"If you say so, sir."

"I think it's a fair guess. Now I'm going to explain my reasons and you'll understand why I couldn't give them in front of the others. I'd like you to fly with me."

This time Hopkinson reacted. "With you?"

"Don't look so surprised. From all I'm told you're the best navigator on the station. And as Squadron Commander I can't afford to lose my way, can I?"

Hopkinson's expression said clearly that it was going to take more than flattery to win him over. "Someone's been stringin' you along. There's half a dozen navigators here as good as me."

"Grenville didn't think so. And the way I see it, if you were good enough for him, you ought to be good enough for me."

The implied compliment to his old skipper, the surest way of modifying the Cockney's resentment, brought a frown to his bony face. "Can I ask a question sir?"

"Why not?"

"Why didn't you bring your old navigator with you?"

"I couldn't. He finished his second tour of ops. a month ago. As he was a married man they wouldn't let him volunteer for a third."

"Where was that, sir?"

"Warboys."

Hopkinson gave a start. "Warboys? Were you in Path-finders?"

Moore looked almost apologetic as he nodded. "John-nie got me in the middle of his first tour and was stuck with me until they stood him down. It came as a wrench to us but there was nothing either of us could do."

The rapid calculations Hopkinson was making brought a new respect to his voice although it retained its char-acteristic Cockney bluntness.

"If you know what it feels like, I don't see why you've done it to me and Larkin."

Moore's eyes lifted to his face. "That's easy to answer. My job is to make this squadron a first-class unit again and that means I can't let individuals' preferences stand in my way. This afternoon we're starting a shakedown pro-gramme that's going to continue non-stop until Wednes-day evening. For that and everything that comes later I need your co-operation because, whatever you say, you're the best navigator on the station. At the same time I don't like making a man fly with me." Moore's lips quirked humorously. "I don't suppose you'd care to volun-teer, would you?"

Hopkinson shuffled uneasily. In the silence a trapped fly could be heard buzzing in the sunlit window. Making an effort to look resigned, the Cockney gave a shrug. "I suppose there's no harm in givin' it a try."

Moore relaxed and the charismatic smile that made the Waaf sergeant dream of cots and cottages reached across the desk to the frowning navigator. "Thanks, Hop-kinson. I don't think you'll regret it. Now let's get over to the Ops. Room and start the briefing."

In a certain large country house not far from Sutton Craddock the security staff were on their toes that afternoon. At the main gate sentries were scrutinizing with extra care the credentials of all visitors whether local tradesmen, artisans, or service personnel. The armed guards with Alsatian dogs who patrolled the inside of the high walls were keeping a watch that would have made it difficult for a squirrel to enter the estate undetected. Davies, who was driving a staff car borrowed from Sutton Craddock, was stopped half-way down the drive as well as at the main gate before he reached the house.

The courtyard on which he parked contained four other cars, one a large American staff car. As he jumped out, a briefcase in his hand, a young Army lieutenant approached him, saluted, and led him down a flight of stone steps to a large lawn surrounded by flower beds. Two uniformed men were sitting at a table in the centre of the lawn, and as Davies approached, the elder of them came forward and held out his hand. He was a Brigadier of distinguished appearance with iron-grey hair and a small, trimmed moustache. An officer in SOE, his role was to work with Davies, the RAF's nominated representative, when close inter-service co-operation was needed. An outstanding example of this co-operation had been the Swartfjord operation. With the Brigadier very British and stiff upper-lipped and Davies volatile, hypersensitive and quick-tempered, it had all the surface appearances of a shot-gun marriage. Instead, by some mystical symbiosis, the two men worked well together and had complete confidence in the other's judgments.

"You're looking well, Davies." The soldier had a quiet, clipped voice that matched his appearance. "Come over and meet General Staines."

The man that rose from the table weighed at least fifteen stone and every ounce of it looked like bone and muscle. In his early fifties, he had spiky iron-grey hair and the face of a boxer. His gravelly voice had a Texan accent. "Glad to meet you, Davies."

Davies saluted, then took the big hand that was offered him. "It's good of you to come, General."

The American shrugged. "Your people said it was important, so I guess I didn't have much choice."

The Brigadier, who had caught the eye of a waiter hovering nearby, turned to the Air Commodore. "What will you have to drink, Davies?"

Davies saw there were two half-filled glasses standing on the table. "Nothing for me, thank you, sir." Seeing the American staring at him, he felt an explanation was necessary. "Drinking during the day always gives me a headache."

The Texan pushed a cigar case towards him. "Then have a smoke."

Feeling he was on trial, Davies opened the case and pulled out something that resembled a toy airship. Discovering with relief his lips could just encircle it, he struck a match and inhaled cautiously. Seeing the Texan's eyes on him, Davies was determined to die rather than cough. When to his surprise he did neither, his normal perky confidence returned.

"Thank you, General. They're milder than I expected."

Staines pulled one out for himself, bit off the end, and lit it. "They're my mid-day smokes. I go on the heavier stuff after dinner." Releasing an expansive blue cloud, he settled back in his chair. "O.K., let's get down to business. The Brigadier has filled me in with the Intelligence details. I understand you've brought some photographs."

Opening his briefcase, Davies passed the prints to the two men. Staines studied them, then pushed them back with a grunt. "All they tell us is that we can't see anything. But I'll grant you that rail track looks suspicious."

"We're nearly one hundred per cent certain the establishment is there," the Brigadier said quietly.

"O.K., suppose it is. Are you telling me you're expecting your boys to go all that way in daylight? And then bomb at low level? Jesus, it's not that far from Salzburg."

"We are using a Mosquito squadron," Davies pointed out.

"I don't care what the hell you're using. The Kraut controllers will vector fighters after them all the way across Europe. When they come down they'll be slaughtered."

Davies nodded. "That's why we need your help. If you lay on a Fortress raid in the Munich area it's certain to draw all their available fighters."

"Not if this rocket establishment is as important as you both think. What happens if they give a couple of Focke Wulf squadrons the job of looking after you?"

"We think we can avoid that happening."

"How?"

Davies spent a couple of minutes explaining. When he finished Staines looked thoughtful. "It might work. Only how many of our ships are you thinking of?"

Davies cast a glance at the Brigadier, then took a deep breath. "To work it has to be a major effort. We'd like a minimum of one hundred and fifty. Preferably two hundred."

The Texan gave a loud laugh of disbelief. "Two hundred B.17s! You've got to be kidding, Davies! What's happened to the RAF? You gone out of business or something?"

Davies stated the obvious. "Our heavies are designed for night bombing: they haven't the armament to fly all that way by day."

Staines's tough face was a study. "You know the range of our Thunderbolt escort? Even with wing tanks we can only reach Cologne. After that we'd get hammered all the way."

The Brigadier's quiet voice drew the American's attention. "We appreciate your losses would be heavy, General. But they have to be weighed against the threat of these rockets which our experts think is very grave indeed."

"O.K., that's as maybe. But we can't release that to the Press, can we? So how do I justify a hundred or two hundred American ships carrying out a support role for one British squadron? If we lost half a dozen the Press would crucify us, and we'd lose a hell of a lot more than that."

"The Press won't know about us," Davies said. "Not if you pick yourself a legitimate target in the Munich area."

Staines was frowning. "Why can't we hit this valley ourselves? Then I'll have a real case to put to Faker."

"We wish you could," the Brigadier told him. "But our agents have gone into it very thoroughly and assure us the configuration of the valley makes it impossible for heavy bombers to make the raid. It has to be done by highly manoeuvrable light bombers."

The Texan ran a hand over his spiky hair before putting his question to Davies. "What outfit are you using?"

"633 Squadron. One of our highly specialized units."

The Texan gave a start. "The outfit that did the Swartfjord job?"

Davies could not keep the pride from his voice. "That's the one, sir."

For a moment the tough American looked impressed. "That was one hell of a job. No question about it." His shrewd blue eyes moved from the Brigadier to Davies and back to the soldier before he spoke again. "So you think this job's important?"

The Brigadier nodded. "We think the Allied air strategy and perhaps the invasion itself could be affected if these rockets are allowed to go into production. But I must warn you that it might not be possible to give you more than twenty-four hours' notice once the target is located."

The Texan raised his bushy eyesbrows. "Why not?"

"We haven't been told yet. But it seems all the notice our agents are prepared to guarantee us."

Staines ran a hand over his spiky hair again. "A hundred and fifty plus B.17s . . . twenty-four hours to put 'em on the line. . . . Jesus, you two really give me a case to put to Eaker. If I pull this off I'll expect a recommendation for that Victoria Cross of yours."

Davies found the temptation irresistible. "I'd stress the threat of those A.A. rockets among your formations, General. They'd make daylight bombing almost impossible."

A less assured character than Davies would have blushed at the look he received. "What the hell do you think I'm going to sell him—the benefit of playing footsy with the British? What's the code name of this A.A. rocket again?"

"Rhine Maiden, sir."

The American emptied his glass, then heaved his big body from the chair. "O.K. Leave it with me and I'll see what I can do."

11

For that day and the two that followed the men of 633 Squadron felt as if a tornado had hit them. Moore's message, fully endorsed by the Station Commander, was as succinct as any message could be. After its heroic efforts in the Spring the squadron had suffered a reaction but its period of convalescence was now over. A massive shake-up and stocktaking would commence, and from now on a hundred per cent effort would be expected from every man.

The message went like a battle order from officers and NCOs down to the lowest erks in the pecking order. Engine fitters like McTyre found themselves doing an exhaustive inventory of their spares and then indignantly checking every individual part to establish its reliability. Crews were sent round the labyrinths of the bomb dump to check for exudation among the older bombs and to list the available stock of pyrotechnics, detonators and fuses. Bomb armourers were made to check the serviceability of pistols, bomb racks, hoists, bombsights, and all the other multitudinous offensive equipment that made up a Mosquito squadron. Gun armourers were dispatched to the range to check the harmonization of all serviceable aircraft and to test spare Brownings and 20mm. cannon, and on their weary return made to strip and oil every propellant unit from Very pistols to signal mortars.

All over the airfield tradesmen were similarly employed. Transport Pool drivers were made to check their vehicles as thoroughly as if preparing to take them into action. Ground gunners were tested on latest German aircraft silhouettes and sent to the range for practice. Photographers had to list their stocks and check every camera; radio operators had to strip and re-tune their sets. Nor was the shakedown limited to the tradesmen. The Clothing Store was made to carry out a stocktaking that would have done credit to Marks and Spencers. The Catering Officer had to match his stocklists with his stores, and great was the consternation thereof. Even Burt the Bastard, the Station Disciplinary Officer, and the Guard Room were not exempted from the shakedown. Before long a rumour ran round the airfield that even the resident blackbirds were lining up for inspection.

To add to the ground crews' resentment, maintenance of the aircraft had to be carried on at the same time. With the Mosquitoes flying as if they were on maximum effort, this meant men working in the evenings and in most cases far into the night.

Yet if resentment was felt on the ground it was nothing to what was felt among the aircrews, old sweats and new men alike, on the first day of the shake-up. Taking the squadron over the moors in the late afternoon, Moore made no attempt to lead them into the complicated drills that those who knew his record expected. Instead, to get the men used to his orders and to familiarize them with his methods, he gave them simple formation practice. Although it was a mere prelude to what was to follow, to men who had flown in action—and that included every man who flew that day—the drilling was an insult, and in spite of the feeling that ran between the reshuffled crews, men took time off their personal feuds to roundly condemn his behaviour.

If on their arrival back at Sutton Craddock they believed their day was over they were bitterly disappointed. During the exercise, cursing armourers had been out on the airfield filling up 11½ lb. practice bombs with smoke-producing stannic chloride. It was a job armourers hated for the chemical was evil-smelling and an irritant to eyes and skin. As the Mosquitoes landed, light-series carriers were hoisted into their bomb bays and these in turn were loaded up with the practice bombs. At the same time bowsers discharged high-octane fuel into the aircrafts' tanks. The choked-up aircrews had barely time for a cup of tea before they were ordered back to Moore who was waiting for them on the airfield. After a quick briefing, he led them into the air again.

This time his destination was Scotland. Ordering the Mosquitoes into line astern, he led them like a file of soldiers between mountains and into steep-sided valleys. After half an hour of this he set a course to Loch Ness where the quadrant huts of a bombing range had been warned to expect them.

Here at both medium and high level Moore sent in each aircraft to test its navigator's and pilot's skill. Most crews obtained reasonable results but some of the newly-assorted ones had problems. Among them, to the York-shireman's chagrin and fury, were Harvey and his new navigator, Blackburn. Clashing over methods of finding wind direction, they saw their bombs falling thousands of feet away from the yellow target. The curses and condemnations that filled the R/T channel brought no more than a smile from Moore who knew the problems minor enough to be solved in a day once the rival factions lost their bloody-mindedness towards one another.

With each aircraft carrying sixteen bombs apiece, the exercise was a long one and before Mosquito No. 16 had dropped its last bomb the Highland mountains were black and the western sky aflame. Although it was dusk when the crews landed, their day was still not over. Lindsay, the Station Armament Officer, had been ordered to give the crews a refresher lecture on the latest bombs and pyrotechnics, and after a quick meal the men were sent to join him in the Ops. Room. Faced with derisory howls and comments, Lindsay could not make himself heard until Moore entered the room and laconically announced that written tests would be given to all crews that week-end and any man who failed them would suffer a curtailment of his freedom until his knowledge improved. Although the hostile silence that followed appeared to have no effect on the imperturbable Moore, it reminded Lindsay of an ocean groundswell before a storm.

The second day brought no relief, in fact the pressure was intensified. Three more flights to Scotland were laid on, and on each Moore stiffened the exercises. On the first flight he led the squadron out on another high-level bombing exercise over the Loch Ness target. This was carried out in two stages, the first at 20,000 feet and the second at 25,000 feet. On the second trip he led the Mosquitoes in line astern through the Highland mountains until their coolant radiators were almost brushing the tree tops and then into a low-level attack on the loch target. On the last flight rockets were used against a special target set up alongside a lake. The day was rounded off by another lecture, this time given by Moore himself, on the latest Pathfinder techniques using ground and sky target indicators.

A gusty wind and a falling barometer on Wednesday morning gave warning that the weather was changing. It was also the morning Harvey's temper exploded. Directly after breakfast he came storming unannounced into Moore's office.

"We're not going up to Scotland again, are we?"

Moore, dragging his flying suit out from a locker, turned unhurriedly. "I'm afraid we are. Is something wrong?"

"Too true something's wrong. I've had a bellyful of being drilled as if I were a rookie at Padgate. Haven't you been told that some of us have flown among mountains a bloody sight more dangerous than those Scottish gnat bites?"

"I know your record, Harvey."

"Then how about showing us some respect? Take the new men if you like but stop treating the rest of us as if we were at OTU. What does it do to you—appeal to your ego or something?"

With some sympathy for the Yorkshireman's anger, Moore was wondering why this man of all his crews could get under his skin so easily. He made an extra effort to be patient.

"I know it's irksome for you and the others, but stick it out a bit longer, will you? I can't practice with half a team and I have a good reason for what I'm doing."

"Is that what you think we are—a football team?" Cursing his disgust, Harvey went to the door and turned. "You can play a reserve today. I'm dropping myself."

Moore met his eyes and held them. "Wrong. You're playing and that's a direct order. Do I make myself clear?"

In the hush that followed the bellow of a Merlin under test could be heard. The seconds seemed endless before Harvey cursed thickly and withdrew. The slam of the ante-room door made the building shake on its foundations.

The weather allowed Moore only two practice flights that day but both exercises were unusual enough to intrigue even the incensed Harvey. The Mosquitoes were led at low level through the Scottish mountains until fifteen miles from the Loch Ness target when they were ordered up to 2,500 feet. From that height they were brought down in a shallow dive, to release their practice bombs at 1,000 feet and continue the dive until they were no more than a hundred feet above the Loch. Twisting through the valleys they stayed at low level until called on to repeat the exercise.

Both exercises ended with gunnery practice on a sea target off the Lossiemouth coast. Rain was falling steadily as they returned to Sutton Craddock and the relieved crews heard that flying was cancelled for the rest of the day.

With all sixteen Mosquitoes to service there was still no respite for the ground crews, however. Squatting on his Mosquito's wing, with rain dripping off his long nose and down his cape, McTyre gave vent to feelings shared by most of his colleagues.

"Talk about a sodding new broom sweepin' clean! What's the stupid bastard trying to do—kill us off before our time?"

The corporal fitter, enjoying the privilege of rank by sheltering under the wing, grinned up at him. "Maybe he's a Jerry in disguise, Mac."

"Stranger things than that have happened, mate," McTyre said darkly. "Look at us lot out here. If we don't get pneumonia in this bloody rain it'll only be because we'll get rheumatic fever first."

Under the nose the cherubim-faced Ellis was struggling to free the ill-fitting 20mm. gun panel. "Did you know Air Commodore Davies is back, Mac? I saw him get out of a car when I went to the armoury."

McTyre's long nose twitched like a greyhound scenting a fox. "Again? Then something big's comin' off. There's always trouble when that little sod's around."

"Who needs trouble when we've got Moore?" the corporal grinned.

Feelings were as high in A Flight crew room where the weary pilots and navigators were slumped in chairs. Grumbles and derogatory comments on Moore were heard coming from even mild-tempered men like St. Claire and Marsh. As Hopkinson entered he saw to his surprise that Larkin and his new navigator, Richards, were drinking tea together. The satirical New Zealander raised a malicious hand on sighting Hopkinson. "Greeting, most favoured one. How does it feel to fly with Nero?"

Hoppy looked uncertain whether to scowl or grin. "You know something? If I had to fly round those bloody mountains once more I'd get hairy knees."

"You'd get more than that, my Cockney sparrow. You'd grow a sporran. Wouldn't he, sprog," Larkin demanded fiercely of his new navigator.

Richards, a plump young man with auburn hair, seemed surprisingly uninjured by the epithet. "I think I've grown one myself, skipper."

"You hear that?" Larkin asked of all and sundry. "Those highlands have given my sprog navigator a sporran. And our Cockney sparrow's got hairy knees."

"I'd say he deserved them, man." The comment came from Stan Baldwin. Negro ex-accountant from Barbados, Baldwin was a comparative rarity even to a service that drew members from all quarters of the Commonwealth. An ebony-faced, heavily-built man with a rich sense of humour, his favourite story was that every time he and his pilot, Paddy Machin, went on a night operation Machin would turn anxious and keep asking if he was still there.

"Why do you say that, my sun-burned friend?" Larkin asked him.

Baldwin showed superb teeth in a wide grin. "Man, anyone who shows that Pathfinder how to play silly buggers with us in those mountains deserves to get hairy. I hope he gets hairy all over."

Hoppy grinned weakly as cheers and catcalls came from old sweats and new men alike. Even Harvey who had appeared in the doorway, was seen to be grinning. Larkin turned towards him with a groan. "What is it now, skipper? More lessons?"

The Yorkshireman shook his head. "He must be sick of you lot. You're stood down for the rest of the day."

There was a howl of relief. "You mean we can go out?" someone asked.

"Why not? You're off duty until the morning."

In the general euphoria that followed Larkin was seen cuffing the plump Richards' face and Clifford, another old sweat, was heard offering his new navigator a lift into town. Similar scenes were in evidence in B Flight crew room. If the crews missed the implications, they were not lost on the officer who entered Adams' "Confessional" half an hour later. Hanging up his raincoat, he approached the Intelligence Officer's desk. "Well, what's your verdict?"

Adams, who had been working as hard as anyone during the last three days, was unsure of Moore's question.

"It's looking good. The average error on the range today was under seventy yards."

At Moore's impatient gesure, Adams understood. "You mean the crews? Oh, yes, it's working. They're still a bit cliquy, of course, but most of their hostility to one another appears to have gone. Those training exercises of yours must be therapeutic."

Moore was looking amused. "You know there's more to it than that. I saw your face in the Mess last night when they were all trying to avoid me."

Adams shuffled uneasily in his chair. "What's your point? That their hostility has transferred itself to you?"

"What else?"

"It's only a temporary thing," Adams muttered. "It'll go as soon as they get to know you better." Then he caught Moore's quizzical expression and gave a start. "You wanted it this way, didn't you?"

Moore shrugged and reached out for the bombing report. "They say you can't beat a common dislike for drawing men together."

Adams was about to reply when the telephone rang. "Yes, sir. He's here now. I'll tell him." Replacing the receiver he glanced up at Moore.

"That was the C.O. He and Davies want a word with us right away. They intend laying on the Hoffenscheim job as soon as the weather clears."

12

The dog, sitting upright in the passenger seat of the car, gave an impatient bark. Harvey glanced at it and grinned.

"Shut up, you stupid old bugger."

A torn rubber on the left-hand wiper, giving a blurred image of the rainswept road ahead, was the cause of the dog's complaint. At the sound of Harvey's voice it wagged its tail and attempted to paw the windscreen. Instead it slipped and stumbled into the well beneath the seat. Looking crestfallen, it scrambled back and wagged its tail at Harvey, who grinned again.

"Serve you right for being such a moaner, mate."

The car was a bull-nosed Morris the Yorkshireman had picked up for thirty pounds when he was promoted to Flight Commander. Its main function before Powell's death had been to transport both men to local race meetings, a pastime they shared, and to take them to Highgate where Harvey was friendly with a middle-aged bricklayer and his family. The family consisted of Jack Lewis, his wife Mary, two sons and a daughter. Both sons were in the Army; the girl, Sarah, who had recently left school, was still at home. Once and sometimes twice a week the shirt-sleeved Harvey could be found in the kitchen helping the family to wash up the evening dishes. To those at the station who saw him as a hard, uncompromising officer, the sight would have provoked either disbelief or hilarity, as Harvey was uncomfortably aware. Powell, however, who had visited the family somewhat less frequently than Harvey, had kept the Yorkshireman's visits a secret to the day of his death.

For Harvey, whose father lived too far away to be visited except on a long weekend pass, the visits had become as necessary as the companionship of Sam, his dog. Elevated by war to command men better educated than himself, secretly embarrassed by the military conferences and Mess functions with their upper-class overtones, the

Yorkshireman found relief and even security in his visits to the bricklayer's house.

Today, Wednesday, had been his first opportunity to inform the family of Powell's death. Sarah's reaction had confirmed Harvey's long-held belief that the girl had a crush on the Australian. Shock had turned into hysteria, forcing Mary Lewis to take the girl to her room. With Jack Lewis on fire-watching duty that night, Harvey had stayed long enough to ensure the girl had quietened down and then, on Lewis's suggestion, had slipped out to have a pint with him at the local before the bricklayer reported to the Town Hall for duty. Left alone in the pub, which held painful memories of Powell, Harvey had found himself growing increasingly restive and moody. Finally, on an impulse that was entirely self-punishing, he had bundled Sam into his car and started back to the station.

With rain falling steadily from an overcast sky, the evening was drawing in early as the old Morris laboured up the long hill that led from Highgate. From its crest, on fine days, the southern reaches of the Yorkshire Moors were just visible. Today the wide counterpane of small fields and dales that lay between them and Sutton Craddock looked as if a spider's web had been drawn across it. It was a sight many members of the squadron would have found depressing but Harvey found an affinity with it. It was not the first time Harvey had been glad the war had not taken him from his native soil.

He was a third of the way to the airfield when he saw a stationery taxi at the road side. A man with a brace was struggling with the rear wheel and a woman wearing a mackintosh and head scarf was standing beside him. On seeing the Morris the man dropped the brace and signalled the car to stop. Braking, Harvey leaned across Sam and wound down the window.

"Puncture?"

The taxi driver, his jacket black with rain, nodded his disgust. "I can't get the bloody wheel nuts loose." Then he noticed Harvey's RAF mackintosh. "Are you going to the station, sir?"

"Yes."

"Then would you give my fare a lift? She's got a room booked at the Black Swan. Give my office a ring too, will you? Here's the number."

Harvey glanced at the smudged card the man pushed

at him and slipped it into his coat pocket. "All right. Tell
her to jump in."

Through the rain-streaked windscreen he watched the
man drag a suitcase from the taxi and follow the woman to the Morris. As he leaned across Sam again to throw
open the door the dog gave a bark of protest. "Put the
suitcase on the back seat," he told the driver. As the man
obeyed, the Yorkshireman picked up the indignant Sam
and deposited him alongside the suitcase. He then ac-
knowledged the waiting woman.

"Jump in."

"You are very kind." Her voice had an attractive foreign accent that Harvey could not place. She gave money
to the taxi driver and then climbed in beside him. Nodding at the man, Harvey revved the engine and pulled
away. With a sigh of relief the woman lifted her hands and
removed her scarf.

"It is good to get out of the rain. Is it true you are going
near to the Black Swan?"

"Yes." Glancing at her Harvey saw she was young with
swept-back dark hair and an oval, intelligent face.

"I hope it isn't far out of your way."

"No. It's right next to the airfield."

"How far away is that?"

"Six, perhaps seven miles. No more."

"You are stationed at the airfield, of course?"

Harvey was unaware of the grimness of his nod. "Aye,
I'm stationed there."

In the awkward silence that followed he could feel the
girl assessing him. One who always found small talk with
women difficult, Harvey was relieved when she broke the
silence.

"What is the Black Swan like?"

"It's not the Savoy. But it's homely and old-worldly, if
you like that kind of thing."

"I do."

"Then you shouldn't find it too bad." Before another
silence could fall Harvey made an effort. "Do you know
someone at the airfield?"

"Yes."

"Might I ask who?"

"Air Commodore Davies."

Harvey could not conceal his start. "You know Davies?"

"Yes. His family and mine are friends."

"But I thought his home was in Kent."

"It is. But I am on holiday and he kindly arranged for me to stay here for a couple of weeks."

Harvey was nothing if not blunt. "He must be out of his mind. What the hell is there here for a girl on holiday?"

"He knows I love walking and felt I would like the moors. They're not far from here, are they?"

"Not too far. But you'll need to pick your weather." Harvey's nod was at the slanting rain. "They don't make you very welcome on days like this."

Her answer made him stare at her. "Like all things with character, I suppose they have their moods."

"They have their moods all right." His laugh was harsh. "Some of 'em black and surly."

"Yet you like them, don't you?"

"What makes you think that?"

"The way you talk about them. Some men pay compliments that way."

Wondering how anyone could discover the truth about him so quickly, Harvey began throwing up his defences. "I was born in this part of the world, so it's different for me. In a couple of days you'll probably hate the place."

"What makes you so sure of that?"

"For one thing you're foreign, aren't you?"

"Yes."

"What nationality?"

"Swiss."

"Swiss what?"

"I don't know what you mean."

"Swiss Italian, Swiss French or Swiss German?"

"My family are of German stock."

"German," Harvey repeated, as the girl looked full at him.

"Yes. Pure German. Does it offend you?"

Harvey was still getting over his surprise. "What do you mean—offend me?"

"That I am a German. Most people in this country today do not like Germans, Swiss or otherwise."

Harvey's laugh was harsh again. "We'd have to be sick or something if we liked them, wouldn't we? Seeing we spend most of our working time trying to kill 'em."

The girl was gazing at him as if she had not seen him properly before. "I suppose that is true. If one felt nothing about one's enemies, war would be an even greater obscenity than it is."

Her words made Harvey start. The nearside wheels of the Morris hit a pool and sent water cascading over the verge. With a muttered curse he pulled the car back to the crown of the road. "So you think war's an obscenity."

"Don't you?"

It was a question that brought out the perversity in Harvey that was always close to the surface. "Not particularly. In peacetime the rottenness of the world is often hidden. In wartime it comes out into the open. I'm not sure I don't prefer it that way. At least you know who your enemies are. Or think you do."

"Think you know," she repeated. "Don't you believe the Nazis are your enemies?"

"Maybe they are. But they aren't my only ones." Suddenly realizing how he was giving himself away, Harvey turned his attention back to the road.

Her eyes were moving over his morose face. "You must have had a very unhappy life to think like that."

The astonished Harvey was wondering how you could want to hurt someone whom you had only known a few minutes. "Why must people like you always rush to Freud? Has Davies had an unhappy life? Because in case you don't know he's about the keenest Hun killer I've met."

Her gaze moved to the stone hedge where a crow, disturbed by the approaching car, was flapping away into the rain. "Arthur has never hidden from us that he doesn't like the Germany of today. But I know he distinguishes between the ordinary Germans and those who support the Nazis."

To hear Davies being called Arthur was enough to bring any Flight Commander down to earth, thought Harvey as the Morris crested another hill and the Control Tower of Sutton Craddock became visible through the murk. "Sorry. I don't know why I'm talking this way. I'm not even sure I know what I'm talking about. Blame it on the weather, will you?"

"You don't need to apologize. People should always say what they think—or how can one get to know them?"

Harvey found he was smiling for the first time that

week. "Then you ought to get on well with the folks around here. They also believe in saying what they think."

He liked her laugh. It was contained and yet spontaneous. "And you said I wouldn't like it here. Now I know you are wrong."

Less than two minutes later Harvey braked outside the private gate of the inn. As he opened the rear car door he found the girl talking to Sam. "What is your dog called?" she asked him.

"Sam."

She gave a laugh of pleasure. "I think he likes me. Look, he's licking my hand."

He dragged out the suitcase. "You're honoured. By and large he doesn't think much of people."

She appeared to be about to say something, then climbed from the car instead. As a loud gust of shouting and laughter came from the inn she glanced inquiringly at him. "What is it? A party?"

From the corner of his eye the Yorkshireman was watching two sergeants who were passing the car on their way to the pub. Catching sight of him and the girl, one man nudged the other and whispered a comment. The sight made Harvey brusque.

"It'll be noisy tonight. The lads have been under pressure this week and they're letting off steam. Things will get back to normal tomorrow."

Closing the door on the barking Sam, he followed the girl down the path. Although the loose mackintosh hid her figure, he saw she was tall and walked well. Opening the front door of the inn he led her into an oak-panelled hall that was in semi-darkness. On the right was a well-worn staircase, on the left an antique table and a wall telephone. Ahead were three doors. One, glass-panelled, only partly concealed the light and gaiety of the bars it served. Putting down the suitcase Harvey struck a bell that stood on the table. He had to strike it twice more before the door opened and a perspiring Kearns appeared. For a moment the din was deafening and among the milling airmen Harvey caught sight of Millburn and Gabby jammed tight against the bar. Then Kearns closed the door and hurried forward.

"Sorry, Mr. Harvey, but it's murder in there tonight. What can I do for you?"

The girl took a step forward. "Are you Mr. Kearns?"

"That's right, Miss."

"I believe Air Commodore Davies has made a reservation for me. My name is Reinhardt."

"Oh, yes, Miss. The room's all ready for you. Sorry we're in such a state tonight."

The girl gave him a smile. "Why are you sorry? Everyone seems very happy."

"I think they are, Miss. But I hope the noise doesn't disturb you too much."

"Don't let it worry you. I'm sure it won't."

Clearly impressed by her manner and good looks, Kearns helped her remove her mackintosh. Beneath it she was wearing a green costume that set off her tall, supple body and dark hair. Picking up the suitcase Kearns hurried up the stairs. "I'll show you your room now and as soon as the rush dies down I'll see you get dinner."

The girl glanced at Harvey. "If you are in a hurry I will phone the taxi people for you."

"There's no need," he told her. "I've plenty of time."

In his hurry to get back to the bar, Kearns was already half-way up the staircase. "Your room's Number Two, Miss."

"Thank you," she called. "I'll be up in a moment." Turning back to Harvey she held out her hand. "Now we know each other's names. Mine is Anna Reinhardt. And you are Mr. Harvey."

There was a grace about her that made Harvey feel clumsy. "Frank Harvey. Would you like me to tell Davies that you've arrived?"

"It is not necessary. He said he would phone me after nine-thirty."

Still uncertain of her relationship with Davies, Harvey could only hope his question was not too obvious. "Will you be seeing much of him while you're here?"

The semi-darkness of the hall hid from him the smile that for a moment touched her lips. "It is not likely. Arthur is a friend of my family but he is far too important a man to have much time to spend on me. Although I am hoping he will take me out to dinner one evening."

Harvey took a deep breath. "Then would you care to have a drink with me when you've unpacked your things?"

She cast a rueful glance at the glass-panelled door. "It

looks very crowded in there. And I have been travelling since this morning."

Nothing more was needed to change Harvey's mood. "Sorry. I shouldn't have asked. I hope you enjoy your stay and don't find our aircraft too noisy."

He was at the telephone and fumbling for the taxi-driver's card when her hand touched his sleeve. "You are a very sensitive man, aren't you? I did not refuse to have a drink with you. I only meant I would prefer it when I am less tired."

Harvey was suddenly aware she had the greyest eyes he had ever seen. Gazing into them, he was lost. "You said you liked walking. Would you care to go on the moors when the weather clears? We could drive to Pick-ering or Whitby and——"

Her smile came before he could finish. "Yes. Very much. When?"

"Can I phone you? We never know from day to day when we're flying."

"Of course. Thank you for asking me. Now I had bet-ter go and look at my room. Auf Wiedersehen."

Harvey watched her until she had vanished upstairs before making the phone call. As he walked down the road towards the station entrance the rain ceased and he could smell the nettles. He took a deep breath and held it. The weather was changing. It would be a fine day tomorrow.

13

Davies, newly-shaved and impatient, was standing near the open door of Henderson's office. Hearing footsteps hurrying down the corridor he turned to the three men by the window. "Remember, as far as these two go, this is just another job. The same applies when we go into the crew briefing afterwards. Watch what you say. All right?"

Henderson, Adams and Moore nodded. Ten seconds later there was a tap on the door and Harvey and Young appeared. Although neither had expected the early morning call, the Australian was the only one showing its effects. He had celebrated the end of the training stint with Millburn and Gabby the previous evening, and the pouches under his eyes showed it. Davies' sharp eyes were on him as he answered the salutes of the two flight commanders.

"You didn't expect this early call, did you, Young?"

"No, sir."

"I can bloody see you didn't. What were you on last night—meths?"

Young made a brave attempt to grin. "No, sir. Just the usual swill."

"You must get a different brew to what I get, lad. Unless you had a bath in it. Can you see?"

"Yes, sir."

The grunt Davies gave suggested scepticism as he walked over to the desk. A large map of Western Europe was pinned on the wall alongside it. Picking up a ruler, Davies motioned the two men nearer.

"We've got a job for you today. Before we go in and brief the crews we thought we'd run over the finer details with you. The target's here."—and Davies held the ruler to the map—"An engineering factory at a place called Hoffenscheim on the old German–Belgium frontier. It's not on the scale of the factories in the Ruhr but it's important because it specializes in precision engineering. You've been chosen for the job because it's situated in a narrowish wooded valley, but as this valley runs east to west you shouldn't have any approach problems providing your navigation is good. All right so far?"

Both flight commanders nodded. Davies moved the ruler across the map. "The distance from the enemy coast is around one hundred miles, so we've decided to make it a low-level job all the way." Seeing both men start, Davies nodded. "I know it means surrendering your altitude superiority but this way you'll get beneath his radar defences. The reasoning goes that to precision bomb the target you'll have to come down to low level anyway, and if Jerry's radar could track you all the way to the target, he could have a reception committee waiting for you. Whereas by keeping on the deck we hope surprise and speed will keep you out of trouble."

Neither flight commander looked wholly convinced. Davies' eyes were on Harvey. "You got a question, Harvey?"

"Yes, sir. If we're going all the way on the deck we're going to need diversions. Have we got any?"

"If you'd give me a bloody chance, I'll come to 'em," Davies snapped. His pointer lifted to the coast of Jutland. "Up here—above latitude 55—the Banff Wing will be out on a sweep. Further south II Fighter Group will be carrying out an offensive patrol over the Netherlands. 12 Group are going to do the same over Belgium and Northern France. Best of all we've picked a day when the Yanks are hoping to clobber Frankfurt."

"Hoping?" Harvey interrupted.

Davies gave him a scowl. "The Met. boys say there's still plenty of thin cloud about, particularly below latitude 50. However it's expected to clear around midday, perhaps before. The plan is that you cross the enemy coast fifteen minutes after the last of the B.17s. That way, if Jerry's defences are on their toes, and they usually are, most of his fighters will be chasing the B.17s."

"Poor bloody Yanks," Young ventured.

Davies allowed the general laugh to die down before continuing. "Lindsay will go into the details of your armament but as I understand it you'll be carrying four 500-pounders apiece. Two will be General Purpose and the other two Semi Armour Piercing. You're taking SAPs in case there is any heavy machinery about. Also the heavier shrapnel will do more damage. I think Lindsay's tail-

fusing with 5.5 second delays, but you must check on this to make certain your kites are far enough apart on the run-in: we don't want you blowing one another up. You'll drop all four stores in one salvo. So unless you make a balls of it you'll only do one bombing run. As for ammo, you'll be carrying full tanks for your Brownings and Hispano, although we're not expecting you'll need them. Don't forget before take-off to check your crews have set their bomb sights for low level or they'll clobber Berlin instead of Hoffenscheim. All right, Moore—you want to finish it off?"

His back to the window, Adams saw Harvey's face cloud in dislike as the immaculate figure of Moore stepped forward. Taking the ruler from Davies, he turned amiably towards his two flight commanders.

"With luck I'm hoping we'll get away by noon. After takeoff I want your men to climb to 1,500 feet and form behind me in echelon right according to your numbers. I shall lead you at that height to Manston where we shall dive right to the deck and make a dirty dash straight for the target. Your navigators will get all details of this track at their briefing. But—and this is the answer if either of you thought I was playing silly buggers over Scotland yesterday—we won't be keeping on the deck all the way. You both know how difficult it is to sight a target, much less avoid over-shooting it, when you're flying at low level. As soon as we reach Viviers—that's about twenty miles from the valley—we're going to make a steep climb to 2,500 feet. Then we'll begin a shallow dive on the target. It has to be shallow because you both know one can't bomb from a steeply-diving Mosquito. This way we'll have time to identify the target before we clobber it. Any questions so far?"

Young nodded. "What's the idea of flying in echelon right all the way to Manston, skipper?"

"This is because we now know that Jerry's long-range radar can pick us up almost as soon as we start orbiting our airfields. If we fly south in echelon right, our images superimpose themselves on his screen and give him the impression we're heavies. So once we dive beneath his screen at Manston he'll assume we've only been air-testing and have landed again."

Surprise and grudging respect appeared on the faces of

both flight commanders. Before Moore could continue, Harvey's gruff voice checked him.

"I'm not happy about the climb to 2,500 feet before we reach the target. According to that map Hoffenscheim is on the south-east fringe of the Ruhr and that means a hell of a lot of fighter stations close by. This climb could give them the chance to reach us."

Moore gave him an amiable nod. "That's one of the reasons we wanted to consult you both before the briefing. I agree it does give them an extra minute or two. But look at it the other way. By making it easier for us to identify the target and so avoid over-shooting it, we might spend far less time over it than if we have to stooge around in a search. If you think about it, I'm sure you'll agree it's the best choice."

When Harvey did not reply, Moore went on: "We're not expecting much opposition. Intelligence believes they've only two small flak posts, and a couple of 500-pounders apiece ought to see them off. In fact with any luck at all we'll clobber them before their radar sets are warmed up. I'll take care of them myself, but if I make a mess of it, then Millburn will take over. Then you come in at pre-set intervals, concentrating on the factory. Orbit afterwards at 2,000 feet until you get my all-clear, then get down to the deck again and make for home. Your navigators will get a track that takes us north-east to Breda and then over to Norwich. This is to make certain Jerry isn't waiting for us on our homeward leg. Now—any questions?"

"What about flak ships on the way out?" It was Young.

Moore glanced at Adams, who pushed himself away from the window. "You pass between a couple code-named Hermann and Otto. Our reports say Hermann's a new ship with much heavier armament. So you're routed nearer Otto to give Hermann the benefit of the doubt."

Davies interrupted impatiently. "12 Group have promised to take care of them, haven't they?"

Adams was thinking of the muted cat-calls and hollow laughs that the crews would make if Davies made the same comment at the briefing. Bomber crews had little if any respect for their fighter colleagues' ground support. "Yes, sir. But we still think it's wise to keep well away from Hermann."

Harvey, whose silent hostility towards Moore had been a feature of the interview, returned with his earlier complaint. "On a normal low-level operation with all these diversions I'd agree we shouldn't have too much trouble. But if we make this climb on the way out, then I feel we ought to have a fighter escort."

It was the kind of remark a flight commander was allowed to make when alone in his Squadron Commander's office but not, because of its implied criticism, in front of others. Davies, with red spots beginning to glow in his cheeks, intervened sharply.

"You've got a fair share of complaints today, haven't you, Harvey? You're not getting a fighter escort because we don't think you're going to need one. All right?"

Seeing Henderson wanted a word with the two flight commanders, Moore stepped aside. Aware Davies' eyes were on him, the big Scot trod warily. "See your kites are air-tested as soon as possible in case the mist clears quickly. We don't want you to miss the Yanks because they could give you a clear run to the target." Torn between his wish for success and the need to keep secret the target's larger importance, Henderson mixed his metaphors with some effect. "As you know, we've a lot to live up to and now we've had this spell of training there'll be plenty of people watching to see how we perform. So turn the wick up a bit and bring your boys back with their tails wagging. All right—let's get to the briefing."

After receiving their detailed briefing and carrying out their air tests, the sixteen operational crews of 633 Squadron had no option but to wait for the weather to clear. Few welcomed the delay, particularly those blessed or cursed with vivid imaginations. The morning sky with its bright film of cloud would have been ideal for their mission. But as the sun shredded away layer after layer of moisture, Larkin's gloomy prophecy was shared by most of the crews. "By the time the Yanks make up their minds we're going to look like goldfish swimming about at the bottom of a lighted tank."

The way men spent the stomach-tightening wait gave some indication of their characters. St. Claire had gone into the Mess after completing his air test. Adams, hearing the sound of a Chopin nocturne being played on the piano as he passed the door, glanced inside. The young artist was seated at the piano in the far corner with Sue Spencer beside him. The girl's expression made Adams feel like a Peeping Tom. Moved, he drew back out of sight and listened until the haunting melody died away.

Harvey had gone back to his billet. Lying on the bunk with his eyes closed, he was running over the briefing session again. Aware his dislike of Moore was an incentive to criticism, he had nevertheless been sincere in his complaint that the attack held built-in risks. One of Harvey's virtues, which Moore had had no time to discover, was his responsibility to the men in his flight. Even those who disliked him admitted he looked after his men like a hen her chicks. It was the reason that pilots like Marsh, who had no death-or-glory ambitions, valued him as a flight commander. To the Yorkshireman the only justification for the risk Moore was taking was a target of special strategic importance.

The thought made his eyes open. Could it be that? It was true that Davies had offered an explanation but somehow it had sounded thin to Harvey. He had taken more notice of Davies' presence at the briefing. It was feasible an Air Commodore found a raid on a precision engineering plant a special occasion but Harvey had his doubts.

He closed his eyes again. Special target or not, the war would go on and one side of him was not sorry. The thought of stepping out of his flight commander's uniform to become a builder's clerk again had long been one of Harvey's secret dreads. What a bloody world, he reflected, when men dreaded peace because of the humiliation it brought them. He lit a cigarette, thought about Anna Reinhardt, and found his mental abrasions became less painful.

At that same moment Moore, seated at his desk in the Squadron Office, was staring at a telegram that had arrived ten minutes ago. "Your father passed away at 2 a.m. His last thoughts were of you and the future. Funeral next Wednesday at Cotsmere. Please try to attend. Your loving mother."

Moore's hands were trembling as they held the telegram. The sight surprised him. For over three years he had seen friend after friend killed, some in ways that beggared description. During that same time in the seventy-nine missions he had flown he must have been responsible for the deaths of hundreds of enemy soldiers and civilians. They were not statistics Moore liked to dwell on but they were ones the young pilot felt he had a moral obligation to face. Death was anything but a stranger to him and yet although he had known for months that his father was seriously ill, the telegram still had the power to shock him.

He rose and walked over to the window where he could see a young ACII chatting up one of the Waafs. It was the severance of the umbilical cord, he thought. While the father lived, the child that lived on in the son saw him as a final refuge. When death took him away, the son knew that he stood alone at last.

And not in a personal sense only. Now John Moore was dead, the empire he had built became the son's responsibility. Exigency arrangements would keep it ticking over until the war ended but if Ian Moore survived, the livelihood of thousands of workers would depend on him having the same business sagacity as his father. The prospect which for a long time had been a cloud on Moore's horizon was suddenly a forbidding mountain. With Harvey having the same apprehensions about the end of the war but for entirely opposite reasons, the situation was not without its irony.

Another loner, Marsh, was sitting out on the airfield in the weak sunlight that was now filtering through the clouds. The young pilot officer had a book on his knees but his thoughts were back in Highgate. On his arrival home the previous evening he had found Julie almost hysterical. The baby had been unwell and cried most of the day, and the younger Miss Taylor had complained at the noise. It had taken Marsh half the night to calm Julie, and the couple had barely fallen into an exhausted sleep before an S.P. had hammered on the front door and told Marsh to report immediately to the airfield. The outcome had been another indignant complaint from Miss Taylor and near panic from Julie at what the recall might presage. With no time to reassure the girl before he left and fearful how she might react during the long day, Marsh felt as if the weight of the world was resting on his young shoulders. The fact he might help or even cure the distraught girl by requesting to be taken off flying duties did nothing to help his state of mind.

The rest of the crews were trying to take their minds off the raid in more physical ways. Some were playing cards and darts in the crew rooms. Others were playing football with members of the ground staff. As Gabby slid a neat pass to Millburn, whose boot missed the ball completely but almost took a corporal's head off, the Welshman gave a yell of derision.

"You clumsy pillock. My kid sister could have put that one in."

The American, whose tousled black hair was wet with sweat, glared at the sharp-tongued Gabby. "Why don't you Limeys play real football? Then I could scatter little punks like you all over the field."

When 1200 hours arrived with no news, the crews were called in for an early lunch. They had just sat down when the bell of the teletype brought the Duty Officer to his feet. He read the orders on the rapidly-moving paper and began making his terse phone calls. A minute later Tannoy loudspeakers spluttered, then blared the alert. Cursing men snatched up what food they could carry and ran to the crew rooms for their flying gear and parachutes.

The indecipherable Tannoy voices could be heard from the upstairs front bedroom of the Black Swan. Switching off the radio, Anna Reinhardt ran to the window. Over the russet leaves of a crab apple tree it was possible to see into the airfield where the scene was one of great activity. NCOs were yelling orders, men were climbing into trucks, and one by one, with their characteristic coughs, Merlins were firing at the dispersal points. As the girl watched she saw the first Mosquito begin trundling southwards down the field. Another plane followed it a few seconds later. By this time the concentrated sound of thirty-two Merlins was making the windows of the inn rattle.

The leading Mosquito had reached the far end of the runway and was waiting for flight permission. As a green Very light soared from the Control Tower its engines began booming and it started forward. Weighed down by its bombload it dropped its wheels twice to the runway before it broke free with a triumphant roar. As it dipped a wing and passed over the pub, the girl saw its wheels locking back into their nacelles. The second plane rose eight seconds later, followed by fourteen more at regular intervals. The sky was now free of cloud, and as the sun shone on the streamlined bodies the girl thought of deadly barracudas streaking towards a distant victim. She stood listening at the window until the deep drone of the engines died away.

14

"Flak ship at two o'clock, skipper," Hopkinson said.

Moore, who had already seen the ship, gave a nod. The sixteen Mosquitoes were flying line-astern across the Channel. Since dog-legging at Manston, they had gone down so low their slipstreams were ruffling the blue-green swell. Every pilot's eyes were fixed on the waves ahead: one slip in concentration at this height meant certain death. The navigators were keeping a watch on the gauges and constantly scanning the sky above.

The flak ship Otto was less than three miles away and Moore knew that warning of their approach was already being radioed back. In minutes fighters would be scrambling from Dutch and Belgian airfields. With luck, the zero height which the Mosquitoes were flying would make them difficult to find and pursue. Difficult that was, Moore thought, until they climbed into the open sky near Viviers.

The second flak ship, Hermann, was now visible on the port quarter. Otto however was nearer and the menacing steel hulk of the floating gun platform was beginning to tower out of the sea. Every armoured post along its deck contained radar-controlled guns and Moore knew these would already be lined up on the approaching Mosquitoes.

Climbing up a couple of hundred feet Moore waggled his wings. With radio silence enforced it was a prearranged signal for the squadron to open out. As the pilots obeyed, a rapid staccato of flashes, visible even in the bright sunlight, ran along the side of the ship.

Spread out and skimming over the waves like a shoal of flying fish, the Mosquitoes were making as difficult a target as possible, but the flak crews showed their experience by concentrating on each Mosquito in turn as it flashed past their port beam. For a few seconds the sea below A-Apple, Moore's aircraft, seethed with spray and a sharp explosion made the Mosquito rock. Then the fury of the attack turned on Young who was flying at Number 2.

With the pressure taken off him Moore was able to see that some fire was coming from Hermann, but with the Mosquitoes flying no higher than the masts of Otto, the gunners were clearly afraid of hitting their companion ship. Marsh, who was flying Number 12, had a shell burst beneath his port engine, and as he almost lost control a vision of Julie's condemning face flashed before his eyes.

At the speed the Mosquitoes were travelling, the action was over in seconds. Hopkinson, staring back through the perspex blister, was trying to count the aircraft as they swung back in line astern. "I think they all got through, skipper."

Although both men were in their shirtsleeves they were sweating. The Mosquito was a warm aircraft and at zero altitude in summer the heat could be stifling.

The flat Belgian coast with its wide sandy beaches was now rushing towards them. Although their point of entry had been carefully plotted Moore caught a glimpse of beach defences and a massive gun emplacement as they skimmed over Hitler's Western Wall. Abandoned holiday villas, nestling among sand dunes, flashed past.

Like all his crews, Moore's concentration was intense. Images flashed and faded on the retina of his eyes in rapid succession. A cobbled road, streaming below like a grey river. A horse and cart. A small enemy convoy of camouflaged trucks. A church steeple. A railway track swinging in beneath them. Half a dozen civilians waiting at a small station. Excited arms gesticulating.

The railway track swinging away northwards. A blur of fields, some green, some golden. A pond with cattle drinking. A canal with bridges. A yell from Hoppy—power cables ahead. Up and down to the canal again. A column of grey-clad soldiers marching alongside it. At this height they were real—one could feel their jack-booted threat.

The canal bending away south. Trees thickening and hills rising ahead. Must be the Ardennes. Down a shallow valley—sunlight glistening on a river. Who said Belgium was all cobble stones and factories? Wonder what the fishing's like?

Six more minutes and Hopkinson tapped Moore's arm. "Viviers, skipper!" Over at ten o'clock Moore saw a smoke haze. If any fighters had tried to follow them, they would know it in a moment.

As Moore put A-Apple into a steep climb, the pilots and navigators behind him shared an ambivalence of emotion. Relief from the killing concentration of hedge-hopping was mixed with apprehension that they were now entering the enemy monitoring screens.

From 2,500 feet it was possible to see the great plain of Liège, the northern limit of the Ardennes forests. The amorphous sprawl of buildings covered by a thin film of smoke was Viviers. Below and to the right of the Mosquitoes the densely wooded hills of the Ardennes spread to the horizon. Catching Moore's glance, Hoppy expressed a confidence he did not feel. "I think we're on track, skipper."

Both pilots and navigators were now turning their heads ceaselessly in their watch for fighters. As Harvey had rightly said, there were many airfields near the great industrial complex of the Ruhr and all must have had warning that a squadron of low-flying bombers had penetrated the coastal defences. The question was whether the German Observer Corps had been able to follow their route. Liverish black spots appeared and disappeared in the great blue bowl of sky as men rubbed their watering eyes and stared again. The white-hot sun drew their gaze like a magnet. Life-giving to the burgeoning earth below, it was a constant source of death to bomber crews.

Even at that height the smoke haze that hung permanently over the Ruhr was visible to the north-east. Below, farms and hamlets had returned to the landscape. A town set among low hills appeared and Hopkinson led Moore towards it. As it swept past they caught a glimpse of a ruin on a hilltop and picturesque, half-timbered houses flanking a river. "Monschau," Hopkinson called with relief.

The line of Mosquitoes swept on towards a chain of low hills. As they fell behind, Hoppy gave a yell of triumph and pointed. "Hoffenscheim! One o'clock!" More hills rose ahead. A wide valley shaped like a boomerang ran east and west between them. On its floor was an untidy sprawl of factories and industrial buildings. Climbing up the hillsides were housing estates. A railway track ran into the valley, spread out in a network to feed the factory complex, and wound on into the hills.

Moore knew that if the town were Hoffenscheim the engineering plant must lie round the bend in the valley. He also realized that the Mosquitoes' speed was going to make it impossible to identify the target and attack it simultaneously. Keeping radio silence in case Hoppy was mistaken, he opened A-Apple's throttles and swept along the rail track into the valley.

The small industrial town, used to the Ruhr being attacked at night, was caught completely by surprise. Workmen, finishing their lunch in factory yards, watched the aircraft streak past in blank amazement. Men on shift work, lying in the sun in their back gardens, decided the planes must be their own and closed their eyes again.

Factories and smoking chimneys flowed past Moore's wingtips. He caught a glimpse of a small marshalling yard with stationary freight wagons. Then A-Apple's wings tilted as Moore followed the southward bend of the valley. As a hill shoulder fell away the engineering plant came into sight.

It stood perhaps three-quarters of a mile from the steeply-rising hills to the south. Although Adams had said it was small in Ruhr terms, it looked formidable enough with its smelting furnaces, pressing mills, machine shops, and dozens of smoking chimneys. Hoppy, feverishly checking his photographs, gave a yell of affirmation. "We're O.K. skipper. This is it."

Moore had already identified one flak post, a concrete tower built up above the trees on the hill shoulder. As A-Apple swept down the valley he spotted the second, a squat blockhouse set alongside the rail track at the western end of the complex. He switched on his R/T. "Zero One to Pygmalion. We'll attack on a reciprocal course. Follow me at twelve-second intervals. Good luck."

A-Apple went into a steep climb and began to turn. Led by Young the string of Mosquitoes followed and began to orbit over the western approaches of the valley. Beside Moore, Hopkinson had abandoned his photographs for the bombsight. His metallic voice sounded in Moore's earphones. "O.K. skipper. Ready when you are."

Below, a siren was hooting hysterically. Frantic gun crews had now reached their charges and were turning on radar sets and tugging off gun covers. Inside the factory workmen switched off lathes and ran towards the deep shelters.

Banking steeply, Moore put A-Apple into a shallow dive. Fast though his circuit had been, the gunners in the nearby post were already firing and a glowing chain of shells was swirling upwards. Lining the Mosquito's nose on the flak post, Moore flicked a switch. "Bomb doors open."

Beneath him he could feel the doors trembling in the slipstream. Peering into the bombsight, Hoppy was chanting his instructions as he guided the first gun post into the sights. "Main switch on. One and two selected and fused. Left, left. . . . Steady, steady. . . ."

The engineering complex was rising from the valley floor like a grotesque castle as the diving Mosquito swept towards it. By this time the flak tower on the hill had also commenced firing and a line of black bursts swung A-Apple off course and cut a gouge in her port wing. Automatic 37mms. and almost dead on target. . . . Moore could feel the sweat running down his face as he listened to Hopkinson's instructions. "Right, skipper. Right. . . . Hold it there."

Unable to take evasive action until its bombs fell away, the Mosquito was bracketed in black explosions for seemingly endless seconds until the flak post entered Hopkinson's sights. Then he yelled "Bombs gone" and A-Apple reared like a frightened horse as two 500-lb. bombs, one GP and one SAP, fell simultaneously and plunged towards the blockhouse.

Sweeping on towards their second target, neither man could see how accurate their aim had been but the crews above saw spurts of dust and gravel rise less than twenty yards from the blockhouse as the bombs struck. Although the gunners must have known their fate, they continued firing at A-Apple as it swept over the factory towards the second flak post. With the Mosquito's speed giving him only a few seconds in which to act, Hoppy's instructions came thick and fast.

"Left, left, skipper. Right. . . . A bit more. Hold it there. Steady. . . ."

Aware now of their peril, the flak-tower gunners were throwing everything they had at A-Apple. Swirling shells appeared to start lazily from the hill, only to snap at vicious speed past the perspex blister. Forcing himself to concentrate Hopkinson squinted down the bombsight and pressed the release. Two more bombs plunged down and disappeared into the trees but the hail of shells followed

A-Apple as it leap-frogged the hill shoulder and dived for cover. That same moment two black mushrooms of smoke and debris erupted from the far side of the plant. As A-Apple flashed over the shocked town and clawed for height, two more explosions, this time heard through the roar of the Merlins, came from the hillside. When the four black clouds subsided, both flak posts had ceased firing. Bathed in sweat, Moore lifted his face mask. "Zero One to Pygmalion. In you go."

Young gave his navigator a nod, peeled off, and dived into the valley. As the huge complex of buildings rushed towards him he saw that only two guns were still firing, a couple of light machine guns high up on the roof whose thin threads of tracer looked innocuous after the flak posts. Moore might be an eager-beaver, the Australian was thinking, but by taking all the risks himself he'd reduced the job to a piece of cake. Dropping all his 500-lb. bombs in a salvo, Young went into a steep climb, then banked steeply in an effort to gaze over his wingtips. "See where they fell, Woody?" he was asking his navigator when four flashes ripped two storage sheds apart and tossed them into the air. Three seconds later the Mosquito rocked like a ship at sea from the heavy explosions.

Bomb doors lowered, the third Mosquito had already begun its attack. Its four bombs fell in a line across a large foundry. As smoke and flame belched upwards, a chimney was seen toppling over. Half-way down, it disintegrated into tons of bricks which half-buried a transport yard.

One after another the Mosquitoes made their strike. By the time the last of Young's flight was peeling off to attack, a great pall of black smoke lay over the valley. As the Mosquito made its approach a parabola of coloured shells reached out towards it from the hillside to the south. Hopkinson sounded startled. "You see that, skipper?"

All the crews realized immediately what had happened. Because of the dense trees on the southern ridge, the PR photographs had failed to pick out this third flak post. With its crews lulled into carelessness by months of inactivity, the post had either been unattended while the men enjoyed the sunshine or some mechanical failure had kept the guns out of action. From the hail of shells now being pumped out, the inference was the crews were doing their best to make amends.

Orbiting above the valley, Moore watched the attacking Mosquito vanish into the smoke of the stricken plant, then emerge unscathed. Relaxing, he changed his mind about ordering an attack on the flak post. Unlike the earlier ones, it was not only farther from the plant but had a much more difficult target as the Mosquitoes swept from right to left across its field of fire. In brutal military terms the risk of an aircraft being shot down was greater if sent to attack the post than to attack the plant. Moreover, with the engineering complex now almost entirely covered by smoke, it was impossible to see how much of it remained undamaged. Conscious of the need to destroy as much capacity as possible, Moore decided to concentrate on the primary target.

Not so Harvey. With all his flight yet to make their attack, the Yorkshireman decided the flak post had to be taken out. For a moment he debated whether to seek Moore's permission, then he clicked off his R/T switch. With he and Moore back-to-front in everything they thought and did, it was more than likely the bastard would refuse it. "The flak post's our target," he told Blackburn. "Set your distributor to 'stick' and make sure all four bombs are fused when I open the doors. Never mind your bombsight—drop 'em when I tell you."

Blackburn sounded a trifle breathless. "O.K., skipper."

Knowing the rest of his flight would stay in orbit until he had completed his attack, Harvey peeled away and made for the pall of smoke. As D-Danny's airspeed increased and the smoke began swirling around its wingtips, a glowing chain of shells reached out from the port quarter. It was followed by a double fork of tracer a couple of seconds later. Holding the Mosquito on course until it almost disappeared into the smoke, Harvey suddenly banked steeply and hurled it straight at the flak post. "Bomb doors open!" he yelled.

Orbiting above Moore caught sight of the manoeuvre. "Zero One to Red Leader. You are not to attack flak post. Repeat. Do not attack flak post!"

Harvey could not hear nor would he have obeyed if he had. Dead ahead of him the flak post was spitting shells like a snake spitting venom. Some streaked past the Mos-

quito like white-hot meteorites. Other burst around it
and threw out nets of lethal shrapnel. Feeling his mouth
turning dry, Harvey cursed, lined up the post in his gun-
sights and pressed the firing button. The massive crash
and recoil of the Hispano cannons and Brownings seemed
to momentarily check the Mosquito before it threw itself forward again. Although Harvey found relief in strik-
ing back, the impact of the Mosquito's fire, equal to that
of a three-ton truck hitting a brick wall at 50 mph, had
no effect on the heavily-armoured post. Two seconds later
the Yorkshireman had to release the firing button as he
levelled the aircraft from its dive.

The lower slopes of the hillside were now streaking
past. From the corner of his eyes Harvey saw the dry
pebbled bed of a water-course. With its guns elevated,
the flak tower was pouring up everything it had and to
the crews above the Mosquito looked like an insect being pierced by brightly-coloured pins. A shell ricocheted
from an engine nacelle and another took a couple of
square feet from the starboard wingtip. Big hands gripping the control column as if it were the throat of his
enemy, Harvey was counting: "three . . . four . . . five . . .
Now!"

Like a stone skimming on water the Mosquito bounced
four times as its bombs fell at half-second intervals and
vanished into the trees. As Harvey heaved back on the
column to clear the rising hill, a shell smashed into the
armour plating at his back and filled the cockpit with
fumes. Then the fury of the fire fell away as the Mosquito found shelter on the opposite side of the hill. The
four explosions sounded like heavy doors being slammed
as Harvey climbed up towards Moore and the other orbiting Mosquitoes. Spouts of black smoke together with
rocks and entire trees erupted from the ground. Westward along the valley, obeying instructions, the first Mosquito of Harvey's flight had already commenced its bombing run. As it reached the drifting smoke and no tracer
attacked it, Harvey's big jaw clamped in satisfaction. With
any luck at all, his lads should now have a clear passage.
The Yorkshireman looked almost benign as he turned to
the pale-faced Blackburn. "You feeling O.K.?"

The stocky young navigator managed a smile. "I think
so, skipper."

Harvey gave him a grim wink. "You did all right, lad. Keep it up."

Sinking back into his seat Blackburn looked unable to decide which incident had shaken him the most: the flak post's fury or the Yorkshireman's praise.

One after the other, as safe now as if on a practice run, the aircraft of Harvey's flight flew along the valley and dropped their bombs. From 2,500 feet Hopkinson was taking photographs. The last Mosquito was just commencing its bombing run when a startled voice sounded in Moore's headphones. "Bandits, Pygmalion Leader! In the sun!"

Turning his head, Moore caught a glimpse of a blurred black shape dropping at incredible speed towards the circling Mosquitoes. Before the white-hot sun forced his eyes away he saw two more. His orders stilled the startled voices that were filling the R/T channel. "Red One-Six— jettison bombs and join defensive circle. At the double!"

The crew of Red One-Six were two of the despised "freshers." Startled by the alarm, the navigator forgot to click down his main switch and wasted precious seconds trying to release his bombs before discovering his error. By the time the bombs fell the Mosquito was less than half a mile from the great pall of smoke.

The enemy fighters were Focke Wulf 190s, the advance guard of a squadron based near Maastricht. For the last seventy minutes they had answered urgent call after call as scores of British fighters harried miscellaneous targets in Northern Europe. Frustrated by the diversity of the fighter sweeps, they had at last come face to face with *Tommi* and although their numbers were only four, they had no intention of holding back until their comrades arrived. Seeing the lone V-Victor still down in the valley, the Focke Wulf leader went plunging after it like a kestrel. Ignoring the odds, the remaining three 190s attacked the circle of Mosquitoes with guns blazing.

Freed from their bomb load, the Mosquitoes could hold their own against any German fighter and the defensive tactics they were employing enabled them to cover the tail of their comrades ahead. As one Focke Wulf, eager to inflict some retribution for the damage below, picked out a Mosquito and dived on it, Millburn, only 150 yards

behind, lined up his reflector sight and fired. The blast
of cannon and Brownings hit the main fuel tank, and the
190 disintegrated into a ball of black smoke and scraps of
wreckage. Millburn's yell made earphones rattle. "See
that, you guys? I got one."

But although the defensive circle could hold against such
small odds, Moore knew it would be a different story if
the remainder of the 190 *Gruppe* caught up with them.
Gazing down he saw the Focke Wulf leader had now
fastened on the tail of V-Victor whose crew had not yet
had time to close their bomb doors. Harvey, also an anxious
observer, saw the fighter's tracer lance out like the tongue
of a chameleon and strike the Mosquito's starboard engine. As a white thread of glycol began to stream out,
Harvey cursed, broke circle, and went plunging down.

To save V-Victor he had to open fire at over 500 yards.
Seeing tracer snapping past his port wing, the Focke
Wulf pilot lost interest in V-Victor and tried to break to
starboard but another burst of fire made him kick his
rudder bar back again. Seeing the dense smoke cloud he
dived into it for sanctuary. V-Victor, freed from the
savage attack, was thankfully climbing for the relative
safety of the circle. Harvey, with the tenacity of his kind,
flew right through the smoke after his prey and followed
the 190 down the valley. Unable to shake him off the
Focke Wulf went down to tree-top level and headed for
the chimneys of Hoffenscheim. For a moment it seemed
Harvey might follow him. Instead he banked reluctantly
and climbed after V-Victor into the circle. Watching them,
Moore waited a few more seconds, then raised his mask.
"Zero One to Pygmalion. That's it, the party's over. Follow me home."

Pushing his control column forward he dived north-
east towards Breda. Like a severed noose unfolding, the
circle of Mosquitoes broke and streamed after him. They
were only just in time: the rest of the Focke Wulf squadron was less than a minute away. Streaking into the valley
like angry hornets they banked over the burning plant,
latched again on the call sign of their colleagues, and
headed after them. As the vengeful roar of their engines
faded, the summer day was left to the wail of fire engines and the muffled thumps of fires and explosions.

15

Over by a dispersal hut a group of mechanics had turned and were gazing expectantly at the southern sky. Motioning Adams and Henderson to break off their conversation, Davies listened. For a moment the only sounds were the distant scream of an electric drill and the background singing of birds. Then, as Davies gave Henderson a nod, a hooter sounded and the engines of crash wagons and ambulances started up. Climbing into a jeep that was standing beside them, the three officers waited for the Mosquitoes to appear.

At the inn Anna had been passing the time reading. Now, hearing the commotion on the airfield, she ran to the open window. The first Mosquito appeared over the poplars at the southern end of the field. As it banked with a shattering roar over the inn the girl saw that its port wingtip was heavily gouged and black scars disfigured its sleek fuselage. Her eyes followed it as it circled the field and settled down to land. Dust rose as its tyres squealed on the far end of the runway. Other aircraft were now orbiting the field. The first Mosquito taxied from the runway to its dispersal point. The three senior officers, who had identified its number, were already bounding towards it in their jeep. As they came alongside its two engines spluttered and died. Hopkinson appeared and dropped to the ground, followed by Moore. As the debonair squadron commander allowed a mechanic to help him remove his parachute harness, Davies jumped from the jeep and hurried towards him.

"Well—how did it go?"

Moore was suffering the temporary loss of hearing caused by two power-packed Merlins at close range. "Sorry, sir. I can't hear you."

Davies put his mouth to Moore's ear. "How did it go?" he bawled.

Moore grinned. "I think we gave it a good clobbering."

"How good?"

"There wasn't any wind to clear the smoke, which was pretty dense, but I'd say three-quarters of the buildings were hit."

Davies' eyebrows shot up a full half-inch. "Three-quarters! You're certain?"

"Pretty certain." Moore, whose ears were now recovering, glanced at a corporal and Waaf who were removing the photographic pack. "We did our best to get photographs. They might tell us more."

"There'll be a PR Mossie going over once the commotion's died," Davies told him. His excitement communicated itself to Henderson and Adams who were now at his elbow. "If three-quarters has been damaged, we'll be dead unlucky if it doesn't slow things down for a week or two." Then, realizing how close he had been to breaking security, the small Air Commodore frowned at Moore. "If the smoke was that dense, how can you be so sure?"

"It wasn't a small target and all the boys had to do was drop their bombs on it. There was practically no opposition."

Davies jerked a thumb at the powder-blackened scars on the Mosquito's fuselage. "What's this? Scotch mist?"

"That was from the flak posts," Moore explained. "Once they were knocked out it was a piece of cake."

As Davies's twinkling eyes met Henderson's, the big Scot got in his question at last. "Any casualties, Moore?"

"No, sir. We got away lightly. MacDougall and Briggs had their starboard engine hit by a 190 but they got back to Manston. Neither was hurt."

With his mind eased on that vital issue Henderson looked as delighted as Davies. "Then it's been a big success?"

"I think so," Moore admitted. His eyes were on a Mosquito with a missing starboard wingtip that was coming gingerly in to land. His attention was jerked back by Davies who, drawing nearer, pitched his question low enough not to reach the mechanics working on A-Apple.

"What's your verdict on the lads? Are they going to make the grade or not?"

To the delight of both Henderson and Adams, Moore pretended to be surprised by the question. "I'm not sure I know what you mean, sir. I'd take these crews anywhere. They're a first-class unit."

It was a rebuke that made Davies scowl with pleasure and Henderson look as if he had been presented with a crate of Highland Dew. As the Scot drew Adams' attention to the deep gouge in the port wing, Moore excused himself and walked over to Hopkinson who was chatting to the Waaf photographer.

"Go over and tell Harvey I want to see him in my office, will you?"

Hopkinson's grin was wry. "Before or after de-briefing?"

"Before. In other words, now."

As Moore turned, he almost knocked over the small figure of Davies who had followed him. The Air Commodore's voice was sharp with suspicion. "What do you want Harvey for?"

The good-looking Moore gave him a blank glance. "Nothing in particular, sir."

"Come off it, Moore. I saw your face when you watched him coming in. And he's had a clobbering. What happened?"

"It's nothing important, sir. Only a small misunderstanding that can be put right in a few words."

Seeing he was getting nowhere, Davies gave a grunt of displeasure. "It had better be. Because this squadron and what it has to do is more important than one bloody-minded flight commander. If you have any more trouble with him, you're to let me know. Is that clear?"

"Quite clear, sir."

Giving Moore a suspicious glance, Davies turned away. He was half-way towards Henderson and Adams when his eyes fell on the shell holes in the fuselage. Halting, he jabbed an irascible finger at them. "There's one other thing. There'll be no more of this nonsense. I can't spare you and you know it; so in the future when a dicey job comes along, you delegate it. Understand?"

When no answer came, he spun round. Instead of being at his elbow Moore was exchanging words with Adams who had walked round to examine the other side of the shell-torn Mosquito. Unable this time to hear what confidences were being exchanged, Davies gave a snort and strode off towards the jeep.

Expecting trouble and in no mood to avoid it, Harvey gave the freckle-faced Waaf no chance to announce him.

Giving the adjoining door a thump with his fist, he marched into Moore's office. Straight from his aircraft he was wearing no tunic, and his rolled-up shirt-sleeves revealed powerful, sinewy arms. "I hear you want to see me."

Moore, seated behind his desk, showed no sign of the anger he was feeling. He glanced at the flushed Waaf who, after trying to stop Harvey, was now standing undecided at the door. "Close the door behind you, sergeant, and don't let anyone in."

"Yes, sir." As the girl obeyed and the door closed, Moore turned back to the truculent Yorkshireman. "I'm assuming you know why I've sent for you?"

"I've no idea. Tell me."

Moore's stare moved up slowly to the man's aggressive face. "You know what my answer is to that, Harvey?"

"No."

"I don't believe you."

The Yorkshireman gave a start, then his voice turned hoarse with fury. "You calling me a liar?"

"If you deny knowing why I sent for you, yes. My orders were to leave that flak tower on the southern hillside alone. You deliberately disobeyed them. I want to know why."

"I never heard your orders. That's why."

"If you're saying your radio was u.s., don't. I had it checked five minutes after you landed."

Harvey gave another start. "You what?"

"I had your radio checked. So let's begin again. Why did you disobey my orders?"

"I've just told you. I never heard your orders. I'd switched my R/T off."

It was Moore's turn to stare. "You did what?"

"I switched it off. There was so much chattering over it I couldn't hear myself think."

"You, a flight commander, switched off your R/T in the middle of an operation. Don't you know that's an offence in itself?"

"What the hell was there to hear? We'd all been briefed. In fact I had two bloody briefings."

Once again Moore, whose self-control was his pride, was wondering why this belligerent man could upset him so easily. He picked up a pencil from the desk and studied it a moment before answering. "One reason you leave your R/T on is that you can hear my orders. And my orders were to leave that third flak tower alone."

Harvey's laugh was derisory. "Then it was a good job I didn't hear you, wasn't it? Because it was a bloody daft order."

Holding himself under tight rein, Moore gazed at him almost thoughtfully. "Tell me why it was a daft order."

"Tell you why? Christ, not five minutes earlier you'd played the Lone Ranger and tackled two gun posts on your own. Why did you feel *that* was necessary? Because they were throwing flowers up at us?"

"Those two posts were right alongside the plant. And they covered either approach. The post you attacked was further away and had only a beam shot at us. You took a greater risk in attacking it than by leaving it alone."

"How the hell do you know? I might have lost a couple of my crews if we'd played it your way."

Moore took a deep breath. "Harvey, when you fly with me, you obey my orders. Whether you like them or not, you obey them. You've been in the Services long enough to know those are the rules of the game. So will you stop pulling different ways and let us both get on with the job?"

He received another laugh of dislike. "Your orders—right or wrong? You know what I believe, Moore? You staged that affair today to show us all how tough you are. And you're fighting mad because someone else took the limelight from you. Why don't you admit it?"

Moore's chair fell over as he jumped to his feet. With battle tension still tight in both men, the atmosphere caught at the throat of the breathless Waaf listening at the door. Moore's loss of control showed in his tone as well as his words.

"It's clear enough why you hate my guts, Harvey. You were hoping to get this job and you didn't. Someday, if you can ever take that chip off your shoulder, you'll understand why you were passed over. Until then you'll obey my orders or Christ help you."

Harvey looked as if he had been struck in the face. With a tremendous effort that drained the blood from his cheeks, he went to the door and turned.

"You think you know my reasons for hating your guts? You bloody tailor's dummy, you wouldn't understand my reasons in a thousand years."

The slam of the door behind him almost brought the roof down. Unaware of the deep wounds his words had reopened in the Yorkshireman, Moore was standing pale-faced and motionless. It took a sharp crack to make him start and glance down. The pencil had fractured in his hand.

A tap on the billet door made Moore turn. In his shirt-sleeves, he was putting on his tie in front of a mirror. "Come in."

To his surprise Henderson appeared in the doorway, followed by Adams. The big Scot was looking a trifle embarrassed. "Sorry about this, Moore, but it can't wait."

Although the chair Moore offered him was the best one available, it creaked protestingly as Henderson lowered his weight on it. Confronted with a choice between the only other chair and the bed, Adams somewhat hesitantly chose the bed. Hiding his curiosity, Moore turned back to the C.O. "Can I offer you a drink, sir?"

The Scot shook his head. "No, thanks. I'll probably have a tankful this evening." His question, although clearly a digression from his main purpose, held its full content of curiosity. "Is it true you're standing the party tonight?"

Moore resumed knotting his tie. "I've suggested it to the Catering Officer. You've no objections, have you?"

Henderson looked surprised. "Why should I have objections? I'm just wondering why you should pay for us drunken bastards to celebrate a success you made possible."

Moore sounded almost curt as he reached for his tunic. "Sorry but I don't see it that way. The boys put up a good show so why shouldn't they get a chance to relax. I can afford it."

Adams' myopic eyes had moved to two photographs standing on a locker by the bedside. In the foreground of one was a middle-aged woman of distinguished appearance cutting roses from a large bush. The warmness of her smile suggested she was on close terms with the photographer, possibly Moore himself. The background showed the lawns, forecourt, and terraces of a large country house. The second portrait was that of a white-haired elderly man seated at a desk. Behind him was a wall of tooled leather books. Although both photographs were set in modest frames, their contents unmistakably spelt out wealth and privilege.

Adams was suddenly aware Henderson was grinning at him. "Never let it be said a Scotsman turned down a free dram. All right, Moore, it's your party. But put a limit on the booze or some of 'em won't be fit to fly for a week. Have you seen Davies since the de-briefing?"

"Davies? No."

Henderson, who was lighting a cigarette, released a rueful cloud of smoke. "He's seen me. He's got a bee in his bonnet that you had trouble with Harvey. He told me to have a word with Adams after the de-briefing and then report back to him."

"Report back about what?"

Henderson was viewing Moore's innocence with some scepticism. "Come off it, Moore. You're forgetting every pilot and navigator in the squadron saw him disobey your order. They're all clamming up but even a hairy-kneed Scot can put two and two together. Do you want me to spell it out or will you tell me in your own words?"

Realizing he already knew the facts, Moore shrugged. "It was one of those occasions when either of us could have been right. I thought we stood a bigger chance of losing a kite by attacking the flak post than by leaving it alone. Harvey thought otherwise."

"So he disobeyed your direct order and attacked it?"

"Not my direct order. He never heard it."

"You're not saying he used that corny yarn that his radio was u.s.?"

"No. It wasn't turned on."

Henderson's chair gave a startled creak. "Wasn't turned on? Jam Bang over the target! That's a disciplinary act in itself. Didn't you tell him so?"

"I tore him off a strip in my office fifteen minutes after we landed."

"How did he react?"

Moore gave a wry grimace. "We had a bit of a ding-dong, I'm afraid. Not that it matters if it helps clear the air."

Henderson swore and turned to Adams. "I'll have the bastard posted. It's the only way."

Adams, who realized he was not expected to offer advice, contented himself by making non-committal sounds and pretended to repack his pipe. Moore, who had gone over to the window, spoke without glancing back. "I'd rather you didn't."

Henderson swung back. "What was that?"

"I said I'd rather you didn't post him."

"Why, for Christ's sake?"

"I think he's a good flight commander."

Henderson stared at him. "He nearly clobbers a fellow officer and then disobeys your orders in front of the entire squadron! He's the best!"

"You're forgetting the reason he nearly clobbered Millburn, aren't you?"

"No. I know Powell was his friend."

"That's what I thought at the time but now I see there was more to it. He's got a strong protective streak towards his men. That was why he went for the flak post today."

"It was still against your orders."

"Yes, but who knows I was right? If he hadn't silenced those guns they might have shot down a couple of kites."

Henderson swore again. "You're not supposed to be a prophet. You gave an order and he disobeyed it—that's the point at issue. Anyway, how can you be so sure he was that altruistic? Perhaps he just wanted to show the other's he's as good as you are."

Adams saw Moore shake his head. "No. He did it again later when the 190s arrived. He took a big chance helping MacDougall and Briggs—if the other 190s had followed him down, we probably couldn't have saved him."

The Scot was beginning to show impatience. "You sound as if you like him."

Moore's laugh was rueful. "Hardly. On a personal level we're like two dogs with their hackles up."

"Then that's it," Henderson grunted. "I'll get the bastard transferred. The squadron's starting to pull together at last—I'm not risking the entire barrel going sour again for one rotten apple."

"Harvey won't turn the barrel sour," Moore said. "Not after what happened today."

Watching Henderson, Adams was certain the Scot understood even though his question seemed to deny it. "What's that supposed to mean?"

"Harvey isn't in charge of old sweats now. Today his

flight contained four fresher crews. Yet he still risked his life twice to keep them out of trouble. What's more, everyone saw it. How can that turn the barrel sour?"

Adams felt that integrity demanded some statement from him at this juncture. "It is true, sir, that at the debriefing all the men were showing respect for the way he helped MacDougall and Briggs."

Henderson muttered something rude and moved towards the door. It was a good fifteen seconds before he turned, and to their surprise both men saw he was grinning maliciously. "What d'ye ken? Harvey the peacemaker! There's a thought to raise Davies' blood pressure."

His chuckle died away as his eyes fixed on Moore. "All right, you can keep him for the moment but don't think this'll be the end of your trouble with him. That's as sure as that Millburn and Gabby will get pissed on your free booze tonight."

The two men listened to his anticipatory footsteps retreating down the corridor. Adams returned Moore's smile. "He can't wait to tell Davies. I think he's browned off at being told how to handle his men. Is Davies going to the party tonight?"

"No. He's seeing this Swiss girl over at the pub. For some reason I've been invited to join them."

Adams, who had not been told of Moore's bereavement, looked offended at the news. "That doesn't mean you're going to miss the party, does it?"

Moore crushed a cigarette in the ashtray. "I wasn't coming in any case."

"But that's ridiculous. It's your party. Can't you come after you've met this girl? As Davies is letting us stand down tomorrow, it's sure to go on all night?"

Moore's sudden abruptness startled Adams. "For Christ's sake, I'm not going. Let's leave it there, shall we?"

The sensitive Adams nodded and moved towards the door. As he opened it, Moore checked him. "Sorry, Frank. I'll explain later."

Adams was always quick to forgive. "That's all right. It's none of my business anyway."

Moore was frowning heavily. "I've noticed you're a pretty shrewd judge of people and what makes them tick. Tell me why Harvey and I don't get along. Why does he get into my hair more than anyone I've ever known?"

Impressed by the tolerance the young Squadron Commander had displayed so far, Adams was curious himself. "I've no idea. Unless it's just the two of you are on entirely different wavelengths. It does happen sometimes."

16

With the ground staff as well as the air crews benefit-
ing from Moore's gesture, the Black Swan was quiet that
evening. The Squadron Commander found Davies and
Anna Reinhardt in the private lounge, the only occupants
in an old-world room of blackened beams and glinting
brass. They were seated at a table beneath the window
and an evening sunbeam set them in deep shadow. As
Moore accepted Davies' invitation to draw up a chair he
had the impression the couple had been deep in conversation before his arrival.

The girl's appearance came as a surprise to him. Although he had not given the matter much thought, he had
expected to meet an older woman if only because of her
friendship with the middle-aged Davies. Instead the girl
who held out a slim hand to him was no more than
twenty-four or twenty-five. She was wearing a black dress
and the dark hair that Harvey had admired was now
swept up into a French roll. With her only jewellery an
emerald brooch, she looked as regal as a queen.

"Like a drink?" Davies asked. Before Moore could reply he reached for a bell push, then dropped back on the
window seat. "Is the party under way yet?"

Moore smiled. "There were audible hints it was as I
came by the Mess."

"The squadron are having a bit of a celebration tonight," Davies told the girl. "It could get out of hand
later—let's hope the noise doesn't drift across here and
keep you awake."

"Shouldn't you both be there?" she asked.

"No. We've other things to do." Davies turned back to
Moore. "Sorry if I misled you but this wasn't meant to be
a social occasion. I've a special reason for wanting you
to meet Miss Reinhardt."

Curious, Moore waited, but at that moment Maisie
entered the lounge. Catching sight of the young squadron
leader, her face brightened and there was an archness in

her steps as she approached the window. "Hello, sir. What can I do for you?"

Moore smiled up at the girl. "What can I have?"

The girl's roguish expression gave him a different answer to her words. "I think I can find you a whisky, sir."

"Then that's what I'll have. Thank you."

Maisie turned her big lashes on Davies. "What about you and the lady, sir? Can I bring you another round?"

As Davies nodded the girl picked up the empty glasses, gave Moore a sidelong look, and made for the door, her skirt swirling invitingly around her legs. Davies was about to make a comment when he remembered the girl alongside him and gave a grunt instead. "Well, they say it's a friendly pub."

Moore, managing to keep his face straight, met the girl's grey eyes and saw they were laughing. "Yes, it is, sir. Very friendly."

Seeing the glance the couple exchanged, Davies frowned. "What's all this nonsense about Harvey? You don't seriously think he's a good flight commander, do you?"

"Yes, sir. I do."

Neither man had noticed the girl's slight start. "You're turning soft, Moore," Davies said contemptuously. "He's the sort that enjoys causing trouble." Before Moore could reply he turned to the girl. "We're talking about a character we've got who puts the back up of everyone he meets. I want Moore to get rid of him."

The girl hid her curiosity with a laugh. "You make him sound quite interesting."

"Interesting be damned," Davies grunted. "He's probably a Bolshie if the truth were known. But we've more important things to talk about than Harvey. As I told you earlier, Moore, Anna's come up here for a holiday and I'm hoping she'll enjoy herself. But there's no reason why we shouldn't kill two birds with one stone and that's why I asked you over tonight. You remember that second specialist factory I want clobbered? Well, Anna knows the place and has agreed to brief us before she goes back."

Seeing Moore's curiosity, Davies felt some explanation was necessary. "Her father's a well-known architect and before the war he used to get commissions from all over Europe. He had two in England in the early thirties. That's why Anna's English is so good—she went to an

English school for over three years. Then he got a commission in Munich. Anna went to university there and on her vacations used to take parties of English and American tourists round Bavarian places of interest. Miesbach was one of those places. Am I coming through?"

Uncertain how much the girl knew and yet feeling it highly unlikely that Davies would have told her the wider importance of the Miesbach factory, Moore contented himself with a "Yes, sir."

At that moment Maisie entered with the drinks. As she fussed about the table with all her attention focused on Moore, Anna was silently assessing the young Squadron Commander. A girl to whom a man's physical appearance meant little, she found his scar a relief in a face that might otherwise have been too good-looking. His ease of behaviour coupled with the vaguest hint of shyness, made her remember a comment her father had once made about the English upper class. "They have the rare ability to express self-confidence and vulnerability at the same time. And that makes them very formidable, Liebchen, particularly with women." The impertinence of such an early assessment amused the girl. Apart from what Davies had told her about the young pilot, there had been time to learn only one more thing about him—he had a sense of humour.

Davies waited until Maisie had swung her skirts round the hall door before returning to his theme. "Before Anna came up here I got her to search through her souvenirs and she found photographs and brochures of the town. Add them to her own knowledge of the place and we're in business."

The mellow shaft of sunlight, filled with shining dust motes, was now slanting directly on the girl. Tinted by it, her smooth neck, composed features and piled-up dark hair were rising like a flower from the black calyx of her dress. Davies' voice drove away Moore's fanciful thoughts.

"I can't give you our reason at the moment but we're not carrying out this raid for a few more days. However, when the green light comes, I'll call in Henderson and Adams, and Anna will give us a briefing. Until then not a word to anyone."

Moore contented himself with a nod. Davies, who had lapsed into his usual terseness when discussing service matters, made an attempt to be convivial as he turned back to the girl.

"How were your parents before you left?"

"Quite well. My father keeps getting twinges of arthritis but for that"—the girl was smiling—"he blames the English weather. They both sent their regards to you."

"I must get to see them on my next leave." Davies glanced at his watch, then drained his glass. "I'll have to be going." As Moore rose with him, the Air Commodore made an impatient gesture. "No, you don't need to come. Stay and buy Anna a drink."

Embarrassed, Moore turned to her. "I wish I could, Miss Reinhardt but I have some rather important letters to write tonight. May we make it some other time?"

The girl, who had been told by Davies of his bereavement, nodded sympathetically. "Of course. Give me a ring when you are free."

Meaning well but more suited by nature to a military two-step than a quadrille, Davies made his suggestion sound like an order. "Why leave it so vague? Anna's on holiday and you're not flying tomorrow. So why not ask her out to dinner?"

Moore managed to keep his face expressionless. "I'd enjoy that very much, Miss Reinhardt. May I?"

There were mischievous lights in her eyes as she turned to Davies. "I'm sorry, Arthur. If Wing Commander Moore would care to take me out some other evening, I'd be very happy to go. But it so happens I have a date tomorrow."

Davies looked both curious and irritable. "A date? Already? Who with?"

"An officer called Frank Harvey. He's taking me for a drive on the moors in the afternoon and to dinner at night."

Davies jumped as if a large dog had suddenly leapt from the shadows and bitten him. "Who?"

"Frank Harvey. The pilot you were talking about earlier."

For once it seemed Davies was caught speechless. "How in hell did you meet Harvey?"

"He was kind enough to pick me up when my taxi broke down yesterday. And today he phoned to make a date."

"Harvey," Davies breathed with the air of a man haunted

by a name. "You don't know what you're doing, girl. An afternoon and evening with him and you'll be a Bolshie with a fur cap on your head."

When the girl only smiled Davies marched stiff-legged to the door. His growl was addressed to Moore. "Well, are you coming or not?"

Without waiting to hear his question answered he stalked out into the hall. Which was as well or he might have noticed the smiles that Moore and the girl were exchanging.

Gabby gave a leer of contempt. "Easy, boyo. Dead easy!"

Hopkinson grinned scornfully. "You think so?"

"I know it, boyo. A piece of cake."

The Officers' Mess that night was a shock to the senses with its noise and drunken hilarity. With the squadron's run of bad luck ended, its members were celebrating in time-honoured fashion. A dozen of the older officers, Adams among them, were clustered round the piano where the Armament Officer, no mean pianist, was playing every request thrown at him. In a far corner a party of younger officers were playing a revised version of the Eton Wall Game with a turnip someone had stolen from the kitchen. Every half-minute or so a ruck of struggling men would surge into the party of songsters but miraculously their cohesion would return when the wave had receded. In the opposite corner half a dozen men were surrounding a chair on which a young pilot was standing. They had stretched out a rope from wall to wall and were loudly encouraging the pilot who was preparing to walk it. A final group of hardened drinkers, which included Millburn, Gabby and Hopkinson, were propping up the bar. Waiters, volunteers for the night, weaved glassy-eyed through the turbulence and dropped almost as many glasses as they delivered.

Someone yelled for "Old-fashioned Anson" and the versatile Lindsay picked up the tune. The song was popular and within seconds even the wall-game players were bawling it at the top of their lungs. Adams, whose innate romanticism was always compounded by alcohol, felt the tug of memory as the singing swelled up and filled every corner of the room. This was like the old times when Gillibrand had led the bawdy choruses. The indefinable camaraderie of the fighting man that transcends fear, self-interest, or the love of women. An intoxication that made a man feel a giant and ready to make any sacrifice for his friends or his country. Because it was a manifestation of war, Adams knew it was a dangerous drug and that he should not glory in it but tonight his heart betrayed his mind. The ranks were closing at last: the squadron was becoming a unit again. At the other side of the singing group Henderson's face showed that the Scot had the same thoughts. At that moment Adams had only one regret: that Moore was not present to witness his handiwork.

The song ended and horseplay was rejoined with additional vigour. Gabby jabbed a finger again at the rope and its would-be walker. "A piece of cake," he repeated. "Not worth walking across the room to watch."

"Think you can do better?" Hopkinson taunted. "You're too pissed to walk a chalk line on the floor."

Nothing more was needed to stir the Welshman's aggression. "Who's pissed, you Cockney twit? I've walked things a bloody sight more dangerous than that. Haven't I, Mush?" he asked Millburn who was turning from the bar towards them.

The American, his black hair dishevelled, grinned and thrust a glass of whisky into the Welshman's hand. "Sure you have, kid. You're a regular little Houdini."

"But I bloody have," Gabby repeated with the insistence of the half-drunk. "What about that church tower near Cromer? You said I couldn't do it with that Force Seven wind blowing. Well—did I walk round it or didn't I?"

Millburn's eyes twinkled at the half-circle of grinning faces. "You did, kid. You nearly broke your goddamned neck but you did."

"And how high was it?" the Welshman demanded.

"Oh, a hundred feet, I guess. Maybe more."

Gabby thrust his sharp nose at the sceptical Hopkinson. "You hear that? A hundred feet!" He jabbed a finger again at the tightrope. "And how high's that? Three bloody feet."

"You still couldn't walk it," Hopkinson insisted.

Across the Mess the young officer, a broomstick extended in his hands, pushed a stockinged foot gingerly out on the rope. He took two quick steps, swayed unsteadily to a chorus of cheers, took two more, then tumbled in a heap to the floor. At the howl of derision that arose, Gabby turned triumphantly towards Hopkinson. "That's why he flies like a kite without a tail. No sense of balance."

"I've a pound to say you can't do any better," Hoppy said.

The challenge was clearly an affront to the drunken Welshman's pride. "Three feet above the deck? I could do it with my eyes closed, you Cockney pillock."

"All right. Do it on something higher."

"Such as?"

As Hopkinson grinned there was a gasp from the onlookers. "There's always the water tower."

It took a minute for the challenge to sink in. Then Gabby beamed. "You're on. Once round the parapet. For three quid."

For a moment Hopkinson was taken aback. "You're bull-shitting."

Gabby fumbled in his tunic pocket and pulled out a couple of crumpled notes. He turned to the grinning Millburn. "Lend me a quid."

The American gave him a note and held three more up to the gathering crowd. "Three quid on little Houdini. Who's on?"

A buzz of excitement rose as men began laying bets. As Gabby, grinning vacuously, downed his whisky and pushed away from the bar, a man caught his arm. St. Claire, one of the few officers still reasonably sober, had overheard the challenge.

"Don't be a fool, Gabby. You'll kill yourself."

The Welshman pushed him away. "Make yourself some money, boyo. Put three quid on me."

St. Claire followed him. "You'll kill yourself. The stones round the tank are bevelled. You'll slide straight off if you try to walk round them."

Gabby paused and focused on him. "You're sure of that?"

"Positive," St. Claire lied. "I've flown over the tower enough, haven't I?"

Gabby frowned. "Any one else noticed it?"

Simpson, St. Claire's navigator, caught his pilot's eye and quickly added his own corroboration. "It's true. The stones are definitely bevelled."

Hopkinson looked relieved the bet was off but the grinning Millburn, who was even drunker than Gabby, put his mouth to the Welshman's ear. A moment later the triumphant Gabby swung round. "Don't put your money back yet, boyo. What about the cannon butts?"

Hopkinson looked puzzled. "The cannon butts?"

"The wall at the back. I'll walk from one end to the other. O.K.?"

"But there's a bloody great pile of sand to fall on," Hoppy objected.

"Not at the back there isn't. It's a straight drop of thirty feet. Maybe more." Seeing Hopkinson's hesitation, Gabby misjudged its cause. "A minute ago you said I couldn't walk along a chalk line. You're getting scared now, aren't you, mush?"

Taunted himself, Hopkinson forgot his misgivings. "You can't walk any sort of line, you Welsh pisspot. You're swaying on your feet now."

Gabby gave a yelp of indignation. "You taking me on or backing out?"

"I'm taking you on. But don't blame me when we pick up the pieces."

As the crowd of onlookers surged excitedly towards the Mess entrance, Gabby cast a glance at the older officers still singing around the piano. "Take it easy or they'll bugger it up. Go out a few at a time."

Outside the crowd regrouped and with Gabby, Millburn and Hopkinson in the van started across the airfield towards the distant cannon butts. The night was dark, with patchy cloud and starlight, and a gusting wind was chilling the crews manning the gun-posts. They gazed with astonishment at the drunken, jostling crowd that passed below them. News that Gabby was up to one of his madcap pranks had spread to both the sergeants' and the airmen's messes, and by the time the butts were reached the crowd numbered a hundred men.

Built to take the impact of 20-mm shells, the butts consisted of a high bank of sand backed by a 35-ft. brick wall. Behind the wall the drop was sheer to the metallized surface of the perimeter road. A loud cheer rose as Gabby removed his tunic and climbed over the fence into the butts. Half-way up the steep bank of sand he turned. "Come up here and gimme a hand!"

Millburn and three other men followed him, sinking

almost up to their knees in the sand. At the top of the
bank there was still six feet of bare wall and it took three
of them to hoist the Welshman up. The crowd cheered
again as he jack-knifed over the wall and then squirmed
round to sit on it straddle-legged. The cheer turned into
a gasp of excitement as a gust of wind made him grab
the wall with both hands. Below, Sue Spencer had joined
St. Claire and her face was pale as she gripped the tall
young pilot's arm. "Shouldn't one of us tell the C.O. or
the Adjutant? Otherwise he's going to kill himself."

St. Claire hesitated, then shook his head. "We can't do
that. But some of the men have gone to fetch blankets.
They might help to break his fall if he slips."

Two men carrying service blankets were already running towards the butts. Yelling for others to follow them,
they ran round the back of the wall and threw the blankets open. From this vantage point the black wall rose like
the face of a cliff. On top of it the small figure of Gabby
was silhouetted against the stars. Gripping the edges of a
blanket, six men tried somewhat ludicrously to position
themselves beneath him. Grinning onlookers followed and
offered their advice:

"He'll need a bloody bombsight to land on that, mate."

"Why not chuck him up a parachute?"

"That'll never stop him. He'll keep going all the way to
Aussie land."

Five seconds later a great cheer sent birds clattering
from trees into the night sky. Gabby, who had got his
breath back at last, was attempting to rise to his feet. As
a gust of wind made him grab again at the top of the
wall St. Claire glanced back at the dark shapes of the
Administration Buildings and the Control Tower. He had
little hope that the size and noise of the crowd would
draw the attention of some senior officer. Most of them
were in the Mess, but in any case the butts were a good
four hundred yards from the airfield's main buildings and
the wind was carrying sound away from them. As Sue's
hand tightened spasmodically on his arm, the young artist
bitterly regretted he had not broken the unwritten law
that governed such madcap pranks as he watched Gabby,
arms out-stretched, begin his long walk along the wall.

High up on the bank of sand Millburn was sobering
fast and growing restive as he watched Gabby take his

first few uncertain steps. As the Welshman paused and swayed, he turned to the three men alongside him. "I'm going up too. Gimme a hand."

The men stared at one another, then obeyed. Dropping face down over the top of the wall, Millburn saw the sheer drop to the perimeter track and muttered a subdued "Christ!" Recovering, he wriggled round, put one cautious leg behind him, and not daring to look down, pushed himself to his feet.

A fresh buzz of excitement rose from the crowd. Here and there the muted screams of Waafs could be heard. Sue Spencer sounded horrified. "What's Tommy doing? Has everyone gone mad?"

It was unlikely there was one aircrew member among the crowd who did not understand Millburn's behaviour. A man shared his comrade's danger in the same way he shared his beer and his cigarettes even when that danger was a self-imposed act of foolhardiness. With the philosophy containing a romanticism that most women found absurd, St. Claire made no attempt to answer the girl's question.

Fascinated by the spectacle, even the drunks in the crowd went silent and Gabby's indignant voice could be heard over the wind. "What's the game, Yank? You think you're sharing the stakes?"

Arms outstretched for balance, a sheer black drop on his right side, and the wind a personal enemy, Millburn was now as sober as he had ever been. "Look where you're going, you little bastard," he gritted. "And keep your bloody mouth shut."

A man who thrived on excitement as a schoolboy thrives on icecream, Gabby began to move more swiftly along the wall. Sue Spencer turned incredulously towards St. Claire. "He's not singing, is he?"

St. Claire was listening. "It sounds like it."

"Singing," the girl breathed. "I don't believe it."

The American, whose purpose was to grab hold of the drunken gremlin if he should slip, felt his heart miss a beat as Gabby swayed uncertainly. As Millburn struggled desperately to reach him, Gabby's off-key chant floated back.

"A man came home one evening,
After working hard all day,

> He found the fire had gone out,
> And his wife had run away...."

"Belt up, you Welsh moron," Millburn hissed, now only four feet away but still too distant to lend aid. "Belt up and watch what you're doing or I'll clober you for sure."

The excitement was increasing the Welshman's drunkenness rather than sobering him. Grinning back at Millburn he actually balanced on one leg for a couple of seconds before starting forward and recommencing his song.

> "Twas then he took to drinking,
> What else was he to do,
> He mixed with bad companions,
> And became a burglar too...."

In spite of the chilly wind Millburn could feel the sweat trickling down his face. Cursing himself for his part in the madcap act, he shuffled after the chanting gremlin. "Don't go so bloody fast," he gritted.

Gabby had actually reached the transverse wall that acted as a buttress when his luck ran out. As he turned to grin his triumph, a sudden gust of wind caught him off balance. Seeing him swaying backwards, Millburn acted instinctively. Throwing himself forward he managed to grab the Welshman's shirt but only at the cost of his own balance. Keeping a bulldog grip on the shirt, he lunged out in desperation and flung himself over the other side of the wall. His weight dragged the Welshman after him and in a flailing of arms and legs the two men plunged down into the sand, to screams of alarm and a drunken cheer.

They rolled half-way down the bank before disentangling themselves. Spluttering and wiping his face, Gabby began to laugh. Reacting, Millburn gave a howl of rage. "You horrible little gremlin! I'm going to kill you."

Sand was thick in his dark hair and plastered all over his sweating face. As he tried to reach the Welshman his legs sank into the sand and he fell back. Taking another look at him Gabby realized he meant business and scrambled indignantly down the bank. "What's the matter with you? You're the one who suggested the bloody wall."

Neither reason nor any other scruple could have halted Millburn at that moment. As his raging figure came plunging down the bank Gabby gave a yelp of dismay, scrambled over the fence and dived into the hysterical crowd. Breathing sand and fire, Millburn vaulted out of the butts and charged after him.

17

Harvey paused on the crest of the hill. "Feel like a rest? Or do you want to go on?"

It was not tiredness but the view that made the girl sink down. To the north and west the moors were covered in heather and cloud shadows. Far to her right the sea was visible between the folds of two hills. The sunlit air was still and filled with the singing of skylarks.

"Sit on this. The ground might be damp." Harvey was indicating a gas cape he had laid down. Obeying him, she leaned forward and wrapped her arms around her knees, a characteristic posture. Thirty yards down the hillside, Sam, who was nuzzling through the heather, noticed they had halted and gave an impatient bark. When neither stirred he grumbled and started back.

"I think Sam likes the moors as much as you do," she said.

She could feel his eyes on her. She was wearing a green cotton blouse and fawn skirt. He lit a cigarette before answering. "What about you? Are you enjoying yourself?"

She turned. Bareheaded, he was sitting on his tunic a few feet behind her. "Of course I am. Why do you need to ask such a question?"

Instead of answering he lay back and stared up at the July sky. The dazzling banks of cumulus that drifted past only accentuated its height and clarity. The dog appeared and gave her bare arm a generous lick. As she rubbed its ears, it sank down beside her.

"There was a party at the airfield last night, wasn't there?" she asked as she bent over the dog.

"Yes. How did you know?"

"Air Commodore Davies told me. Did you go?"

"No."

She was suddenly aware why she had mentioned the party. "Why not?"

For a moment his voice was gruff and hostile. "Be-

139

cause I didn't want to." Then, less brusquely: "I had
some friends to see in Highgate."

"I met your new Squadron Commander last night.
Arthur Davies brought him over."

"Why?"

She did not want to lie to him but Davies' instructions
left her no choice. "I suppose Arthur just wanted me to
meet him."

The sudden harshness of his laugh made the dog lift
its head uneasily. "Oh, I see. He wants you to have some
nice, upper-class company while you're here. Did Moore
ask you to go out with him?"

"Yes, but only because Arthur virtually ordered him
to. He was as embarrassed as I was."

"Oh, come off it. When are you seeing him?"

"I don't know."

"But you've just said he asked you."

His change of behavior both puzzled and annoyed
her. "If you must know, he asked me to go out with
him today."

"Why didn't you say yes? I wouldn't have held you to
a promise. All you had to do was ring me."

"Why on earth would I do a thing like that?"

His laugh jarred her. "I'd have thought Moore was
every girl's dream of paradise. A bachelor, clean-cut, well-
educated, and stinking with money. Didn't Davies tell
you he paid for the party last night?"

"Is that why you didn't go?" she asked.

His hard face stared at her aggressively. "I could have
worse reasons, couldn't I?"

"I don't know. Moore seemed a nice enough person to
me."

"He would, wouldn't he? Good-looking and the heir to
a fortune."

"I suppose you do realize you are insulting me?"

With a growl Harvey sank back on his jacket. "Don't
blame me. Blame the way the world operates."

"Why do you dislike Ian Moore so much? Is it a personal thing or is it only dislike of what he represents?"

"Only?" The word was a denunciation.

"Does that mean it isn't personal?"

"For Christ's sake! If you're going to talk about Moore
all the afternoon, you might as well have gone out with
him in the first place."

"It's not Moore I want to talk about. I'm curious to know why you're so bitter towards people like him."

He exhaled smoke resentfully. "Well, you can stay curious as far as I'm concerned."

Her wish to make peace surprised her. "I'm sorry. I know I've no right to ask you such questions." Bending over the dog again she ran her fingers through its wiry coat. "I think I must blame the war. It leaves one with such little time to learn about people."

It was a change of tone that for a moment made her sound alone and vulnerable, and it was enough for the loner in Harvey to respond. "That's all right," he muttered. "I just don't want to talk about it, that's all." A man who found apologizing an effort of will, he frowned and glanced away before making his gruff compromise. "Forget it if I was rude a minute ago, will you? I get carried away sometimes."

She gave him a forgiving smile, then turned back to the sunlit hills. Cloud shadows were moving across them like armies and with her arms wrapped around her knees she watched them in fascination. It was the dog, shifting its position in the heather, that broke the spell. Glancing at Harvey and believing him asleep, she lay back on the cape. As she half-closed her eyes the sunlight splintered on her lashes into iridescent shafts and whirls. With the hum of insects a distant organ note, her eyes turned heavy and closed.

When she awoke the organ note was louder and more insistent. Drugged with sun and sleep she sat upright, trying to trace the sound. Harvey's voice made her start. "It's all right. It's one of ours."

He was lying on one elbow. From the cigarette in his hand, he appeared to have been awake some time. At his nod she glanced westward. A four-engined aircraft was moving south over the ridge of hills.

"A Lancaster," he told her. "Doing an air-test."

She noticed now how far the sun had moved. "I must have been asleep some time."

"Over an hour."

"Haven't you slept?"

He was watching the steady progress of the Lancaster. "I think I dozed off for a while. Can't be sure. I saw three others ten minutes ago. There'll be a Main Force raid on tonight." With one of the abrupt changes of mood that characterized him, he turned towards her half-mockingly. "More Terror-Flyers over the Fatherland. How do you feel about us?"

She knew he had been wanting to ask the question since their first meeting. "You mean how do I feel because I'm of German descent?"

"Yes."

She hesitated. "I'm not happy about the bombing, if that is what you mean."

"No one expects you to be happy. But do you resent it?"

"No. I know the Nazis have to be defeated."

"Then you see a difference between the Nazis and the Germans?"

"Of course. Nazism has been imposed on the Germans."

"They didn't have to accept it if they didn't want to."

"Hadn't history something to do with that?"

"Never mind history. The Germans accepted Nazism because it promised them wealth and power. So shouldn't they take some of the blame?"

She was aware he was provoking her. At the same time she wondered if she was being fair to him in the answer she gave. "It isn't only Germans who can be seduced by promises. But in any case how can you speak for an entire people? Even in the democracies there are some who do not like the way they are governed. Then think how many more there are in Germany who hate Nazism."

His harsh laugh was full of respect. "At least you're right about the democracies. We've got a bloody nerve to be throwing stones around."

His resurgence of bitterness made her wish she had not made the point. "You must not make the mistake of thinking things are as bad here as in Germany. I spent some time there before the war. This is paradise compared to life under the Nazis."

"Paradise?" he sneered. "Here? You should have seen this country in the thirties."

"I did see it. I learned my English here." Seeing his sceptical glance she went on: "We moved about a great deal when I was young because my father is an architect. We spent over a year in Plymouth and nearly three years in Canterbury."

His nod was full of disgust. "In the south. I thought so. If you'd been up in these parts you'd have different ideas about paradise."

"Nothing is as bad as Nazism," she said quietly. "Take the word of someone who has seen it first hand."

A small bird, landing on a bush close to them, checked his reply. To her surprise he motioned her to keep still. Balancing like an acrobat on a swaying twig, the bird lifted a wing and preened itself. Then its bright, alert eyes caught sight of the sleeping dog and with a chirrup it launched itself upwards and flew inland.

Harvey jumped to his feet and stood watching it. Tieless, with his shirtsleeves rolled up and his tall, bony body braced against the summer sky, she thought he looked more like a farmer than a soldier. A moment passed and then he gave an embarrassed laugh. "Sorry about that. But it was a dipper. You don't see many of them in this part of the world."

He straightened again and gazed across the moors in the direction the bird had flown. She saw his shirt tighten as he took in a deep appreciative breath. "God," he said. "What a perfect day."

There was a catch in her laugh as she rose. The reflections of the moors were still in his blue, puzzled eyes as she faced him. "I'm glad that happened."

"What?" he muttered.

"The way your mood changed when you saw that bird. You are a fraud. You don't hate this country as you pretend to do. You love it. Passionately."

He turned away; then, with a curse, he ripped up a clump of heather and thrust it almost into her face. "All right. I love this! And this!" And a sweep of his arm embraced the moors and the distant sea. "Why shouldn't I? No one's spoiled them. But the rest!" He almost choked on the words as he swung away. "They've laid their dirty fingermarks on everything else, haven't they?"

Startled by his outcry the dog had jumped up and was barking. Glad of the interruption he cuffed its ears and quietened it. As she stood watching him, it was suddenly clear to her why she had an affinity with this lonely, embittered man.

"You don't need to fight me," she said quietly. "Who could understand you better? Don't I have much the same problem as you?"

18

The front gate of No. 30 Wilberforce Street, Highgate, had a notice that read: No Tradesmen and No Vendors. Wincing at its antagonism Adams pushed the gate open, crossed the path, and pressed the door bell.

He had to press it three times before the slide of a bolt and the rattle of a chain brought him encouragement. The woman who faced him was the archetypal elderly spinster with primly-permed hair, a voluminous blouse, tweed skirt and brogues.

"Yes. What do you want?"

"Good afternoon. I have an appointment with Mrs. Marsh."

"Are you Squadron Leader Adams?"

"That's right, Miss Taylor. I met your sister when I visited Mrs. Marsh a few weeks ago."

The woman's eyes moved from the rings on his sleeve to the crest on his cap. Adams, who suffered a permanent complex about his non-military appearance, decided she was finding it difficult to believe he was not a tradesman. Behind her was a hall and staircase decorated in sombre shades of brown. A large mahogany hallstand stood against the side wall. With a last stare at Adams the woman withdrew to the foot of the staircase.

"Mrs. Marsh. There's that officer to see you. Squadron Leader Adams."

Adams heard a girl's voice on the landing above. The woman gave him a nod and stood aside. "You'll find her upstairs. The second door on the left."

Feeling her eyes on his back, Adams started up the stairs. Half-way up he encountered two sepia photographs set in identical oval frames. One featured a bulky man in a frock coat, all bristling moustaches and Imperial arrogance, and Adams had barely recovered from the confrontation when he ran into the haughty stare of a *memsahib* wearing pearls and a Victorian hair-do.

Reaching the landing with some relief he found Julie

Marsh, baby in arms, waiting at her sitting room door to greet him. Adams held out his hand.

"Hello, Mrs. Marsh. It's good to see you again."

As the girl struggled to free a hand, Adams saw he had made the wrong move and closed quickly on the baby instead. "How's young Marsh getting along?"

Nervousness made the girl sound breathless. "He's not very good today, I'm afraid. That was why I couldn't get downstairs to let you in. I've just had to change him."

Adams, who had already noticed the smell of vomit that surrounded the child, wished he did not sound so hearty. "Never mind. We all have our bad days, don't we? How old is he now?"

"Nearly nine months." The girl backed into the sitting room. "Won't you come in?"

Adams followed her into the combined sitting room and kitchen where the girl indicated an armchair. "If you care to sit down I'll make a cup of tea."

Adams sank into the armchair. Its padding was compressed and he could feel the pressure of a spring. Julie, after gazing round the room somewhat helplessly, excused herself and took the baby into the bedroom. Barely five seconds passed before there was a loud wail. Hearing the girl trying to soothe the infant, Adams hesitated, then made his gesture.

"Why don't you give Mark to me?" he called out. "Then you'll have your hands free to make the tea."

She appeared in the doorway with the wailing bundle. "Are you sure you don't mind?"

"Not a bit," Adams lied.

Somewhat hesitantly she deposited the bundle on Adams' lap. Leaning forward Adams drew back the blanket with one finger. The small, red face that appeared told Adams beyond any doubt that his intrusion was resented. Seeing him at the same time, the infant let out a howl of outrage, stiffened, and kicked its feet furiously against the arm of the chair.

Busy filling a kettle at the sink, Julie glanced back anxiously. "If you could rock him a little he might settle down."

Hoping fervently the infant would not exact revenge by peeing on him, Adams obeyed. The effect was counterproductive: the yells turned hysterical but with no other recourse open to him Adams went on rocking. Setting the filled kettle on a gas ring the girl hurried towards him.

"I'll give him some orange juice. That usually quietens him."

The subterfuge worked and the replenished infant was replaced in his cot. When the girl returned and busied herself making tea, Adams was at last able to pay her attention. Her dress, cheap but neat, suggested she had made some effort to be presentable but her hair looked straggly and needed combing. Months of stress had given her skin an unhealthy pallor and her face had a pinched appearance that made her look older than her years.

She handed him a cup of tea, then sank on the settee as if the effort of coping with him and the baby was too much. "I'm sorry I haven't any cakes. I meant to go out this morning to the shops but it was difficult with Mark off-colour."

Adams was wondering how to begin. "I never eat between meals. I have to think about my figure." As the girl made an effort to smile, he took the plunge. "You do know why I've come, don't you?"

Her nod was jerky. "Yes. Peter told me he was going to ask you."

"Is there anything you would like to say to me first? It will all be in confidence, of course."

The girl hesitated, then shook her head. "What is there to say? I want Peter to give up flying and he says he can't. I think he'd like to but he's too ashamed to ask. I can't see why."

Adams took the first gentle step forward. "It is difficult for him, you know."

"Why?" Her voice was suddenly hostile. "He's done forty-four trips. That's a tour and a half. On other squadrons men are rested after thirty operations."

"I'm afraid that's your answer. This isn't an ordinary squadron. Like the Pathfinders, crews can only achieve maximum proficiency by staying on beyond their normal tour."

"But that's unfair! Most men don't live to finish a tour. Twelve raids is the average. Peter's done nearly four times that number."

Adams realized the size of the task facing him. "I'm afraid that's why he is so valuable. We've recently had to bring in a large number of new men, so the experienced crews like Peter are worth their weight in gold."

The suddenness with which her emotion died and her eyes filled with tears told Adams the state of her nerves. "What's the use? You all say the same things."

Adams tried a different approach. "Aren't you rather looking on the dark side of things? Have you ever thought how lucky Peter is to be flying the Mosquito? It's probably the safest plane in the RAF. It can get up higher than any German fighter and it can also go faster. This gives him a far better chance of survival than if he were flying heavy bombers."

Adams was conscious of his blunder even before the girl's bitter reply. "Peter has said this to me too. But it didn't help in May, did it? One plane back—from an entire squadron! If Peter hadn't been in hospital at the time, he'd already be dead."

"That was an exceptional operation. In the normal run-of-the-mill raids, Mosquito losses are well below the Main Force average."

Hypersensitive to a degree when discussing other men's lives, Adams imagined the girl's resentful eyes rested a moment on his wingless left shoulder. "You've just said this is a special squadron. That means it carries out special operations."

In desperation at the hash he was making of things, Adams played the liar. "The May raid was exceptional because of its importance and because the Germans had caught wind of it. It doesn't mean the squadron is going to be given anything as dangerous in the future."

The girl was staring blindly at the worn carpet between them. With Adams having disappointed her, she had withdrawn into her private world and was no longer listening to him. Disgusted by his lies and his failure, Adams took another sip of tea and found it was growing cold. The feeling he was letting the young pilot down brought a plea from him when a minute or two of silence might have been wiser.

"I know how hard it is but have you ever tried to see it from Peter's point of view? He's part of an élite group— the few who survived from the old squadron—and a part of him can't help being proud of it. Also men grow very close in wartime and try not to let one another down. I

know how desperately he wants to ease your mind but
it is a huge step for a pilot to ask to be grounded. In fact
it's just possible it might be the worst thing we can ask of
him."

Her expression made Adams realize he now sounded
more like an enemy than an ally. Resentment drew on
the last dregs of her nervous energy. "Men with their
stupid pride and fear of being thought a coward. . . .
What do I care what people think of him? Who'll remember any of this in ten years' time? I want a father for my
baby, not a dead hero."

The difference between man and woman, Adams
thought, frozen in his chair. The woman who since the
dawn of time has resolved her morality within the walls
of her cave and the children's mouths she has to feed. The
man, out-going and finding both survival and success needing collective effort, adopting a morality that takes into
account the interests of his fellow-hunters. One morality
rational and therefore often selfish. The other equally
rational and yet often sentimental. On occasions such as
this totally incompatible.

With her efforts to show a brave face spent, the girl
was now sobbing uncontrollably. More upset than he
could remember, Adams forgot his role as a senior RAF
officer. "I know how you feel. It's my job to talk to these
boys before they go out on a raid and I can't think how
many times I've asked myself how men can find glory in
killing one another."

He broke off, too horrified by his confession to know if
the girl had heard him or not. A glance at her made him
doubt it: her sobs appeared to be tearing her thin body
apart. Adams stole an uneasy glance over his shoulder.
The door was ajar and the girl's distress must surely be
heard downstairs. Then Adams reviled himself. It was a
poor man who weighed up his personal interests when a
fellow human being was suffering like this. Dropping on
the settee, Adams put an arm around the girl's shoulders
and defied any dragons who might see him.

"You mustn't torture yourself this way. The worst
doesn't usually happen, you know. I don't believe it will
happen to Peter."

She tried to speak but her sobs choked her. Adams
drew her closer. "What exactly were you hoping I could
do, Julie?"

"I'm not sure. . . . Couldn't you talk to his Flight Commander . . . or perhaps to the C.O. himself?"

"I could, but you must see they will do nothing until Peter himself asks to be grounded."

"Then talk to Peter for me. Please."

"I already have, Julie. I advised him to go straight to the C.O."

"Then try again. Please. I can't go on like this much longer."

Adams could feel the wetness of her tears on his cheek. "I will. And if I can think of anything else, I'll let you know. But I don't want to disappoint you, so please don't bank on it."

Her lack of response told him that that was unlikely. Not allowing her to go downstairs with him, he remembered little more of his exit than the haunted, tear-ravaged girl saying goodbye to him at her sitting room door. In fact Adams' mind only began to function again on his drive back to Sutton Craddock. In the entire history of war were there ever more pathetic victims than these young fliers and their wives? The monstrous daily charade of women waving goodbye to their husbands as if they were going to the office instead of into mortal danger contained all the elements of pure sadism. For the rest of that day and a considerable part of the night Adams remembered the girl's bitter remark that all the present heroism would soon be forgotten. He had the feeling she was right and it upset him. Adams, the idealist, would have liked these young couples to be remembered forever.

19

With a cheerful toot of its siren, the pleasure boat nudged the pier and swung in alongside it. Behind it the Chiemsee was bright and blue in the July sunlight. As a gang-plank rattled down, the brass band on the pier, all shiny faces and glinting instruments, took a deep breath and burst into a popular tune. With café tables crowded, children playing, and soldiers on leave sauntering up and down with their girl friends, the scene was relaxed and colourful. The war was still a long way from Bavaria and people were making the most of the Sunday afternoon.

Outside a café back on the main road that ran to Prien a burly man nudged his companion's foot under the table as the first passengers disembarked. "As you'd expect, the arrogant bastards are the first off."

The two men, wearing local defence force uniforms, were Hausmann and Meyer. Both worked in the timber yards during the week but like the rest of their fellow workers wore the defence force para-military uniforms in the evenings and on weekends. Although most of the men were over military age or medically unfit, the uniform staved off embarrassing questions as to why they were not in the Services. For Hausmann and Meyer their uniforms were a shield against a more serious embarrassment.

The burly Hausmann was watching a party of four high-ranking German officers who were walking up the pier. Local girls were clinging to their arms. Although the officers were sharing jokes with the girls, there was an arrogance about them that made civilians move aside. His back to the pier, Meyer took a sip of beer.

"Is it the Herrenchiemsee boat?"

"Yes."

The gaunt-faced Meyer had a satirical sense of humour. "That fits. They'll have been strutting up and down the corridors imagining themselves Louis XIV."

The party had reached the pier entrance. As they

150

moved towards two large cars parked there, Hausmann nudged Meyer again. "He's the tall one with a girl on each arm."

Meyer turned casually. The officer Hausmann indicated was a slim and erect man in his late thirties. Arrogant-featured, he had a schläger scar on his right cheekbone. His manner and the deference shown him by the rest of his party made it clear he was their superior in more than rank. Waiting for one of his fellow officers to open the rear door of the larger car, he stepped inside. The two giggling girls followed him a couple of seconds later. Hausmann glanced back at Meyer.

"Colonel von Löwerherz. Wealthy with an aristocratic background. Studied at Heidelberg and was brilliant. Used to be a designer at Mercedes Benz. Now he's Co-ordinator of Research and Development, so he has access to all parts of the project. His weakness is women and rumour has it he's a sadistic bastard. He's in Prien most week-ends and doesn't waste any time. We've learned that on at least three occasions he's taken a woman back to Ruh-polding." Hausmann allowed himself a brief grin. "He must find the weekends too far apart. It's against all the rules of course, but apparently his technical know-how, aristocratic background and rank allow him to get away with it."

Meyer's gaunt face betrayed his frustration. "Three little tarts get taken right inside and we can't even man-age a look through the bloody fence. Can't we question them in some way?"

Hausmann shrugged. "How can we do that without making them suspicious? Anyway, what would be the point? They wouldn't be interested in what was going on, and Löwerherz would hardly take them on a conducted tour."

Back at the pier entrance the two cars were now moving away. As they swept past the café both men looked engrossed in their beer. Hausmann waited until they vanished round a bend before leaning forward again. "London have been in touch while you were in Munich. And this is the idea they've come up with."

He spoke in a low tone for nearly three minutes. When he finished Meyer was showing both shock and disgust. "You haven't agreed to this, have you?"

Hausmann's own distaste for the scheme did nothing to improve his temper. "What the hell can I do about it? I'm here to obey orders, not give them."

"But it's inhuman. No one has the right to ask another human being to do a thing like that."

"Apparently no one has asked. It's Lorenz's own idea."

"Knowing Lorenz, it probably is. But London shouldn't agree to it."

"What alternative have they got? We haven't come up with any ideas ourselves."

"Maybe we haven't. But this one's suicidal. For Christ's sake, Hausmann, have a word with. . . ."

Hausmann's expression made Meyer break off in midsentence. A young Gestapo officer had come round the corner of the café and Meyer's raised voice had caught his attention. Both men froze as he approached their table. He paused behind Meyer's chair as if to question him, then appeared to change his mind and walked on. He was twenty yards down the pavement before Hausmann drew breath again. "Have you gone out of your bloody mind?"

"Sorry," Meyer muttered. "Only it's a filthy thing to ask anyone to do."

Nerves and twinges of arthritis made Hausmann uncharacteristically short-tempered. "It's a filthy world—or haven't you heard? And it could be a damn sight filthier unless we can break this security and locate that plant." He glanced at his watch. "I'm on duty in an hour, so the rest is up to you. Get into Prien and follow Löwerherz around. Find out his haunts and everyone he sees. Keep on him all night if necessary because we've only got this weekend and next to get the information London needs. O.K.?"

Meyer nodded and emptied his glass. Down the pier the band had broken into a rousing march. As Hausmann rose, another twinge of arthritis made him grab hold of the table. "It's those damned damp forests," he growled at Meyer's inquiry. "If we don't get this business settled soon I'll be in worse shape than my old mother."

Davies straightened up from the photographs and brochures that covered the bed. "All right, that's your target. Any more questions?"

When no one spoke he nodded at Anna, who began collecting up the briefing material, and moved into the centre of the room. Henderson, Adams and Moore, the other men present, hesitated a moment and then followed him. Seeing Henderson give Moore an apologetic glance, Davies turned irritable.

"Someone say something, for Christ's sake."

Henderson's comment was addressed to Moore. "You wanted to get away tomorrow, didn't you?"

"What's that?" Davies asked.

The Scot turned to him somewhat disapprovingly. "He was going on leave tomorrow to attend his father's funeral."

Davies allowed himself a single moment of compassion. "Sorry, Moore. It's damned bad luck. But that's how things go." Dropping the disappointment as another casualty of war he went on: "You're all being bloody coy about this raid, aren't you?"

Challenged, Henderson took the plunge. "I suppose that's because it seems a hell of a long trip, sir."

"It is a hell of a long trip," Davies snapped. "But what else can we do? Until the green light comes, we have to slow down production somehow." He turned to Moore. "What do you think? You're the one that has to go."

All eyes turned on Moore who took a few seconds to answer. "With a bit of luck we ought to get there all right. But as we have to go down to five thousand feet or under to obtain accuracy, I think we must expect losses."

"You mean their radar will track you to the target?"

"Yes. I know you've plenty of other activity planned tomorrow night but they can't miss picking us up if we penetrate as deeply as this. And that means night fighters will be waiting when we go down."

To avoid his expression betraying him, Davies turned to the window. "So it's primarily a problem of their tracking system?"

Moore looked surprised at the question. "That and their night fighters. When isn't it the problem?"

Instead of answering Davies gave himself a few seconds more at the window before turning back. "Maybe when it comes to the night it won't be as bad as you think. I'll have another word with the three of you before we brief the crews tomorrow afternoon. In the meantime, if you've no more questions, let's thank Miss Reinhardt for her help and leave the pub as unobtrusively as possible. There's no point in making people curious."

Thanking the girl, Henderson and Adams left first. As Davies led Moore to the door, the young pilot turned back. "I understand Harvey is on duty tonight. So I'm wondering if I might be sneaky and ask for that dinner date you promised me?"

Anna returned his smile. "I'd like that very much, Wing Commander."

"Good. What time will suit you? Seven o'clock?"

"Yes. I'll be ready. Thank you."

Davies followed Moore out on the landing, then reappeared in the doorway. "You're starting to get some sense at last," he grunted.

She laughed at him. "I'm relieved to hear you say that, Arthur."

Davies gave her a wink and closed the door behind him. Left alone the girl drifted across to the window. From it she could see Henderson and Adams walking down the road to the airfield. The field itself was sunlit but a bank of dark clouds were massing over the southern perimeter and a Mosquito flying on air-test could be seen silhouetted against them. The girl was about to turn on the radio when her telephone rang. "Hello, Miss." The voice was Maisie's. "Someone from the airfield wants a word with you."

The someone was Harvey. "Anna? Hello. I thought I'd phone while I had the chance—you never know in this game when they're going to cut communications."

"Hello, Frank. I'm glad you did."

"It doesn't look as if I'll get a chance to come over today but what's the situation tomorrow?"

"I'm not doing anything if that's what you mean."

"Then am I going to see you?"

Aware he knew nothing yet about the forthcoming raid she chose her words carefully. "If you'd like to. What about the morning?"

"The morning?" Harvey sounded disappointed. "If we're not flying, couldn't we make it the afternoon òr the evening?"

"Yes, of course. But it would be good to see you in the morning if you can manage it."

When other men might have made egotistical assumptions, it was typical of Harvey that he only sounded puzzled. "All right. Around 1030?"

She was trying to resolve this inhibited, diffident man with the belligerent trouble-maker portrayed by Davies and failing on every count. They talked for nearly five minutes before Harvey was interrupted. "Sorry, Anna, but there's a bit of a flap on. I'll have to go."

She was surprised to hear her voice pull him back. "Don't forget about the morning. Come as early as you can."

She lowered the receiver and as if the airfield were a magnet found herself drawn to the window again. The bank of clouds, moving rapidly, had now covered the sun and in its shadow the entire aspect of the airfield had changed. Hangars and Nissen huts, whose outlines had been softened by the sunlight, now looked gaunt and impermanent. Stains of oil on the runways, refracting prismatic light, were now ugly bruises on grey flesh. As the Mosquito under air-test flittered like a shadow across the threatening sky, a chill ran through the girl.

20

Across the packed room the three-piece band was playing "Only Forever." Waiters, some with trays held above their heads, were struggling through the circle of tables. On the small maple dance floor, locked together in the fashion of the time, couples were doing their best not to collide with one another. Although a number of civilians were present, servicemen and their girl friends were in the majority. A blue haze of tobacco smoke hung over the tables and the air was filled with the frenetic chatter and laughter of wartime.

Moore's eyes were on the girl seated opposite him. An American sergeant and his girl, ignoring the fox-trot tempo, were jitterbugging on the crowded floor, and she was watching their performance with amusement. She was wearing a green evening dress that set off to perfection her dark hair and creamy skin, and Moore, who had already decided she was the most unusual girl he had ever met, was wondering whether it was her appearance or her personality that intrigued him the most. He gave her a rueful grin as she turned back.

"I'm afraid it's hardly the Dorchester but it's the best we've got in these parts."

Her grey eyes reproved him. "Don't apologize for it. I'm enjoying myself."

"You are? That's marvellous. I suppose the food wasn't too bad. Would you care to dance?"

"If you promise not to jitterbug. I don't think there is room on the floor for two of us."

"Jitterbugging isn't my style. I'm the close-in, smoochy type."

A dimple came into her cheek. "I'm not sure I know what that means."

Smiling, he led her towards the floor. "Come and find out."

He was not surprised to discover she danced well. As the floor grew more crowded, dancing turned into little

156

more than a shuffle, but with her tall and supple body pressed against him Moore had no complaints and it was nearly fifteen minutes before he led her back to their table. Seeing the champagne bottle was empty he checked a passing waiter. "Bring another bottle, will you?"

He ignored the girl's protest as he sat back. "You mustn't argue. This is a special occasion."

"It is?"

Moore's eyes were admiring her. "It is for me. It isn't every day I get the chance to take out an Air Commodore's beautiful girl friend."

She took his banter the way it was intended. "Poor Arthur. He never seems able to relax, does he?"

"He doesn't need to. He enjoys his work. God knows what he'll do when the war's over."

"I think you are right. He will be very bored."

Moore's mood changed. Lighting a cigarette, he frowned down at it. "He won't be the only one. A good many of us are going to find peacetime difficult to take."

"But why? Surely you can't like all this destruction and killing?"

His smile was wry. "Between the two of us it disgusts me."

"Then why will you find peacetime so difficult?"

He shifted in his chair before answering. "I suppose with me it's because I dread responsibility."

"Does your father's death mean you are now the head of the company?"

He wondered how much Davies had told her. "Yes, I'm afraid it does."

"And you don't like that?"

Never one to share his forebodings easily, Moore wondered at the special qualities of this girl who could make him admit them now. "Frankly, I dread it. Thousands of men and their families dependent on me for their livelihood. . . . I'm a coward—it'll turn me old before my time." Then he saw she was laughing. "What's the joke?"

"You are a Squadron Commander. Every time you lead your men out on a raid you are responsible for their lives. Yet you are afraid of being responsible for their livelihood. Can't you see how funny that is?"

He laughed with her. "It's a different kind of responsibility. I'm not the strategist, only a tactician. But as the Chairman of the company I'll be responsible for policy every inch of the way. And that thought frightens the life out of me."

"I still think it is very funny," she told him.

Over on the dance floor there was a loud cheer as the American and his partner completed their marathon dance. Moore's question came as the girl turned to look. "Anna! Why did Davies arrange for you to come here?"

For a moment her gaze remained on the group of cheering servicemen as if she had not heard him. Then, without haste, she turned back. "Arthur told you why. I came for a holiday and also to tell you all I know about Miesbach."

"But Davies could have had you interrogated at home and had the photographs sent to us. There was no need for you to waste your leave here."

"I am not wasting it. I wanted to see this part of England."

"A northern market town? An airfield?"

"No. The scenery. It is very beautiful up here."

"There's beautiful scenery in the south."

"I know that. But I wanted to see another part of the country. Is that so strange?"

It wasn't at all strange, Moore thought, wondering why he was asking his questions. "Where did you go yesterday?"

"To the moors. Somewhere near Whitby, I believe."

"What did you think of them?"

"They are everything I expected. Very beautiful."

The question came before Moore could check it. "How did you get on with Harvey?"

She picked up her glass of champagne. "Quite well, I think."

"You didn't find him a difficult character?"

He discovered that instead of avoiding a challenge her inclination was to meet it half-way. "Are you another who doesn't like him?"

He avoided a direct answer. "One can't deny he has a pretty large chip on his shoulder."

"Perhaps there is a reason for that chip."

"Perhaps. But he's not the only man in the war who's had a hard life. Half of my squadron are working class but they don't go round acting like martyrs."

"Perhaps his life was harder than most." At his glance

she shook her head. "No, he did not speak about it. But I am sure something has happened to make him the way he is."

"Aren't you a bit suspicious of people who blame society for their behaviour? Isn't it often an excuse to hide their own short-comings?"

Although it was a remark made deliberately to disturb her composure he found the tables were turned as her grey eyes met his own. "But Harvey does not use it as an excuse. He will not talk about it."

"But the inference is there, isn't it?"

"It is easy for you to talk this way—society has been kind to you. For the same reason it is easier for you to fight to preserve that society."

Although quietly delivered, it was a rebuke that made him smile wryly. "You're very frank."

"Would you want me to be anything else?"

"No. I like you as you are. But if Harvey is so bitter with society, why does he fight for it? We're not Nazi Germany. He wouldn't be shot if he were a conscientious objector."

"Haven't you ever thought this could be one of the conflicts he suffers from? He believes he hates England for her indifference and yet deep inside he might love her passionately. I think he does. Not the society but the fields, the hedgerows, the villages—the visions men have when they think of England."

Moore was trying to associate visions of rural England with the brooding Harvey and failing on every count. "Isn't that rather romantic?"

She smiled at her analogy. "Isn't love itself romantic? Harvey makes me think of a man in love with a cruel mistress. He curses her and wants to escape but must always be there when she needs him."

"He seems to interest you very much," Moore said curiously.

"He does. I have not met many men like him."

"You will if you stay in this country long enough. We've got more than our fair share of them."

Her quiet reply made him start. "Then you are lucky."

"Lucky?" Moore had to glance at the girl's earnest face to be certain she was not teasing him. "Warts and all, I'll take Harvey as a flight commander because a good part of his bloody-mindness rubs off on the enemy. But in peacetime his type are a menace. Harvey would call a strike if someone took just a minute off his tea break."

"He probably would," she said quietly. "But it is a bad thing to defend one's rights?"

"Oh, come off it!" Moore's sudden outburst of impatience was uncharacteristic. "When I was a boy I remember seeing someone like Harvey take a swing at my father simply because he was trying to rationalize a production line. Don't tell me that's defending one's rights. It's just bloody-minded obstructionism."

It was a moment before she answered him. "Have you ever thought that men like that are the price one has to pay for democracy?"

He stared at her. "Now I know you're pulling my leg."

"No, I'm serious. Men who can't be cowed by authority can't be conquered by authoritarianism. If there had been half a million of them in Germany ten years ago —perhaps only a few thousand—there would be no Nazism today."

"There might be Communism though, mightn't there?"

She saw he was recovering his good humour and allowed herself a smile. "I find that rather funny. I doubt if Harvey knows what a Communist is."

"If he doesn't, he's trying hard," was Moore's wry comment.

"I think you're wrong to lump Harvey with the kind of man who struck your father. I believe he has a much deeper reason for his bitterness towards society."

Too intelligent to miss her inference, Moore gave a sudden start. "What are you getting at? That I might dislike Harvey because when I was a boy I saw someone like him strike my father?"

She held his stare without flinching. "It is possible, isn't it?"

His laugh was a mixture of disbelief and respect. "I suppose anything's possible. Are you sure you're not a teacher of psychology?"

For the first time she showed embarrassment. "I have no right to make such suggestions. But it was you who began talking about Harvey."

"I don't mind your suggestions. As a matter of fact I'm grateful for them. As I said earlier—Harvey's a good flight commander and acts like a father to his men. When you come across a man like that you resent not liking him."

"You are very generous to someone you don't like and who doesn't like you. I don't think you would find Harvey so generous."

His reply teased her. "You're forgetting your own credo. Everything is that much easier when society has made you the top dog. Remember?"

The dimple reappeared in her cheek. "You can't deny it's true, can you?"

"I'm not denying anything. But you have got Harvey insured all ways." Moore's smile turned quizzical. "Harvey—the pillar of democracy! The archetypal Saxon defending his rights against the Norman oppressor! I must tell this to Davies. He'll never be the same man again."

She laughed with him. "I'd rather you didn't. It might come between our two families."

It was approaching midnight when they made the journey back to Sutton Craddock. Although its roof and walls were silvered by the waning moon, the inn had a stillness that made her turn to him. "I'm sorry I can't invite you inside for a cup of coffee but Mr. Kearns and Maisie are usually in bed well before this time."

He nodded and slipped an arm around her shoulders. For a minute or more she responded to his kisses with a warmth that surprised him. Then abruptly she drew back. Her expression in the shadowy car gave him the thought —until he dismissed it as absurd—that the evening had induced her to discard her armour of self-discipline and that she was suddenly alarmed by its absence.

"What is it, Anna?"

For a moment she did not respond. Then she began fumbling for the door handle. "I must go now."

He checked her. "It isn't Harvey, is it? Or someone else?"

Her exclamation of distress was in German. "I cannot talk about it. Please do not ask me."

His hand fell away from her arm. "Very well. Am I going to see you again?"

"Yes, of course. You can always phone me. Thank you for the evening. I have enjoyed it very much."

He made no further effort to detain her. With the car door open, she suddenly turned back. "You and Harvey —you will both come back tomorrow night, won't you?"

It took him a moment to understand what she meant. "Don't be silly. Of course we shall come back."

Outside she paused by the wicker gate. Although she was a lovely monochrome picture in the moonlight, there was a loneliness in her expression Moore had not seen before. As he was telling himself it was a trick of the light she turned and hurried up the gravel path.

He waited until she had disappeared into the inn before reversing the car and driving to the airfield. It was just on midnight when he entered his billet. Although it was a habit of his to listen to the late news, he made no attempt to switch on his radio. Instead he undressed, slipped into bed, and lay gazing up at the dark ceiling.

21

The staff car pulled up with a squeal of brakes outside the Administration Block. A young Leading Aircraftman chatting up a pretty Waaf near the entrance stiffened as Davies, with the agility of a man half his age, leapt from the car and came bounding forward. Trousers flapping round his legs, he snapped a salute at the frozen couple and disappeared into the building. As he hurried down the corridor he glanced at his watch and his footsteps quickened. Five seconds later he reached the C.O.'s office, rapped on the door and threw it open.

The room was full of the officers who conducted crew briefings. Among them were Henderson, Moore, Adams, and the two flight commanders, Harvey and Young. Ignoring the salutes, Davies slung a briefcase on the desk and turned. "You all heard the BBC news this morning?"

When some of the men shook their heads Davies marched over to a radio perched on a filing cabinet and switched it on. A boisterous chorus of singing indicated the end of Workers' Playtime. Turning the volume down for a moment, Davies glanced at Henderson. "Everything going all right, Jock?"

"Yes, sir. Everything's fine."

"What time are you holding the briefing?"

"Directly after the men have had their evening meal."

"I take it the Target Indicators have arrived?"

"Yes. They came an hour ago."

Davies' eyes shifted to Moore. "Your men do understand this technique of bombing on flares?"

"Yes, sir. We did an exercise last week."

"Who are you using as backers-up?"

"Harvey and Young, sir."

Davies slanted a look of dislike at the heavy-jowled Harvey. "You're sure they've got it buttoned-up? If the flares go down in the wrong place you could end up dropping bombs in Lake Constance."

163

"They both know what to do, sir. They're experienced pilots."

Before the scowling Davies could reply, the chorus of singing turned into a loud cheer, then faded away. Reaching out hurriedly, Davies turned up the volume. Six pips sounded and then the measured, resonant voice of the news reader. As Davies motioned for silence, the intrigued officers crowded nearer to listen.

"Last night over seven hundred of our heavy bombers raided the important enemy port of Hamburg. Great damage was done and crews reported that the entire centre of the city was set ablaze. Because of new defensive tactics employed, our losses were slight. In all only twelve aircraft failed to return."

A stir of excitement ran through the listening men. As their questioning voices rose, Davies turned off the radio and swung round.

"Sensational, isn't it? 1.5 per cent casualties. Until last night our average losses over Hamburg have been six per cent. So last night we saved around thirty-five heavies."

Henderson asked the question all wanted to ask. "How, sir?"

The grinning Davies was revelling in the moment. "Anyone got a new packet of cigarettes?"

As the officers stared at one another Lindsay shrugged and held out a packet of Player's Navy Cut. Opening it Davies pulled out a strip of tin foil. "You won't be seeing this stuff in cigarette packets much longer." Releasing the foil he allowed it to flutter to the ground. "That's how it's done. Too bloody simple, isn't it?"

He grinned again at the blank stares he received. "Tin foil's the secret. If bundles of it are thrown out every minute by an approaching heavy, they reflect back the impulses from Jerry's radar beams and throw his direction-finding to hell. We've known about it a long time but no one dared use it until we were sure it would benefit us more than Jerry. Now the time has come and Butch Harris chose Hamburg as his first target." Davies turned his exultant eyes on Moore. "That's why I set up this raid on Miesbach—I knew it wasn't going to be as dangerous as it sounded. Once the Hamburg raid was over and the cat out of the bag, you could get the benefit of it."

Excitement was growing among the listening officers.

Adams put the question they all wanted to ask. "Does it affect all types of radar, sir?"

"Everything except long-range detectors," Davies told him. "That means his searchlights and gun predictors as well as his night fighters' Airborne Interception Equipment. From what I heard early this morning his searchlights were all over the place and his flak fire a shambles. It's been given the code-name "Window" and sounds like the greatest thing since Father Christmas. Of course Jerry will find a counter to it in a month or two but until he does we're going to make hay while the sun shines. You can't carry the stuff yourselves because there isn't room for the bundles in a Mossie cockpit but you can still benefit from it as you'll see in a minute."

Quelling their curiosity with difficulty, his listeners watched him unlatch his briefcase and pull out a file. Opening it, he gave his attention first to Moore and his two flight commanders.

"Let's take the attack itself first. As you know, because accuracy is so important on this operation, we're using the Pathfinder technique. Wing Commander Moore will corner the factory with green target indicators and the rest of the squadron will bomb within those flares. But because flares burn out or get buried beneath falling rubble, it's important you two backers-up keep a beady eye on things. If Moore's flares don't suffer any damage, back up with your own at the intervals given you. If they go out earlier than they should, make certain they are replaced before any more bombs are dropped. When you do the main briefing this afternoon, be sure all the men understand this because we don't want any bombs wasted. O.K.?"

As the three men nodded Davies flipped over a page in the file. "All right—now to the ways and means of getting there. Here is a list of our activity tonight. Up north we've got 4 Group and the Canadians doing a spot of mine-laying in the Baltic. 8 Group will be doing their nightly milk-run to Berlin and they're also laying a spoof raid on Karlsruhe. But the operation that's going to help you most is a Main Force raid on Augsburg. Your run is timed so that you'll approach Jerry's radar beacons at the time the bomber stream is running through them. Main Force will be twenty-five miles north of you, so you don't need to worry too much about collisions, but their presence alone ought to draw every fighter for two hundred miles. Better than that, however, they'll be dropping "window" from the moment they're within range of the beacons. Which we believe will make your trip a picnic."

While talking, Davies had been watching Harvey examine the large map of Europe on the wall. His sharp question made the Yorkshireman turn. "What's the trouble, Harvey? You found something to gripe about?"

The gruff voice that answered him was Harvey's characteristic response to attack. "I'm thinking we can't keep twenty-five miles from the heavies all the way. What happens when we peel off for Miesbach?"

"For Christ's sake—you're getting cover ninety per cent of the way! Do you want your hand holding over the target as well?" Aware he had shown his dislike of Harvey too openly, Davies turned back irritably to the others. "What do they say—you can't please everybody? Because this is the first time the night fighters in the south have encountered "window" we believe they'll spend the night chasing their arses. But however it turns out, it ought to be a damn sight easier operation than you expected. Any more questions or gripes?"

When nobody spoke Davies handed the file to Henderson and picked up his briefcase. "All right, Jock. Take over, will you? I have to run off now to see somebody but I'll be back in time for the crew briefing."

Klaus gazed around the night sky disconsolately. A month ago, even a fortnight ago, it would have seemed impossible that he might go with Heidi to the altar without his Iron Cross. Now the odds seemed all in its favour. Why, of all places, had he to be stationed in Bavaria? The Reich stretched from the Russian steppes to the French seaboard, from the Arctic Circle to the foot of Italy, and nearly everywhere there was air activity. In Russia it was well known that even third-rate pilots were registering two and three kills a week, and in Belgium and Northern Germany it was action all the time.

Hamburg seemed to be the latest battle centre. It was true rumours were running wild that the *Tommis* had introduced a new radar interference device but it took more than rumours to convince Klaus that if he were in the air with six or seven hundred *Tommi* bombers he wouldn't make his presence felt.

What infuriated Klaus and his younger colleagues were the reports that selected squadrons of night fighters had recently been given freedom from the chains of the radar beacons. Using them as mere assembly points, the fighters were being allowed to follow the bomber streams to their targets. Not only did the tactics, christened Wild Boar, give the fighters longer contact with the bombers, but over their objectives the backdrop of fires and searchlights made them an easier target. The new system meant refuelling at remote airfields but the risks entailed were a small price to pay for the extra kills being recorded. However all the fortunate squadrons were based in the north where enemy activity was high. In the south, as sleepy as the country it protected, the old Kummhuber "tied-system" still held sway.

Behind Klaus, little Fritz Neumann was also in low spirits, although for a very different reason. Earlier that day he had received news that his mother had suffered a severe embolism and been rushed to hospital. Fritz had put in immediately for compassionate leave but felt his chances of getting it before Klaus became due for leave himself were nil.

With little to do until a bomber entered Kassel's radar beam Fritz gazed out through the cupola. It was a good night for bombers, he noted, with a low, waning moon, plenty of breaks in the clouds for star navigation, and reasonable cover from searchlights and fighters. The Messerschmitt was circling the station at 20,000 feet and the clouds had an eerie appearance in the faint moonlight. A black hole in them directly below made Fritz think of a drop into a bottomless dungeon. As he peered into it, a narrow smear of light appeared, to go out like a snuffed match thirty seconds later. A night fighter taking off, was Fritz's guess, and he felt a sense of comradeship in the thought.

The feeling died as he gazed upwards at the spangled dome of stars. Millions of them, all icy and impersonal, and reaching up to infinity and beyond. This was the time Fritz always felt lonely. Waiting for the bombers to come and aware that one night you could be the one slithering down that terrifying hole to oblivion. Tonight, with his mother close to death, Fritz marvelled at the madness of men who could deliberately create suffering when so much suffering existed already.

Feeling it was a thought with an undertone of disloyalty he tried to push it away, then shrugged. Why bother? Thousands of other men must think the same. Yet when the moment came only a handful failed to press the trigger or drive home the knife and they were shot as traitors or reviled as cranks. Man was a victim of both his destructive instincts and his moral cowardice.

As if to prove his point, Fritz bent attentively over his A.I. set as a sharp voice crackled in his earphones. "Bearcat Two! A hostile force is approaching. Steer Zero Six Five. Altitude 6,400 metres. . . ."

Before the Controller at Kassel had completed his instructions the eager Klaus was banking on a wingtip. Settling on its new compass course like a wolf taking scent, the black 110 raced across the starlit sky. When a correction came fifteen seconds later it veered five degrees and streaked on, its exhaust stacks aflame.

Back at Kassel the Fighter Controller discovered his calf was itching. Intent on vectoring Bearcat II towards its first victim, he rubbed the afflicted spot with his foot. The blue coordinates on the Seeburg Table that represented Klaus's 110 had travelled another five miles nearer the eight red traces that were British bombers when the Controller forgot his itching calf and gave a grunt of shock.

"What the hell's happening? The bastards look as if they're spawning in mid-air."

His assistant, who had been fine-tuning the radio, swung round to see the eight traces had burst into a thousand and turned the entire screen luminous. "What is it? Interference?"

"It must be. But what's causing it?"

While the two men stared at the flashing screen, other beacons in the defence chain were experiencing the same phenomenon. Shouts and curses rang out, some reaching out across the air to the puzzled fighter pilots.

"This can't be happening, Max. It's crazy."

"Christ, there are thousands of the bastards!"

Hearing the tumult, Klaus turned to Fritz. "What do you make of it?"

"It must be the interference the *Tommis* used over Hamburg."

"But how the hell does it work?"

Before Fritz could answer the Fighter Controller at Kassel recovered his poise. "Bearcat Two! I can't vector you because of interference. Try to make contact on your Emil-Emil."

In other words we're on our own, Klaus thought with mixed feelings. "You hear that, Fritz? Get that scanner of yours working."

Ahead, its upper layer silvered by moonlight and its belly dark and sullen, a long bank of cloud stretched from horizon to horizon. The muscles of Klaus's face tightened as he estimated its height. 6,800 metres and maybe more. Even the elements were on the *Tommis*' side tonight.

Fritz's first contact came when the ghostly peaks of the clouds were swirling beneath them. "I've got something, Hans. Six hostiles. No, eight. . . . 6,000 metres."

Klaus felt his mouth water. "What bearing?"

The radar operator ignored his sharp question. "4,000 metres . . . 2,000 metres . . . they've gone past!"

"Gone past? What the hell are you talking about?"

"They've gone past. At a hell of a speed."

"But we're behind them. So how could they go past?"

Fritz's voice quickened. "Another contact. 8,000, 6,000, 4,000, 1,000. . . . This is crazy! They've gone past too."

"But they'd have to be flying on a reciprocal course to do that. Are you sure there's nothing wrong with your set?"

Before Fritz could answer his screens lit up again. This time there were too many traces to count. "It's hopeless, Hans. According to my set there are thousands of hostiles flying in different directions."

Biting his lip, Klaus stared down at the sullen vastness of the cloud. The *Tommis* were inside it somewhere and although it was a hundred-to-one chance of making contact with them without A.I. help, he wasn't going to fart about any longer while Fritz reported ghost images. He pushed his stick forward and cloud vapour was swirling past his wingtips when Control came on again.

"Attention, Bearcat Two. There are more hostiles south of Beacon Kassel. Passing through map reference Hans-

Wolfgang on a bearing of approximately 150. Speed and number indefinite because of interference but are believed to be a much smaller force. The main force is your priority but if contact is impossible, seek out the new hostiles."

Klaus kicked the rudder, drew back on the column, and the 110 came howling out of the cloud. As he rammed the throttles right up to the gate he heard Fritz's uneasy voice.

"Didn't he say the main force had priority?"

Klaus switched off the R/T before replying. "Forget what he said. If we can't depend on your Emil, we have to see the bastards. And there's much clearer weather to the south."

22

With the moon hidden behind the bank of cloud, the Überlingen stretched to the south and east like a vast sheet of unpolished steel. Miesbach, a solid shadow around its western reaches, lay huddled under the cover of darkness. For nearly three minutes the night sky above the town had been filled with the roar of engines as Mosquito after Mosquito arrived and began orbiting at preset heights. Flying in the lowest orbit of the stack, Moore had been giving time for any stragglers to arrive. The stack was now complete, from Moore at 4,000 feet to Marsh at 14,000.

Uncertain as to whether it was the target or only the assembly point, Miesbach was playing it safe. Air Raid wardens were frantically ensuring not a light was visible. Defence crews, tensely watching the darkened moon, were standing ready beside their unlit searchlights and warmed-up flak guns. Townsfolk, huddled in basements and shelters, were talking in whispers and swallowing to lubricate their dry throats. Tension was like a static charge in the warm night air.

At 7,000 feet Millburn and Gabby, who had arrived a minute ahead of their ETA, were high enough to see the red glow that was Augsburg, the Main Force target. As the Welshman looked away he saw a tiny flame appear in the sky east of the glow. At that distance it looked no more than a burning match being dropped from a giant's fingers. Gabby's comment was cynical. "That's one poor bastard Davies' Father Christmas hasn't saved. Do you think it's working?"

Millburn, a dark shape in the eerie blue light of the cockpit, shrugged. "It's been quiet enough so far."

"So what? Since when could Jerry intercept us at 35,000 feet? Harvey was right, boyo. This is where it counts."

Millburn pushed a stick of chewing gum into his mouth. "Some guys expect everything. If we get a clear passage here and back, I'm not complaining."

"You know what I think," Gabby said maliciously. "All that tinfoil will do to Jerry is make life easier for him. They say he's getting low on bumph. I'll lay odds he's already got his Strength-through-Joy Boys running around collecting it."

Millburn grinned. "It's a bit on the flimsy side, isn't it? And kinda narrow."

"Then he'll probably melt it down for tin cans. Jerry's an ingenious bastard, boyo."

"If you're so worried about bandits, stop nattering and keep your eyes open."

Gabby, who was in a touchy Celtic mood that night, took instant umbrage. "You make a lot of noise for a taxi driver, Yank. Without me you couldn't go from Leeds to Liverpool without getting lost."

"Sour grapes'll get you nowhere, kid. It's like with women—some guys have it and others don't. So why bellyache so much?"

Gabby scowled darkly. "What would happen if an 88 got me tonight? How would you get home? Go on—tell me!"

The grinning American turned to him. "All right, kid, I will. I'd go down on the deck and backtrack that tinfoil. Didn't you know that's what it's for? So we can get rid of little ponces of navigators who're always belly-aching."

At the base of the stack Moore was ready to lay his target indicators. As Hopkinson, crouched over the flare chute, gave him a nod, he levelled A-Apple and swept over the centre of the town.

"O.K., Hoppy. Let's have some light."

The barometrically-fused, hooded flare slid down the chute and fell to its pre-set height of 2,500 feet where its parachute broke free. At the same moment its magnesium candle burst into brilliant luminescence and hung suspended in space.

The effect was startling. A petrified vision, the town seemed to leap upwards and freeze in the icy light. Set in relief by their jet-black shadows, factories, streets, even flak batteries with their toy crews, could be seen. To St. Claire, the artist, who was circling at 6,500 feet, the effect was that of a black cloak being torn from a naked body.

Hopkinson had no time for such fantasies even had his

Cockney mind indulged in them. Dropping a second flare from the chute he edged forward and peered down. Five seconds later he gave a yell. "There it is, skipper. Over to the right. At two o'clock."

Moore dipped a wingtip to take a look. Along the northern bank of the lake was a complex of factories, railway sidings and docks. As A-Apple swept towards the complex Hoppy's confident voice came again.

"We're O.K. Our target's over on the far side. Three parallel sheds and a rail siding. Just like the photographs."

Waiting to hear no more, Moore put A-Apple's nose down. It was the moment the petrified Miesbach came to life. Not knowing whether the flares expressed uncertainty on the part of the *Tommis*, so that they might still sweep past, the defence crews had held their fire. Now, as Moore dived into the light, their last doubt vanished and every flak battery in and around the town began firing. To Hopkinson, concentrating on the target ahead, coloured chains of tracer seemed to be coming up from every point of the compass. A series of explosions rocked the Mosquito and shell fragments beat a tattoo on her wings. Five seconds later three searchlights coned her. If the cursing Hopkinson, a veteran of forty-three operations, had not already pulled down his smoked goggles, their combined 21,000,000 candle power would have blinded him.

"Skipper, for Christ's sake call some of the others down. We can't take all this stick ourselves or we'll never make it."

The heavy defences of the town had come as a surprise to Moore. Before he could react to Hopkinson's entreaty, four more Mosquitoes dived down beneath the hooded flares. Harvey had sized up the situation and brought down three other crews with him.

A-Apple was jinking violently to escape the searchlights. Two slid off like fingers trying to hold a slippery fish. The third clung on tenaciously, forcing Moore to dive and then bank on a wingtip. The manoeuvre lost the searchlight but forced A-Apple to swing east in a wide arc to make a fresh approach on the factory. With the two flares now close to the ground, Moore ordered his high-level Mosquitoes to drop four more. As they ignited Hopkinson guided him back to their target.

On the perimeter of the flares, the factory was a study

of elongated shadows. To gain greater accuracy Moore dived down to 1,200 feet, a target for every light gun in the district. Like nets thrown up to ensnare a bird, tracer soared up from flak posts and factory roofs. As he drove the Mosquito on Moore could feel his toes clenched up inside his flying boots. "O.K., Hoppy. Drop it!"

A-Apple reeled from a sharp explosion as the first target indicator fell away. It burst in a huge splash of green fire on the factory's railway siding. The second fell fifty feet from the corner of a large shed. As Moore banked and banked again, Hopkinson dropped two more T.I.s to complete the square. His relieved yell made Moore's earphones rattle.

"I feel like a ping-pong ball in a shooting gallery, skipper. Let's get the hell out of here."

"All right, Hoppy. We'll drop our GPs later."

Followed by the flak, A-Apple clawed for the cover of darkness. Still orbiting at 7,000 feet Millburn gave a grin of appreciation. "You've got to hand it to that guy—he's got some hard bark on him."

The flares were dying out and as the town sank back into darkness the only lights came from searchlights and gun flashes. Yet the very darkness that brought an illusion of safety to the townsfolk only emphasized the square of green fire burning within the factory complex. Orbiting at 8,000 feet Moore directed his crews towards it. As each Mosquito, flying at 4,500 feet, swept over the square it dropped a stick of bombs.

Heavy explosions and fires betrayed the damage that was being done. Seeing one of the target indicators die out as a factory wall toppled over it, Moore called in Teddy Young. The experienced Australian dropped his T.I. within twenty yards of the original marker and completed the square for good measure. In less than thirty seconds the raid was in progress again.

When Peter Marsh, flying No. 16, was called down great clouds of crimson smoke and flames almost hid the factory from view. But the flak was still heavy and a couple of seconds after Marsh's navigator had released his bombs a chain of 37 mms. bracketed the Mosquito. An explosion at the rear of the starboard engine sent something spinning off into space and a massive crump beneath the fuselage almost turned the plane over. As Marsh fought for control he could smell cordite and burning rubber. Heart in his mouth, he tested the controls and then turned gingerly away. As he began climbing he heard Moore's sharp voice. "Marsh! What's the damage?"

"I think it's my undercart, skipper, and I've lost the exhaust shroud on my starboard engine."

"Can you make it home?"

Marsh hoped the R/T static would mask his unsteady voice. "I hope so, skipper."

"All right, get on your way." Moore was about to wish the hapless crew good luck when a distant cry of shock checked him. It was followed by a voice hideously distorted by terror and despair. "We're hit, skipper . . . Finished. Look out for bandits."

The cry came from one of the Mosquitoes already making its way home. As Moore and Hopkinson stared round they saw a flame appear in the night sky. Rapidly expanding into a long tongue of fire it slithered down and vanished into the hills west of the town.

The fires at Miesbach were staining the Überlingen red and forming a crimson cloud in the night sky. Klaus had spotted the fires five minutes ago and although the 110 was flying under full boost he was trying to urge it along even faster with his body.

"See any *Tommis* yet, Fritz?"

"Not from here. Perhaps they've finished and gone home."

Klaus winced. "We'd have had a contact of some kind, wouldn't we?"

"Not if they're Mosquitoes. They could be three thousand metres above us by this time."

The knowledge Fritz could be right did nothing to improve Klaus's temper. "Sometimes I think you don't want to find the bastards. How do you know they're not doing a dog-leg home?"

About to ask how they were going to overtake Mosquitoes if they were, Fritz decided it was wiser to keep quiet. To the south, shaken by the raid that had taken place so near to their frontier, Swiss gunners were firing shells that exploded like red poppies in the sky. As he turned back to his radar set Fritz gave a start. "Hans, I've got a reading! A clear one."

Adrenalin began pumping immediately through Klaus's bloodstream. "Hang on to it, for Christ's sake. What's its range?"

"Maximum. But it's closing fast. I think it's a Mosquito."

Exultant one moment, Klaus cursed the next as the stars vanished and dark cotton wool pressed against the cupola. He breathed a sigh of relief ten seconds later as the 110 swept out into an enormous chasm of starlight. At a word from Fritz he broke to port, then circled in a wide arc to starboard until he had completed 180 degrees. He could still see no shape in the vast black bowl of the sky. But if Fritz was reading his Emil correctly he should now be behind the hostile bomber.

His nerves were tight as he waited for Fritz's readings. If the hostile was a Mosquito and it had enough fuel, it could both outpace and outclimb him. But if its fuel reserves were low it might just be flying within his own maximum speed.

Fritz had begun his counting again. "7,000 metres. . . ." A pause and then: "6,500 . . . 6,200 . . . 6,000." Klaus's jaw clamped with relief. Luck was with him at last.

He spotted the Mosquito ninety seconds later. Its dark shape, climbing all the time, was three hundred feet ahead of him at eleven o'clock. Klaus touched the rudder and drew the stick back an inch. Gently, he told himself. Don't get overkeen or you might lose it.

Like a cat creeping on its prey, he closed the range to a hundred and fifty yards. The Mosquito's crew, Elliot and Jameson, a solicitor's clerk from London and an apprentice printer from Salford, flew on unsuspectingly. Their "boozer," the red bulb on the dashboard activated by the AI set of an approaching radar-controlled fighter, gave two weak blinks and then went dead, the victim of a short in the receiver. With both men gazing intently out into the night sky, neither noticed its abortive alarm.

With only seconds of life left to them the two young men were allowing their thoughts to wander. Elliot, who had played for the Harlequins before the war, was wondering if he would be picked by Group for their trial in two weeks' time. Jameson, the apprentice printer, was wondering what he could buy his girl friend for her birthday next week.

Beneath them Klaus had crept forward until the 110

was almost directly below the Mosquito. Then, with the cry of a man driving home a spear, he hauled back on the stick and pressed down hard on his firing button. With a crash that seemed to split the sky open, three heavy Orlikon cannon raked the Mosquito from nose to tail.

The effect was almost indescribable. The first shells blasted off the Mosquito's nose and released a howling banshee into the cockpit that turned loose objects like charts into lethal projectiles. The ones that followed sliced open the fuselage like some giant buzz saw. A shell pierced the buttocks of Jameson and burst somewhere in the region of his lungs. The right leg of Elliot was blown off, and he sat staring blankly at the pumping stump. Hydraulic and oil pipe lines burst like arteries and began discharging their vital fluid. The stricken aircraft lurched like a pole-axed animal, then miraculously righted itself as the dying Elliot crooked out his warning. Then Klaus fired a second burst and the port tanks caught fire.

Satisfied, Klaus allowed the 110 to fall away. When he righted it the Mosquito was little more than a blazing torch falling into the hills. Klaus's exultant shout, the cry of the German fighter who had made a kill, made Fritz's earphones rattle. "Pauka! Pauka!"

Hidden behind his radar set, Fritz was silently retching. When that *Tommi* bomber hit the ground, they would need sacks to pick up the pieces of meat. Yet it too had probably killed men tonight, and if he, Fritz, had not helped to destroy it, it might have killed women and children tomorrow. There was no stopping the lunatic game now—as each side provided the other with more justification for revenge the slaughter grew more vicious and indiscriminate. As Fritz gagged again, Klaus expressed his jubilation aloud.

"Eight, Fritz. Only two more to go and I've still a fortnight left."

Ten kills—anything between thirty and seventy men slaughtered. In a mad world, Fritz thought, what better basis on which to build a marriage and have children? As if to mock him, traces flickered on his screens again.

"I've got two more readings, Hans."

Still quivering from excitement, Klaus gave a laugh of disbelief. "*Two* more!"

"Yes. They're heading this way."

"Then put me behind the bastards! As fast as you can!"

Fighting his stomach, Fritz concentrated on his A.I. set again. Five seconds later the 110's port wingtip dropped and the deadly black shape cut across the summer night like a reaper's scythe.

23

Harvey peered through the windshield at the dark shape and twin exhausts three hundred yards ahead of him. "Marsh! It's me, Harvey. What shape are you in?"

Marsh exchanged a glance of disbelief with his navigator. "Hello, Skipper. How did you find us?"

"You've an exhaust shroud missing, remember? What other damage is there?"

"The engines seem O.K. but I think there must be elevator and aileron damage—she's very sluggish."

"That's probably because your undercart's half down. Listen—I'm going to try to give you cover home. We can see you as long as the weather stays clear—if it closes in we'll have to work something out. Don't use your R/T unless it's necessary—we don't want to make it easy for the bastards. Just keep an eye on your boozer. O.K.?"

Marsh's voice could not hide his relief. "Thanks, skipper."

Sinking back into his seat Harvey turned to Blackburn. "Don't go to sleep for the next two hours," he grunted. "We might have visitors."

Blackburn, tense in his seat, swallowed before answering. "No, skipper."

The two Mosquitoes droned on through the starlit sky. With Marsh's crippled plane doing no more than 230 knots, Harvey was finding his own sluggish on the controls. Two bloody beetles floundering across the surface of a pond, he thought. With God knows how many hungry birds on the hunt for food.

Unlike the rest of the squadron who, after dropping their bombs, had started for home, Harvey had remained behind to see how his flight fared and so had witnessed Marsh being hit by flak. A professional, the Yorkshireman bore no resentment that Moore had allowed the young pilot to find his way home alone. Moore's job was to stay and assess the damage to the factory, and even if his crews had been present and volunteered to a man to give Marsh cover, no responsible Squadron Commander would have sanctioned the gesture. Apart from the difficulty of keeping contact at night, Marsh's crippled Mosquito would have to limp back at the altitude in which the enemy night fighters were at their deadliest, and without A.I. equipment two Mosquitoes would be as vulnerable as one. Like any other raiding party in enemy territory, bomber crews accepted the hazard that if they were hit they were on their own and Marsh was no exception.

Harvey had no quarrel with the reasoning behind the unwritten law but tonight could not obey it. A man protective by nature, his impulse was reinforced by his knowledge of Marsh's personal problems. The reason he gave himself was that Marsh's exhaust shroud was missing. The exposed flame would make it easier to keep contact and so the effort was worth making. The fact that the same flame might attract fighters as blood attracts sharks, Harvey chose to ignore.

As he watched the flickering exhausts ahead of him he tried to work out the pros and cons. His hope was that in spite of their jammed radar equipment the majority of the night fighters would go on trying to track the heavies both to and from their target. If they did, there was a chance Marsh and he might sneak through unobserved. On the other hand there was always the chance that some pilots, like the one who had shot down Elliot, might have decided that the pickings were easier to the south where the weather was clearer and the radar interference less marked. The real facts were anyone's guess.

Harvey's main ambition at that moment was to reach the cloud front they had passed over on their way to Miesbach. Met. had told them it would widen during the night and spread north—and in fact it had already doused the crescent moon half an hour ago. Not only would it give reasonable cover against fighters but the bomber stream would be returning through it and Harvey remembered they would be dropping "window" until out of range of the enemy beacons. If he and Marsh could latch on to the stream, the odds on their getting home would rise dramatically.

In R-Robert the numbness Marsh had been feeling since the flak had crippled him was wearing off. Everything indicated that this was the trip Julie feared, the one when his luck ran out. Over and beyond his personal fear of death, Marsh had his greater fear. If he were killed and Julie's mind snapped—and he was certain it would—what would happen to her and the baby? Sweat began to run down the young pilot's body. Dear Christ, I mustn't be killed. Not until they're both safe. Please take me back to them.

Fear that his anguish was showing made him glance guiltily across the cockpit. Seeing Douglas, his navigator, staring anxiously out into the darkness, he sank back in relief. Knowing there were still four hundred miles to the coast, Douglas was probably as scared as he was. Then Marsh shook his head. Douglas wasn't married. He had no hostages to fate.

His envy turned immediately to guilt. He loved Julie and it wasn't her fault the war had torn her nerves into shreds. Marsh had discovered that many men, by blaming the war for their family's problems, were able to carry those problems lightly. It was something Marsh could not do. If you loved someone, you cared. Here or at the far end of the world.

The baby's sobs fell into a whimper and died away. Holding her breath, Julie tip-toed to the cot and laid the child down. Replacing the coverlet she sank wearily on the edge of her bed.

It was 3 a.m. and she had hardly slept. Lying in bed she had been tortured by fears for Peter. Then Mark had woken up and, perhaps sensing her overwrought condition, had fretted for over an hour. As a result the girl was now physically as well as nervously exhausted.

A thin figure in her nightdress she moved to the window and drew aside the blackout curtain. Although the gardens of Wilberforce Street, with their small lawns and patriotic vegetable patches, were in shadow, the waning moon gave a faint sheen to the roofs of garden sheds and the houses that stood opposite.

Her eyes lifted to the hard, glittering stars that the moon could not extinguish. Those same stars would be gazing down on Peter and indifferent to whether he lived or died. A shiver ran through the girl and her heart rate increased. Both she and Peter had been wicked to bring a child into such a pitiless world.

For the hundredth time that night she wondered where

Peter was. As it was a night raid he was probably over
Germany. Two lonely men in a tiny wooden box, plunging through a sky filled with searching enemies while below them an entire nation willed their death. The realities
were terrifying enough before her feverish imagination
added its own hazards. Engine failure, navigation error,
maintenance neglect, a structural defect, any of these
and a dozen more could be added to the massive defensive
strength the Germans could muster over their own territory. If Peter should escape this time, what chance did
he have of escaping next week or next month? The people who lectured her for her lack of faith either lied
about the odds against him or were blindly ignorant of
them. Even if Peter were a different kind of man, the
outlook would be no better.

It was an ironical fact that while Julie Marsh lived in
constant fear of Peter's death in action, she could at no
time accept him as a fighting soldier. Men like the big,
brooding Harvey or the handsome, devil-may-care Millburn one could see any night at the cinema, charging a
machine gun nest single-handed or clubbing half a dozen
Japs to death with a rifle butt. But to Julie, Peter was still
the gentle accountant's clerk who had been almost too
shy to ask her for a date. The fact that every night
over Germany the skies were filled with men like Peter
giving battle to the enemy was lost on the girl. To her,
Peter was miscast, a stripling among men, and it was one
of the reasons she felt no guilt in begging him to give up
operational flying.

But she knew now that he never would. False pride,
perhaps the hope he might grow one day into someone
like Harvey or Millburn, kept him going. The knowledge
that he had a baby and that she, Julie, needed him made
no difference. A sudden massive spasm of resentment
made her body contract. Damn him! Damn him! If she
had to go on suffering this torment with no hope of his
survival at the end of it, then it was better he died tonight!

The thought was like a massive explosion in her mind,
leaving the room hushed and her face pale and shocked.
God in Heaven, what have I done? If he doesn't return
now I shall know I have killed him. . . . Closing her eyes
she concentrated until she felt her brain would burst.

Dear God, please listen. I didn't mean that about Peter. I don't know where the thought came from but it wasn't from me. I love Peter. So please forgive me and bring him safely home!

When she opened her eyes her nightdress was icy with perspiration. Her prayers had brought some relief but she knew a new fear had been created alongside the old. If Peter were killed now she would never be sure whether or not she was the cause. Why had the thought come to her? Was she going mad?

She glanced at her watch. It would be dawn in two hours. Allow him another three hours for de-briefing and the journey from Sutton Craddock and he should be home by 8 o'clock. No, give him another hour. If he were not home by 9 o'clock she would have reason to fear the worst.

A movement in the garden caught her eye. A black cat was creeping soundlessly along the wall beneath the window. As she watched in fascination it suddenly leapt down and bounded forward in one movement. A second later the girl imagined she heard the faintest of cries rise from the garden.

Hand at her throat, she backed away. The whimper she gave as she threw herself on the bed was a sound of pure terror.

"Peter! Look!"

The sharp cry came from Douglas. Red pulsations from the bulb on the dashboard were suddenly staining the cockpit interior and the navigator's alarmed face. Torn brutally from his thoughts of Julie, Marsh was paralysed for a moment. Then he snatched at his mask.

"Skipper! Do you have a contact on your boozer?"

Harvey sounded both startled and puzzled. "No. Have you?"

"Yes. A strong one. Maybe your set's not so sensitive or it's u.s."

Harvey's grim answer came five seconds later. "We've got it now. All right, start a banking search. But take it slowly in case I lose you and for Christ's sake don't go off course."

Ahead the flickering exhaust tilted as R-Robert banked to port. Without taking his eyes off the plane as he followed it, Harvey addressed the pale-faced Blackburn. "We'll probably be the first he'll try to take, so keep your eyes skinned. Underneath and behind—the bastard might come in either way."

As the Mosquitoes zig-zagged across the sky both pilots lowered one wing and then the other to give their navigators a view below. In the black sky behind them Fritz noticed the manoeuvres on his screen. "They've started to take evasive action, Klaus."

Neither German was surprised. For some time now German night-fighter crews had known the *Tommis* were carrying an A.I. detection device although as yet they did not know how it worked. The important thing, Klaus was thinking, was to make certain it did not help them to escape. As Fritz estimated the range at 1,000 metres, Klaus made his first visual contact, a slim black shape arching across the starlit sky ahead and above him.

"There's one of them! See him? He's swinging over to 2 o'clock."

"Shall I switch off the Emil?"

"No. Let's get in closer first in case I lose him. I'll tell you when."

Fritz sounded puzzled. "What are they?"

"Mosquitoes. I'm sure of it."

"But why are they only doing 370 kph?"

"I suppose they got damaged in the raid and they're trying to sneak home."

Fritz could understand Klaus's excitement. Among fellow pilots if not by High Command, the high-performance Mosquitoes were considered a greater prize than Lancasters. At the same time Fritz shared the respect most of his kind had for the versatile wooden aircraft. "One might be giving the other cover. So take it easy when you go in."

Klaus grinned. "At night? If he is, he's a bloody fool. Doesn't he know he's likely to be picked off first?"

The two Mosquitoes were now dipping their wings constantly in their efforts to locate their hunter. Like blind man's buff, Harvey was thinking, his big hands gripping the control column. Two blind men on one side and on the other a man with eyes that could see in the dark. . . . "Marsh, listen. If he attacks me first—and if the bastard is any good he will—then you piss off. No heroics.

You've got the crippled kite, so you get the hell out of here the moment he opens fire. That's an order."

Marsh caught a glimpse of Douglas's expression in the red, pulsating light and read his thoughts. Maybe he was a moody bastard and maybe he could be bloodyminded too. But when it counted Harvey was there.

"Marsh! Do you hear me?"

"Yes, skipper. I heard. Thanks."

None of the four men was certain who would be attacked first. If the hunter made the deduction the leading plane was the only one crippled, he might give it priority under the argument that a bird in hand was worth two in the bush. All four men hoped that if the worst happened it would be swift. An aircraft could take minutes to reach the earth from 20,000 feet and minutes could be an eternity in a tortured, screaming body.

With tension as tight as a bowstring the cat-and-mouse chase continued. Ahead it looked as if a mountain had risen into the sky and was hiding the stars from horizon to horizon. Sweating freely, Harvey tried to estimate how long it would take them to reach the cloud front. Five seconds later he growled at his own stupidity. The enemy pilot would be making his own calculations and be certain to attack in good time. As if to prove him right the pulsating red light suddenly went out, the sign the hunter was close enough to switch off his A.I. for fear of damage. Although he had been expecting it for the last minute, Harvey was momentarily frozen in the darkness. Then his urgent but steady voice reached out across the black sky to Marsh.

"Steady, lad. He can't be far away now."

The attack came as Harvey had known it would, very suddenly. The blackness beneath his Mosquito was ripped apart by a series of vivid flashes, and although the Yorkshireman's response was almost instantaneous there was a deafening explosion at the rear of the cockpit which hurled both men against their straps. A second shell smashed brutally between their legs and exploded somewhere beneath the instrument panel. In a second the cockpit was full of choking fumes. As the half-stunned Harvey fought for breath, the Mosquito went out of control and spun earthwards. As it passed him, Klaus gave a yell of triumph and followed it down. The other *Tomm.* might have the chance to reach the clouds before he could climb back but that couldn't be helped. He mustn't let this, his ninth kill, escape.

For Marsh the way to life was open again and no one could have condemned him had he taken it. He had Harvey's express order to escape and moreover there was a strong possibility his crippled plane might break up in combat. And beyond those clouds were Julie and the baby. For a moment the temptation was like the tearing of flesh. Then the young man whom Julie could never see as a soldier pushed the control column forward.

A second burst of fire from Klaus had brought flames from Harvey's port engine. With the stunned Yorkshireman still unable to take evasive action, Klaus closed in for the kill. The thought of the crippled Mosquito following him down never entered his mind because he believed the darkness made pursuit impossible.

What the excitement of the chase made him forget was that the burning engine of Harvey's plane silhouetted the 110 to any aircraft diving after it. In addition his last burst of fire had given Marsh a reference point. It was little more than a flitting shadow but enough for Marsh to sight on.

His first burst, which brought startled shouts from both Klaus and Fritz, ripped past the fuselage like a flight of luminous arrows. His second burst passed beneath the violently banking 110. Neither attack appeared to do any harm except to Klaus's temper. Yelling at Fritz to get his scanners working, Klaus came raging round to take revenge on the crippled *Tommi* who had shown such impertinence.

It was then that his starboard engine coughed and died. The first burst of fire that had seemed innocuous had in fact severed the armoured fuel lines. There was no fire because the shells had been armour-piercing instead of incendiary, but the effect was a useless power unit. In vain Klaus put the 110 into a dive in an attempt to restart. Unlike the Mosquito, which remained capable of a high performance even on one engine, the 110 had no such power reserve and it was soon clear to the frustrated Klaus he had no chance of re-engagement. All his skill would now be needed to find a landing field. Nor was

there any question of his claiming the first Mosquito as a
kill. Fritz had already reported that its engine fire had
gone out as its pilot switched on his extinguisher.

As Klaus was about to ask the Controller to give him
a fix he gave a grunt of disbelief. His other engine was
playing up now. Oil or coolant trouble—whatever it was
the thermometer needle was steadily climbing. Cursing
his luck he asked the controller to vector him towards
the nearest airfield.

Keeping a wary eye on the gauge he lowered the 110
down. As the needle entered the red zone the danger of
fire forced him to throttle back. Below, the defence sys-
tems were now alerted and two searchlights were laying
their luminous beams in the direction of the nearest airfield. By this time Klaus knew he was not going to make
it: the overheated engine could be seen glowing in the
darkness. At 5,000 feet, in a series of enormous bangs
that both men felt would tear the wing off, it seized up.
In the silence that followed the men could hear the forbidding scream of the airfoils. Hidden by his radar set,
Fritz crossed himself.

All Klaus could do now was steer towards one of the
searchlights and hope its crew would choose him a reasonable landing site. As he drew nearer he saw the hori-
zontal beam was lying across a field of rye. Conscious
that one mistake would be his last, he dived more steeply
to avoid overshooting, then levelled off and lowered the
110 into the surrealistic flare path. The searchlight crew
ducked down as the plane, airfoils screaming, passed no
more than thirty feet over their heads.

The rye was tall and hid the undulations of the field.
Klaus's landing was good and for the first hundred yards,
although juddering violently on its oleo legs, the 110
remained intact. Then one wheel dropped into a hole, the
port wingtip struck the ground, and with a massive
rending of stressed metal and spars, the plane ground-
looped, half rose on its nose, and crashed down again.

Although half-stunned, both men were able to climb
out and run a safe distance from the ominously-smoking
plane. A trickle of blood was running down Fritz's face
and Klaus was nursing a badly-bruised arm. In the distance the shouts of the searchlight crews could be heard
as they ran towards the field. Seeing Klaus's expression

and thankful for the pilot's skill, Fritz felt a word of comfort not out of place.

"We're lucky. It could have been a hell of a sight worse. And we're certain to get a new plane fitted out well before you go on leave."

Klaus did not answer. His young face, petulant with disappointment and anger, was gazing vengefully up at the night sky.

24

The siren that awoke Anna sounded just before dawn. The sky was clear as she threw open her bedroom window although red pennants on the eastern horizon foretold a deterioration in the weather later. The two windsocks showed the breeze was fresh and southerly. Across the airfield ground crews who had been snatching a few hours sleep were emerging from billets and dispersal huts. Engines were starting up and a couple of ambulances were already moving alongside a runway. Ten seconds later a crash wagon followed them.

As Anna threw on a wrap against the morning chill, the first Mosquito flew in. Wheels and flaps down, it swooped so low over the inn the girl could see the blackened scars of flak on the underside of its fuselage. There was a cloud of spray and a squeal of rubber as its wheels touched the runway. Half a mile down the field, all grace gone now it was earthbound, it turned and taxied towards its dispersal point.

One by one at irregular intervals the Mosquitoes came back. The sun was above the horizon and turning the dew on the crab apple into crystal gems when the thirteenth Mosquito, like a weary traveller in sight of home, swept towards the inn. Although its wings bore flak damage, they wagged a couple of times before it settled down on the landing strip. Leaning from the window Anna saw a buxom figure in a dressing gown waving from the wicker gate below. Early though it was, Maisie was not one to let the squadron's return go unwelcomed.

As the Mosquito came to rest at its dispersal point a tense silence settled over the field. Groups of men formed, their eyes on the empty sky. When five more minutes passed their tension turned into resignation and they began to disperse. Below Maisie drew back disconsolately from the gate and vanished into the inn. Discovering she was chilled to the bone, Anna closed the window.

Three aircraft missing. She was wishing now that she

had found out beforehand the identification numbers of Harvey and Moore. She reached for the telephone, then drew back her hand. The crews would be at de-briefing; for her to interfere with personal questions would be an unpardonable act in Davies' eyes.

On going down to breakfast she had hopes that Maisie might know whom the missing planes belonged to, but the subdued girl had seen only the last three Mosquitos fly in. Returning restlessly to her room, Anna was listening to the news when her telephone rang. She ran across to it. "Hello."

"There's a call from the airfield for you, Miss."

Her heart was beating hard as she waited. "Hello. Anna?" It was Moore. "I'm sorry to phone you so early but I wondered if I could come across to see you."

Her pleasure at hearing his voice was countered by a sudden numbness. "Yes, of course. When will you come?"

"Right away, if I may."

"I see. Come straight up to my room. I will have coffee sent up."

Her face gave nothing away when she went downstairs to make her request. The curious Maisie brought up a coffee tray and had barely left the bedroom when Moore entered. Her first impression was how much older he looked. His hair was dishevelled and his eyes bloodshot from strain. He had shed his flying suit but the uniform beneath was not the immaculate one she had become accustomed to. It was old and oil-stained and smelt of combat in its every crease. For once Moore looked the combatant pilot that he was.

His smile was wry as he paused in the centre of the room. "Sorry about this. I know it's a poor time to visit a girl."

It was the kind of deliberate banality she had learned to expect from the British when emotion was involved. She indicated the tray on her bedside table.

"Will you have coffee?"

"Yes, thanks."

"Black or white?"

"Black, please."

From the corner of her eye she saw him pull out a packet of cigarettes and then hesitate.

"Please smoke if you wish to," she said.

As she began pouring she heard a match strike and

the sound of his inhaling. "You know why I've come, don't you?"

She handed him his cup of coffee before answering. "I think so. Harvey hasn't come back, has he?"

He seemed puzzled by her self-control. Inhaling again, he walked across to the window. "No. I'm afraid he hasn't."

"Does that mean he is dead?"

He took a sip of coffee, then laid the cup and saucer on the window ledge. "I'm afraid it's too early to say what happened."

"Then no one saw him shot down?"

"No. When he was last seen over the target area he appeared to be all right. After that we don't know what happened because each of us made our own way home. But one of my boys heard him talking on R/T to Marsh, a member of his flight."

"What does that mean?"

"Marsh had been crippled by flak fire. We think the fool tried to escort him home."

Every muscle in her body stiffened. "The fool?"

The tension of the night had not yet worked out of Moore. His bloodshot eyes accepted her challenge and threw it back. "Yes. No one can give cover at night. If it were possible I'd have seen Marsh got it. It only means the cover is the first to be shot down."

She believed him and yet found she was shivering with resentment. "You don't see it as a brave gesture?"

"Bravery's not enough. It was stupid. No one can match German night fighters without A.I. equipment. All he did was throw good money after bad. And there's no profit in that."

It was a remark Harvey himself could have made but her desire to hurt him made no concession to fairness although afterwards her comment appalled her. "Perhaps men like Harvey aren't so interested in profit. Perhaps they had a different education and upbringing. Have you thought of that?"

At first he appeared to find difficulty in believing what she had said. Then his cheeks turned pale. Grinding out his cigarette in an ashtray, he started for the door, only to pause as he reached her. Close enough to see dislike as well as fatigue on his good-looking face, she was about to apologize when with a curse he jerked her towards him and kissed her full on the mouth. Unsure of him, she

tried to break away but the grip of his arms was too
fierce and she had to wait for the paroxysm of emotion
to die away. As his grip slackened, the telephone rang.
Answering it, she held out the receiver.

"It's the airfield. For you."

Discovering she was trembling she crossed over to the
mantelpiece and leaned against it. Behind her his voice
was expressing relief. "Thanks for letting me know, Frank.
Yes, I'll be right over."

He was gazing at her as she turned. "That was Adams.
They've just received news that Harvey's safe. He landed
on an emergency airfield."

A small ornament stood on the mantelpiece and she
fingered it for a moment before speaking. "What about
the other crew?"

"They ran out of petrol just after crossing the coast
and had to crash land. Marsh is badly shaken up but
he's alive. His navigator's dead."

He went to the door. "They're flying Harvey back
some time this morning. After we've had a word with
him, I'll see he comes over."

As if they were challenging one another, their eyes met
and held. Then he turned and the door closed behind him.

It was nearly noon when a small single-engined aircraft circled the airfield and landed. Expecting Harvey's
arrival, Anna was sitting in a deckchair in the garden
behind the inn. Putting down her book she went upstairs
to her room. From it she could see the aircraft taxi-ing
to the nearest hangar. In spite of its distance away, she
felt certain she recognized the big-boned figure of Harvey
as two men jumped out.

Knowing Moore would not keep him long she stayed
at the window waiting for him. To her surprise he had
still made no attempt to contact her when Maisie rang
the lunch bell. Concerned at his behaviour she returned
to her room after lunch and put a call through to the airfield.

The moment he spoke she knew she had given him offence. "Hello. What is it?"

"Frank, why haven't you come over to see me? I've
been worried about you."

"Sorry. But I've been busy since I got back."

"Didn't Ian Moore ask you to come over?"

His reaction at her mention of Moore told her everything. "What the hell has it to do with Moore?"

"I want to see you, Frank. Please come over as soon as you can."

In the pause that followed his pride seemed at war with his wishes. "All right," he said sullenly. "I'll see what I can do."

She was back on the lawn when he appeared half an hour later. As he crossed the grass she saw there was a heavy contusion on his left cheek. She rose quickly. "You've been hurt. I didn't know."

He gave a shrug of indifference. "It's only a bruise. What do you want?"

"Want?"

"Yes. Why do you want to see me?"

"What a strange question. I thought we were friends."

"So did I," he said bitterly.

She walked right up to him. "Someone saw me having dinner with Moore, didn't they? Is that why you didn't come across yesterday morning?"

He avoided her eyes. "What do you think?"

"Frank, there's something you must understand. I'm free to go out with anyone I like. So I wasn't going behind your back when I had dinner with Moore."

He cursed and swung away. "Go out with the bugger every night if you want to. I know he's got a damn sight more to give you than I have."

She did not know whether to be angry with him or sympathetic. "Frank, you're acting like a jealous child. It doesn't make any difference to me how wealthy a man is. I went out with Moore because I'd promised to go out with him." She drew another deckchair alongside her own. "Now please sit down. You must be worn out."

When he still did not respond she found herself searching for conversation that would prevent his leaving. "Where's Sam today?"

"In the billet. Asleep."

"I hear he sometimes flies with you. Is that true?"

"Sometimes."

She caught hold of his hand. "Sit down, Frank, please. I'm worried about you."

Muttering something she could not catch he ignored the chair but sank down on the grass. It was, she realized, a compromise amnesty. "I intended telling you I'd had dinner with Moore," she said. "But so far I haven't had the chance."

His eyes, sunken and half-closed with fatigue, were following the clouds crossing the sky. Her thoughts had a bitter flavour as she watched him. He was a man to whom responsibility was a sacred trust, who would put his life between an enemy and a friend. Yet he was also a man hounded by a sense of inferiority that could diminish those qualities to those who did not understand him. The greatest evil of privilege was not the uneven distribution of wealth, she thought. It was the crippling of personality.

"Tell me what happened," she said after a minute had passed.

He turned his head. "Nothing much. One of my kids got his exhaust shroud knocked off by flak and was showing up like a roman candle. As I had to come back the same way home I thought I'd keep him company."

Her eyes were on his swollen face. "How did you get that injury?"

His laugh was self-derisive. "A hell of an escort I turned out to be. A night fighter clobbered me and young Marsh had to turn back and give me a hand."

"That was just what Moore said would happen. By trying to help him you made yourself the first target."

His look of dislike returned. "Moore might have been a bloody Pathfinder but he doesn't know everything."

"What do you mean?"

"He doesn't know much about his men. Young Marsh is carrying a hell of a load. The doctor reckons his wife will go mental with worry if he doesn't pack up operational flying. And to make things worse they have a kid of nine months. Adams keeps on having a go at me but what the hell can I do."

"Can't you recommend that he's grounded?"

Harvey's voice had never been more gruff. "No, I bloody can't. It's something a man has to do himself. Otherwise you might do him more harm than good."

She could understand that. When the malicious whispers began and the self-doubts followed, the cure might be as destructive as the illness. "His navigator was killed this morning, wasn't he?"

"Yes. We stayed with him until he put his kite down in a field. It didn't look too bad a prang—there wasn't enough fuel left for a fire—but he was the only one who got out. Later on we got a police report that his navigator's neck had been broken. That won't make him feel any better either—they were close friends."

She winced. "Was Marsh hurt?"

"No. Only bruised and shocked. They took him to the nearest hospital. I'd like to have seen him but they put him under sedation. So I. . . ." Harvey broke off, then his breath sucked in. "Jesus Christ!"

As he leapt to his feet she rose with him, oddly frightened. "What is it?"

"His wife—Julie," he muttered. "I wonder if anyone's thought to get in touch with her."

"Can't you phone her from here?"

"The people she stays with aren't on the phone." Harvey was showing more alarm than he had shown throughout his entire ordeal over Germany. "I'll have to go. I'll take Adams with me."

"Let me come too," she pleaded.

Ignoring her he began running down the gravel path to the gate. She hesitated a moment, then ran after him.

Over at Group Headquarters, Davies was deep in conversation on a scrambler telephone. His appearance suggested relief and excitement. "So they've got the ground prepared at last, have they?"

The Brigadier's clipped words were the gentlest of reminders that scrambler or no scrambler their dialogue should be as uncommunicative as possible. "Yes. The next stage begins tomorrow."

"Tomorrow?"

"Yes. The participants will be notified later today."

Although surprised, Davies decided he had better play it as cautiously as the Brigadier. "How long is the next stage expected to take?"

"We're hoping no more than a week to ten days. The final stage is more difficult to assess. However, let's take first things first. The briefing will take place tomorrow night at the usual place. In the meantime there is one more thing I want you to do." The Brigadier spoke for a couple of minutes before ending: "In view of his importance in the affair, I feel he ought to attend. If it is done in the way I suggest, it should look like a perfectly natural occurrence. Do you agree?"

Davies was thinking that it might cause some speculation among these close at hand and then realized that that very speculation would be a cover in itself. "I'll see to it, sir. Have you spoken to the Americans yet?"

"Yes, they're being kept fully informed. Of course, like you they'd prefer definite dates but I'm afraid there are too many imponderables for that. Is there anything else you'd like to know before I ring off?"

Excited that events were on the move at last, Davies was mentally rubbing his hands. "No, I can't think of anything."

"Very well. Then we'll meet tomorrow night."

25

Abandoning the bell Harvey hammered on the door with his fist. Embarrassed, Adams made an attempt to restrain him. "Give them time, for heaven's sake. They're two elderly spinsters."

Ignoring him Harvey was about to assault the door again when a chain rattled and the younger Miss Taylor appeared.

"What on earth are you doing? Trying to break the door down?"

Harvey took an aggressive step forward. "We want to see Mrs. Marsh. It's urgent."

"Do you, indeed? You don't have to smash the door down. I've a good mind to complain to your Commanding Officer." Giving the black-faced Harvey a glare, Miss Taylor went to the foot of the stairs. "Mrs. Marsh! There's Squadron Leader Adams and a man and a woman to see you. In a great hurry from the way they're behaving."

There was no reply. The woman called again, then strode back to the doorway. "She must be out. She does sometimes go shopping on Tuesday mornings."

Harvey's eyes were on the hat and coat the woman was still wearing. "When did you last see her?"

"Yesterday evening."

"You haven't seen her this morning?"

"No. But that's not unusual. She often sleeps late and my sister and I have spent the morning with our cousin. In fact we've only been back a couple of minutes before you arrived. Why are you asking all these questions?"

Adams broke in in an attempt to lower the temperature. "I'm sorry, Miss Taylor but we're very worried about Mrs. Marsh. Are you saying she's been alone all the morning?"

"Of course she's been alone. Why shouldn't she be? She's a woman, not a child."

At Harvey's growl, Adams felt like a man trying to hold

back a bear with a piece of string. "May we go upstairs for a moment? Just to make certain she is all right."

A glance at the scowling Harvey decided the woman. "No, you can't. I don't know this man and I'm not having strangers wandering all over my house. In any case, why shouldn't she be all right? I'll get her to phone you when she comes home."

Before she could close the door Anna stepped forward. "I don't think you understand, Miss Taylor. Her husband has been hurt and she doesn't know yet. We've come to break the news and to reassure her he'll soon be out of hospital."

Before the hesitating woman could change her mind, Harvey's patience exploded. With a snarl he shoved aside both the door and the squealing woman and went up the stairs three at a time. Not daring to think what they were doing, the dazed Adams followed him with Anna close on his heels.

Harvey had already disappeared into the bedroom when they entered the empty sitting room. Anna was about to follow the Yorkshireman when he appeared in the doorway. His appearance shocked her: the bruise looked huge and livid on his pale face. With a curse he lurched towards her, half-dragged her out on the landing, and pushed her roughly against the wall.

"Don't go into that bedroom! You hear me? I'm going to get an ambulance."

As he ran downstairs the startled Miss Taylor tried to question him but he ignored her and disappeared into the street. Anna, who ran straight back into the apartment, saw Adams was approaching the bedroom door. As he reached it he stiffened, then began gagging. "Oh, my God!"

She waited to hear no more. Pushing Adams aside as he tried to stop her, she ran into the room.

The air was heavy and close that evening with yellow clouds prematurely darkening the sky. As Anna sank wearily on her bed, Harvey crossed over to the window and threw it open. A crow, taking a rest on the crab apple, gave a caw of indignation at the disturbance and flapped away towards the airfield.

Loosening his tie, Harvey lit a cigarette. His laugh made the girl wince. "So that's that. Another sample of man's inhumanity to man."

For a moment reaction made it an effort to answer him. With Adams they had remained at the hospital until it was certain no more news on the girl would be forthcoming that day. The theory of the doctors was that the half-crazed girl had given her baby the last of her sleeping tablets before slashing her own wrists. A fit of vomiting, coming after Julie had lost consciousness, had undoubtedly saved the baby's life but the girl was in a more critical condition. Although given massive blood transfusions, she was still unconscious and it would be another twenty-four hours before an assessment of her chance could be made.

"At least we got there in time to give her a chance," Anna said. "And we know the baby is safe."

He gave a shudder of hatred. "It's no thanks to those two old bitches, is it? They knew the job Marsh was doing but although they were sharp enough to grab his rent they couldn't help him by keeping an eye on the girl. That's what it's all about, isn't it? Sod you Jack." Harvey was breathing like a man trying to rid his lungs of a pestilence. "And they tell us man's born in the image of God. If he is, Christ help us."

Since their discovery of the stricken girl his mood had grown blacker as the day wore on. Even on the harsh terms of the tragedy Anna was finding it difficult to accept a bitterness of this magnitude. "You mustn't take it so personally. You did all you could to prevent it happening."

From his glance she might have been an enemy. "Did I? Then why the hell didn't I remember to get news to her earlier?"

"You can't remember everything. You'd just spent the night risking your life for her husband. It was the others, the ones who were safe on the ground, who should have remembered."

Her resentful words reminded Harvey of Adams. A sensitive man at the best of times, the Intelligence Officer had looked as if his moment of forgetfulness would haunt him for the rest of his life. "They were thinking about us. You can't expect them to think of wives and girl friends as well."

"Then neither can you. You're the least guilty of anyone. When you get over the shock you'll realize that."

His brooding voice suggested he had not been listening. "It's going to be hell for Marsh when he hears about it."

"When will they tell him?"

"Adams is going to ask Henderson to wait until he gets back. It shouldn't be more than a day or two. The poor sod can't help her and he'll go out of his own mind trapped in a hospital two hundred miles away."

"Will Henderson agree?"

"Christ knows. People do queer things, don't they? He might prefer to pass the buck to someone down there. Not that he needs to."

"I suppose by that you mean you intend breaking the news yourself," she said quietly.

His aggression leapt back. "Why not? He's one of my men, isn't he?"

Not for the first time she wondered how a man could feel such bitterness towards his fellow men and yet be so protective towards them. "You can't carry every load. No one's got that strong a back."

"I've done a great job so far, haven't I?" he sneered. "If you hadn't had the presence of mind to put tourniquets on the girl while I was downstairs yelling for help, she'd have been dead before she reached hospital."

Again she was angry with him. "The only reason I thought of tourniquets was because I've had a nurse's training. Stop blaming yourself. You're making a sin of it."

The tortured thing inside him was only too ready to take offence. "What the hell do you expect—one of Jesus's little sunbeams?" Cursing, he snatched up his cap. "I'm getting back to camp. Give Moore a ring. Nothing affects that bastard—he'll cheer you up in no time."

Controlling her nerves with an effort, she rose and went to the door. "Sit down while I fetch us both a drink."

"Don't bother. I can get all the drink I want in the Mess."

"Frank, we've both had a shock today—that's why we're acting like this. Please sit down until I get back."

He muttered something, hesitated, then flung his cap into a corner of the room. "For Christ's sake—you don't let up, do you? All right. But ask Maisie to look under the bloody counter."

As the girl disappeared Harvey lit another cigarette and turned moodily away. Every protective element in his make-up resented the part the girl had been called to play in the harrowing affair. At the same time her willingness to help and her resourcefulness had deeply impressed him. Although unaware of it in his present mood, the Yorkshireman had lost his heart without trace to this capable and courageous girl.

She returned three minutes later with a couple of glasses half-filled with whisky. "Maisie's an angel," she smiled.

"Aye, she is," he muttered, taking a glass from her. "And so she's another one the bloody world has kicked in the guts."

She dropped on the bed and watched him. The cords of his neck stood out as he half-emptied the glass. As he slumped into a chair she had hopes the neat spirit was acting as a tranquillizer. Instead, as his eyes rose to challenge her, she realized it was inflaming rather than mellowing his mood.

"Do you know what drove that kid to suicide today?" When she did not speak his arm swung out like a man swinging a sword. "It wasn't just her fear of young Marsh being killed. It was that filthy world out there. If those two old bitches had shown her some charity she could have lived with it. Even if buggers like me had gone to see her occasionally instead of getting pissed in the Mess it would have helped. But no—she was left to sweat it out alone. It's not the fear or the pain or the hunger that kills—it's the feeling nobody cares. Once you believe the world's as callous as that, who the hell wants to go on living in it?"

She swallowed to ease the dryness of her throat. "Do you feel that yourself sometimes? That nobody cares?"

"Me?" His derisive laugh jarred the heavy evening air. "What the hell have I to do with it? I learned how to be a loner when I was knee high. But some never can. When they find out what an uncharitable world it is, they can't face it." He took another gulp of whisky and a cough almost drowned his words. "People like my old woman."

She realized that the events of the day had somehow inflamed the festering sore within him and his pain needed relief. At the same time his old, distrusting self was bitterly resenting his weakness. Afraid of slamming the door that had unexpectedly swung open, she moved with great care. "Tell me about your mother, Frank. And your father. I'd like to know them better."

He stared at her, then jumped up and went back to the window. The first breath of the storm stirred the blackout curtains. As they sank back against the wall he exhaled smoke.

"It's bloody morbid, going back into the past like this. Why don't we go downstairs and have a drink with the boys?"

His offer was a measure of his desperation, for she knew how much he disliked sharing her company with his colleagues. "Please, Frank. As a favour."

His bruised face had a baleful appearance as he turned to her. "Why do you want to hear about my parents? You feel like going slumming?"

Unable to find a suitable reply she did not answer him. With his hostility finding no opposition his desperation seemed to grow. "You know what my parents were?"

She shook her head.

"They were a pair of bloody criminals." At her start his voice jeered at her. "That's right. Criminals! Stupid and uneducated but worst of all, poor. And that's the worst crime you can commit in this bloody world. Or didn't you know that?"

As she relaxed, he lifted his glass again. "Want to hear any more? Or is that enough?"

"No, I want to hear more," she said quietly.

"Then you're crazy. What's interesting about a couple of old fools?"

"I'd like to decide that myself if you'll give me the chance."

Defeated but offering a last gesture of defiance he slumped back in the chair and lit another cigarette. "What the hell do you want to know?"

"Tell me the things you remember most. When you were a child."

His swollen face twisted. "The thing I remember most was moving from house to house to find one we could afford. I believe the old man had a job before the Depression but he lost it with three million others. Then there was the old woman selling her bits of furniture. Their idea was to open up a pastry shop. Looking back it was a crazy idea—if they hadn't money to buy decent food, who else had?—but the daft old fools never did have any business sense. Although looking at it another way, what alternative did they have? Every factory had a queue of men a hundred yards long outside its gates and the old man had been trudging round 'em for years."

She was afraid to move or speak as his sullen voice led her down the dark corridors of memory.

"The old woman was the hardest worker I've ever known but she had one obsession—an onyx table her father had left her. It was a handsome thing but looked bloody ridiculous in the rat-holes we lived in. She wouldn't part with it, however, although it might have brought in enough money to buy a shop. You only needed a few quid in those days because everyone else was getting rid of 'em, but although she wasn't well she preferred to take in washing and go out charing rather than sell it." Defending his mother now, he lifted his bruised face. "When you're really poor, you need something to value. Maybe it has something to do with self-respect or security, or maybe it's a life-line. I know the old woman felt selfish in keeping it but as it was the only thing of value she had, my father never thought of asking her to part with it."

He ground out his cigarette and lit another. When he started again his voice had subtly changed as if his bitterness had momentarily slid away and he was living his childhood days again.

"By selling nearly everything they had, they finally got their shop. It had to succeed, so they put everything into it. My father was up every morning at 5 o'clock to light the ovens; my mother never finished until 9 in the evenings. For six years it was hand-to-mouth living. No one took a tram if he could walk—every penny counted. Holidays were something you read about. The incredible thing was"—his laugh was meant to be derisive but in fact was full of pride—"they made it. They managed to pay a woman to work in the bakehouse and even bought a second-hand van for twenty quid. They began thinking about employing someone to look after the shop so we could have a holiday. And then, bingo, it blew up around their ears."

The light was fading fast and a rumble of thunder sounded. "What happened, Frank?"

His laugh was a sound she knew she would always remember. "The system took over, love. A quarter of a mile down the road one of the City Fathers had a grocery and bottle store. I suppose he'd been watching us for years to see if the struggle was paying off. When he saw it was he got himself a few ovens and a couple of bakers and put the boot in. It's as easy as hell if you've got the capital. You just undercut the other poor sod until he folds up. It's called good healthy competition. Only they don't tell you how the bastards get their money. This one had made his by fiddling municipal contracts."

His expression told her she was near the source of his bitterness. The curtains at the window stirred again. "Did they go bankrupt?"

"Of course they did. No one would buy the shop now this alderman bastard was bleeding it to death. They had to stop trading and sell the stock and fittings to pay the bills. When they got the debts down to sixty pounds, my mother tried to sell her table, but now that everyone knew the mess we were in, no one offered more than a few quid. While she was trying to find an honest buyer the Receiver was called in and it went anyway."

"You are saying they lost their personal possessions because they went bankrupt?"

His gibing voice mocked her. "Why not? I told you my people were stupid old buggers. They'd never heard of limited liability and even if they had, they'd never have crawled behind it. To them a debt was something you paid in full no matter what it cost you. So when the Receiver's hearing was over, all they had was a bit of kitchenware and the beds we slept in. And none of that was much use when the landlord kicked us out into the street."

She was finding it difficult to believe what she was hearing. "You were made homeless too?"

"Why not?" he sneered. "We'd no money. Who wants people without it? Worst of all we'd gone bankrupt. So even the couple of friends they approached for help said they were sorry but they had relatives staying with them that week."

"But why was going bankrupt such a crime? It wasn't their fault."

A vein was swollen on his forehead. "You don't know how the system works, do you? It's not enough to have a power structure that means the wealthy always win. You have to make sure the peasants don't see through it. So you condition them to feel ashamed of the debts you've driven them into. Where we lived it was a hell of a disgrace to go bankrupt. My poor old mum went around with her head down as if she'd been caught stealing the Crown Jewels."

"Where did you go to live?" she asked in the silence that followed.

He swung away but not before she saw the sweat on his forehead. "They put us in a couple of hostels," he muttered. "My father and I in one, my mother in another."

"How old were you at this time?"

"I don't remember. Fourteen. Maybe fifteen."

"But you were still at school?"

"Yes. I'd got a scholarship to a secondary school and although it was a hell of a sacrifice for them they wouldn't let me give it up and find a job."

With his background she had often wondered how he had obtained his education. A flash of lightning lit up the window and rain began pattering on the leaves of the crab apple. Although she flinched from the pain it would give him, instinct told her the last door of his memory must be opened.

"Your mother must have suffered at being separated from both of you like that."

He started as if a knife had been driven into him. "Of course she suffered. It was the first time she and the old man had been apart."

She braced herself. "It killed her, didn't it, Frank?"

The bruise seemed to rise from his pale, sweating face as if it had a life of its own. As a loud peal of thunder sounded, she thought for one bizarre moment he would leap from his chair and strike her. Instead his eyes closed and he sank back. As the peal of thunder died she could hear his heavy breathing. She crossed over to him and stood beside his chair.

"What happened? Did she commit suicide?"

He nodded, his eyes still closed. His jaw muscles were bunched like a man fighting a life-and-death struggle. As the rain began drumming down she went to the window and spent a few seconds closing it. When she glanced back he was fumbling in his tunic pocket for cigarettes. "I'm sorry, Frank, but you've held that inside you too long."

"Aye," he muttered. "You could be right."

She pushed the cigarettes back into his pocket. "You've had a hellish twenty-four hours. Come and rest for a while."

For a moment he resisted her. Then he allowed her to lead him to the bed where she helped him remove his tunic and shoes. "Lie back and close your eyes."

Exhausted by emotion he tried to argue and sank back instead. His forehead felt feverish as she ran a hand across it. Her touch seemed to dissolve his tension and he felt himself sinking into a voluptuous brown sea. Although he did not want to leave her his weariness was too great to resist. As he sank slowly down he heard the strident ring of the telephone. Although it drew him back to the surface he was not fully awake when she answered it.

"Yes. Who? Oh, yes, thank you. Please tell him to wait a moment. I'll come downstairs to speak to him."

With a backward glance at Harvey, the girl slipped from the room. When she returned four minutes later he was sitting up in bed. "Was that the phone?"

Half-asleep he missed the unsteadiness of her voice. "Yes. It was for me." To hide her expression she crossed over to the dressing table where she spent a few seconds fumbling in a drawer. When she turned back to him her face was composed again. "I thought you were supposed to be asleep," she chided.

He sank back but as she approached the bed she saw he was staring at the ceiling. Aware of his suspicions, she knew only a lie would comfort him. "I took it downstairs so as not to disturb you. It was Arthur Davies. He wants to come over tomorrow morning to see me. That's all it was."

She saw his features relax and his eyes close again. She sank down on the bed alongside him and as sleep quietened his breathing she reached out and touched his arm. A gesture too gentle to disturb, it suggested an impulsive desire to remain in contact with him. A flash of lightning showed her face was pale and strained. For long minutes she sat motionless, lost in some desolate world of her own. Then, with a sigh, she rose and began undressing.

Her white body, with a flat stomach and long, slender legs, returned to the bedside. Her shapely breasts lifted as she raised both hands to release her hair. In a black cascade it tumbled down her smooth back.

She drew back the coverlet with care and slid into bed. To avoid disturbing the sleeping Harvey she kept as far away as possible but a lock of hair slid like silk across his cheek. Drugged as he was by exhaustion, some magic of communication made him stir and reach out a hand. As it made contact with her naked shoulder he gave a start and awoke. "Anna!"

She turned and leaned over him. "I'm here. What is it?"

"You're cold," he muttered. "Why are you cold?"

She put a hand on his lips and whispered to him. Obeying her he undressed and rejoined her in bed. Now he could feel the entire nakedness of her, the firmness of her breasts, the smooth length of her thighs. His desire was a throbbing ache and yet Harvey, who had never known such love for a woman before, was held back by uncertainty.

"There's something wrong, isn't there? What is it?"

She pressed closer to him and her lips touched his bruised cheek. "Why do you ask such foolish questions?"

His head lifted from the pillow. "You're not doing this because of what I told you? Because if you are. . . ."

Her denial was spontaneous and fierce. "No! No, no, no! Stop talking like this."

She saw he was still not convinced. As his head dropped back she ran a hand across his forehead. "What are you afraid of?"

His tough, battered face tried to grin up at her. "This is one time I have to be sure. I happen to be in love with you."

Tears filled her eyes. "You can be sure," she whispered.

"Then tell me why you're trembling like this."

Her sudden cry startled them both. "Stop asking these questions! Just put your arms round me and don't talk any more." Then, seeing her outburst had fed rather than allayed his doubts, she forced a laugh. "You don't know much about women, do you, Frank?"

"What does that mean?"

"Don't you know that women often act this way when they're happy?"

"Happy about what?"

She bent down and kissed him. "I was crying because you trusted me with the story of your mother. Can't you understand that?"

As he searched her face she kissed him again. This

time his wish to believe her was too strong. Gently she slid beneath him, her hands running through his hair and down his naked back. He was the one who was trembling now and the implications in a man so strong reached into the depths of her womanhood. As his blue eyes, oddly vulnerable in their masculine setting, gazed down she reached beneath him and drew him forward.

The fervour of her love-making surprised them both, tossing them about like two branches in a cataract. The climax was a shuddering drop into a whirlpool of storm-tossed water and glittering droplets of sunlight. Yet thirty seconds later, when his eyes opened to gaze into her own, she wondered if the very intensity of her love-making had betrayed her.

Footsteps sounded on the road outside as Maisie sent the last of the airmen home. A young man's voice could be heard telling a ribald joke. The laughter that followed faded as the group of men crossed the road and made for their barracks. Harvey, dressing in the dark, slipped into his tunic and approached the bed.

"I'm not sure what's on tomorrow but I'll ring you the first chance I get."

She was glad he had not turned on the light. "Yes. Please do."

He bent down to kiss her. "God, it's hard to go," he muttered.

She caught hold of his hand and gripped it tightly. "You will take care of yourself, won't you?"

He misunderstood her as he was meant to do. "It's not likely there's an operation tomorrow or Adams would have contacted me."

"I'm glad. But in the future don't take any more risks like you took last night, will you?"

Again Harvey was puzzled by her behaviour. "You don't have to worry about me. Don't you know I'm bullet-proof?"

Smiling at his clumsy attempt to reassure her she kissed his hand, then pushed him gently away. "Of course you are. I'm just being sentimental, that is all. Now you had better go." At the door he heard her voice again, an unsteady whisper. "Auf Wiedersehen, Liebchen."

It was one of the few times he had heard her speak

German and its emotional undertones disturbed him. "Are you sure there's nothing wrong?"

"Yes. Don't worry about me. God bless you, Frank."

He hesitated, then, impatient with himself, closed the door and hurried downstairs. Left alone she sat motionless until his footsteps sounded on the gravel path below. Then a sudden urgency stirred her and she ran to the window. The sky was still heavily overcast and she could see only the silhouettes of the hangars and Control Tower. As the wicker gate clicked, the shadowy figure of Harvey could be seen walking down the road towards the airfield entrance. Half-way there he turned and although she knew he could not see her at the darkened window, she waved. A moment later his shadow merged with the shadows at the camp entrance and the sound of his footsteps died away.

She walked to her small table and sat there. Inside the inn she heard footsteps on the creaking staircase and a door close. Outside, raindrops were dripping mournfully from the eaves and pattering on the leaves of the crab apple. The silence seemed to close in and isolate her in time and space.

Stirring herself with an effort, she drew the curtains, switched on the light, and carried a notepad over to the table. The task she had set herself appeared immensely difficult. Four times she tore sheets from the pad and threw them away, and when the letter was completed at last and she read it through she gave a cry of despair and buried her face in her hands.

26

Harvey turned briskly down the path that led to Adams' "Confessional." Pattering alongside him, Sam paused to cock his leg against a gas detector post. Coming in the other direction, with mugs, knives, and forks in their hands, were McTyre and Ellis. Last in and last out of breakfast as usual, McTyre, with his dishevelled hair, unshaven chin, and unpolished buttons, was a sight to make any self-respecting S.P.'s mouth water. Seeing the big Flight Commander turn down the path, McTyre was about to make a smart detour by the Photographic Section when he heard Harvey whistling. The unprecedented sound either stunned the old sweat or brought out the touch of bravado to which he was prone from time to time. Giving the faltering Ellis a shove he shambled on down the path, transferring his mug and cutlery from right hand to left as he went. Three yards from the briskly-stepping Harvey he brought up his arm in what for McTyre was a respectable salute.

The glance the Yorkshireman gave the two airmen was almost benign. "Morning, McTyre. Morning, Ellis. You going to find out what's rattling in my starboard engine today, McTyre?"

McTyre halted. "I'll find it, sir. No need to worry."

Harvey grinned. "You'd better find it bloody fast because if something drops off I'll have your giblets for dogmeat. All right?"

"Just relax, six. Leave it to me."

Nodding at both of them, Harvey turned down the path that led between two small flower beds to Adams' sanctum. McTyre nudged the speechless Ellis' arm as the couple moved on. "You ever seen 'im as friendly as that before, mush?"

"Never," the youngster said truthfully.

His long nose as curious as a pointer's, McTyre watched Harvey and the dog enter the Intelligence Room. "I wonder what the 'ell it is? Maybe he's heard they're postin' him to Burma or the Russian Front."

Inside the "Confessional" Harvey was approaching Adams' huge desk. "The Old Man gave me a buzz ten minutes ago and said I had to see you. You know what it's about?"

Adams, still shocked and full of guilt at Julie's attempted suicide, was taking in the Yorkshireman's cheerful appearance with some surprise. "Yes. He wants me to brief you." Before Harvey could comment, Adams' tone changed. "Have you heard anything from the hospital this morning?"

"I phoned half an hour ago," Harvey told him. "They said there was a slight improvement."

Adams, who had spoken to the hospital three times during the night, looked worried. "After all the blood transfusions she's had she ought to be sitting up in bed by this time. The doctors have a theory she doesn't want to recover."

Twenty-four hours ago Harvey would have shared his concern. Today he found pessimism difficult. "She'll feel differently when Marsh gets back and visits her." He nodded at the photographs that littered Adams' desk. "What's all this bumph for?"

Adams made an effort to concentrate on the task in hand. "Didn't the Old Man tell you that you're to lead a training exercise up to Scotland this afternoon?"

"A training session? This afternoon?" For a moment Harvey's disappointment and dislike of Moore broke through. "Doesn't the Wonder Boy give us our lessons any more?"

"He went off on leave this morning. He hasn't had a chance to go home since his father died."

Harvey gave a shrug of sarcasm. "Who would tell me? I'm only the bloody Senior Flight Commander." He picked up a photograph. "What's the exercise?"

"A simulated low-level attack in a wooded valley. The Observer Corps have got everything marked out for you. You're to use 11½ lb. practice bombs. Accuracy's very important."

Harvey was studying the photographs which were all of the same valley. "It's bloody narrow, isn't it?"

"Fairly narrow," Adams admitted, continuing quickly: "It's not our choice. Group sent us the photographs last night."

Harvey's bruised face frowned at him. "You know what the job is?"

Adams hesitated. "I've got an idea, yes. But it's very hush-hush at the moment."

"Oh whose instructions? Moore's?"

"No. Davies'."

Harvey's resentment cooled. "So it's something big?"

To Adams' relief the sound of an aircraft taking off brought a change in Harvey's questioning. The noise, little more than a purr compared with the throaty roar of a Mosquito's Merlins, made the Yorkshireman glance at him.

"Davies," Adams ventured. "He said he was off somewhere or other this morning."

Harvey strode to the window and peered out. His expression as he returned to the desk puzzled Adams—of late Davies' comings and goings had become so frequent that the squadron had grown used to them.

"Is he expected back this morning?"

"This morning?" Adams looked surprised. "Nobody said anything. But I shouldn't think so."

"Are you sure?"

The Yorkshireman's insistence puzzled Adams. "Nothing's sure with Davies. But there's no reason for him to come back today that I know of—not unless he wants to see how the exercise has gone." Feeling a change in Harvey's mood and unable to account for it, Adams indicated a chair. "If you'd like to take the weight off your legs, I'll run through the details."

He talked to Harvey for ten minutes. His feeling the Flight Commander's mind was on other things persisted —twice he had to repeat details that normally Harvey would have taken in his stride. But by the time the briefing was over the Yorkshireman appeared to have recovered something of his earlier mood. "Did you say the Old Man wants the crews briefed this morning?"

Adams nodded. "Will 1100 hours suit you?"

"I'd rather make it 1200 hours. I've a couple of things to do this morning. Will that be O.K.?"

"I don't see why not. Providing the air-tests are done beforehand."

Harvey pushed back his chair. "They'll be done. See you here at 1200 hours then."

Calling Sam, he was half-way down the hut before Adams remembered. "You do know that Henderson has agreed to keep quiet about Julie until Marsh gets back?"

Harvey turned. "Yes, thank Christ. The M.O. told me at breakfast."

He glanced at his watch as he left the hut. There was plenty of time to organize the exercise and nip over the road to explain the situation to Anna. Giving Sam a playful cuff round the ears, Harvey went to his flight office. He was on the phone talking to his Flight Sergeant when a young S.P. knocked on the door and entered. Finishing his conversation, Harvey replaced the receiver.

"Yes?"

The S.P. saluted, then held out a letter. "This was dropped in the Guardroom this morning, sir."

Harvey gazed down at the envelope. Addressed to him, it was written in a handwriting he did not recognize. "Do you know who brought it?"

The S.P. looked embarrassed. "No, sir. It was there when we came on duty."

"You mean it had been forgotten?"

"I'm afraid so, sir."

Harvey scowled. "All right. I'll see to it."

The S.P. thankfully withdrew. Dropping into his chair Harvey tore open the envelope. As his eyes ran down the brief letter he gave a grunt of shock. A moment later his chair clattered over as he leapt to his feet and ran from the office. Startled by his behaviour, Sam gave a bark and scampered after him. Ignoring the sentry's salute as well as the startled glances of airmen and Waafs, Harvey ran out of the station and down the road to the Black Swan. Breathing heavily he reached the front porch only to find the oak door bolted. He had to hammer three times on the iron knocker before Joe Kearns appeared. Still in his shirtsleeves, the innkeeper looked startled by the Yorkshireman's urgency.

"What's the trouble, Mr. Harvey?"

"I've come about Miss Reinhardt. Has she left yet?"

"Yes. Didn't you know? She went just after seven-thirty this morning."

The panting Harvey cursed. "Do you know the time of her train?"

As Kearns hesitated, Maisie appeared in the panelled hall. Drawn to the door by curiosity, an apron round her shapely hips, she could guess why Kearns was reluctant to answer Harvey's question and pushed forward. Although a kind-hearted girl, Maisie considered herself a realist.

"She didn't go by train. That new Squadron Commander of yours called for her."

Harvey's violent start confirmed Kearn's suspicions. "You mean he took her to the station?"

Maisie shrugged. "No. I think she was going all the way with him, wherever that was."

The Yorkshireman's swollen face turned thunderblack at the suggestion. "Why the hell should you think that?"

It was a reaction that would have made a lesser girl draw back. In Maisie it produced a hostility she was to regret almost at once. "Because it looked that way, that's why. They'd both got their luggage in the car. And anyway, there isn't a train going to London at that time in the morning."

Without another word Harvey swung away. Meeting Kearns's glance, Maisie looked immediately defensive. "He wanted to know, didn't he? An' anyway, what's wrong with a girl taking a lift? It isn't exactly the end of the world, is it?"

Kearns did not answer. His eyes were on the tall, big-boned figure of Harvey. With the anxious dog gazing up at him, he was walking heavy-footed down the road as if from the death of a dream.

The Mosquito was darting through the mountains like a swift chasing gnats. Banking left, then skidding right round an outcrop of rock, it entered a valley and flattened down to zero height over a narrow but fast-flowing river. On either side dense forests of firs shivered to the roar and fury of the aircraft's passing. Inside it Harvey was hunched over the control column like a man who was demonstrating his hatred of life. At his side young Blackburn was as tense as a man in a dentist's chair as he glanced again at the pilot's huge and forbidding figure.

Ahead, a mountain spur diverted the river a full forty degrees. Holding on course until it seemed the Mosquito would crash into the shelving rock face, Harvey swung the column over and heaved it back. Hanging on its wing-tips, curving in its flight like a bent bow, the plane flew parallel to the rock face for a few seconds, did a reverse bank, then swooped down to the treetops again. Fighting to keep his stomach down, Blackburn peered ahead and jabbed his finger.

The valley ran straight for another five miles before another mountain spur formed a barrier across it. As Harvey climbed a couple of hundred feet for better visibility, a distant clearing among the firs on the left bank of the river could be seen. In its centre was a white target. As Harvey opened the bomb doors, his growl sounded in Blackburn's earphones. "I'll drop the bloody things myself. Four at a time."

Blackburn's nod expressed profound relief. To miss the target with the Yorkshireman in this mood did not bear contemplation. The Mosquito's nose dropped again and the tops of the firs shivered like green water in its slipstream. With both main and selector switches on, Harvey waited, then began counting as the clearing flashed towards him. "One, two, three—gone."

The bombs fell away and were flung like stones into the clearing, but Blackburn made no attempt to see where they burst. His eyes were glued on the mountain spur that was hurling itself at terrifying speed towards them. For a moment it seemed Harvey's plan was to fly straight into its boulder-strewn slopes. Then sky and earth tilted dizzily and Blackburn felt as if his stomach was sagging to his knees. A moment later the Mosquito came shooting out of the valley like a sky rocket.

Glancing back Harvey saw columns of smoke rising only a few yards from the white target. His orders to the planes circling above were gritty with sarcasm.

"That's the way I want it doing this time. No poncing about at 2,000 feet—get right down on the deck. You don't have to worry about the Laird's gamekeepers—they've been told not to shoot to kill."

In T-Tommy Gabby glanced at the tousle-headed Millburn. "Our Tike's in a happy mood today. You think he might be constipated?"

The American grinned as he followed St. Claire in the squadron's orbit above the valley. "Could be. If he is, he's going the right way to shake it loose."

In numerical order the Mosquitoes followed one another down. Mutters and curses filled the radio channel as planes came shooting out like corks from bottles, their nervous pilots fighting clear of the mountain spur. The old hands felt misgivings about the severity of the exercise which reminded them of the training they had received before the Swartfjord raid.

The strain of flying the fast-moving Mosquitoes in the narrow confines of the valley was considerable, but Harvey's orders had been to work the crews hard and he was in no mood to compromise. The older hands had little difficulty in planting their bombs within the clearing but the new members found the threatening mountain spur a distraction and Harvey kept them at it until the last of their bombs had been dropped. By that time jumpy nerves had become abrased ones, and when at last the crews formated to return home, the mood of some almost matched that of their deputy leader.

27

Millburn flipped a coin and slapped it down on the back of his hand. "Heads you've got the back seat. Tails you're in the bushes. Call."

Gabby, sitting behind him in the car, eyed his hands suspiciously. "What's that coin you're using?"

"A Coin of the Realm, kid. One of your English pennies. What does it matter anyway? You're calling."

"Heads," Gabby said impulsively.

Millburn removed his upper hand. "Tails! Into the bushes, my young love birds."

The girl sitting beside Gabby let out a wail of protest. Small but buxom, she had a chubby face and a mass of curly fair hair. "That's not fair. We should take it in turns. I got prickles all over me on Sunday."

Millburn grinned at her. "Try another position, honey. Teach our little Welsh friend to share and share alike."

The girl next to the American turned with some impatience. A taller girl, she was modelled on Veronica Lake, the current sex symbol, from the long blonde hair that half hid her face to her pseudo-sophisticated voice. "For heaven's sake, Dolly. . . . Don't be such a bad sport."

"Who's a bad sport?" Dolly demanded. She jabbed her finger at the grinning Millburn. "He fiddles that coin. I don't know how, but he does."

Millburn tut-tutted. "You'll never go to heaven if you have thoughts like that, Dolly."

"It's you who should be worrying about heaven, Tommy Millburn. I know you're cheating."

Veronica Lake, whose real name was Gwen Dawson, gave a cry of impatience. "Please, Dolly. You're just wasting time."

Millburn's twinkling eyes ran suggestively down the taller girl's shapely body. "That's right, Dolly. You're wasting time. So what about it?"

Grumbling, Dolly swung her stubby legs out into the afternoon sunlight. "This is the last time, Tommy Millburn. You're cheating—I know you are."

Eyes glinting like a stoat after a rabbit, Gabby followed her into a clump of bushes, an army blanket over one arm. Watching them, Millburn leaned his good-looking tousled head from the car window. "Watch out for the thistles, you guys. They look the kind that could do you a real mischief."

Veronica Lake tinkled. Millburn grabbed her round the waist, and planted a kiss in the centre of her very low-cut dress. Then he jerked a thumb at the empty rear seat. "Come on, honey. Let's be comfortable."

The American's car was parked on a rough hillside covered with clumps of bramble and broom. Below it the grassy common sloped down to a small lake that had once been a gravel pit. The two airmen had brought the girls to the village the previous week and found it ideal for their needs. Seldom used by the villagers, the common offered privacy for their present activities while Fenleigh's two pubs were on hand for refreshment later.

Millburn helped the girl into the rear seat and slid in after her. As he put an arm round her waist she pushed him back. "Don't be in such a hurry. It's all you Yanks think about. Can't we talk for a while?"

Millburn looked shocked. "Talk? What about?"

"Well—there's you and me, isn't there?"

"You've got a point there, honey."

"Well, go on then. Talk about yourself first."

"O.K. I'm an American. I was born in El Paso. I'm 23 years old and I'm in the RAF. Oh yeah, and I'm a man. How's that?"

She suppressed a giggle with difficulty. "Neither of you seem to do much in the Air Force. How do you manage to get so many afternoons off?"

"You get half-days. We get half-days. Union regulations, honey."

"But we only get one a week, like today. Are you both on leave?"

Millburn put a finger on his lips and glanced furtively around. "Can you keep a secret?"

"Yes. Why?"

"We're in training, honey—that's why we're getting time off just now. It's a special mission. When we're ready we're flying straight to Hitler's Chancellery in Berlin. We're going to land on the roof, capture him, and hand him over to Churchill. Not bad, uh?"

Her long hair, slanting across her face, was preventing her seeing his expression. She tossed her head. "You're pulling my leg. Aren't you?"

He grinned. "Don't be like that. In a couple of months you'll be able to go and see the guy in the London Zoo. Will you believe me then?"

She pouted. "Aren't you ever serious?"

Behind her back Millburn was undoing the buttons of her dress. "I'm serious now, honey. Deadly serious."

"You haven't said a word about me yet," she complained as he slid down one shoulder of her dress.

"That's right, I haven't." Millburn slid down the other shoulder and took her bra with it. As he eased her down and lowered his head, his voice took on a muffled sound. "That's easy, honey. You're beautiful."

Her hands clamped behind his back. "Do you think so?"

"No doubt about it." Half a minute more and Millburn came up for air. "Mind you, I'll be able to tell you more when we get this dress off."

She felt Veronica would forgive her one small giggle. "You're very naughty, Tommy Millburn."

Millburn was too busy with the dress to answer. Although blessed with considerable expertise, he had learned long ago that every new case presented its own problems. As the girl's wrigglings made matters worse, the American was tempted to throw open a door and undress her outside. Then, to his relief, the dress slid to the floor.

Millburn discovered he was breathing hard and doubted if it was all passion. "Thank God for that."

The girl had taken refuge behind her mask of hair. "Don't sit there staring, Tommy Millburn. Do something."

Millburn complied by climbing out of his own clothes. When he was down to his vest and underpants, she drew him down. "Give me a kiss first, darling."

Millburn had to part her hair twice to find her mouth. Her deep sigh was Veronica Lake at her best. "That's wonderful, Tommy. Do it again."

Millburn was obliging when there was the sound of a heavy vehicle braking on the road above. A moment later it began trundling down the hillside. Beneath him the girl stiffened. "What's that?"

Millburn peered cautiously over the window sill. To his consternation a bus was following the track through the bushes. For a horrendous moment it seemed it would halt nose to bumper with the car. Instead it swung past and continued down the hillside. Before he ducked down the American caught a fleeting glimpse of a full load of passengers.

"What is it?" the startled girl asked again.

"It's a bloody bus," Millburn hissed.

"A bus? It can't be."

"It's a bus, I tell you. Christ knows where it's going."

The two of them peered over the front seats. At the lake fifty yards away the bus halted and its doors opened. Millburn blinked. "I don't believe it!"

The passengers who were disembarking were all women aged between forty and sixty. Chattering and laughing they formed into groups alongside the lake. Millburn stared at the girl. "Who the hell are they?"

"It looks like a works' outing."

"A what?"

"A works' outing. You know, a factory giving its staff a day in the country."

Before Millburn could react the bushes near the car twitched violently. A moment later, wearing nothing but her dress, Dolly appeared and flung herself into the driver's seat. "You do what you like, Johnnie Gabriel, but I'm not risking being seen by a bunch of old women. If you want me, you can come back into the car."

Hastily buttoning up his trousers, Gabby climbed in beside her. "They couldn't see us from down there," he complained.

"You don't know old women. They've got eyes in the back of their heads. Anyway, I was getting bitten. There are ants out there."

Millburn tapped on the back of the seat. "What's the matter with you guys? You think talking's more fun?"

Gabby grinned, then turned towards the indignant Dolly. "He's right. We're wasting time."

Dolly sniffed. "It's all right for him. He fiddles it so he always has the best spot."

Her complaints died as Gabby nibbled at her ear. Soon whispers and giggles could be heard as the two of them

egan undressing again. For a few seconds there was si-
ence. Then the car rocked violently and Dolly let out a
ell of pain. "Look out! Something's sticking into me."

Gabby fumbled beneath her. "It's only the handbrake."

"Only! Can't you put something over it?"

Gabby could see nothing suitable, then remembered the
rmy blanket. Seeing the party of women were still
lustered round the lake he threw open the door and
ived into the bushes, an apparition wearing only a pair of
egulation underpants and blue socks. Running back to the
ar with the blanket over his arm he stumbled, gave a
owl of pain, and clutched his foot. Millburn, his cheeks
eddened by Veronica Lake's lipstick, gave him a wither-
ng glance. "You want to bring those old women on top of
is?"

Groaning, Gabby hopped back into the car and
lammed the door. "Those bloody thistles!" He shoved
he blanket beneath Dolly's ample buttocks. "How's that?"

"A bit better," she muttered. "But it's still sticking into
me."

Gabby's retort was interrupted by a hiss of fury from
Millburn. "Sonofabitch, there's no wonder you two can't
make it. You're worse than two old women."

The insult stung Gabby into action. To the accompani-
ment of grunts, giggles, and sighs of ecstacy, the car began to rock in unsynchronized rhythm. A minute passed
and then a stifled groan came from Dolly. "I can't. . . .
It's sticking into my back. Get off me!"

In concert with Millburn on the back scat Gabby was
far enough gone to make such a request unthinkable.
Fumbling under the squirming girl he found the handbrake and pushed it to the floor. Dolly gave a sigh of bliss.
"Oh, that's better, luv. That's better. . . ."

Millburn, who was half-way to the summit of his joy,
did not even know the handbrake had been released. At
first the car moved no more than a couple of inches.
Then, as its rocking became more uninhibited, it began to
roll forward, slowly at first, then faster as the declivity of
the hillside steepened.

It took a heavy bump as the car ran over a ridge to
alert Millburn that something was wrong. His startled
voice came over the mounting rumble of the wheels.
"Gabby! We're moving. Goddamn it, we're moving."

For the little Welshman the entire world was moving

at that moment and he wanted it no other way. His ec-
static mumble was an attempt to reassure. "That's all
right, boyo. . . . That's how it feels sometimes."

With self-preservation having an edge on sex, Millburn
was now trying to extricate himself. "The bloody brake's
slipped, you Welsh moron! Do something, for Christ's
sake."

Alert at last to danger, Gabby fumbled beneath the
pulsating Dolly, only to discover her plump buttocks were
anchoring the handbrake firmly to the floor. He gave a
desperate tug. "Get up! Get off the brake."

Wooed one moment and unwanted the next, Dolly's
reaction was bitter. "How can I get up? You're lying on
top of me."

Wriggling sideways Gabby tried again but the girl appeared to be jammed between the two seats. With the
car now in full flight down the hill, Gabby had no time
for niceties. Grabbing a piece of flesh between his finger
and thumb he nipped hard. With a howl of indignation the
girl shot into the air, only to drop back on the brake and
trap Gabby's arm. Behind them Millburn had struggled to
his knees. "The foot brake," he yelled. "Get your bloody
foot on it."

He could have asked nothing more difficult of Gabby.
With his left arm trapped beneath Dolly, the Welshman's
skinny bare legs were kicking feebly at the car roof. Down
by the pond the party of women were gazing with astonishment at the runaway car. Bouncing and bucking over
the uneven hillside, gathering speed with every second, it
was plunging straight for them.

Millburn, baulked from climbing over the front seats
by the couple lying across them, could see the startled
women and the pond through the windscreen and his yell
was hoarse. "Do something! Get that footbrake down."

With a desperate heave Gabby managed to free his
arm from Dolly's buttocks and with a contortion that
would have done credit to Houdini managed to reach the
foot pedal. Closing his fingers round it he pressed down
as hard as his restricted position would allow. To his
surprise the car came to an abrupt halt. Screams and
curses followed as Veronica Lake and Millburn collapsed
in a heap on the floor. Dolly was likewise pitched forward, taking Gabby with her. Although her fleshy charms
wrapped themselves round his face and almost suffocated

him, Gabby miraculously kept his hold on the pedal until he was able to drag up the handbrake. With a groan of relief, he sagged back.

With the two couples fully occupied recovering themselves, it took a scream from Dolly to give the alarm. "Oh, my God. Look!"

Women's faces were pressed against every window. As they saw the tangle of nude bodies, there was an outburst of laughter, screams, and cackles. Gabby's nerve broke. Dragging Dolly to one side, he squeezed past her into the driver's seat. There, clad only in his socks, he turned towards the equally horrified Millburn. "The keys! Where are the bloody keys?"

Agonized seconds passed while Millburn sought for his trousers which were buried beneath the sobbing Veronica Lake. Finding the keys in his tunic pocket instead he pushed them at Gabby. As the Welshman fumbled to insert them in the lock, there was a loud cackle from an old woman standing alongside the American's door. "Let's get 'em out and take a better look at 'em."

Millburn grabbed the door handle and hung on tightly. "What the hell are you doing? Get the bloody thing off the ground!"

For an answer the car lurched forward, scattering the group of hysterical women. Swinging round it fled back up the hill, followed by a storm of boos and cheers. Dolly, whose crossed hands were struggling unsuccessfully to contain the bouncing of her charms, glared tearfully at the pale-faced Gabby. "That's it, Johnnie Gabriel. That's absolutely the last time."

Too shattered to think of a reply, Gabby swung the car on to the road and drove as if the entire German Air Force were on his tail.

28

Sitting in Henderson's swivel chair, Davies discovered his feet barely touched the floor. Reaching down for the height adjustment knob, he found it was jammed. His instant tetchiness betrayed the lack of sleep he had suffered during the last few days. Bloody raw-boned, hairy-kneed Scot! Why the hell couldn't he keep his equipment serviceable? As he leaned down and put both hands to the task, there was a tap on the door. Cursing, the small officer straightened. "Come in!"

Harvey appeared in the doorway. The sight did nothing to improve Davies' temper. "Afternoon, Harvey. Come in and close the door."

The Yorkshireman obeyed and approached the desk. A less-prejudiced observer would have detected signs of diffidence in him. Davies was wondering suspiciously why he'd asked for a private interview. He debated whether to invite the Yorkshireman to sit down, then decided against it. Let the bloody-minded bolshie stand. "All right, Harvey. What can I do for you?"

Harvey's nervousness showed itself in a defiant tightening of his features. "It's a personal request, sir."

"Personal?"

"Yes, sir. I'd like you to give me Miss Reinhardt's address."

Davies jumped. "Say that again."

"I'd appreciate it if you'd give me Miss Reinhardt's address."

A sudden wariness superimposed itself on Davies' irritability. "Why didn't you get it from her yourself?"

"She left before I'd a chance to ask her."

"You're saying she left without telling you?"

A muscle twitching on Harvey's swollen cheek was the only indication of his grief. "Yes, sir."

Davies sat back. Although secretly conceding it was rough on Harvey he could see no other course of action open to him. "In that case I'd try to forget about her. If

224

she'd wanted you to keep in touch she'd have made it possible."

Harvey, who had suffered the same thought a hundred times already, managed to keep his pain hidden. "If it's a brush off I shan't pester her. But I'd like to write her to make certain."

"Why haven't you asked me before? She's been gone over a week now."

"You haven't been here, sir. You left the same morning she did."

Davies realized that was true. "What else could it be but a brush off?"

"I don't know but I want to find out. That's why I need her address."

"Well, I can't give it to you. Not without her consent."

"All right, then ask her. Will you do that for me?"

Davies was beginning to breathe hard. "You think I've nothing better to do than sort out your love life? It's as clear as a duck's arse she wants to drop the whole thing. So why can't you accept it?"

Frustration and pain brought out all that was aggressive in Harvey. "I'm asking you for her address, not the bloody moon. But you wouldn't help a lame dog over a style, would you?"

Feeling guilty already, Davies needed to hear no more. He came out of the chair like a sprinter from his blocks. "One more word out of you and you're under close arrest. If Anna Reinhardt's had a bellyful of you that's all right with me because I've had a bellyful too. Now get out of here!"

For a full five seconds Harvey stared him right in the face. Then with a growl of hatred he strode from the office, leaving the door wide open. Davies stood glaring after him. "By the bloody centre. . . ." His yell brought a sergeant running into the office. "Go and get the C.O.! At the double."

Henderson hurried in fifteen seconds later. He found Davies glowering beside the swivel chair. "What is it, sir?"

"That bastard Harvey—Christ—I've a bloody good mind to put him under close arrest."

"What happened, sir?"

"The stupid sod's got a crush on Anna Reinhardt and wanted me to give him her address. When I wouldn't he was bloody rude."

"I'm sorry about that, sir. Do you want me to discipline him?"

Davies cursed again, then appeared to relent. "No, leave it," he muttered. "I gave him a fair old bollocking before I kicked him out. What time's Moore back today?"

Used to the Air Commodore's moods and aware of his dislike of Harvey, the Scot was astonished how quickly Davies' temper was cooling. "He's back now. He phoned me twenty minutes ago."

Davies gave a start. "He is? Then get him here right away, will you?"

Henderson put a call through to the squadron office. "He's just changing. He'll be here as quick as he can."

Davies wandered restlessly round the desk and ended up at the window. "You'll be glad to have him back."

"Of course," Henderson said, watching him.

Davies' eyes were following but not seeing the trim figure of a Waaf who was walking past the block. "Sorry about those two ops. Group pushed on you this week but I couldn't persuade 'em to keep you in reserve any longer. But you got off lightly, didn't you?"

"Yes. Only one kite damaged."

"No one injured?"

"No, sir."

"That's what we can't afford while we're waiting—the loss of trained men. Who led 'em? Harvey?"

Feeling considerable sympathy for Harvey, the Scot took the chance to raise his credit. "He did a good job both times. He's also kept the training up. Allowing for the way he must be feeling, I think that's pretty commendable."

Davies' only response was a grunt. "Keep all the kites serviceable you can, Jock. We can't say when we're going to need 'em."

Five minutes later Moore entered the office. Although he was newly-bathed and changed, his appearance caused the Scot concern. "You're not looking too good, Moore. Is anything wrong?"

Wheeling round, Davies saw the young pilot's face was paler than usual and bore considerable signs of strain. He broke in before Henderson could question Moore further. "Hello, Moore. How were things at home? Is your mother bearing up all right?"

Although his questions seemed amiable enough—even considerate for one of Davies' temperament—Henderson imagined there was resentment in Moore's glance. "She's taken it very well, thank you, sir."

"That's good." Courtesies over, Davies got down to business. "Does Harvey know you're back yet?"

"I don't know. I haven't seen him."

"He's just been in here. He wants Anna Reinhardt's address. I wouldn't tell him anything, so he might try you. If he does, you're not to discuss her with him. All right?"

This time Henderson was not surprised to see Moore's face tighten, although the pilot's reaction suggested bitterness rather than resentment. "If that's what you want, sir."

"It is what I want," Davies snapped. "In fact it's an order." Seeing Henderson staring at him he stared back challengingly. "She's obviously given him the brush off. So why should he go on pestering her?"

When Davies defended his actions to subordinates, the Scot knew it had to be an unreal afternoon. Wondering if he ought to comment, he was relieved when the red telephone on the desk began ringing. Answering it, he glanced at Davies. "It's that call you've been waiting for."

As Davies took the receiver from him, Henderson jerked his head at Moore and the two men left the office, Davies waited until the door closed before speaking. "Davies here. Yes, sir. I got back an hour ago. What's that? They have? Already?" As he listened Davies gave a jump of excitement. "That's the luckiest break we've had so far. Yes, of course I'll come round. Give me forty minutes. Goodbye, sir."

Both Henderson and Moore noticed the change in him as they were called back into the office. An elderly puppy given a rubber bone could not have looked more bouncy or pleased with itself. "I've got to run off," he told Henderson. "Can I borrow your car?"

More mystified than ever, the Scot nodded. "Do you expect to be long, sir?"

"A couple of hours. Maybe less." Slapping on his cap, Davies almost bounded to the door. "See you both at dinner."

As his footsteps hurried down the corridor, Henderson gave a groan. "First he tells us this operation is our pigeon. Now he's acting like a spy in a fifth-rate thriller. What the hell's going on? Do you know?"

When Moore did not answer the Scot walked moodily

back to his desk. "I'm not happy about the way he's treating Harvey either. The poor bastard was a different man after meeting that girl and I think he's entitled to some explanation why she dropped him flat like that."

When Moore still did not answer Henderson gave him a hostile glance. "Well. Don't you think so?"

To his surprise the good-looking pilot gave a shiver of disgust. "Don't ask me what I think. All I know is that war's a filthy business."

Henderson's brows came together. "You're starting to act like Davies. I don't see what the war has to do with a man finding out why a girl's dropped him. He's been on the piss every night since she left."

Moore turned sharply away and lit a cigarette. With the pilot's mood as enigmatical as Davies', Henderson could not decide whether the impulsive act was related to his question or not. Then, as the sunlight from the window emphasized the lines of strain on the younger man's face, the Scot drew his own conclusions and became sympathetic.

"The last few days can't have been easy for you. Are you sure your mother's all right?"

He saw Moore start, then draw in smoke. "Oh, yes, thanks. She's taken it very well, considering."

Having just made up his mind he understood Moore's behaviour, Henderson now felt his question had come as a surprise. There were bloody undertones everywhere today, he decided. With a growl of frustration he made for the door. "It's early but I'm going for a drink. You coming or not?"

Harvey ran Moore down on the airfield. The Squadron Commander was at the dispersal point of A-Apple, listening to his Flight Sergeant explaining why a new magazine was needed for its starboard cannon. Harvey gave the N.C.O. no more than a couple of seconds before breaking in. "I'd like a word with you. In private. It's important."

Giving him a curt nod, Moore turned back to the N.C.O. "Strip the panel off, Chiefy, and I'll take a look. I'll be back in a couple of minutes."

The indignant Flight Sergeant watched the two officers move away from the dispersal point. "You see that?" he demanded of the three mechanics clustered around the nose of A-Apple. "No apology—nothing. Just broke right in. I hope Moore tears a strip off the bad-mannered sod."

Neither officer spoke as they tramped across the grass. It had been cut that day and had a sweet smell in the late afternoon sunlight. A flock of birds, grubbing for worms, rose and flew away. The dispersal point was a good forty yards away before Harvey halted. His hostility, fed by a week of brooding, prevented his noticing the strain Moore was showing.

"I'm putting in a recommendation that Peter Marsh is grounded."

Braced for questions and a possible quarrel about Anna, Moore was taken by surprise. "How is his wife?"

"She's conscious again. But that's about all. The doctors are afraid she doesn't want to go on living."

Moore gave a wince of sympathy. "I must get over to see her. How is Marsh taking it?"

Harvey's glance expressed contempt such a question was necessary. "I haven't seen him for a couple of days. I asked the Adjutant to bring his leave forward. He's spending it visiting her in hospital."

"When is he due back?"

"Next Monday. That's why I want him grounded this week."

"Has he applied to be grounded?"

"No. The poor bastard can't face it. That's why we have to take it out of his hands."

"But you know we can't do that. A man has to make the first move himself."

Harvey needed nothing more to justify his personal animosity. "What do you mean—we can't do it? This isn't some kid who's just started operational flying. He's done nearly as many ops. as we have. He's entitled to a rest."

"If you mean a rest between tours, I agree with you. I'll see he gets one as soon as his present tour ends."

"You know bloody well that isn't what I mean. The kid's been suffering hell for months. What's he going to feel like now, knowing the next time he goes on an op. she might finish herself off. For Christ's sake, we've got to help him."

"We will, if he helps himself. Tell him to put in a request and I'll add my recommendation. There's no other way. You know the rules."

Harvey cursed. "I know effing rules can be broken if there's a will to break them. You're a personal friend of Davies—why won't you talk to him?"

Moore was trying to imagine Davies' reaction at this moment in time to the suggestion one of his most experienced pilots was grounded. "He wouldn't wear it, Harvey. Not for a minute."

"You mean you won't ask him? Right?"

"It's not that. You've just picked the worst possible time to ask. Give it a month, perhaps only three weeks, and I'll do what I can. But not now."

Harvey's suspicious eyes were searching his face. "What's so special about now?"

Aware how the Yorkshireman's questions were endangering security, Moore's voice turned unintentionally curt. "I've promised I'll do all I can later on. Now let's drop it, shall we?"

In spite of his animosity, Harvey's urgent need to learn Anna's address had determined the Yorkshireman to keep his self-control until his questions were asked. But with his concern for Marsh high up on his list of priorities Moore's curt rejection was like petrol vapour coming into contact with white-hot metal. In a sheet of flame his resentment exploded.

"You're really something, aren't you? The big businessman, used to pushing his workmen around like effing pawns. Never mind about their personal problems! Work the sods until they drop, then sack 'em and get in a fresh lot. Success and profit first, last, and all the time. Jesus Christ, your kind make me bring up."

A cloud shadow, drifting slowly across the field, reached the two men and isolated them in their hostility. Although Moore's good-looking face turned very pale, his reply was astonishingly quiet and controlled.

"I'm sorry I can't help you, Harvey. I really am very sorry."

Conscious now that pride would never allow him to ask any favours of this man, Harvey let all his self-destructiveness burst to the surface. "You know something, Moore? The Japs and the Nazis operate the way you do. Cannon fodder for the Fatherland. Chuck 'em in and let 'em die. That's where you ought to be—on the other side." A shudder of desire ran through the Yorkshireman. "Christ, don't I wish you were."

It was an orgasm of bitterness that gave him no chance to read Moore's expression. When the retaliatory attack that he was thirsting for still did not come, Harvey gave a snarl of fury, swung away, and began trudging across the grass towards the billet.

Henderson was propping up the bar in the Mess when Davies found him. Although clearly excited and in a good mood, the small Air Commodore gave a glance of disapproval at the glass of whisky the Scot was holding.

"I've been hunting all over the station for you. Bit early for that stuff, isn't it?"

Henderson, who had already seen off two glasses, was in no mood for apologies. "It's been that kind of a day, sir. Can I get you one?"

"Not bloody likely. I never drink before dinner. Where are Adams and Moore?"

Henderson rebelliously drained his glass before replying. "I don't know, sir. Probably in their offices."

"Well, put out a call for them," Davies snapped. "I want the three of you in your office in thirty minutes. And lay on full security precautions in the meantime."

Alcohol made the Scot's queston overtly sarcastic. "That couldn't mean you're going to give us an idea at last what's going on, could it?"

Davies gave him a sharp stare. "What's the matter with you? You feeling the-little-boy-nobody-loves all of a sudden?"

Henderson's grin expressed both embarrassment and defiance. "Would you blame me if I did?"

Davies' satisfaction at the news he had received proved adequate for the occasion. "For Christ's sake, Jock, you know how these things are—these last few weeks I've even had to tell lies to myself. We haven't got all the problems solved yet—the last one might prove to be the biggest—but although it's still strictly hush-hush, things have gone far enough for you to be brought in. Give me thirty minutes and you'll get the full story."

Henderson's voice was heavy with feeling as he pushed himself away from the bar. "Thank God for that."

29

Adams was almost past the billet door when he heard the dog whimpering. Turning, he listened. It came again, an anxious, entreating sound. Hesitating for a long moment Adams tapped on the door.

There was a loud, relieved bark and the sound of the dog scampering across the floor. As Adams tapped again its paws scratched on the woodwork. Waiting no longer, Adams pushed the door open.

The dog leapt up in relief against his legs, then ran back. The shadowy billet reeked with the smell of whisky. Reaching the bed the dog turned its head and barked impatiently.

Crossing the floor Adams patted the dog absent-mindedly. His eyes were on Harvey sprawled out face downward on the bed. In his shirtsleeves the Yorkshireman had one arm doubled beneath him and the other dangling over the bedside. An empty whisky bottle and a glass stood on the nearby locker. The dog had awakened him and his face, unshaven since the previous day, lifted a few inches from his pillow as Adams approached. "What do y' want?"

Adams found it was difficult to know what to say. "Are you all right, Frank?"

"Course I'm all right."

"Is there anything I can do?"

Harvey dropped back on his pillow. "Yes. You can bugger off."

Irresolute, Adams stood back. Tail wagging, the dog gazed up at him. Feeling unable to meet its eyes, Adams hesitated, then retreated to the door. As he closed it behind him the dog's disappointed whimpering commenced again. With his movements suddenly full of purpose Adams went looking for Moore.

Moore was in his office writing a letter when Adams found him. The chain of a block and tackle had broken that afternoon and a young fitter working beneath it had been badly injured. The Adjutant, on whom the unpleasant task of notifying relatives usually fell, had been surprised and gratified when Moore had said he would write the letter himself. He did not know it was a responsibility Moore had taken on himself since his early days of command at Warboys.

With a shaded desk lamp concentrating its light downwards, Adams' myopic eyes could not distinguish Moore's features clearly as he approached the desk. "Sorry to bother you at this time of the night, Ian, but I've come about Harvey. I heard his dog whimpering a few minutes ago and took a look in his billet. He's in a hell of a state—plastered to the wide."

There was a pause before Moore answered him. "I noticed he wasn't at dinner tonight."

"Tonight? I don't know when he ate last. It's been going on for weeks. Christ knows how he manages to do his job."

There was the click of a lighter as Moore lit a cigarette. Still not able to see his expression, Adams drew nearer the desk. "This thing's destroying him, Ian. He must have loved that girl to distraction."

There was a sharp exclamation, then the sound of a chair pushed back. "Just what the hell are you trying to say?"

Coming from one as controlled as Moore, the outburst both dismayed and startled Adams. At the same time the Intelligence Officer had his own brand of tenacity which became evident now. "I'm wondering if it's necessary to let the poor devil suffer any longer. After all, unless the final stage is a failure, the big show must be on soon. I know it means breaking orders and security, but the hell with it. There's a limit to what a man can see another man suffer."

Bitter and resentful, Moore's reply was not the one Adams expected. "Do you think he'll suffer any less if he hears the truth?"

"Perhaps not," Adams admitted. "Perhaps it might make some things worse. But at least he won't go on believing the whole world has betrayed him."

"Won't he? He's capable of going beserk and grabbing Davies by the throat."

"No. He'll realize that any stupid move might harm Anna. He'd sooner shoot himself than let that happen."

"There's still Davies. If he discovers security has been broken he'll be ruthless."

It was Adams' turn to explode, an event totally out of character. "Damn Davies! He's nothing but a military machine. No feeling, no pity—just eyes down and on with the job."

"The type of man that wins wars."

"God damn his war and God damn his type. I can't sit back any longer and let a man like Harvey destroy himself. You've said often enough he cares about others. Then isn't it time someone cared about him?"

There was a brief silence, then a clatter as a pen was thrown on the desk. "Fair enough. Only let's hope you're right and it doesn't make things worse for him."

Adams showed dismay as Moore came round the side of the desk. "I don't want you to do it. I just wanted to talk to you first, that's all."

Ignoring him Moore made for the door. Adams hurried after him. "Ian, wait. You're needed for this operation. If Davies finds out I've broken security it won't matter."

At the door Moore glanced back. "You were right to come. I'll let you know how he takes it."

Before Adams could protest again Moore had disappeared.

Followed by the relieved Sam, Moore approached the bed. "Harvey, I'd like a word with you. It's important."

The sound of the voice he hated brought Harvey's eyes open. As consciousness seeped back into them, he twisted round and recognized the man standing over him. With a curse he switched on his bedside lamp. "Wha' the hell d'you want?"

"I want to talk with you. Mind if I sit down?"

Bruised, black-jowled, ravaged by alcohol, the Yorkshireman's face was a forbidding sight in the lamplight. "I'm off duty, Moore. So piss off out of here."

Moore was hardly aware of the deep breath he took. "I'm not here on service business. I've come to talk about Anna."

The girl's name was like an electric shock to the man, making him start violently, then lift up on his elbows. "You heard from her?"

"No, it's not that."

Harvey cursed again, then sank back. "Then what the hell is it?"

Needing a moment to compose his thoughts Moore dragged up a chair to the bedside. A radio in the billet next door could be heard playing "As Time Goes By." Seeing the dog wagging its tail, Moore reached impulsively down to stroke it. Immediately Harvey's voice leapt at him.

"If you've got something to tell me about Anna, then bloody tell me. Or is this some dirty new game you're playing?"

The intensity of the man, the way the girl's name had sobered him, made Moore wonder if he had been wrong to take Adams' advice. Pushing back his forebodings he straightened in his chair.

"What I'm going to tell you is top secret. If Davies ever finds out I've broken security, we'll all be for the high jump. Worst of all it might put Anna in great danger. So for God's sake don't go haywire, and keep everything you hear to yourself."

From Harvey's reaction there appeared to be only one sentence he understood. "Put her in danger? What do you mean?"

Moore had already decided that the quicker the knife went in the less prolonged the pain. "Frank, Anna isn't the girl we thought she was. She's a German working for British Intelligence."

Harvey's cheeks drained of blood. Sensing his shock, the dog leapt up and tried to lick him. For a moment the Yorkshireman was too stunned to resist. Then he pushed the dog away. "It's a joke, isn't it? A bloody sick joke."

As Moore shook his head, beads of sweat began forming on the man's unshaven face. "Who told you?"

"Davies, the night before she left here. He ordered me to attend her briefing at Tempsford before they flew her back into Europe. That was the reason we left together the next morning."

Harvey let out a muttered "Christ" and dropped back on his pillow.

"She was under the tightest security orders while she was here—that's why she could say so little in the letter she left you. Also, as she knew she was going back to Germany, she felt it was fairer to you if she made a clean break. She knew it would hurt you at first—but what choice did she have?"

Moore saw the Yorkshireman's sunken eyes close. Moved and wanting to inflict no more pain, he knew one last thing had to be said or the pain already inflicted was without purpose. "It hurt her like hell to leave you that way —she broke down twice in the car. As she wasn't a girl to show her feelings, it could mean only one thing. You couldn't be more wrong about the way she felt about you."

A glance showed Harvey to be lying very still. Rising quietly Moore started for the door. He had almost reached it when a curse of protest echoed round the billet.

"For Christ's sake, you can't go now. If she's an agent there must be a connexion between her and the training we've been doing."

Turning, Moore saw the Yorkshireman had swung his feet to the floor and was sitting facing him. "I've told you all you need to know, Frank. The rest doesn't concern you."

"Doesn't concern me! You'd better believe this, Moore —if you don't tell me everything you know, I'll go straight to Davies and get it out of him. Tonight!"

Knowing he had lost, Moore walked heavily back to his chair. "You must have felt the same as me—I couldn't believe she was only a schoolteacher. But I never guessed the truth until Davies told me the night before she left. Most of her background story was true enough—she had spent a number of years in England and she had worked in Bavaria. But her parents were German, not Swiss, and she was born in Munich."

Jumping up, Harvey pulled another bottle of whisky from his locker. As he swilled the spirit into his glass, Moore noticed the violent trembling of his hands. "I don't get it," the Yorkshireman muttered. "If she's a German, why is she working for us?"

The signs of distress that both Henderson and Davies had noted in Moore on his return to the station showed again as he sank back into the chair. "I'd have thought that obvious. She's too intelligent and fair-minded to fall for that damned adage 'My country, right or wrong.' She's fully aware the majority of Germans would see her as a traitor but she feels that's a small price to pay if she and her friends can help to rid Germany of Nazism."

There was the cartilaginous sound of Harvey swallowing.

"You still haven't told me how she's connected with the training we've been doing."

Knowing that all escape routes were now closed, Moore told him about the experiments being conducted inside the valley. "All that can be seen from the air is a railway track disappearing into a dense forest. That's bad enough but a few days ago Davies learned the establishment is built underground."

"Underground? Then how the hell can it be bombed?"

"It seems there might be a way but Davies is keeping that up his sleeve for the moment. He says he hopes to have something definite any time now."

Sidetracked for the moment by the news of the rocket establishment Harvey returned to his original question. "I still don't see where Anna comes in all this." Then he noticed Moore's expression and his breath sucked in. "You're not telling me she's inside the bloody valley?"

Moore found he could not meet his eyes. "None of the men agents could infiltrate the security screen. So she came up with an idea herself."

"What idea?"

Moore felt he had had enough. "Leave it there, Frank. Please."

A hand like a vice gripped his wrist as he attempted to rise. "If none of the men could get inside, then how the hell could she? I want to know."

It was one of the few times in his life that Moore felt panic. "I don't know that, Frank. She didn't tell me."

The grip on his wrist tightened. "You're lying! She went over there to offer herself to one of the bastards, didn't she? If none of the men could get in, it has to be that."

It was Moore's own feelings for the girl that betrayed him. Staring at his expression, Harvey sank slowly back on the bed. "Oh, Christ," he muttered. "Oh, Jesus Christ."

The music next door had started again. A man was singing "All The Things You Are." Still on the bed, the dog tried to scramble on to Harvey's knee. Blind with grief, seeking relief in movement, the Yorkshireman jumped to his feet and walked round the bed. When he turned at last his appearance shocked Moore. His facial lines looked as if they had been slashed with a razor and his eyes were bloodshot with torment.

"Do you know who the bastard is?"

"No. Some executive officer, I suppose."

"How soon can we make the raid?" Harvey's question was full of a terrible hunger.

"That depends on her coming up with the answers Davies wants." The suddenness of Moore's decision surprised himself. "You won't be going. Not now you know she's in there."

"Not going?" Harvey looked horrified. "But I've got to go."

"No," Moore said again. "We can manage without you."

The big man looked panic-stricken. "If it's so important to her, I must go. Surely to Christ you can see that."

Moore could see it as clearly as if he were in the man's mind but it still took him another thirty seconds to reach a decision. "If I let you go, do you promise to play it straight from the book? No emotional gestures or any nonsense like that?"

"I'll play it straight," the Yorkshireman muttered.

"Very well. We'll leave things as they are." Held by the man's appearance Moore hesitated. "Are you going to be all right?"

In Harvey's harsh world a man hid his wounds, knowing the indication of them was all that the predators were waiting for. Muttering something he sank down on the bed and began stroking the relieved dog. "Of course I'm all right."

As Moore nodded and went to the door, Harvey looked up. "This raid's going to be a rough one, isn't it?"

"It depends. It could be."

"Yet you did say you could spare me?"

"Yes. I can use one of our reserve crews."

"Then, as I'm coming along, you could spare someone in my place?"

"What are you getting at?"

"I want you to leave young Marsh behind. Will you do that?"

Moore gazed at him in astonishment. Bloody, his head bowed, he still tried to protect others. It was suddenly very clear to Moore what Anna had seen in this man. "All right. Marsh won't go. Satisfied?"

Harvey's nod was sullen, yet his every word reached

the door. "I appreciate what you've done, Moore. And the chance you've taken. Thanks."

Strangely moved, Moore opened the door and stood on the step outside. "I'd get some sleep if I were you. The green light could come at any time."

This time Harvey nodded without speaking. Moore's last glance showed him bent over the dog as if ashamed of his gratitude.

Moore's last words to Harvey were more prophetic than he knew. Not fifty minutes later Henderson was called by the Duty officer to the red telephone in his office. Davies was on the line and his excitement alone told Henderson the weeks of waiting were over.

"She's done it, Jock. I'll give you all the details later but the big show's on tomorrow. I want your lads briefed and your air-tests completed by 0900 hours. All right?"

Henderson could feel his heart beating rapidly. "Yes, sir. When will you be coming?"

"I've a few things to clear up with the Yanks and then I'll be on my way. Should arrive before midnight with luck." Davies' enthusiasm came over the line as if he were in the office himself. "Thank Christ we've got word at last. I was getting scared they'd got on to Anna and arrested her. You'll be getting your operational details through the usual channels. See you later."

In fact the teletype in the Operations Room was already clacking. Fetched by the Duty Sergeant, Adams began taking down the details while S.P.s stood guard at the door and windows. The Duty officer, making certain outside communications were cut, began to alert ground-crew N.C.O.s. At the same time all available S.P.s were driven at high speed to Highgate and adjacent villages where they rounded up indignant airmen and officers and shepherded them into waiting transports. The scene of intense activity at Sutton Craddock on their arrival convinced the most phlegmatic of them that something big was afoot. They were soon to learn how big that something was.

30

The only men at Sutton Craddock who slept that night
were the aircrews, and with the excited speculation at
what the morrow might bring added to the activity around
them, their sleep was only fitful. They were called at
0500 hours, given breakfast half an hour later, and at
0627 the station tannoy ordered them into the Operations Room. There, on the platform beneath the huge
map of Europe, Davies, Henderson, Moore, and the rest
of the briefing officers were waiting for them.

Only Moore, who was to fly with the squadron, had enjoyed more than two hours' sleep. The rest had been
kept busy by Henderson and the dynamic Davies as they
made certain the squadron was in one hundred per cent
state of readiness. In fact, as far as the aircraft were
concerned they had only to be air-tested and bombed up
and they would be fully operational.

The state of the crews was less desirable. Caught by surprise at the speed of the emergency, allowed only a
few hours' sleep to counter the effects of the previous
night's beer, the rows of young men looked bleary and
bewildered as they stared at the large cloth-covered
mound that stood on a table in the centre of the platform. As Davies and the other officers conferred behind
the table, the men's nervous eyes pulled away and wandered round the slogan-covered walls of the room. Whispers sounded, nervous laughs broke out, and matches
scratched. Cigarette smoke, drifting into a misty layer
beneath the ceiling, made the dangling models of German aircraft look as if they were flying through high-
level cloud.

The group on the platform ended their conference and
after a brief introductory comment from Henderson,
Davies stepped forward. Murmurs died away and tension caught at the throat as his ferret-sharp eyes travelled along the rows of expectant faces. His high-pitched

voice, trying to ease the tension, ironically only drew it tighter.

"You chaps are not exactly Strength-through-Joy boys in the morning, are you? I've never seen so many dogs' dinners at one sitting. Never mind. In a couple of minutes I'll guarantee to have you as wide awake as if I'd dumped you into a tub of cold water."

On this highly expectant note Davies walked back to the table and laid his hand on the cloth that covered the large mound. "Before this briefing's over you're all going to have the chance to take a closer look at this thing. But first I'm going to explain what it's all about."

With that he jerked off the cloth. Leaning forward in anticipation, the crews saw a large, papiermâché model of the Ruhpolding valley. Their blank stares were shared by Young and Harvey, sitting in their isolated chairs on the other side of the aisle. Leaning towards Harvey, the Australian muttered a question. Harvey, whose face showed the ravages of a sleepless night, shook his head curtly.

Davies moved behind the scale model and picked up a pointer. "This is the valley you're going to. Your target is somewhere in a dense forest along its floor. I'm not allowed to tell you what Jerry's making there, but I can say that they are devices that could make our invasion hellishly costly or even impossible. So it's an establishment we must destroy and we shall destroy it. But there are snags."

He paused so that his young audience could assimilate his words. Their faces were a study of their characters. Some looked pale and tensed. Some looked excited. In the second row of chairs, for all the world like a mischievous schoolboy being given details of a day's outing, Gabby was whispering something to Millburn, who grinned broadly. Further along the same row the Byronic features of St. Claire were calmly attentive. Sue Spencer, sitting at the large table alongside Adams and the only member on the platform unbriefed about the raid, had her eyes on the young pianist. One of her slim hands, holding a pencil, was doodling on a piece of paper as if it had a life of its own.

"Snag Number One is the distance," Davies went on. "You've been nearly as far before—I've seen to that

—but not in daylight, and for reasons I'll explain in a moment, that's when the job must be done. The establishment is in a Bavarian valley south-east of Munich."

There was a loud buzz of consternation. A voice called out: "Christ, that's impossible!" Used to demonstrations of shock, Davies used the shout to advantage.

"Someone's surprised? You shouldn't be. You're an élite squadron with a record no other unit in the RAF can match. So what's so surprising about a daylight raid into Bavaria? You should be glad I'm not sending you to Tokyo."

A ripple of nervous laughter ran through the general alarm. "Snag Number Two," Davies said. "The target's underground. Snag Number Three adds insult to injury. The target's somewhere in this bloody great forest. A railway track runs to it but Jerry's been clever as always—the firs grow tall in this part of the world and so he's only lopped off the lower branches. Add camouflage to that and it means you can't see the track from the air."

In their bewilderment men began to forget discipline. Loud murmurs of protest and even a muted cat-call could be heard. A born actor, Davies allowed the hubbub to run on for a full ten seconds before walking to the front of the platform and holding up his hand. His grin was wicked.

"I said I'd wake you up, didn't I? Now you're awake, let's see how we can get round these snags. Number One first. We all know that if you fly that deep into Germany in daylight, Jerry will have half his Air Force waiting for you. But what if you fly on the backs of a hundred and fifty American B.17s going out to bomb Jerry's Me.109 factory at Regensburg? Jerry will throw everything at the B.17s, who'll be screening you from his detectors, and you'll have a cushy ride nearly all the way to your target." At the stares of amazement he was receiving Davies grinned again. "That's how it's going to be. The Yanks are going out at 29,000 feet and you're going to ride 'em piggy back at your maximum ceiling. They'll drop their bombs on Regensburg and keep going straight on to North Africa. When they reach Munich you'll peel off and with any luck at all, you'll have a free dive down to the target."

The muttering among the crews died down as the feasibility of the scheme sank in. "It'll work," Davies assured them. "The Yank daylight raids have been hurting Jerry and a hundred and fifty heavies penetrating into Bavaria will cause a hell of a reaction. All right, snag Number Two. This has been our biggest headache. We've known for some time that a tanker train containing thousands of gallons of highly-explosive fuel arrives every nine or so days and discharges into underground tanks. What we haven't known is when the next tanker is due. Last night we heard it should reach the establishment at 1300 hours today and will start discharging fuel fifteen minutes later. The job takes about ninety minutes. Our boffins calculate that for maximum effect we want fifty per cent of the fuel left in the tanker and fifty per cent in the underground tanks when we clobber the train. After that it doesn't take much imagination to realize what will happen. The burning fuel will pour down, the underground tanks will explode, and up goes Jerry, establishment, and all. Nasty but necessary if we're to win this war and get back to our families again."

The attention of his audience was now fully held. As a few faces, St. Claire's prominent among them, winced at the method of destruction Davies allowed no time for reflection.

"That leads us to snag Number Three—how do we find the tanker in the first place? The answer there is that some very brave people in Germany have got an agent inside the valley and that agent will indicate to you the position of the train when you arrive. With everything happening in a hurry because of the train's arrival today they haven't been able to work out yet what the signal will be but we're assured we'll get one."

From the platform Moore was watching Harvey. Until this moment the Yorkshireman's face had shown little expression as if the long night had burned his emotion to ash. But as Davies spoke of the lone agent in the valley the tell-tale muscle in his cheek began contracting.

"From all this you'll realize timing is vital," Davies went on. "You'll strike the tanker at 1400 hours precisely and the entire operation, Yanks and all, is scheduled around that time. You'll top up your tanks at Manston and wait for the Yanks to formate over Dungeness. After they've had a good start you'll follow and climb up on their backs. Both of you must be at your maximum operational height before you reach Mons. You have an escort as far as our fighters' extreme range—after that you'll be on your own.

"As for diversions, 12 Group will be on the offensive in the Netherlands and 11 Group will be on a similar sweep in Central France. One way and another"—Davies' grin moved along the row of faces—"you're being mollycoddled all the way. That's the general picture. Any questions before I pass you over to your specialist officers?"

To Adams the Operations Room felt cold that morning. Davies had a knack of making the most hazardous operation sound routine, but Adams knew there was no guarantee the enemy controllers would not guess the Mosquitoes' target when they broke away from the B.17s. Even if they did not, the marauding German fighters would be on them like wolves if they wasted any time over the target. The sight of Teddy Young rising to his feet interrupted Adams' forebodings.

"What are your contingency plans if this agent doesn't get his message up to us, sir? I take it this could happen?"

Young did not notice the black look Harvey gave him. Forced into an admission he did not want to make, Davies displayed irritability. "If you don't get a signal your leader will use his initiative. You'll get full details of the alternatives in a minute, but, briefly, one method is to try to estimate the line of the railway track and each kite to plant bombs along it until the tanker's reached. The other way is to pattern-bomb the area. Operational conditions would decide which method to use. But we're feeling confident neither will be necessary."

Young opened his mouth again, then changed his mind and sat down. Adams read his thoughts as if they had been expressed. If they had to spend time looking for the target, the hostile fighters must reach them. Across the room MacDougall lifted a hand.

"Won't the Germans shunt the train away from the target the moment they get warning of us, sir?"

This time Davies was more at ease. "They can't. We've established they're using steam locomotives. So any attempt to move the tanker would immediately give its position away."

A question came from Ross, an ex-Edinburgh student.

"The underground tanks won't have access to oxygen, sir. So how can you be sure they'll explode?"

Davies conceded the shrewdness of the question. "The answer is it's a fuel that contains its own oxygen content." Aware it was a give-away reply to anyone who was technically-minded, Davies moved on swiftly. "All right. I'm now going to pass you over to your specialist officers. Then you can take a look at this model and the photographs we've got."

If any man among the crews remained unconvinced of the importance of the mission, the detailed briefing that followed put an end to his doubts. It was ninety minutes before the men returned to their seats and Moore spoke to them for the first time. Although sharing Harvey's concern for Anna, he gave the appearance of being relaxed and confident.

"We are using our full operational strength of sixteen Mosquitoes. Going out we shall fly in sections of three, line abreast. As we're hoping to go unnoticed above the B.17s we shall keep radio silence all the way. When I break it over the target, don't talk unless you've something worth saying. I don't want the channel cluttered up with comics, so all those with guilty consciences take note." As Moore's eyes rested on the hurt Gabby, rows of tensed faces began grinning. "Study your charts carefully. I want all navigators to keep individual logs so they can get home alone if necessary. In other words don't think this is a doddle and all you have to do is follow the Yanks to Munich."

"You think there'll be any left by that time, skipper?" The mordant quip came from Stan Baldwin.

"Let's hope for our sakes there are," Moore said dryly. "Once we break from them at Munich we'll fly in line astern until we reach Ruhpolding. In case anyone should fall asleep and come adrift, your marker is a bloody great castle on an island in the Chiemsee. Ludwig II, the mad king of Bavaria, built it and it's a near replica of Versailles. So when you see it don't think you've gone mad or the Yank navigators have ballsed things up and taken you back to Paris. We enter the valley at the Ruhpolding end and follow the railway until it disappears into the forest. At this point, if all goes well we'll get our indication where the tanker is. The first kites will make their attack, the rest will orbit and give cover in the usual way. With any luck we'll have the job done and be away before Jerry can get his trousers up!"

"Supposing we don't get our signal, skipper." It was Young again, still worried about the problem of location. "It seems a hell of a big forest. How can we be sure which way the railway runs?"

Moore's honesty brought a scowl from Davies. "I suppose the answer to that, Teddy, is that we can't. We'd have to play it as it came. If we'd used up all our bombs and still hadn't clobbered the train, we could still try cannon fire, so we'd have quite a few bites at the cherry. But this is looking on the black side. The chances are the first wave will blow the thing sky high and the rest of you will be stuck for a target."

The thought of Mosquitoes strafing a tanker loaded with explosive fuel at tree-top height made Adams turn pale. Moore gave the crews no time for such speculation.

"My guess is that the hardest part of the operation will be in one sense the easiest. I don't need to tell any of you that Jerry's air defences have made a big comeback recently and their tails are right up. So it's a safe bet the Yanks are going to get a hell of a clobbering and it's not going to be much fun for us riding on their backs and watching it. However"—and Moore was gazing straight at Millburn—"it's imperative we conserve ourselves and our ammunition for the job in hand. So no gallant gestures. The Yanks won't hold it against you—they've been told what to expect."

Heads nodded dubiously, Millburn's among them. "The squadron call sign will be Longbow and the station call sign Harry. When you hear me transmit Crispin you'll know you'll be drinking champagne tonight. Any more questions?"

When none came Davies returned to the front of the platform. Solemn after his earlier enthusiasm, he brought a hush to the room.

"I've this last thing to emphasize. If these new weapons come into production they won't just affect the grand strategy of our combined Air Forces, they could delay the invasion itself. The cost of that in human lives and misery doesn't bear thinking about. Also some very brave people, among them the Americans who are setting themselves up as decoys, are taking some frightening risks for us. So I know you'll all do your best. Now off you go and get your kites air-tested. Take off time is 1045 prompt."

The tap on his billet door made Adams turn. With the briefing over he had slipped back to rummage for a letter he wanted to answer that day. As he straightened he saw the tall figure of Harvey standing in the doorway. The Yorkshireman was wearing flying overalls and had an oxygen mask and earphones slung over one shoulder.

"Sue Spencer said I'd find you here," he muttered. "You got a minute to spare?"

"Of course. Come in."

Turning his head, Harvey whistled. A moment later Sam appeared and gazed up at him expectantly. Without preamble Harvey led the dog into the billet.

"I want someone to leave Sam with. Will you take him on? You seem to like dogs and he seems to get on well with you."

Adams gave a start. "Then you're not taking him with you today?"

The man's laugh was hard and humourless. "All that way? What would the poor sod do for a lamp post?" Bending down he cuffed the dog's head. Reacting immediately, Sam leapt up against him. Ashamed of the demonstration of affection, Harvey pushed the animal back. "Sit down! Stay!"

Wagging its tail, the dog sat back on its haunches. The Yorkshireman turned his grim face towards Adams. "Well, will you have him? You'll find he does as he's told."

Adams, who had drawn closer to read the man's expression, pulled himself together. "Of course. I'll be glad to look after him until you get back."

Harvey showed resentment. "You wouldn't take him for longer?"

"If it were necessary, yes. But it won't be. You'll want him yourself again this evening."

Harvey relaxed. "Fair enough. Thanks. We're taking off soon so I'll leave him here. O.K.?"

"Yes. I'll shut him in when I go to the Control Tower."

Nodding his appreciation, Harvey moved towards the door. The dog, eyes full of worship, gave a sudden anxious bark. As the Yorkshireman turned, his expression betrayed him. "Shut up, you stupid old bugger. Behave yourself."

The dog barked again. Moved by the scene, Adams forgot the rules and took a step forward. "You feeling all right, Frank? You will be back for a drink in the Mess tonight?"

The man's expression changed. "What the hell are you talking about? I'm just taking precautions, that's all. Of course I'll be back."

Without another word he turned and closed the door behind him. Jumping to its feet the dog ran forward and began scratching the woodwork. Adams took a precious bar of chocolate from his locker, broke off a couple of pieces, and held them out in his hand. Although well known for his love of chocolate, Sam ignored the offer and continued to scratch at the door.

31

At 36,000 feet the vast dome of sky was a pitiless blue and the sun blinding even through the smoked goggles Moore was wearing. Behind him, in five ranks of three aircraft apiece, the Mosquitoes were like a troop of horsemen. Painted PR blue for the occasion, with the brilliant sunlight giving a halo to their spinning propellers, they yawed gently in the rarefied air. With the crews airborne long enough for the roar of engines to have faded into a neutral background, the sensation was one of almost disembodied detachment. In this bright beautiful world of the stratosphere, war was nothing more than an obscene thought in the mind.

Until a man gazed down and saw the massive armada of war 7,000 feet below that was heading relentlessly towards the heart of Germany. With each one of the 146 giant bombers emitting condensation trails from its wingtips, the effect was that of enormous rockets pouring out gas as they streaked through the sky. The great trails linked together and formed a wash that spread back into the windless stratosphere as far as the eye could reach.

An English voice on a low signal strength drew Moore's attention. "Sorry but that's as far as we can go, Oklahoma Leader. We'll buy you tea and muffins when you get back. Good luck. Out."

A humorous voice with an American drawl followed. "We can't wait for those muffins, Turpin Leader. Thanks for your help."

Moore and Hopkinson exchanged glances. The German monitoring service, picking up the heavy activity over the American airfields, would have guessed from the B.17s' assembly point at Dungeness that the operation was aimed at central or southern Europe. Fighter groups would have been moved to airfields west of Reims and those same fighters would certainly be airborne and in visual contact by this time. Their brief was to wait until the Allied fighter escort reached the limit of its range and then

hurl their unimpaired strength against the unprotected
bombers. The ground below was hidden by a thin film
of mist but the news the escort was turning back gave
a general indication of the armada's position. Within minutes it would be crossing the German frontier.

Pouring out their tell-tale wake, the Fortresses droned
on while their crews peered out into the dazzling, deadly sky. Flak, which had followed them right across Belgium and France, grew fiercer as they turned south in
a dog-leg. As predictors got their range and ugly black
mushrooms burst into the heart of the formation, a
Fortress was hit in its inner port engine. Yawing clumsily,
it began to sideslip, then to gyrate as the port wing
broke up. The white puffs of two parachutes appeared
but before more could follow there was a vivid flash
and an eruption of oily smoke. Fragments flew in all directions and the fuselage, a metal coffin for the eight
men still strapped inside, plummeted down and disappeared
into the veil of cloud. Above, the armada closed its
ranks and droned on.

Inside the huge planes gunners were either standing or
crouched behind their heavy-calibre Brownings. With each
Fortress carrying thirteen machine guns the concentration of fire directed on an enemy aircraft attacking from
the rear or even below could be devastating. The weakness, as the Americans knew too tell, was up front.
Still not modified with a two-gun "chin" turret, the
Fortresses were vulnerable to a head-on attack. This
weakness had been discovered by the Focke Wulfs of
11/JGI earlier that summer and they were the first to
attack the armada just as it crossed the German frontier.
A highly-experienced unit, they came straight at the Americans like a pack of wolves attacking a stampede of bison.
Sweeping down from head-on and above, they opened
fire with cannon at 800 yards. Guns firing until the last
split-second before collision, they dived beneath the formation and swung violently away to avoid the fire from the
bombers' ventral and side gun positions. Then, while the
second wave made its attack, the first wave climbed back
into position for a repeat performance.

The result of the first attack was instantaneous. One of
the leading Fortresses took a burst of cannon fire full in
the forward cockpit. The effect on flesh and bone was
indescribable. With its controls locked by the explosions

the bomber did not fall at once but like a blinded animal reeled from the main pack and began a bizarre course of its own. With the side and rear gunners unaware of the carnage up front, they continued to defend the doomed plane against the triumphant wolves that came snarling after it. One gun after the other ceased firing: then the entire massive structure lurched, turned over, and disappeared into the haze below.

The entire sky became threaded with cannon and machine-gun tracer as the ferocious battle continued. With their homeland threatened by the armada and the hideous carnage of Hamburg still fresh in their minds, the German fighter pilots displayed the same desperate courage as their British counterparts of three years earlier. Some Focke Wulfs, ignoring the massive fire-power of the Fortresses, plunged straight into the formation, spraying cannon fire in all directions as they dived. One, hit by at least fifty heavy machine guns, literally disintegrated in mid-air. Another crumpled like a shot pheasant and dropped as lifelessly. Yet another collided with a Fortress and the two planes, welded together, fell in a welter of flame and oily smoke. The radio channel, on which the Mosquitoes above were tuned, was filled with the sounds of battle.

"Bandit, Tex! Three o'clock high!"

"Close up, you guys. Keep formation."

"I got the bastard! See that, Stan? I got the bastard!"

The minutes of fury seemed endless to the B.17s' gunners. When at last the Focke Wulfs' ammunition ran out and they had to withdraw, some of the younger hands believed a victory had been won. The older hands dragged out new ammunition boxes, reloaded, shifted their gum from one cheek to the other, and waited.

They did not have to wait long. Two more fighter *gruppen* were already hurling themselves towards the armada. Others, Hans Klaus's night-fighter unit among them, were lined up on airfields waiting for their turn to attack. Aware the Americans would not be making such a deep penetration unless they had a target of high importance, the Germans had called up their night-fighter units to augment their defences, a build-up of strength that was massive and intimidating.

One of the two *gruppen* about to attack the armada was another of these night-fighter units. Equipped with

110s, its crews made up in courage what they lacked
in daylight training. The other unit was an experienced
squadron of 109s. Both units carried 21cm. rockets on
their wings and as the first wave swept in they released the rockets at 900 yards. Two Fortresses were
hit. One kept going with smoke pluming from an engine.
The other had a wing shorn clean off and its asym-
metrical remains went spinning earthwards.

Seven thousand feet above the running battle, the Mosquito crews were reacting according to their tempera-
ments. While every man wanted to go to the help of the
Americans, some had enough phlegm to accept the situation. Others, Harvey, Moore, St. Claire, and Baldwin among
them, found their passive role painful to a degree. In
T-Tommy, Gabby was eyeing Millburn with concern.
With his forehead above his oxygen mask furrowed and
beaded with sweat, the American was clearly in torment
as he watched the trial by fire of his fellow countrymen.
Noticing Gabby's glance, he stiffened and reacted bellig-
erently.

"What the hell are you afraid of? That I might give
the poor bastards a hand?"

It was one moment in his life when Gabby knew that
silence was golden. The American glared at him, then
indicated the chart strapped to the Welshman's thigh.
"How much further, for Christ's sake?"

Gabby decided it was unwise to tell him the truth. "Not
much further." In an effort to take the American's mind
off his equivocal answer, he pointed at an Me.109 that
was plunging earthwards trailing smoke. "Anyway, your lot
are giving as good as they get."

"You expect anything else?" Millburn muttered, gazing
down again.

It was an unfortunate moment to choose. A B.17 had
just received a direct hit from a 21cm. rocket and the
mutilated body of a gunner could be seen dropping out
of the ruptured fuselage. The curse that broke from Millburn was bitter and unprintable.

Beside its usual complement, the Operations Room
contained two extra officers that afternoon. One was the
Brigadier, a dignified if somewhat pale figure sitting beside Henderson and Adams at the large table. The other
man was the Texan, General Staines. He had telephoned

Davies the previous night to say he would like to be at Sutton Craddock during the operation, and when Davies had expressed surprise as well as pleasure, the American had made the wry comment that as he had accepted the pigeon he might as well see it home to roost. It was a comment of such ambiguity that Davies had felt unable to pursue it further. The Texan's one request was that a telephone should be connected directly to his USAAF Headquarters, and Marsden had set this up during the night. The benefits were now evident. 633 Squadron were still bound by radio silence but now the Americans were under attack it was expected of them to report successes and losses to their headquarters. Reports were coming in almost by the minute and these were being passed on by Staines to the grateful Brigadier and Davies.

An unlit cigar in his mouth, the Texan had the receiver clamped to his ear. Davies was pacing restlessly beneath the huge map of Europe. As he heard a metallic crackling in Staines's earpiece he halted. Half a minute later the American turned to the motionless Brigadier.

"They've reached Wiesbaden. Losses—eight so far and six damaged. The Krauts are throwing everything at them."

Catching the Brigadier's glance, Davies opened his mouth, then discovered he had nothing to say. Adams, the most imaginative man in the room, was mentally counting the losses in human terms. Eighty young men lost already and that did not include the casualties on the damaged B.17s. His eyes moved to the large clock above the map. At least another forty minutes to ETA. He could see the massive Fortresses rising and falling in the afternoon sky, the attacking fighters with their lethal cannon and rockets, the agonized cries of wounded men, the flames that swept into choking lungs, and the silence of the room seemed to mock him. Once again Adams hated the age and infirmity that had relegated him to a role in which he felt so ashamedly safe.

The painful, loss-filled minutes dragged by. Behind the table Davies had resumed his restless pacing. The occasional glance Staines gave him indicated that the Texan was not as free from strain as his extrovert appearance suggested. Down the room the earphones of the Signals corporal who was waiting for the first message from

Moore remained silent. It was Staines, expressing a pride
that Davies understood well, who gave the news that the
armada had reached its target.

"Regensburg–Prufening! You hear that? They've broken
through!"

Davies gave a little skip of relief, then remembered himself. "Well done. That means our boys won't be idle
much longer."

The Texan waved him silent as he listened. "The
Krauts are pouring it in but we're hitting the target O.K.
Your guys are going on to Munich with the first wave."

Reports of the air battle raging over Regensburg were
now coming in thick and fast and Staines's tough face
seemed to grow older by the minute as he listened to his
B.17 losses. "Sonofabitch, this is costing something," he
muttered. At 1337 he glanced at Davies. "Your guys
have broken off contact. So they can't be far from the
valley."

With the photographs of the district etched in his mind,
Adams was instantly there. Dry-mouthed navigators trying to identify the valley as the blue Chiemsee swept
towards them. The lake shivering in the air-blast of thirty-
two propellers. The island ahead with its columns of trees,
statues, and bizarre halls of Versailles. Brief glimpses
of terraces and flowerbeds, then belly down on the lake
again with spray hissing on red-hot engines. Over the
autobahn and on towards the great semi-circles of mountains that lay between Bavaria and the Austrian Alps.
. . . Adams' graphic vision was shattered as the sudden
blip of Morse sounded down the room. Moving as fast as
a man half his age, Davies jumped down from the platform and ran towards the corporal who was scribbling
the message on a pad. Davies scanned the signal, then
read it jubilantly aloud.

"Longbow leader to Harry. Valley identified. Stand by."

Red spots glowing in his cheeks, Davies turned back to
the corporal. "Harry to Longbow leader. Have you a contract with Lorenz? Over."

Over three minutes passed before the Morse blips came
again. As Davies bent eagerly down, Adams saw his expression change. Henderson rose sharply to his feet.
"What is it, sir?"

Looking frail and anxious, the elderly Brigadier moved
up alongside Davies. Turning as if his small body had

become arthritic, Davies tore off the top sheet of the pad and offered it to him. As the soldier gave a start, Staines frowned and removed an unlit cigar from his mouth. "What's the problem? You two lost your tongues?"

Forgetting both courtesy and rank in the stress of the moment, Davies conferred urgently with the Brigadier. As the soldier nodded, Davies scribbled on the pad and thrust it at the corporal. "Send this! And make certain they receive it."

As the tap of the Morse key began again, he walked towards Staines and laid Moore's message in front of him. When the American gave a curse of dismay, Davies walked back to the Signals bench. As he and the Brigadier stood waiting for news, their appearance made Adams think of two men who had gambled their all on a throw of the dice and the throw had failed.

32

Hopkinson's sharp eyes were busy identifying the prominent features of the small Bavarian village as it swept towards him. The river, the Byzantine-style church steeple on the right, the railway station, the Steinberg Alps ahead. . . . "Ruhpolding, skipper! Bang on the button."

Moore nodded. Two valleys lay ahead and he was already banking A-Apple towards the narrower. Flying in tight line-astern formation the string of Mosquitoes curved and followed him. The village swept past and a few seconds later the sunlit plain gave way to high mountains that closed in on either side. A road and single-track railway followed a stream that wound through isolated hill farms and grassy meadows. Ahead the bearded chin of a mountain split the valley into two branches. A wooded spur half-blocked the entrance to the eastern branch. The stream and road ran on into the western branch which was wider. The rail track parted company and looped round the foot of the spur to enter the eastern valley.

Nodding at Hopkinson, Moore followed the railway. Dense firs flowed beneath him, then he was over the spur and into the valley. His first glimpse of it confirmed all Davies' deductions. Seven or eight miles long, flanked by high mountains and with an even higher mountain sealing its far end, it could only be entered from its northern entrance by highly-manoeuvrable aircraft flying at low level. Once the target was located every Mosquito would have to circle back to Ruhpolding before launching its attack.

Moore switched on his R/T. "Longbow leader. Orbit the valley and stand by. Keep watch for bandits. Red Section Leader, follow me into the valley."

Conscious his time in the valley was governed by his speed, Moore throttled back. Harvey, summoned up by his call, was swinging into position alongside him. Both men had their eyes on the single track rail that had now straightened out and was running along the floor of the valley. Afternoon sunlight, filtered by the thin mist above, glinted dully on the massive steel gates that lay across it. Two tiny uniformed figures could be seen running into the massive blockhouse that stood close by. The shape of the security fence could be traced by the scars that ran along the lower slopes of the wooded mountains. The sheer size of the cordoned-off area and its impression of brutal efficiency added a nightmarish quality to Harvey's fears for the girl.

Moore's voice crackled in his earphones. "You see anything?"

"Not yet," Harvey muttered.

Scattered haphazardly among dense trees were a few small farms and handkerchief-sized meadows. Alpine-yellow in the sunlight, hay was already stooked for the winter feed. Here and there were foresters' huts and the thread of paths and fire breaks. Otherwise the valley was a dense forest of trees, sweeping down from the mountains and covering the ground in a vast, bottle-green carpet.

To gain a better view the two Mosquitoes climbed another four hundred feet. Below them the railway had already disappeared into the trees. Searching for unspecified instructions, Harvey was unsure whether he wanted those instructions or not. They would be evidence Anna was still free but their implementation might put her in mortal danger.

He glanced at Blackburn, who shook his head. "Sorry, skipper, but I can't see anything either."

The huge mountain at the end of the valley, with a boss of naked rock at its summit, was sweeping perilously closer. The carpet of forest, reaching in all directions, was ominously still. Harvey's guess was the Germans were playing it canny to make certain first that the valley was the Mosquitoes' target. With an establishment of such importance hidden there, heavy defences must be present to guard it.

Like Harvey, Moore was growing increasingly anxious. Apart from concern for Anna, which he shared with the Yorkshireman, he realized that her role in the operation was more important then perhaps anyone had believed. Commonsense dictated that the Germans would not have continued the rail track in a straight line once it disappeared into the forest. The rocket establishment could be anywhere beneath the green quilt, perhaps even in the shadow of the bald-topped mountain itself.

A few more seconds and that same mountain was a threat the Mosquitoes could not ignore. With a word to Harvey, Moore banked steeply and began climbing up to the orbiting squadron. His decision was made. With only minutes left before enemy fighters reached them he could afford no more time waiting for Anna's instructions. However remote, there was the possibility the rocket establishment was within a mile or so of the forest fringe and the possibility had to be catered for. "Longbow leader to Zero Two, Three, Four, and Five. Adopt Scheme A. In you go!"

The four Mosquitoes named peeled away and dived towards Ruhpolding. As he waited for them to return through the mountains Moore shared his attention between the valley and the sky above. The thin layer of mist worried him. Fighters could assemble behind it and attack with the minimum of warning.

Circling with him Harvey had settled his own private dilemma. If no message came from Anna the chances were high her role had been discovered, and the thought of her, a German, in the hands of the Gestapo made the Yorkshireman's hands sweat. A signal would at least mean she was free. But although Harvey was now scanning the valley with binoculars he could see nothing that remotely suggested a signal.

The first of the four Mosquitoes Moore had dispatched was now winging back through the mountains. Flown by Teddy Young it leapt the spur and made for the visible end of the rail track. The sight of its open bomb doors was what the hidden German gunners had been waiting for. Half a dozen prongs of tracer lunged at the plane as it rocketed past the steel gates. Young, who was holding the release button himself, pressed it a couple of seconds later. The automatic selector released his full complement of eight bombs at one second intervals. Delay-fused, they began exploding along a half mile stretch of forest as the Australian came corkscrewing out of the valley. Trees were flung upwards and fire blazed around the points of impact, but from the height Moore and Harvey were flying the forest looked as dense and invulnerable as ever.

Zero Three followed twenty seconds later. It had the

ad luck to cross the mountain spur three hundred feet igher than Young where a 20mm. crew were crouching. As the Mosquito swept past a fork of tracer raked it rom nose to tail. Turning over like a gaffed fish it somer-aulted among the trees in a tangle of wreckage. Seeing he danger Moore dived down on the spur. The Mos-quito could not drop bombs in a twenty-degree plus dive, out it could strafe with its cannon and Brownings. Crouched behind the nest of rocks, intent on spearing the next plane that swept past them, the gun crew were late in seeing the threat from above and before they could swing their gun-mounting round, Moore opened fire. The hose of shells severed branches from trees and hurled the men aside like broken puppets. Giving the sweating Hopkinson a word of reassurance he did not feel himself, Moore climbed back into orbit.

Zero Four crossed the spur safely and jinked towards the fires ahead. Now that the Mosquitoes had declared their intention, flak posts were springing up like dragons' teeth on every side of the valley. Jinking to evade the blizzard of fire, the Mosquito laid its stick of bombs ten degrees east of the line laid down by Young. All eight bombs burst as it climbed from the valley but the limited size of the explosions made it obvious the train had not been hit.

By the time Zero Five made its strike tracer was rising in sheets from the valley floor. Rolling in the dense ex-plosions it laid its bombs ten degrees west and clawed for the safety of height. From above, the pattern of the bombing was a Y branded on the fringe of the forest. Catching Moore's eye, Hoppy gave a grimace. "It's hope-less, skipper. We'd need a thousand kites to find it. And now they know what we're doing they'll shoot us down like bloody ducks."

Moore knew he was right. Had the tanker been located, the losses incurred in its destruction could be justified. As things were the cost would be senseless. "Get base on again," he told Hopkinson. "Tell them we've been in the valley nearly three minutes and there's still no signal from Lorenz. We've tried Scheme A but the flak is heavy. Ask permission to operate Scheme B."

The answer that caused Davies so much heartbreak came thirty seconds later. Formating the squadron in sections of three, Moore led them back along the valley. With

the need for pinpoint accuracy gone, they flew a couple
of hundred feet above the surrounding mountains. Guessing their intent the gunners below fired as fast as their
loaders could feed the guns. K-Kenny received a direct
hit just as Moore gave the order to jettison bombs. As
the sticks of bombs fell in an extensive pattern and disappeared among the trees, K-Kenny turned in an instant from a bird of grace and power into a miscellany
of wings and broken spars falling out of a ball of
smoke.

Moore was holding his breath and counting as he led the
Mosquitoes to safety over the western mountains. As he
dipped a wing, the bombs began exploding in rapid succession among the trees. The air-blast made the Mosquitoes rock like canoes in rough water. Waiting in case
the train exploded, Moore swept along the valley rim.
Although columns of black smoke were rising and drifting together, the fires, smothered by the dense trees,
looked as innocuous as a hundred burning cigarettes
scattered over a lawn. Hiding his feelings from Hopkinson, Moore lifted his face mask. "Longbow leader.
That's all we can do. Let's go home."

He had barely finished speaking when a lone Mosquito dived past him. Certain that Anna had been killed
or captured Harvey had no intention of leaving the valley until the cause of her sacrifice was found. Afraid for
his safety Moore banked after him. "Harvey! You're dis-
obeying orders. Get back into formation!"

He expected no answer nor did he receive one for a
full six seconds. Then Harvey's eager shout made him
start. "Moore! Something's happening down here. Come
and take a look."

Ordering Young to keep watch, Moore dived into the
flak after the Yorkshireman. He saw D-Danny three thousand feet below, banking steeply towards one of the handkerchief-sized Alpine meadows. With two columns of
smoke rising from the meadow Moore thought for a moment that two bombs had fallen on it. Then Hopkinson, who was gazing through binoculars at the field, turned
his sharp face towards him.

"They're hay stacks, skipper. Someone's set them alight."

The throttles of A-Apple nearly went through the gate
as Moore rammed them forward. As the meadow grew
larger in the windscreen he saw that two stooks of hay

were pouring off black smoke. A shadow swept across
the ground as at zero height Harvey flew over the meadow
and waggled his wings violently. As the Yorkshireman
swept away Moore saw a tiny figure crouched beside a
stook of hay wave back. Hopkinson, staring through the
binoculars, saw something else. "Soldiers, skipper! Coming out of the woods on the other side!"

Moore switched on his fire-and-safe button. The party
of soldiers, six in all, had now run out into the meadow.
Urged by an N.C.O. they dropped down and took aim
at the girl fifty yards from them. As she tried to find
cover Moore opened fire. His first burst, fired at extreme
range, served only to draw the soldiers' attention. His
second burst, fired from less than two hundred yards,
caught them as they were running back towards the trees.
Like blades of grass beneath a reaper's scythe they were
flung in all directions. Keeping his thumb on the button
until the last moment Moore drew back the stick and
went rocketing up the wooded mountainside.

Across the valley Harvey had banked steeply to return
to the field and was in time to see Moore's devastating
attack on the soldiers. As he came raging back he saw
the girl wave her acknowledgment to Moore and run
across to a fourth stook of hay. Three were now burning and as Harvey skimmed the field smoke began pouring from the fourth. For a moment, in spite of Blackburn's imploring glance, it seemed Harvey would attempt
to land on the tiny field. Then, as the girl waved her arms
frantically and pointed towards the woods, he abandoned
the suicidal idea and headed across the valley.

In A-Apple Hopkinson was jabbing an excited finger
downwards. "It's the French Resistance trick, skipper.
Giving us a bearing."

Moore saw he was right. The four fires, set in converging
lines, were aiming at an imaginary point deep in the
forest. Debating whether to bring the squadron back into
the valley, Moore decided there was time for that if his
own attack failed. Giving Young instructions to keep the
squadron out of flak range unless he was shot down,
Moore turned to Hopkinson. "Have you got a fix?" When
the Cockney nodded Moore put A-Apple's nose down.

Below, the track of Harvey's Mosquito could be traced
by the brightly-coloured pins of tracer that were trying
to spear it. Aware their attackers were on the scent at

last, the enemy gun crews were throwing everything at D-Danny. Black-faced and tormented, Harvey was driving the plane through the torrent of fire as if by will-power alone. Blackburn, helpless in his role of navigator, could do nothing but cling to his seat and pray. A deafening explosion almost turned the Mosquito over; a 37mm. shell tore a gaping hole in its starboard wing. Yet ironically it was a light machine gun which neither man saw that did the most damage. Opening up as D-Danny swept past, it stitched a line of holes the full length of the fuselage. Flung against his safety straps, Blackburn stared with disbelief at the charred holes in his overalls. Harvey, grunting with pain and doubling up like a boxer receiving a blow in the stomach, recovered and went raging on.

An isolated farmhouse appeared. It would be years before men would learn the secret of its hinged roof and the motor testing beds that lay beneath it. But as Harvey swept north of it he caught a glimpse of two green, cylindrical wagons standing beneath the firs. As the stricken Blackburn tried to draw his attention to them, Harvey put D-Danny into a climbing turn and came sweeping back.

Like some enormous green snake hiding from predators, the train was stretched out beneath the trees almost as far as the farmhouse. Switching on his firing button Harvey pushed the stick right forward. Still out of range Moore called an urgent warning.

"Harvey, you're too low. Attack at extreme range."

Nothing but a bullet in the brain would have diverted Harvey at that moment. This was the prize Anna was risking her life for and Anna was going to have that prize. As the first wagon entered his sights he thumbed the firing button and held it down. The ashen-faced Blackburn closed his eyes as the Mosquito flew along the line of wagons. Twenty cannon shells a second, packed with high explosive, smashed through the skin of the tankers and ran on in a series of bright explosions. Overalled figures, working on couplings beneath the train, gave hoarse cries of warning and ran for their lives into the trees.

To Moore and Hopkinson time seemed to slow down in the breathless moment that followed. They could see Harvey's fire spearing into the trees but at first without result as if the rearmost wagons had already been drained of fuel. Then an odd cascade of liquid fire squirted into the sky. With black smoke pluming from its edges, it resembled a bizarre fountain. The pyrotechnical display seemed to last for seconds before a shimmering flash ran through the trees below. It was followed by a ball of fire that expanded at terrifying speed in all directions. The blast that followed it, a deafening peal of thunder, shot A-Apple upwards as if on the back of some gigantic lift. As Moore righted the aircraft a dense monolith of smoke, shot by fresh explosions and debris, began to cover the floor of the valley. Glancing at his watch Moore saw it was 1414. Incredibly they had been over the valley only eleven minutes. About to order Hopkinson to send the message that would transform Davies from a shattered man to a euphoric one, Moore saw the navigator was already tapping the Morse key.

The R/T channel was swamped by shouts of triumph from the orbiting crews. Warning them not to relax their vigilance Moore turned again towards the dense column of smoke. Guessing his intent Hopkinson showed scepticism. "He'd never survive that explosion, skipper. Not from that height."

Parabolas of coloured shells soaring up among the black smoke proved Hopkinson wrong. Flak crews who had survived the tanker explosion had now recovered and were trying to take their revenge on D-Danny. Like a naked man who had lost half his skin in a fire the Mosquito was a hideous sight. Most of its paint was burnt away, great holes gaped in its wings, and its tail fin and one elevator were only naked spars. As Moore, ignoring the flak, drew in closer he could see Harvey's head lolling against the heat-blistered canopy.

"Harvey! Are you hurt?"

The Yorkshireman sounded dazed and far away. "Aye. I've been hit."

"What about Blackburn?"

"He got it too. But he's alive."

"Can you make it home?"

There was no reply. A second wave of massive explosions was hurling up trees and debris from the tortured valley floor but Harvey had eyes only for the empty meadow in which the hay stooks were still smoking. Moore's voice turned sharp. "She got away. In any case there's nothing more you can do. You've Blackburn to think about. Head for home and we'll give you cover."

For a long moment D-Danny went on circling the field. Then, with immense reluctance, it began to climb painfully from the valley where the rest of the squadron closed around it. Like a party of soldiers carrying away a wounded and valued comrade they rose and disappeared into the veil of clouds.

33

Davies waited to hear no more than the word "Crispin." Like a man reprieved from execution he swung round on the onlookers who had risen to their feet. "They've done it! They've bloody well done it!"

Adams was the first to find his voice. "But how, sir? They'd already dropped their bombs."

In his euphoria Davies forgot code words and everything else. "The girl got a message through to them at the last minute. So someone went down and strafed the train."

Adams' jubilation came to a dead halt. "Who, sir?"

Davies turned back to the corporal. "Does the message say?"

"Yes, sir. It was Flight Commander Harvey."

Davies jerked violently. "Who?"

"Flight Commander Harvey, sir."

"My Christ," Davies said blankly.

Henderson pushed forward towards the corporal. "Is he dead?"

"The message doesn't mention losses, sir."

"He must be dead," Adams said.

"He'll get a decoration," Davies told them. "Posthumous or otherwise."

As the two men stared at him, Staines's gravelly voice drew their attention. Alone alongside his telephone, the big American was frowning heavily. "So the Rhine Maidens won't get airborne and my boys haven't given their lives for nothing. Congratulations."

The bright-eyed Davies hurried over to him and shook his hand. "Sorry, sir. We were carried away for a moment. It was your lads who made it possible for us to get there. We're deeply grateful."

The mollified Texan shook hands with the Brigadier and Henderson in turn. "In the long run we're the ones who'll profit. Those rockets would have knocked hell out of us

if they'd gone into production. I'm putting your whole
outfit up for Congressional Commendation, Henderson.
In the meantime, if any of your boys get thirsty and
drop into our airfields, I've a hunch they'll do all right."

Even his Scots phlegm could not hide Henderson's delight as he nodded at the phone the American was picking
up. "Thank you, sir. What's the latest news from your end?"

"The serviceable ships are on their way to North Africa.
It's the crippled ships we're concerned about. They've no
choice but to turn back for home and it's a hell of a way
before they can get fighter cover."

"How many are there, sir?"

"Twenty." The Texan did not notice the look Davies
gave Henderson as he put his ear to the receiver again.
"And some are in bad shape. The way the Krauts are
hammering 'em we'll be lucky if half of 'em get home."

After a whispered word to Davies, the Brigadier walked
over to a red telephone at the far end of the room.
Adams was the nearest to him and although the soldier's
clipped voice was low, its semi-reverential tone suggested
a distinguished presence on the other end of the line.
"Hello, sir. Yes, the news is good—they've done it again.
A complete success as far as we can gather. Losses?
We don't know yet but I'll keep you informed. Thank
you very much, sir."

In the minutes that followed Adams' feelings were mixed
—jubilation at the squadron's success was tempered by
lack of details of its losses. Nor could Adams, a hu-
manitarian, banish from his mind the gruesome deaths
hundreds of workers must have suffered in the underground factory as the raging fuel swept in. Another harrowing factor was the stream of reports Staines was receiving about his crippled B.17s. Even Davies, once his
euphroia had cooled, showed sympathy as he sat down
alongside the Texan.

"Where are your boys now, sir?"

"Just short of the Rhine. Still a long way from fighter
cover."

"I shouldn't worry too much. Things mightn't turn out
as badly as you think."

Adams felt the resentful glance Staines gave him was
justified. Jumping to his feet as if too excited to stay
in one place for long, Davies went over to Henderson
and began whispering to him, both men continually throw-

ing glances at the American. Two minutes later a sharp
exclamation from Staines sent both men hurrying over to
him. "Well, I'm a sonofabitch!"

Eager red spots were back in Davies's cheeks. "What is
it, sir?"

The Texan remained glued to the telephone for another
fifteen seconds. Then his tough, incredulous face lifted
up to the grinning Davies. "My crippled B.17s report
those boys of yours have caught up with them and are
giving them fighter cover. You never told me this was
part of the deal."

Davies transferred his twinkling glance to Henderson.
"We weren't certain they'd have any ammo. left after
the Rhine Maiden affair. But assuming they had, we made
the private point to Moore that as your lads had carried
the can all the way there, it would be a nice gesture
if we carried it part of the way back." As Staines grinned
appreciatingly, Davies felt that in the circumstances in
Americanism would not be out of place. "In other words,
sir, we're an outfit that likes to pay its debts."

From above, the tightly-packed formation of B.17s
looked like a school of wounded whales being attacked
by killer sharks. Bleeding from a hundred wounds, they
were defending themselves desperately but the attackers
were hungry and ruthless. Boring in, snapping and tearing,
they would strike at one aircraft until, dazed and blinded,
it lost the security of its own kind. Immediately half a
dozen shark-like fighters would close in for the kill.

Two units of German fighters were engaging the crippled B.17s. One was a Focke Wulf squadron recently
withdrawn from the Italian front: the other was Hans
Klaus's 110 squadron, thrown into action at last. On
first sighting the formation of B.17s the young pilot's
mouth had begun watering. Here, surely, with his tenth
kill at last. Picking out a Fortress he went after it like
a gun dog after a wounded boar.

It was a reckless attack that exposed Klaus's inexperi-
ence against the heavily-armed B.17s. Although some of
their comrades were wounded or dead, the remaining
American gunners were still full of fight and the hail of
fire that greeted Klaus made him dive hurriedly for
safety. Flushed with embarrassment and anger he remembered the instructions given him before take-off and

turned west to catch the formation head-on as it made for home.

At the same moment Klaus turned west, Moore sighted the air battle ahead. His order made Millburn clamp his jaw in satisfaction. "I think it's time we showed the Yanks our appreciation. Green Section Leader, prepare to attack. I'll stay and give Harvey cover."

As Teddy Young led the squadron into the sun, Moore dropped behind Harvey. From the rear the Yorkshireman's aircraft was a hideous sight with its parboiled skin and skeleton holes.

"How are you feeling, Frank?"

The man's gruff voice gave nothing away. "I'm all right. But the kid came round so I had to give him morphia."

The two Mosquitoes were now four thousand feet above the air battle. At any moment Moore expected an attack but the fighters seemed drunk on the blood of the mammoths they were engaging. In his earphones Moore heard an Australian yell. "Green section leader to Longbow. Pick yourself a target and let's go!"

Freed from their bombloads, the Mosquitoes came dropping out of the sun like a pack of gannets. Believing no hostile fighters within seventy miles, the Germans were caught by surprise. On the first strike three of them went reeling earthwards trailing smoke and fire. In T-Tommy Millburn was displaying relief that was near to ecstacy as he came climbing back and fastened his sights on a 110. Outmanoeuvred by the faster Mosquito, the Messerchmitt's propellers looked like waving arms in the sunlight as it tried to escape. Closing in, Millburn fired a burst full into its tanks. The acrid smell of the explosion entered the cockpit as T-Tommy flew right through the fireball. Yelling his triumph Millburn went in search of a fresh victim while the American gunners, resigned to death even as they were putting up a gallant fight for life, rubbed their eyes in astonishment at seeing the British squadron reappear in the role of fighter escort.

This new phase of the battle had been reached when Klaus returned on his head-on course. His shout of disbelief made Fritz start. "Mosquitoes! Where the hell have they come from?"

Acutely aware that without the cover of darkness a 110 was no match for a Mosquito, Fritz felt his heart miss a beat. "If you're right, be careful how you attack."

With his personal enmity against the aircraft impairing his judgment, Hans was contemptuous. "What the hell for? We still outnumber them two to one."

Although duels between fighters were taking place far from the Fortresses, the epicentre of the main battle was now some miles away. As he aimed to dive on the approaching B.17s, Klaus saw two Mosquitoes a thousand feet below and heading in his direction. Snatching up a pair of binoculars he took in the tattered condition of the leading aircraft. Immediately he turned into the sun. He could dive on the two Mosquitoes, continue on and wheel into the path of the B.17s. It was a safe enough manoeuvre; even if he missed the rearmost Mosquito it would not dare to leave its charge and follow him.

Fritz made an immediate protest. "Our job is to go for the heavies."

"We are going for them," Hans grinned. "We're just going to swat a Mosquito or two on our way."

The vectors of the 110 and the Mosquitoes were shortening fast. Banking tightly and allowing the crippled plane and its escort to pass westward beneath him, Klaus confirmed their speed was less than his own. Manoeuvring with great care so that the sun was directly behind him, Klaus launched his attack.

It was the greatest mistake of the young German's life. With years of combat experience behind them, both Moore and Hopkinson had been keeping special watch on the sun. Moreover Hopkinson's binocular-sharp eyes had picked up the 110 seconds before A-Apple had been spotted by Klaus. Bracing himself, Moore spoke quietly to Harvey.

"We've got company, Frank. Break when I tell you."

Above them a blurred, black shape was growing raipdly larger in the dazzling orb of the sun. Moore waited another two seconds, then shouted his warning. "Corkscrew starboard!"

Sluggish on its controls, Harvey's Mosquito fell into a sideslip as he swung it away but the manoeuvre was still effective. As Moore banked to port three lines of tracer appeared past his wingtip. It was followed a couple of seconds later by the 110, already banking steeply in a desperate attempt not to overshoot.

But in the deadly way of air combat, there was to be no second chance. No longer aided by darkness, the 110 was as doomed as a rabbit chased by a stoat as the graceful, more manoeuvrable Mosquito closed up behind. In vain Klaus hurled it about the sky. Inexorably its tailplane came creeping into Moore's sights. The fuselage followed and then the cockpit canopy. Steadying the Mosquito like the precision instrument it was, Moore fired a single burst. The 110 crumpled and began spinning earthwards, and one of the war's many millions of minute issues was resolved. Fritz Neumann would never learn if his mother was to survive her embolism—in fact she was to outlive him by only two days. And it was now very certain that Hans Klaus would not attend his wedding wearing the Iron Cross.

34

Pouring smoke from both its starboard engines the B.17 lurched drunkenly from the tight formation. As its pilot tried to bring it under control, two Focke Wulfs attacked from opposite sides. With five gunners already slumped over their weapons, the end was near. Cannon shells blasted huge holes in the massive wings and tore off the weakened tail assembly. With air screaming eerily inside its fuselage, the B.17 began its long fall to earth. Incredibly a gunner in the upper turret, his parachute pack blown to ribbons by gunfire, went on firing defiantly as the two Focke Wulfs followed the bomber down.

It was the first B.17 to be lost since 633 Squadron had come to the Americans' aid but all the Mosquito crews knew it would not be the last unless help came soon. In spite of the wing tanks they had carried to Bavaria, the extra demands of combat were a massive drain on fuel reserves. Two Mosquitoes had already been lost and there were wounded among the surviving crews. Gabby would no longer need to fake wounds to glamorize his image: blood from a wound in his thigh was splattered over the cockpit floor and on Millburn's overalls. Young Flemming of B Flight had been struck on the head by a cannon shell and his hideously mutilated body kept nudging his ashen-faced pilot. Blood was running down St. Claire's left arm, but the calm young artist continued to attack every Focke Wulf that came within range. The battle had now moved into France but the enemy fighters had been reinforced by a crack *gruppe* from the Paris area and the odds were now heavily in their favour.

Six miles to the north Moore was keeping an anxious eye on the battle. Three hundred yards ahead of him Harvey's crippled plane was also causing him concern. During the last five minutes it had been flying an increasingly erratic course. As Hopkinson glanced at him, Moore addressed his microphone.

"You're off course again, Frank. Five degrees."

A thick curse answered him. "We're not going to make it, Moore. So get over and help the lads."

"How badly wounded are you?"

"How the hell do I know?"

"Where is the wound?"

"Somewhere in my guts."

"Are you losing much blood?"

"Enough."

"Have you put a field dressing on it?"

"Yes, I've stuffed one down." A pause and then another curse. "Who the hell cares. Piss off, Moore. It doesn't matter."

Above his face mask Moore's face was drenched in sweat. "Stop talking like a bloody fool. If you don't care about your own life, think about Blackburn."

There was a long pause and then D-Danny swung sullenly back on course. Alongside Moore, Hoppy gave a start and pointed ahead. A swarm of liverish black spots were swimming in the bright sky. Hopkinson snatched up a pair of binoculars, then sank back in relief. "Spitfires. We've come into their range."

A few seconds more and shark-like bodies, waggling their wings, streaked past and hurled themselves into the battle. Three flights of Thunderbolts were next. One detached itself and an American voice drawled in Moore's earphones. "You don't mind my company, do you, Limey?"

"I love your company," Moore told him. "Stick around."

The Thunderbolt began patrolling the sky a mile behind him. Seeing the Allied escort was now engaging the German fighters, Moore gave the order that brought relief to his hardpressed crews. "Longbow Leader to Green Section Leader. Disengage as soon as you can and take the boys home."

Ahead D-Danny was flying like a bird with a damaged wing. "Frank! You're losing height. Keep her nose up." A pause, and then: "Frank! Can you hear me?"

The voice that came sounded very distant and very drunk. "What d'you want?"

"I said you're losing height." Moore turned to Hopkinson. "How much longer to the coast?"

The Cockney looked apologetic. "At least fifteen minutes, skipper."

Moore winced. "Frank, listen. Use your oxygen. Turn it up until your head clears. All right?"

After a long pause Harvey's voice sounded louder. "The Spitties have come, haven't they?"

"Yes. We should make it now."

"That's good. The boys deserve it. Go and join 'em, Moore. You're sticking your neck out flying alone like this."

"The same way you left Marsh?"

When there was only a growl for a reply, Moore went on: "Frank, for all you know Anna could have got away. They'd have more than her to worry about when those tanks went up."

To one as deep in despair as Harvey, an offer of hope had to be rejected swiftly unless it was to bring more pain. "Why don't you piss off? And take that bloody Thunderbolt with you."

Moore glanced back. The dogfight was now little more than a dancing cloud of gnats in the summer sky but the American fighter was still behind them. "Anna wouldn't quit, Frank. If there's a way out of that valley she'll find it."

There was a sudden snarl from D-Danny. "What's that supposed to mean? That I'm quitting? All I'm saying, Moore, is that I can do without you."

This was better, Moore thought. "Why do you tykes love being independent? Does a piece of help stick in your gullet?"

"We get by without it, Moore. We always have."

Hopkinson was peering into the sun. Glancing back Moore saw the Thunderbolt was coming down like a blunt-nosed meteor. As his earphones rattled to the American's warning, Moore yelled his own to Harvey, "Break, Frank! Fast!"

Acting purely on reflex, Harvey sent D-Danny slithering round. Moore side-slipped to port, corrected A-Apple, and took a full deflection shot at the Fock Wulf that dived in front of him. The hastily-aimed burst missed but the German pilot, aware the Thunderbolt was also making towards him like an infuriated bulldog, continued to dive into the haze below. Harvey, who had lost nearly two thousand feet in the sharp action, was struggling to get D-Danny on an even keel again. Moore closed up behind him.

"You all right, Frank?"

He could hear Harvey's heavy breathing and knew loss of blood was taking its toll. "Aye, I think so. Thanks."

"Watch your compass. We're off course again."

The slow minutes dragged past. With the Focke Wulf pilot deciding the air battle to the east offered easier pickings, the American pilot had climbed back into station again. In D-Danny Harvey's sunken eyes were half-closed. The rise and fall of the Mosquito, the limitless blue sky, the background drone of the engines, were all becoming a part of the light-headed world into which he was slipping. Beside him the unconscious, blood-stained figure of Blackburn was slumped against his straps. Frowning, Harvey turned to him. "You're quiet, kid. What's wrong?"

Moore exchanged glances with Hopkinson. "He's turning delirious. Frank, turn your oxygen full on!"

Once again the erratic course of D-Danny began to steady. "That's better, Frank. Can you hear me all right?"

"Aye," Harvey muttered. "Just about."

"What are your plans after the war?"

"After the war! What the hell are you talking about?"

"Like a job in my company?"

There was a silence, then a disbelieving laugh. *"Your* company! What as? A lavatory attendant?"

Moore relaxed again and smiled. "No. I might do a bit better than that."

"All right. A bloody sweeper. No thanks."

The grim humour, coming from a tortured body, moved even the hard-bitten Hopkinson.

"Tell me what makes you tykes so bloody-minded?" Moore asked.

"That's easy." Harvey had to pause for breath. "It's living with toffee-nosed bastards like you. Turns anyone's milk sour." Another pause for breath, and then: "I thought you didn't fancy taking on your old man's job."

"Who told you that?"

"Anna."

Moore's answer, although spontaneous, came as a surprise to himself. "I seem to have different feelings about it now."

"What's changed your mind?"

"I'm not sure. Maybe it's one or two people I've met recently."

Hopkinson was jabbing a relieved finger at the coast that had appeared ahead. Although Moore knew its packed defences represented a last major threat, he had never seen a sweeter sight. "We're nearly there, Frank. Hoppy will guide us through. Keep your oxygen full on and stick right on my tail."

With A-Apple now in the lead the two Mosquitoes swept over the coastal defences. For half a minute the sky around them turned lethal with black explosions and lashing steel. Then they were through and the blue water of the Channel was below them. Dropping back Moore took guard behind Harvey again.

A few more minutes and the chalk cliffs of the Isle of Wight rose on their starboard side. They crossed the coast near Christchurch Harbour and swept over the green-quilted New Forest. By this time D-Danny was down to five hundred feet and slithering all over the sky. Sweating with fear for the Yorkshireman, Moore tried to revive him. "Don't crack up now, Frank, for God's sake. Holmsley airfield's only a minute away."

There was no reply. D-Danny's nose was dropping like the head of a weary animal. Taking a deep breath, Moore closed right in.

"Harvey, you cowardly Yorkshire bastard! Wake up or I'll splatter your guts all over the forest!"

Harvey jerked against his straps and his blood-streaked eyes opened. Behind him Moore switched on his firing button. Before the startled Hopkinson could protest he took careful aim and sent a long burst just below D-Danny's fuselage. A second burst ripped no more than fifteen feet above its canopy. Crash crews, standing by on the emergency landing field, heard the firing and gazed at one another in astonishment when they saw only two Mosquitoes sweeping towards them.

The reflexes of a man who had learned to fight almost before he could walk brought life back to Harvey. Ahead of him he saw the airfield with crash wagons and ambulances waiting alongside its east-west runway. With an enormous effort he steadied the Mosquito and made for it. As his eyes kept losing focus he heard Moore talking him down.

"Watch your flying speed as you lower your flaps. Left, left—steady. Your starboard wing's dropping. Up, up—that's better. Now back on the throttles. Back, back. . . ."

The runway was now streaming beneath Harvey like a black ribbon. Forty feet . . . thirty feet . . . he was sinking to a safe landing when his damaged control surfaces suddenly betrayed him and D-Danny dropped like a stone. A tyre burst immediately, pitching the plane off the runway and digging one wingtip into the soft ground. With a massive snapping of spars the Mosquito went spinning round and round, tearing off an engine in its gyrations.

Hoppy gave a horrified murmur: "Oh, my God!" Ignoring traffic rules and personal safety, Moore put his wheels straight down on the runway. Behind him crash wagons, with sirens howling, were bearing down on the smoking wreckage. With brakes squealing and pouring off smoke, A-Apple bucketed down the field, turned off the runway, and came back at almost take-off speed.

As both men leapt out they saw a party of medical orderlies were carrying Harvey away from the crumpled cockpit while a crash crew struggled to free Blackburn. Leaving Hopkinson to see if the crew needed help, Moore ran on to the orderlies who were lowering Harvey on to a stretcher.

The Yorkshireman's appearance horrified him. His overalls were soaked in blood from the waist downwards and his face was hollow and ravaged with pain. He appeared unconscious but as Moore knelt beside him, his eyes opened.

"The kid! Young Blackburn! Is he all right?"

Glancing back Moore saw the crash party were bringing up metal-cutting equipment. Hopkinson, approaching from the wreckage, shook his head. Bending down again Moore tried to hide the scene from the supine Harvey. "They're taking care of him, Frank. Lie back and relax."

A medical orderly was trying to unbutton Harvey's bloodstained overalls. The Yorkshireman pushed him back impatiently. "Wait a bloody minute!" Fumbling for Moore's hand he gripped it and drew the Squadron Commander closer. Seeing he wanted to keep his words private, Moore bent over him. "What is it, Frank?"

The man's hoarse whisper seemed louder than a cry of pain. "What do you really think? Could she have got away?"

Moore would gladly have lied his soul into Purgatory at that moment. "Why not? After all that hell you raised, they'd be too busy to bother about her."

The man's eyes, blood-streaked and oddly vulnerable, tared up at him. "I'm grateful, Moore. Particularly for ıelping her."

Over their heads airfoils were whining as battle-scarred Mosquitoes came in to unload their wounded and to re-uel. Moore discovered the Yorkshireman was still grip-ıing his hand. "It's time they got you to hospital, Frank. I want you back on duty in three weeks' time."

Harvey's lips quirked in grim humour. A Mosquito with a line of blackened shell holes running from a wing root to its cockade came bumping down the runway less than thirty yards from them. The air disturbance swung one of the ambulance doors on its hinges. As the sound of the airfoils faded, Harvey's slurred voice arrested the or-derlies who were about to pick up his stretcher.

"You know what I'd do, don't you, Moore? Probably the first day I was there."

For a moment Moore thought he was turning delirious again. "What, Frank?"

"I'd call a bloody strike, mate. You hadn't thought of that, had you?"

Moore gazed in awe at the ravaged, undefeated face. As the orderlies bent down again, there was a coughing roar from D-Danny followed by shouts of alarm as asbestos-clad figures scattered in all directions. Seeing the ball of fire that had suddenly engulfed the wreckage, Harvey cursed frantically and tried to push the order-lies aside. It took four men to hold him down as he fought to reach the fire that was incinerating Blackburn. Feeling deathly sick and telling himself it was caused by the stench of burning glycol and rubber, Moore knelt alongside Harvey again.

"I'm sorry, Frank. They did all they could. He didn't suffer. They think he was dead when you landed."

Astonishingly, a muffled sob broke from the Yorkshire-man. For a moment the column of black smoke seemed to darken the entire sky for Moore. Then, taking a deep breath, he rose and faced the senior medical orderly.

"Tell your doctors they've got to save this man's life. Make certain they understand that. Do you hear me?"

The N.C.O. glanced at his face, then looked away in embarrassment. "We'll do our best, sir."

Moore could not control his trembling. "You'll do more than your best! You'll save his life!"

It was Hopkinson who hastily drew him away. "It'll be all right, skipper. They'll take good care of him."

The orderlies lifted the stretcher into the ambulance and closed the doors. Moore turned to watch the vehicle as it drove away. Ammunition was now exploding in D-Danny, a lethal pyrotechnical display that brought shouts of warning from the crash crews. When Moore took no notice, Hopkinson touched his arm.

"Hadn't we better get moving, skipper? Most of the boys are down by this time."

Moore's eyes remained on the departing ambulance. It took another anxious reminder from Hopkinson before he turned and took in the dense smoke and the bursting cannon shells. Giving the Cockney a curt nod, he started across the airfield towards the Control Tower.

Standing aside for the Brigadier to enter the staff car, Davies glanced at the two men standing on the kerb. No gnome or gremlin could have looked more maliciously wicked than the small Air Commodore at that moment.

"Pity I can't stay for the party. But think of me when I get back to Group tomorrow. The bastards wanted to shove you back into Main Force! I can't wait to see their faces now."

With that Davies jumped gleefully into the car. Henderson gave Adams a rueful grin as the car disappeared through the station gates. "See that look in his eyes? He's had a successful operation and this time the casualties aren't too heavy. That means in the future he'll volunteer us for every sticky job that comes along."

The same thought had occurred to Adams. "Eight dead and three wounded—I wouldn't call them light casualties."

"No, but he expected far higher ones. He told me so this morning."

"He nearly got them," Adams said. "If the girl had given her signal earlier and Moore had kept to the original plan, they'd have been shot down like partridges. Our estimates of the number of guns sited along the valley were miles out."

"Could she have done it deliberately?"

"No. If she'd known there were so many guns she'd have told us. She probably ran foul of the soldiers on her way to the field and was late in escaping from them."

Black against the evening afterglow the Mosquitoes looked like resting birds on the airfield. Although it was growing too dark for them to be seen, Adams knew that four of the dispersal points were empty. Down the road the sound of music and high revelry was coming from the Mess as the crews celebrated their victory. Davies had stood everyone down except essential personnel and there were similar celebrations in the N.C.O.s' and airmen's Messes. In the shadows between two huts opposite something moved and a moment later the figure of Sam slunk dejectedly across the road. As Adams called its name, the dog gave a whimper of recognition and made towards him.

"He keeps going back to Harvey's billet," Adams said, bending down to stroke the dog. "Did Moore phone the hospital again?"

"Yes. Harvey's had an operation and they gave the usual spiel that he's doing as well as can be expected. We're going to phone again in a couple of hours."

An outburst of cheering floated towards them. Adams glanced in its direction. "Moore has gone to the party, hasn't he?"

Henderson nodded. "The boys didn't give him a choice this time. They practically carried him there. Not that he appeared that keen," the Scot added as an afterthought. "This business of Harvey and the girl seems to have got under his skin."

Adams was rubbing the dog's ears. Before the senior officers had left, he and Henderson had shared a bottle of malt whisky with them. Never one who could take much alcohol without the effects showing, Adams was showing them now. "It's a funny thing about those two. In a way they both had a love-hate for their countries. I suppose that was one of the things that first drew them together."

Henderson's eyebrows knitted. "Love-hate?"

"Yes. Harvey's hardly rapturous about our society, is he? And Anna hates the Nazis." Needing someone to talk to tonight, Adams did not notice the big Scot's expression. "She was a lovely girl. But I know I'm going to wish she'd never come here."

Overhead the heavy drone of engines was moving across the late evening sky. Lost to Adams' meaning, the practical Henderson gave an impatient grunt. "We'd have been bloody pushed to do the job without her, wouldn't we?"

Behind his thick spectacles Adams looked surprised. "Oh, I didn't mean that. I meant that after a few years of war you manage to convince yourself that all the people on the other side are bad. After knowing Anna you can never think that again. So she's made everything that bit more difficult."

Thinking what a load of bullshit Adams could talk after a few drinks, Henderson decided it was a night to be charitable. "Don't go soft on me, Frank, for Christ's sake. There's a lot more war to go yet."

Adams winced. "Do you think so?"

"I'm sure of it. Jerry might be retreating here and there but he'll fight all the harder when we get near his frontiers."

"I suppose you're right," Adams muttered dejectedly. Another outburst of cheering down the road made the dog lift its head and bark. Taken to the confessional by three large glasses of whisky, Adams forgot whom he was talking to as he nodded at the source of the sound. "That's where I'll be in a couple of minutes. And I won't be thinking of our dead boys or the dead Yanks or the dead Germans. I won't even be thinking about Harvey and Anna. I'll be downing the drinks they pass me, singing the old songs, and I'll be so proud of this squadron and what the lads have done I'll feel fifteen feet tall."

"Is that bad?" Henderson asked, staring at him.

To his dismay Adams realized he was going to be misunderstood again. "I don't mean I shouldn't be proud of the squadron or the boys themselves. They're a fine crowd and they've done a wonderful job. It's just that I don't feel one should. . . ." Suddenly realizing that whatever he said tonight would sound wrong, Adams' voice trailed away. "I think I've had too many glasses of that whisky."

It was a capitulation that brought Henderson relief. "You know what's wrong with you, Frank? You're only half-sloshed. Have a few more drams and it'll all swing back into place again. Now let's get over there before those young buggers drink the place dry."

Trying to match the big Scot's strides as they headed for the Mess, and with Sam pattering at his heels, Adams glanced up again at the evening sky. Another heavy bomb-

r was trundling across it, its passage only visible by the
stars it extinguished. Soon it would join the main stream
that would already be sweeping across the skies of occupied Europe. The armada would reach its target without undue difficulty because night one thousand, four
hundred and thirty-nine of the war was calm and starlit.
For the same reason enemy night fighters would have no
difficulty in finding the Lancasters and Stirlings. As he
pushed into the deafening, smoky carousal that was the
Mess, Adams was reflecting what fine sport the War Gods
would have tonight.

It took only two of the large glasses of whisky that
were thrust at him from all sides to bring about the
change in equilibrium that Henderson had predicted. Fine
sport or not, Adams reminded himself, the bastards still
wouldn't be having it off with those Rhine Maidens in
the months ahead. Eyes glinting triumphantly behind his
spectacles, he carefully located the piano and steered
Sam and himself towards it. Half a minute later, his head
back and his cheeks pink, Adams was singing the roof
off with the best of them.

ABOUT THE AUTHOR

FREDERICK E. SMITH joined the R.A.F. in 1939 as a wireless operator/air gunner and commenced service in early 1940, serving in Britain, Africa and finally the Far East. At the end of the war he married and worked for several years in South Africa before returning to England to fulfill his life-long ambition to write. Two years later, his first play was produced and his first novel published. Since then, he has written twenty-four novels, about eighty short stories and two plays. Two novels, *633 Squadron* and *The Devil Doll,* have been made into films and one, *A Killing for the Hawks,* has won the Mark Twain Literary Award.